Penguin Boo
Blood on the

Emanuel Litvinoff was born in London's Whitechapel. Largely self-educated, he has published several highly praised novels, poems, an autobiographical book of stories, and has contributed about a dozen plays to television. He left school at the age of fourteen and then, prior to the war, worked in various occupations, including tailoring and cabinet making, interspersed with periods of unemployment. From 1940 to 1946 he served in the British army, reaching the rank of Major. He spent two years in West Africa, seconded to the Royal West African Frontier Force, and also served in the Middle East. His other publications include *The Lost Europeans*, *The Man Next Door* and *Journey Through a Small Planet* (Penguin). *Blood on the Snow* is the second book in Litvinoff's epic *Faces of Terror* trilogy; *A Death Out of Season* and *The Face of Terror* are being published simultaneously in Penguins.

Emanuel Litvinoff

Blood on the Snow

Penguin Books

Penguin Books Ltd, Harmondsworth,
Middlesex, England
Penguin Books, 625 Madison Avenue,
New York, New York 10022, U.S.A.
Penguin Books Australia Ltd, Ringwood,
Victoria, Australia
Penguin Books Canada Ltd, 2801 John Street,
Markham, Ontario, Canada L3R 1B4
Penguin Books (N.Z.) Ltd, 182–190 Wairau Road,
Auckland 10, New Zealand

First published by Michael Joseph 1975
Published in Penguin Books 1979

Made and printed in Great Britain by
Richard Clay (The Chaucer Press) Ltd, Bungay, Suffolk
Set in Monotype Plantin

The date by the Gregorian calendar was Wednesday, 25 October 1917. The weather is recorded as raw and chill. Black clouds gathered in the sky. Quite early it began to grow dark.

In the guise of an old man but impatient as a bridegroom, Lenin waited in a small room of Petrograd's Smolny Institute, a former high school for aristocratic girls. Just before 9 p.m. the cruiser *Aurora* opened fire across the Neva with blank cartridges and Red Guards stormed the Winter Palace.

Two hours later Bolshevism inherited the destiny of Russia.

Lenin worked during the night drafting a decree to expropriate all landed estates. Next morning he threw open the curtains of the window and addressed the iron-grey city in a voice of awe and prophecy.

'Greetings,' he said, 'on the first day of the Socialist Revolution.'

Part One

'We have made a pact with death'

LEON TROTSKY

Chapter One

The horseman slumped tiredly in the saddle as he cantered up Ekaterinburg's Glavni Prospekt on a torpid afternoon in July 1918, that first summer of famine, terror and civil war. Patches of sweat stained the armpits of his grey-green tunic and eyes of desperate innocence stared from a boyish, dirt-streaked face. Dismounting at the Hotel Palais Royal, he tethered the horse and respectfully doffed his pointed cap with its red star before entering the building.

Inside there was noise, heat and confusion. Russia was an ant-heap upturned by a giant hand, its multitudes startled into blind and seething confusion. Peasants and townsmen, young, old, male and female, people of different nationalities arbitrarily thrown together by the upheaval, were crowded into the foyer. Others like them invaded churches, railway stations, former mansions of the rich brought to abrupt ruin, all seeking shelter from the violence that had shattered their centuries of servitude. And as they huddled together in that ravenous summer of bloodshed, lice and hunger, another, insidious, army went about its deadly work – the bacilli of typhus.

Lifting his muddy felt boots to avoid stepping on reclining bodies, the soldier advanced into the hotel lobby and gazed with interest at several posters displayed on its walls. He could understand only the pictures, not the words, but they made sense of things for him. There was one of a fellow like himself galloping into battle, and Comrade Lenin smashing the imperialists, and workers in great ranks marching towards the sun of socialism. It gave him a good feeling, like drinking hot soup.

'Can you tell me where I can find Comrade Byeloborodov?' he asked a scowling Red Guard standing sentry at the entrance to a corridor.

The man looked at him as if he was a cockroach and said: 'There's lots wanting to see the Commissars. What's your business?'

'I've come from Ostrovskaya with a message from the Commander.'

'Show us your bit of paper, then.'

The soldier searched in his tunic and produced a crumpled page torn from a field notebook. It had his name on it, Vassily Petkovich, and the rubber stamp of his unit over words that said he was travelling to Ekaterinburg on official business. The Commander wrote it out in a hurry and sent him off when the field telephone no longer answered.

'Mind you get there as quick as you can, Vassily, or I'll drag the shit out of you,' he said.

Truth to tell, Vassily was glad to get away for a bit. They were shaking the earth in Ostrovskaya with their mortars, the enemy. Took the legs off one of the boys when he went out for a minute to have a leak. And for all you could do about it you might just as well shoot your bullets at the moon.

'Third door on the right,' said the sentry with a flick of his head. 'Knock respectful and wait till you're called.'

Byeloborodov, Chairman of the Ural Soviet, was a barrel-chested ex-miner of medium height, about forty years old. He had the muscular jaws of a practised orator and was smoking a thick hand-rolled cigarette. Staring at Vassily across a desk submerged in chaos, he rapped out: 'What is it, lad?'

'A message from Ostrovskaya, your Honour,' replied Vassily, quite forgetting that he was not supposed to say 'your Honour'. He handed over a sealed envelope and stood stiffly to attention.

The Commissar's hectoring face sagged as he read the dispatch. Blue smoke drifted in the stagnant air and he rubbed his red-rimmed eyes as though they smarted. More bad news. The front was in a state of near collapse. Well-armed, well-trained, efficiently commanded, the Czechoslovak insurgents were advancing on Ekaterinburg from two sides. In contrast, the revolutionary forces consisted of improvised factory units and illiterate peasants terrified of the noise of their own rifles. Men sneaked back to their own villages, often only to die of typhus. There was a shortage of everything – food, ammunition, horses.

As long as the Czechoslovaks controlled the Trans-Siberian railway, supplies and reinforcements could not get through. On the industrial front, workers fainted at their benches from hunger. 'Bread or we're done for!' was the cry.

Vassily dutifully waited for the representative of Soviet power to command his obedience until the hollow craving in his belly for simple nourishment could stand it no longer.

'Your Honour, sir,' he said in a hoarse voice, tears glistening in his candid eyes, 'I've rode seven hours and nothing in my mouth except a spoonful of gruel for yesterday's supper.'

'Try the kitchen,' Byeloborodov said, rousing himself, 'but you'll be lucky to find even a herring-bone. There's a shortage of everything.'

Especially time, he reflected, thinking grimly of the prisoners held in the mansion confiscated from the engineer Ipatiev. The advancing Czechs were under orders to rescue them at all costs. It would be a bad fright for the Revolution, absolutism rising from its grave. The liberated Tsar would preside over a carnival of White terror. As soon as the enemy captured a town they began their savage and rapacious killing. A look into a man's eyes and if there was something there that didn't please them he was finished off by rope, bullet or bayonet. And under every pile of corpses were the Jews and commissars, always first to go.

They had been debating what to do about Nicholas II ever since he'd been transferred from Tobolsk in Siberia to Ekaterinburg with his family and entourage of four, three months before. The Anarchists wanted the lot of them done in right away and threatened to do it themselves if there was any squeamishness. There was talk of staging a public trial of Nicholas with Trotsky as prosecutor, but it was too late for that now. Bykov, Commissar in charge of Mining Industries, also argued in favour of immediate execution, quoting in support Lenin's remark that if the cultured English had thought it right to behead a crowned brigand then in Russia it was necessary to liquidate a hundred Romanovs. Grinich, the former watchmaker, a moderate Bolshevik, pointed out that the English monarch had been condemned by an act of Parliament. Taking a life, any man's, without due process of law was unprincipled terror and he, personally, refused to have anything to do with it. To end the wrangling another moderate, Goloshchokin, was sent to obtain instructions from the Central Committee. But Moscow was more than nine hundred perilous versts away. Half the intervening countryside was in the hands of White insurgents and bands of Cossack freebooters roamed through towns and villages in a frenzy of rape and murder. If Goloshchokin failed to return . . .

Byeloborodov hunched his massive shoulders under the burden of decision. Destiny was reaching out to grip him by the throat. It was an incredible thought that he, a miner and the son of a miner, could issue a quiet order and in no time at all a dynasty that had ruled Russia for centuries would cease to exist. History should reverberate like the voice of God on a mountain peak. But if it fell to his lot to do the Revolution that service, so be it.

As daylight dwindled rumours of further disaster filtered in from the smouldering battle-front. A special unit of Red Guards deployed to hold the north bank of the river Ufa had been overwhelmed. Kamnishlov, seventy-five versts to the east, was said to have fallen to the Czechs with scarcely a shot from its demoralized defenders. In Ekaterinburg itself, a riot over food broke out among the thousands of refugees sheltering in the railway station and people were trodden to death.

Some time after midnight Byeloborodov stretched out on the camp-bed in his office to try to snatch a bit of rest. Fragmentary messages of alarm sparked and fizzled through the inflamed circuits of his brain. Sleep struck him like a blow on the back of the skull.

When he returned with groaning reluctance to sensibility Goloshchokin's moonstruck shadow was there in the room. He seemed dejected to have survived his difficult journey, closing the door in silence, switching on the light and passing a hand wearily over the back of his neck as he collapsed into a chair.

'Well?' Byeloborodov said quietly.

Goloshchokin stared at him through a glaze of fatigue and turned his thumbs towards the ground.

Byeloborodov rose slowly from the bed. 'All of them?'

'Even the servants,' Goloshchokin replied and a hard lump appeared on the hinge of each jaw.

Byeloborodov nodded. 'Have you got it in writing?'

'Yes, I insisted. The order must be read and destroyed.'

Goloshchokin undid his shirt and produced an oilskin packet. Inside was an envelope. It bore no mark, no official seal, and was limp from the heat of his body. Byeloborodov again experienced amazement at the lack of ceremony attending this symbolic end of an epoch. Across his mind passed an instantaneous vision of Russia's last emperor, shabby and subdued, digging a vegetable patch in the Ipatiev garden under the jeering eyes of peasant lads on sentry duty. A Romanov ruler for whom no requiem would be sung in the cathedrals of Muscovy, whose grave would be anonymous.

He opened the envelope. It contained a terse message written in Sverdlov's angular, scholastic hand authorizing execution. There must be no survivors. Sentence to be carried out with least possible delay to avoid danger of rescue by counter-revolutionaries but precise time left to local discretion. Remains of deceased to be totally obliterated and Moscow notified by telegraph immediately action completed.

It was the fifteenth of July. Byeloborodov did some mental arithmetic, tapping the arm of his chair with blunt fingertips. So many lorries, so many men, so many versts to a suitable mineshaft already selected. The deed must be done under cover of darkness and be over before dawn.

'Tomorrow at midnight,' he said quietly.

'Who will do it?' Goloshchokin asked in an agonized voice. 'Supposing the men disobey the order to shoot?'

'It will be done even if I have to fire every bullet myself,' said Byeloborodov. The hair on the back of his hands bristled. Sweeping the clutter on his desk aside, he pulled the telephone over and called an immediate meeting of the regional soviet . . .

A rough wooden pallisade had been erected around the engineer Ipatiev's house, partly to screen the royal prisoners from curious onlookers but mainly to strengthen security. At dusk the following day sentries were doubled, sharpshooters were posted at upper-storey windows of the long white building. If a citizen so much as loitered to fasten a bootlace he was driven off with curses and rifle-butts. One by one at irregular intervals tarpaulin-covered lorries assembled at the rear of the house.

For the unsuspecting prisoners the evening seemed no different from others they had spent in captivity. The deposed Tsar played chess with Dr Botkin, his personal physician. Alexandra, the Tsarina, wrote letters to German relatives which would never be delivered. Demidova, her lady-in-waiting, passed the time with needlework. The four boyish-looking princesses – their hair had been shaved after an attack of measles and was still short – read, embroidered and did what they could to amuse fourteen-year-old Tsarevich Alexei, who could bleed to death from a cut unless lovingly protected. How the male cook and manservant occupied themselves in the last hours of their lives goes unrecorded.

Darkness spilled over the rim of mountains and filled the valley. The fevered, besieged town settled down for the night to a silence broken by the whimpering of famished children. Lamps were extinguished in the Romanov sleeping quarters. Chairman Byeloborodov and other members of the regional Soviet, pale and sweating as if their own last moment was approaching, kept glancing at their watches in the adjacent barrack house. A special ration of vodka had been issued to the Latvian execution squad, one of whom was playing a concertina as boisterous voices sang in shrill falsetto:

I'm cursed by my mother,
My dad's gone berserk.
A Bolshevik kissed me
In Ciechochinek . . .

Byeloborodov gave a wincing smile, recalling that in a pit disaster trapped miners also sang to keep their courage up. He felt the approach of midnight as a fist closing on his stomach. With fifteen minutes to go he nodded at the bearded, villainous-looking Jacob Yurovsky who nodded back and immediately left the room. The others dispersed to the trucks to supervise loading of the corpses.

The clear, moonless sky reached upward to infinity. Byeloborodov's lapsed Christian soul shuddered and was instantly suppressed. He watched Yurovsky and his firing squad unsteadily cross the courtyard and enter the Ipatiev house. Everything would happen quickly. A few minutes to rouse the sleepers and order them to dress on the pretext that counter-revolutionary forces were about to attack the building and they must be moved to the cellar for their own safety. Hurry them down before they could properly ungum their eyes. Yurovsky steps forward and reads the sentence. To respect legality: a concession to the pedantry of Grinich. 'Nikolai Alexandrovich Romanov ... order of the Bolshevik Central Committee, etcetera, etcetera,' and the shooting begins with a revolver bullet between the Tsar's eyes.

The worst thing was having to shoot women. Revolutionary justice: cruel but necessary.

Byeloborodov drew back his sleeve and glanced at his wrist-watch. The hands converged. Midnight.

Gripping the starting handle of the leading lorry, he swung vigorously. An irregular series of explosions began as one by one engines belched gasoline smoke. Soon they were all roaring together loud enough to drown a clap of thunder, never mind the business going on in the Ipatiev cellar.

Presently the first bundle was brought out wrapped in a dirty blanket.

The very next night in the small industrial town of Alapayevsk, four hundred versts north-east of Ekaterinburg, there was another lot of shooting. Four grand dukes, one grand duchess, a prince and princess, all finished off in the basement of a disused school and dropped down a mineshaft.

The workers had settled their account with the Romanovs.

And in far-off Moscow the people's government, Sovnarcom, was busily changing the world, building Communism without ceremony.

'Living socialism is the work of the popular masses themselves,' Lenin had declared. 'Not one pound of bread will escape accounting.'

So delegates from factory, farm and ghetto sat on rough benches in the dilapidated former restaurant of the Hotel Metropole. Faded patches showed on walls where pictures in gilt frames had paid homage to the Imperial order. Cigarette stubs were trodden into the carpet and a stone fountain that once splashed to the tinkling of a string orchestra was now waterless. In this drab forum the commanding voice of proletarian dictatorship was heard for the first time on earth. Soldiers in battle-stained tunics, graduates of brilliant universities, gnarled, taciturn men who spoke their minds with blunt gestures and words as slow and heavy as spadefuls of clay soil. Day by day they uprooted more of the old life and laid down foundations for the new.

On this particular day Commissioner Semashko occupied the rostrum, presenting the draft of a decree on public health, as Yakov Sverdlov, Chairman of the Central Executive, a tall sickly-looking intellectual in a worn leather jerkin, entered the chamber and walked briskly to his place behind Lenin. The two bearded faces came together in whispered consultation.

As soon as Semashko finished speaking, Lenin rose to his feet and said: 'Comrade Sverdlov requests the floor to make an announcement.'

Sverdlov's pince-nez flashed as he gazed along the rows of upturned faces. A celebrated orator whose resonant voice came surprisingly from the sound-box of a meagre chest, he spoke now entirely without rhetoric.

'I have received information that Nicholas has been executed by shooting at Ekaterinburg on the order of the Regional Soviet. Nicholas wanted to escape. The Czechoslovaks were approaching. The Central Committee has approved the execution.'

In total silence he descended the platform and left the chamber.

'We will now continue with a detailed examination of the draft decree,' said Lenin in practical tones and called on the next speaker.

In the meantime, Sverdlov hurried back to his office and sent for Felix Dzerzhinsky, chief of the Cheka.

'Comrade, I have to report a grave act of negligence in connection with the liquidation of the Romanovs in Ekaterinburg,' he said. 'A body is missing.'

Except for a slight narrowing of watchful sardonic eyes, the Pole's harsh aristocratic features remained impassive.

'Missing?' he inquired softly.

'Eleven people were brought to the cellar. Only ten corpses were acccunted for.'

'In that case we are dealing with sabotage, not negligence.'

Sverdlov gave a short, impatient nod. 'It cannot be ruled out until a full investigation establishes otherwise.'

'Whose is the missing body?'

'Byeloborodov is not sure. There was a good deal of mutilation. But he is certain it was one of the daughters, probably the youngest, Anastasia. I can only,' Sverdlov said gloomily, 'hope the girl is dead. Lenin, the Central Executive – all of us – regard it of the utmost importance that there be no survivors.' His voice deepened and moved into rhetoric. 'If as much as a finger of the Tsar was found, in no time the priests would have it performing miracles, but a seventeen-year-old princess risen from the dead! The Whites would rally a crusade around that living banner!'

Dzerzhinsky's thin lips became compressed behind his shaggy, drooping moustache. He gazed at Sverdlov with uncontrolled severity.

'That,' he said icily, 'the Cheka will never permit.'

2

Byeloborodov turned from the tiled stove where he was burning papers, startled by the sombre, clean-shaven stranger who had silently entered the office. Dressed in the leather jacket of a Chekist, a Mauser pistol strapped to his waist, the man's sudden appearance gave the Regional Chairman an unreasonable feeling of having been caught doing something shameful.

More trouble!

'You've arrived at a bad time,' he said ungraciously.

Sweat ran down his face and drenched the collar of his grimy, unbuttoned shirt. In contrast, the visitor looked as fresh as if he'd stepped out of a propaganda poster – the tall, resolute, hard-eyed Bolshevik in his early thirties whose profile cleaved the dawn red sky of Russia.

'Peter Pavlovich Piatkov at your service,' the apparition declared with the faintest of ironical smiles at his grudging welcome. 'I believe you were informed I was coming.'

'Yes, of course. Dzerzhinsky telegraphed. The inquiry . . .'

'My instructions are to conclude the matter and report back to Moscow as quickly as possible. You have everything ready?'

Byeloborodov gestured helplessly. 'I'm doing the best I can. Frankly, these last few days . . .'

A despondent smile trembled on his lips. Everything was out of control. He was losing the faculty of decision. Look, comrade, he thought savagely, what the hell do you want of me? I'm coping with hunger, disease and military disaster. My body is screaming out for a decent night's sleep. The earth is breaking up under our feet and you fellows can think of nothing but smelling out a counter-revolutionary conspiracy!

'The situation here is desperate and getting worse every hour,' he said huskily. 'There's no alternative but to evacuate. I've given orders to burn every single piece of paper that could be of use to the enemy. It's doubtful if we can hold out more than another two days.'

'Then we must lose no time,' said Piatkov, calmly drawing a chair up to the desk and flicking open a thick notebook. 'There are a number of people I shall have to see. The Commander of the local Cheka, Yurovsky, members of the regional soviet –'

'Yes, yes! Of course.' Byeloborodov's heart beat irregularly with the effort of controlling his impatience. 'Write it all down. I have to go now, but I'll send an orderly. He'll bring the ones you want.'

'But, Comrade Chairman, you are the first on my list.'

'I'm sorry, I have a list of my own.'

A hardness slid under Piatkov's smooth dark skin and pin-points of fire shone in his watchful eyes, but he spoke almost solicitously.

'Please don't think I'm being difficult. There are certain things I must find out from you before I speak to anybody else. You would oblige me by being cooperative.'

'Cooperative!' The Chairman laughed as though he was choking. He stamped towards the door, stamped back again and glared at the Chekist across the width of the desk. 'I'm as loyal as anybody, Comrade, but don't lecture *me* on cooperation. We've been under siege here for weeks. I've practically gone on my knees to everybody begging for help. If we could stick it out here, we'd save the Urals for the Revolution. Give us a daily ration of one herring and a hundred grammes of bread like they get in Moscow and we'd fight like lions.' A nerve vibrated wildly: suddenly it snapped. Holding out a rigid arm, he pointed shakily at the street. 'There are people out there – sick, wounded, desperate for a few crumbs – human beings living in hell! What's going to happen to them? Are they to be abandoned to White butchery? Don't tell me what the priorities are, comrade,' he yelled, and struck his breast. 'I feel them here, *here*.'

The air was stifling. Transparent cylinders of dusty sunshine beamed heat into the room. A glossy bluebottle as large as a honey-bee buzzed against the grimy window. Piatkov took out an immaculate handkerchief and wiped the perspiration from his broad, pale forehead.

'I understand how you feel,' he said neutrally. 'No one underestimates your difficulties. But the Central Committee also has its priorities. This is only one sector of civil war. The inquiry has been ordered because it is important. The sooner we begin, the sooner it will be over. You will not be detained a moment longer than necessary.'

The tone was adamant. It could have been Dzerzhinsky himself speaking. An instinctive shudder travelled the length of Byeloborodov's spine as he recalled the melancholy face of that merciless defender of the republic whose tall, untidy figure could freeze the temperature of a crowded hall the moment it entered. What had he said scarcely a month ago? 'We stand for organized terror. Terror is an absolute necessity in time of revolution. The Cheka is obliged to defend the revolution even if its sword sometimes falls on the heads of the innocents.' Quite suddenly the Chairman was a hollow man: defiance was an empty gesture. Lowering his bulky body into a chair in sheer exhaustion, he stared into the other's sardonic eyes and said: 'What do you want to know?'

'Everything,' was the laconic reply.

Byeloborodov began talking.

In a deliberately perfunctory manner, as if submitting a report on the rationing of potatoes, he described how the slaughter of eleven human beings had been prepared – the choice of a suitable time; the provision of axes, sulphuric acid and of gasoline to burn the remains and render them unrecognizable. It was felt that Russians could not be relied on to obey an order to shoot the Imperial family, so Yurovsky was told to select an execution squad of Latvian Red Guards, men whose reputation for ruthlessness and efficiency would be well-known to Cheka headquarters. The burial party, however, consisted mainly of local workers and peasants. Fears of mass-hysteria should news of the liquidation circulate among the fevered populace caused a degree of haste in collecting the bodies. Only when they reached the mineshaft and began to chop up the corpses limb from limb was it discovered that one body – almost certainly that of the Grand Duchess Anastasia – was missing. An immediate search was ordered and was still in progress.

Piatkov nodded and wrote it all down, his manner also matter-of-fact. So, a sack of potatoes short, it seemed to say. We must get to the bottom of it.

'Did you question everybody involved?'

'Goloshchokin did . . . but not everybody.'

'Why not?'

'Some men from the burial party had already dispersed. There was a delay, you understand. First we held a meeting of the soviet –'

'You allowed men to leave? After what they'd witnessed?'

Byeloborodov's heavy shoulders jerked defiantly. 'Why not?'

'Because,' Piatkov pointed out quietly, 'it was not exactly the kind of news they should have been permitted to take back to their wives.'

'They did not know who they were burying. Class-enemies, that's all they were told. Not the first, nor will it be the last. There's nothing more bloodthirsty than class-war.'

Piatkov drew an elliptical ring around Goloshchokin's name. 'Or more treacherous,' he insinuated. 'Tell me, am I right in thinking that some of your commissars objected to executing Nicholas?'

The wrinkles in Byeloborodov's weathered face deepened as he stared at the encircled name. It was vaguely sinister. In these days of civil war, spies, traitors and saboteurs could crop up anywhere and this created an obsession with revolutionary purity. A man's past came under scrutiny at the least suspicion and heaven help him if somewhere along the line there'd been a flirtation with the wrong party. Nothing there to worry a good

Bolshevik like Goloshchokin, but there was more than one former Menshevik and Socialist Revolutionary on the regional soviet. So, what of it? The ambiguous, cold-eyed and obviously non-proletarian Chekist, Piatkov, was himself an unlikely political virgin.

Yes, there had been some who didn't agree with finishing off the Tsar the other night, but it would be a bad thing if comrades got to biting one another like spiders in a jar as soon as something went wrong. If Moscow wanted to start a witch-hunt, they'd get no help from him.

'Where did you hear that?' he demanded, the dull rage reviving. Trembling, he reached into his pocket for a cigarette but found it empty.

Piatkov shrugged. 'You know the saying. Rumour travels fast.'

'I'll give you a short answer. Three words, no, four. It's a damned lie! Write down that I said so.'

Piatkov wrote it down.

'Sometimes a tiny grit of truth is buried in rumour,' he said. 'Let's dig about a bit and see if it's there. You say there was no disagreement?'

'None at all. Only differences of opinion on how we should set about it.' Byeloborodov cleared his throat huskily. His anger subsided: there was not enough energy left in him to fuel defiance. 'Goloshchokin explained it all to the Central Executive. We would have preferred to see Nicholas Romanov brought before a revolutionary tribunal. The shooting of workers on Bloody Sunday alone justifies his execution as a criminal assassin, never mind all the atrocities since 1905. When that became impossible because of the situation at the front we accepted the necessity for immediate action.'

'All of you?'

'Have you ever been on a committee where there was no disagreement? One or two were in favour of liquidating Nicholas and the Tsarevich, but not the women and servants. That's when we decided to consult Moscow. No one opposed Lenin's decision.'

'Not even Grinich and Goloshchokin?'

'Nobody, comrade. Not a single one,' Byeloborodov said with weary emphasis. 'Have you finished with me? Can I go now?'

'Not quite.' Piatkov glanced meditatively at his notes. He produced a paper packet containing a single army biscuit which he broke in half, handing one piece to the Regional Chairman in a gesture of friendliness.

Then the cross-examination began. And after Byeloborodov, each member of the Regional Soviet in turn came under the same relentless examination.

The heat still burned with a harsh malevolence some hours later as Peter Piatkov accompanied by Goloshchokin went on foot to continue the investigation at the Ipatiev house. It must, he thought, be the fiercest summer for years. The famished town stirred feebly now and then before relapsing into a quiescent stupor like a creature that had lain down in the dust to die. Two shabby middle-aged men pulling a handcart piled with refuse gave them a servile greeting, former bourgeoisie performing their compulsory labour. Sensing the approaching doom, an assortment of refugees carrying children and bundled belongings were in hurried flight, but apart from distant rifle-shots sounding haphazardly among the surrounding hills there was little sign of war. The struggle against starvation was more in evidence in the crowds camped outside a food cooperative on Glavni Prospekt, hopelessly waiting for a miracle to fill its empty shelves. Spidery infants with stick-like limbs and distended bellies watched the two men pass, their eyes huge and blank.

Peter doggedly averted his gaze, denying himself the indulgence of pity. One must look beyond immediate suffering. When enthusiasm swept liberated Petrograd after the storming of the Winter Palace, a German poet spoke of the Revolution as an orgasmic union of Russia with her destiny. Now, nine months later, she was a mother writhing in the monstrous pangs of parturition.

But from the very beginning the new life forming within her was attacked by virulent bacteria – dispossessed landlords who buried vast quantities of food in secret stores, peasants refusing to surrender grain, merchants draining the nation's capital away in gold smuggled abroad, profiteers who forced the price of bread up by 800 per cent. In outlying provinces armed freebooters destroyed crops, cattle and human beings indiscriminately. One vital task of the Cheka was to destroy these vermin. But the crisis of birth itself had now come for the Motherland with civil war and foreign intervention. Either a living future would struggle from the blood and slime or the outcome would be death. Death . . .

Walking through the drab despondent town where Tsardom's last representative so improbably met his provincial fate, a town now passively awaiting his strutting avengers, Peter Piatkov was invaded by a dull, grinding anxiety. Omens could be disregarded but not the realities of war. With the Ural front in collapse nothing could stop the enemy pouring across the plain of Sviazhsk. And beyond Sviazhsk exposed to everything was central Russia, the dear heartland. He began to walk faster, irrationally, driven by alarm. It was as if danger threatened the love of his life.

The inquiry resumed in the engineer Ipatiev's spacious, high-ceilinged study. It had been cruelly vandalized. Shelves were stripped of books and ornaments, the carpet had been ripped up, official notices stuck on the walls announced this, that and the other in threatening terms, the huge empty fireplace was littered with glass from a splintered mirror. There was a dank smell of urine.

Jacob Yurovsky, commander of the local Cheka, presented himself for interrogation with the swaggering truculence of someone who felt his place in history was controversial but assured.

'Take my word for it, comrade, no one came out of there alive. Not after we finished our job. You can tell them that in Moscow.'

His coarse piratical face gazed good-humouredly at Peter through its bush of black hair.

'There was no two ways about it,' he went on, sucking the last bit of smoke from a crumpled cigarette and letting it trickle through his thick snout. 'Everything was done according to orders. Listen you lot, I said to the lads, we're Bolsheviks, the dictatorship of the proletariat, and these are enemies of the people. So we're going to finish them off quick and without mercy. And don't none of you go pulling the gold rings off their fingers and hiding them up your arses. You won't get away with it. Never mind gold. If I find as much as an inch of tobacco a man's not entitled to, his mother will be wailing for his soul by the next morning.'

Peter watched him impassively, with cold distaste. Villainous in appearance, stinking like a Kalmyk herdsman in his filthy clothes, the man was not entirely what he seemed. His Tsarist police record, now deposited on file in Lubianka Street, was succinct and sardonic. 'Yurovsky, Jacob Volfovich, son of a ghetto innkeeper. Wits sharpened in some rabbinical school, he can spout Marxism like the rest of them if it suits him but affects the speech and manner of an illiterate drayman. Only the coin has a hollow ring. Give it a bite and the teethmarks will show.' It was an accurate description even with the anti-semitism subtracted; and from a revolutionary point-of-view Yurovsky's record was not ignoble. There had been nothing counterfeit in his underground work or the prison sentences it incurred.

An orderly brought in two steaming glasses of carrot tea. Jacob Volfovich gulped the insipid brew and wiped his mouth with his sleeve.

'It was like this,' he said. 'Outside they started up the engines. When the noise was good and loud we lined them all up like they were going to have a photo taken. I stood opposite Nicholas Romanov, gabbled out the order of execution, then whipped out my revolver and shot him between his two blue eyes. The boys did their shooting at once before there was too much screaming. Anybody moved or groaned, he was finished off with bayonet and rifle-butt. When they came to load them on to the lorries there was only death in that cellar, you believe me.' Suddenly he knitted his bushy eyebrows and scowled across the desk. 'I don't like the way you're looking, comrade. Don't think we took pleasure in it. Killing in hot blood's one thing, but a job like that revolts the stomach. Some of the lads were sick afterwards.'

'I can well imagine,' Peter said. Abruptly, he got up from the chair and began restlessly pacing the room, pausing at the fireplace to stare down at his fragmented reflection in the splintered mirror. His severed lips were compressed and bitter, and glittering among the debris a solitary eye burned the moment into his memory – Ekaterinburg, summer 1918, the dying and the dead . . .

'Tell me,' he said slowly, 'if nobody was left alive can you suggest why anyone should want to steal a dead body?'

Yurovsky poked his tobacco-stained teeth with a dirty thumbnail and shrugged.

'Looking for hidden jewels, maybe. Even worse, it could be something unnatural. It's not unknown for degenerates to violate a female corpse.'

That, too, was possible. Anything was possible, given the scope of human depravity. But, revulsion apart, there was no point in raking up more of that filth.

'It's time I inspected the cellar,' Peter said. 'Will you please accompany me.'

'You'll find nothing down there. It's all been tidied up.'

'Let's have a look, anyway. I can hardly tell Dzerzhinsky that I didn't even see the place where it happened.'

'True enough,' Yurovsky agreed. His eyes twinkled merrily. 'That cellar's now part of revolutionary history, like the fall of the Bastille. One day citizens will come from far and wide, in pilgrimage, you might say.'

'You might say,' Peter echoed dryly.

He had expected to find something not unlike a prison cell, dank, constricted, gloom filtering from an iron grating. Instead an alcoved double door led into a large room that still retained traces of elegance. It had striped wallpaper of a pattern fashionable among the pre-revolutionary bourgeoisie, with a decorative cornice round the ceiling, a pinewood floor of narrow planks and wrought-iron brackets for hanging lamps. In a curious way, this made it more macabre – bullet holes, fallen plaster, bloodstains on the floor, splinters of wood dug up by the points of bayonets, a row of terribly empty chairs. And yet what touched the mind was not a sense of horror but something hopeless and forlorn that lives in all rooms left derelict and abandoned.

Like a stage-manager evoking a successful production, Yurovsky strode around on short legs setting the scene, explaining where each departed actor had stood or sat, reassembling his cast of executioners. Bullets flew again, bodies fell, blood mingled with blood as vividly as if the smoke of burning cordite still choked the air.

'Were your men drunk at the time?' Peter interrupted brusquely.

Yurovsky turned, arrested in mid-gesture.

'Drunk?' he asked plaintively. 'My men? Now who could've told you a stinking slander like that?' He shook his head several times and spat at the floor. 'Maybe you've had the experience, comrade, maybe not, but taking a life's not just a question of bang-bang you're dead. My lads aren't murderers. Send 'em into a room to butcher peaceful-looking people, you've got to tell 'em why it's right for the cause. And then you've got to dish out a ration of vodka to stop their knees trembling. Right?'

'Stiffen the knees and confuse the brain,' Peter remarked, lifting his hand to forestall the inevitable protest. 'The point I'm getting at, Yurovsky, is that somebody's sight might have got a bit blurred, especially if his heart wasn't in the killing.'

The questioning proceeded interminably, hour after hour, as daylight faded and a haunted darkness loomed beyond the long windows of the study. A procession of men filed into the room one by one, and the more they ransacked their memories, the more an impression of panic and confusion emerged. Like victims of shock, they could only recall fragments of horror, retreating into baffled amnesia when asked to supply precise details of their unnerving experience.

A tow-haired Latvian of about twenty, sturdy and sunburnt, suddenly burst into tears.

'We – we was ordered to do it! Ord-ord . . . ordered.' He began to shiver violently. 'They . . . they even shot . . . their dog!'

Late in the night came the first concrete indication that a premeditated escape may have been effected. Someone had seen a horse-drawn peasant cart filled with straw at the rear of the house, just outside the perimeter. It was unattended. Perhaps it meant nothing: many such carts brought fugitives from outlying villages into Ekaterinburg. On the other hand, it would have proved ideal for removing an injured girl to a prepared hiding place. And two members of the burial party were still missing. Oddly, nobody knew their names, not Byeloborodov, nor Goloshchokin, nor those with whom they had supposedly been working. They were described as dark, stocky men of about thirty years of age, with prominent cheek-bones and small eyes, who spoke like mountain people. It was believed they were brothers.

A faint dawn crept up from the West Siberian lowlands and crested the distant mountains as he left to walk back to the hotel, lifting his face gratefully to the cool, cleansing breeze. No gunfire could be heard: war had surrendered to the truce of sleep. There was a brief sensual pleasure in physical movement, in solitude, in the illusion of peace created by boarded-up shops, silent factories, deserted foundries smelling of sulphur and cold metal.

There was also disquiet, a mistrust of appearances. Passing the derelict Church of the Ascension on Vosnesensky Prospekt, he saw a spectral procession emerge from the foetid interior. Further along, groups of ragged people were leaving a school they had been using as a dormitory. The whole town was in stealthy movement. Quietly, stumbling like sleepwalkers, refugees in their thousands were abandoning primitive shelters and migrating westward. The low multitudinous murmur, the sound of shuffling feet, was like the vast susurrus of leaves in a windswept forest. A lorry, heavily loaded and guarded by armed men, started up abruptly and moved off, soon joined by others. Horse-drawn carts rattled along uneven roads. And, although the noise of flight increased, furtiveness and stealth remained.

Peter was suddenly engulfed by the mood of depression that had begun to settle on him the moment he drove into Ekaterinburg on his motor-cycle. He would always think of the town despondently, not only because of his disagreeable duty here and the apathetic sufferings of its war victims, but also because here the spirit of Russia languished in provincial squalor, and in that sloth even the Revolution could sink without trace.

When he arrived, the Hotel Palais Royal was being hastily

vacated. Red Guards aided by civilian clerks staggered beneath wooden crates heavy with the bureaucratic impedimenta of Soviet power and loaded them into waiting lorries.

Peter pushed past them and entered the building. Voices came from Byeloborodov's office, one of them a woman's. It had a contralto timbre, husky and familiar. After the shock, his heart moved painfully. Lydia. It needed little to evoke in him the vivid memory of her haunting face. It interposed itself achingly across the years as indestructible as time, never losing its power to torment his dreams and fill his waking hours with the hope that he would turn a corner, enter a room, make an unexpected journey, and find her waiting.

Trembling absurdly, he stood listening to the blurred conversation on the other side of the door. A paralysis of will prevented him from entering. The telephone rang. Byeloborodov answered it, speaking in guttural fury. 'No, it's impossible! What the devil do you think I am, a miracle worker?'

'Will that be all, Comrade Chairman?' the heart-contracting voice inquired.

There was a further muffled exchange, an interminable pause then, abruptly, the door opened.

A small dark woman emerged carrying some papers. Her melancholy Jewish eyes surveyed him curiously. 'Yes, comrade?' she said.

He shook his head. How often it had happened, the wild surge of hope, disappointment as acrid as grief. There was nothing to say, nothing at all.

'I am the secretary to the Regional Soviet,' the woman said. 'Is there anything I can do for you?'

Not even the voice . . .

Byeloborodov shouted from inside: 'Who is it? What's going on there? . . . Oh, it's you, Piatkov,' he said in an unfriendly tone as Peter entered. 'Well, have you come to any conclusion?' There was a demented look in his bloodshot eyes.

'Not yet,' Peter said. 'This is only the beginning.' Back in Moscow he would open a file and start the search that could only be concluded when it was known for certain if the missing victim in the Ipatiev cellar was alive or dead. It would be better for her if she was dead, he reflected abstractly.

Outside it was growing light, the dawn-blue sky shot through with horizontal rays of pallid sunshine. A distant machine-gun stitched a seam in the silence, followed by the sharp crackle of rifle fire. The truce of sleep was ended.

'We're pulling out this morning,' said Byeloborodov. 'I can offer you a lift to Perm.'

'I'm going in a different direction,' Peter replied. He held out his hand.

Byeloborodov seized it in a convulsive grip. Red tears glittered in his eyes and he swallowed hoarsely. For a moment he found difficulty in speaking.

'Good luck to you, then,' he brought out at last, still holding Peter's hand. 'We'll meet in better times. I'm sure of it!'

Thinking of Lydia and the imponderable future, Peter said: 'Let us hope so.'

Chapter Two

The Ural Regional Soviet barely squeezed through the narrow escape route to Perm before the Czechoslovak Legion swarmed triumphantly into Ekaterinburg. It was 26 July and Peter had been three hours on the road. Somewhere in the Sarapul region he came under machine-gun fire from an enemy group hiding in a forest and interrupted his journey to organize and lead a counter-attack by the local detachment of Red militia. This unrehearsed delay caused him to arrive at the Volga city of Kazan just too late to experience an extraordinary coincidence, prefigured perhaps by the confusion aroused in him by Byeloborodov's secretary's voice. Some ten minutes before he called at military headquarters to obtain a requisition to refuel his motor-cycle, a six-hour conference of guerrilla commanders had concluded and dispersed. One of those attending had been Lydia Alexandrova, the woman who was dearer to him than life itself.

Back in Moscow, on 6 August he heard the shock news that Admiral Kolchak's White Guards, sweeping up from south of the Urals, had combined with the Czechs and captured Kazan, seizing the entire gold reserves of Russia deposited there for safe-keeping. Lenin's home town of Simbirsk had also fallen. A mood of desperation gripped the dedicated defenders of the beleagured Republic. 'Comrades, we are alone,' the proletariat was told. Workers vowed to slave at their machines until they dropped. Elderly men, schoolboys, disabled war veterans volunteered for front-line fighting. The Central Committee went into continuous session as the military situation steadily worsened. A British army of intervention with an American contingent had already occupied Archangelsk in the north. In Vladivostok and elsewhere in eastern Siberia, Japanese invaders were joined by British, French and American units. General

Dutov's counter-revolutionary Cossacks held extensive territory around Uralsk, the borderland region between European Russia and the Kazakh steppes. The trap of steel was closing. But the greatest immediate danger was posed by the doughty Czechoslovaks. Hurriedly assembling the railway coaches that formed his mobile headquarters, Commissar of War and Commander-in-Chief of the Red Army Leon Trotsky, determined at all cost to halt their advance, raced towards the vital strategic town of Sviazhsk, on the west bank of the Volga opposite Kazan. If Sviazhsk fell, nothing could stop the death-thrust at Moscow itself.

It was better in any case to die fighting than fall into enemy hands. Kolchak's White Guards were indulging in an orgy of vengeful massacre in all the captured towns and villages. Naked corpses of Reds and those denounced as Red were left in the streets for days before burial, throats slashed, eyes gouged, noses and tongues cut off, genitals mutilated. It was as though the slaughterers had frenziedly sought to obliterate everything that was recognizably human in their victims. Dazed survivors who managed to reach safety spoke of men and women dragged into the streets and beaten to death by infuriated bourgeois mobs in reprisal for humiliations they believed had been inflicted upon them.

Despite attempts at sabotage on the line, within forty-eight hours of Kazan's capture Trotsky's train arrived in Sviazhsk. Calm, indomitable, his eyes glinting shrewdly, he entered a staff car and drove among the disorganized, panic-striken Bolshevik soldiers, rallying them with his mordant, electrifying oratory, awakening men from the trance of defeat. In contemptuous disregard of danger, he led them personally back into battle. Messengers were sent to contact Red guerrillas still operating behind enemy lines. 'Keep on fighting. We are going to win,' they were told.

2

A rifle bolt clicked. 'Stop, or I'll blast your head off!' A dark shape separated from the web of shadow thrown by a clump of birches and a cold muzzle jabbed the ragged intruder's neck.

'Who are you?'

'Love of Christ, Dmitri, it's me. Vladimir Svirsky! Take that thing away before it goes off.'

White teeth shone in the sentry's blackened face. He lowered his rifle.

'Volodya! What the hell are you doing here? Your lot are supposed to be the other side of the river.'

'I've got a message, you cunt. What else?'

'As long as you didn't come for grub,' the sentry laughed. 'We're down to digging worms.'

'Can't think of nothing but your gut,' Volodya said in mock disgust, 'and you defending the blessed soil of free Russia. Where's the commander?'

'Sleeping peacefully. Come along.'

Patches of moonlight stippled the black earth as they moved softly through shadows of gently stirring trees. They crossed a small stream, stooped under overhanging branches and entered a clearing where a score or so of partisans lay in huddled sleep on the ground or resting against tree-trunks. 'Wait here, Vova,' Dmitri said, stepping forward and pausing beside a slight figure wrapped in a worn army coat lying apart from the others.

'Comrade!' He bent and touched the sleeper's shoulder.

Light eyes gleaming in a taut, youthful face, the guerrilla commander stared upwards and said: 'What is it?'

'A messenger,' Dmitri whispered. 'Volodya Svirsky, from Frumkin's unit.'

'A message from Joseph! Send him over.'

The young commander's voice was husky and unbroken, a woman's, but Dmitri seemed to take it for granted. She threw aside her coat and stood up, half a head taller than him. Thick dark hair roughly cropped, leather jerkin accentuating the breadth of her shoulders, the swell of her hips and her long shapely legs concealed in ill-fitting breeches, except for the contralto voice she could have been a tall smooth boy.

'What's it like over your side of the river, Volodya?' she asked, buckling on her belt with its heavy revolver and taking the message from him.

Volodya rubbed his snub nose. 'We're still alive,' he replied grudgingly.

'It's going to be all right, you'll see,' the girl said, striking a match. Her eyes picked up the flame's reflection, catlike, as she read the message. 'Wake up Igor Ivanovich,' she told Dmitri, glancing at her wristwatch to check the time. He nodded obediently and left. She smiled at Volodya. 'Homesick for Novgorod?'

'All the time,' he said. 'Do you know it?'

'Do I know it!' The commander laughed softly as if to imply that her happiest memories were of that ancient city. 'When I was a kid in Petersburg my father used to take me there to visit an elderly aunt. She lived near the Cathedral of Sophia, in one of those very narrow old streets.'

'The Sophia Side. Posh, eh?' Volodya grinned mischievously. 'I wouldn't say too much about that, comrade Lydia. Better shift the old lady to the Commercial Side, where we live. We're woodcarvers, the Svirskys. Have been for hundreds of years. Fancy you having an aunty in Novgorod!'

'It's a good place. Independent people. I like the old proverb, how does it go?'

'If the prince is bad, into the mud with him,' Volodya recited happily. 'And that's how it's always been in our town,' he said with amused tenderness, staring into the darkness.

The sentry reappeared, accompanied by a slouching battle-scarred man in his middle twenties, one eye covered by a dirty bandage.

'What's up?' he demanded laconically.

'I have to see Joseph,' said the girl. 'Something important.'

'Why don't he come to see you?'

'Because, Igor Ivanovich, in this area he commands all guerrilla forces. He is also the political commissar.' She looked steadily into his one good eye. 'I'm only in command of this unit.'

'Yeah, sure,' the man said, his mouth twisting cynically.

'I'll be gone about two hours. Put everybody on the alert, we may have to move out tonight.'

'Very good, comrade commander,' Igor Ivanovich said. Slowly, still staring at her, he put his hands between his legs and scratched his genitals.

'Let's go, Volodya,' said the girl, walking swiftly away with a swinging stride. She merged into the shadows and became invisible.

'No wonder we're fucking well on the run,' the one-eyed man muttered viciously.

Lydia Alexandrova's guerrilla group was one of a few scattered formations left behind in the general retreat and hiding in the forests south of Kazan. It was Tatar country, a region of small towns and sheep-raising villages, each with their shallow-domed mosque, wooden slavonic church and muddy market square. A half moon shone in the starry sky, deceptively peaceful, but somewhere in that quiet country enemy patrols were hunting them. Capture meant certain and hideous death.

It took them almost an hour of stealthy movement to reach the woods outside Kovali where Joseph Frumkin's partisans were concealed. Odd, artificial-sounding cries rose from the dark fields as they crept along ditches. Each hidden fold was a potential ambush. As they approached the vicinity of the village there were muffled voices, the red glow of lighted cigarettes. Sentries. Lydia's foot slipped, dislodging a small shower of stones. The talking stopped in mid-sentence. There was the crack of a rifle-shot, then another and another. Bullets loosed off at random. She lay quite still, Volodya by her side, waiting for the sentries to resume their conversation, guessing that they'd fired out of boredom or nervousness. Somewhere in the sleeping village a dog howled with a note of human desolation. A man said something and laughed. It was safe to move again.

A thin mist floated above the river, just discernible in the moonlight.

'Ready to swim for it?' Volodya whispered.

Lydia nodded. Taking off her gun-belt and holding it over her head, she slipped cautiously into the water. The chill was unexpected, as sharp as a knife-thrust. Suddenly she was exhilarated, plunged into a memory of crystal winters a long time gone, the heart-leaping sight of snow glittering in an early morning garden: that aching innocence. And even when she pulled herself on to the opposite bank, shivering in her wet clothes, a feeling that had become unfamiliar was retained: optimism, the simple belief that things were going to get better.

It was two months since she'd left Moscow, early in June, to take part in the fighting that broke out when the Czechoslovaks armed themselves secretly, seized control of large stretches of the Trans-Siberian railway and occupied the southern Ural town of Chelyabinsk. Two months by the calendar, but time no less than reality was hideously distorted by war and a single day's bitterness and loss could seem longer than all the years of one's life. The death of one friend destroyed perspective, the agony of thousands darkened the very meaning of human existence. It was a price her generation had known it would have to pay to create for the first time a truly humane social order, yet it was hard to hold on to that abstract ideal when a starving child cried for food beside the body of its dead mother.

There had never been a revolution without the spilling of innocent blood, but not since Ghengis Khan had Russia seen such atrocities as were being perpetrated by defenders of the old order. In Finland alone the victorious Whites killed the wounded, machine-gunned thousands of workers in batches of hundreds at a time, and massacred women whose husbands or sons were Red Guards. But they couldn't machine-gun the future of 130 millions in the great territories of Russia. We are going to win, she told herself. It was not just rhetoric. One only had to recall those first intoxicating weeks when the people took over their own destiny after centuries of slavery and the great cry 'peace, land and bread' began to be answered. Bitterly though it must be fought for, that freedom was indestructible.

Yes, things are going to get better, she thought with conviction, glancing back at the village, now a huddle of dark buildings against the sky. The forest closed around them protectively, given over it seemed only to trees, birds and solitude. Volodya began to whistle under his breath. 'Halt! Who goes there?' someone called. The password was given. They were among friends. Joseph came towards her with open arms. 'Lydia,' he said, crushing her against his bony chest in a tight embrace. His body burned with a dry fever. They were old friends, this erstwhile Marxist critic of literature and herself. His whole life was dedicated to the revolution, and its present peril raged in his veins with malarial virulence.

'Great things are happening,' he said, leading her over to a small group of men sprawled on the ground near by. Among them was the gipsy-faced Platon Jorgashvili, a forty-year-old Georgian bandit turned Red guerrilla, who led a mixed group of Caucasian mountaineers operating north of Simbirsk. When asked why they were so far from their home territory, his cheerful answer was: 'Why not? It's good to see the world.'

'Come, little falcon, sit by me,' he said to Lydia, baring his strong white teeth in a rascally grin. 'I've been saving a bit of tobacco for you.'

'Real tobacco, Pasha?' she inquired, raising a sceptical eyebrow.

'*Makhorka*, sweetheart. What do you expect, Turkish?'

He rolled a cigarette in a piece of newspaper and she lit it eagerly, the first smoke for days. Bitter and strong, it produced a light-headed happiness. 'Here, comrade,' she said, passing the cigarette over to one of the other men who drew on it hungrily before handing it to someone else.

'Comrades!' Frumkin began in his arresting voice. Tall and thin, he gripped a low branch with one hand and stared down at them with a strange tenderness. The wind ruffled his thinning hair. Moved by something he saw in their faces, he seemed about to burst into tears and it was some moments before he resumed.

'For weeks we've been fighting a desperate campaign against counter-revolution and foreign intervention,' he said. 'We've lost many of our dearest comrades, boys we fought alongside, who shared their last crust of bread with us, as precious to us as our own flesh and blood. Each day it's been getting worse. Our forces have been driven away, we're isolated in enemy territory, short of arms, bellies empty. Bloodthirsty Kolchak' – his mouth twisted as though about to spit out something loathsome – 'says that no-one would give two brass kopecks for proletarian Russia and boasts he will hang Lenin and the Central Executive from the lamp-posts in Nevsky Prospekt.'

'We'll nail those kopecks into Kolchak's eyeballs,' Platon Jorgashvili growled, looking round at the others. He found no response: they were too weary for bluster.

'Kolchak will be dealt with,' Joseph said very quietly in

tones as dispassionate as justice itself. 'Comrades, it's fallen to our lot to be present at a crucial moment in history. A proclamation has reached us from Sviazhsk written by the Commissar for War himself.' He produced a typewritten sheet from his pocket and held it up. 'Platon, you have eyes that can see in the dark. Will you read it?'

Jorgashvili stood up, a short man with a barrel chest, and took the message. With obvious pride, but haltingly – like a backward pupil performing a recitation – he inflated his lungs and began to read.

'Comrades, soldiers of the Red Army, we are facing the decisive battle for the Republic. There can be no more retreat. Do not yield an inch of ground. From now on we take the counter-offensive. Kazan will be recaptured, then Simbirsk, Samara and every town and village until the White Czech forces are driven out of the entire Ural region. Be bold and courageous. Show no mercy to the class enemy. Long live the Revolution. Signed L. D. Trotsky.'

The Georgian stood in an orator's posture, head thrown back, waiting for the applause. There was silence. Somebody muttered: 'And I suppose the Commissar's gone back to his desk in Moscow.'

Tea by Vysotsky, sugar by Brodsky, Russia by Trotsky. The current anti-semitic joke. Jews own the country but won't fight for it. One even heard it from people who called themselves Bolsheviks.

Slowly, all expression drained from his face, Joseph turned to confront the speaker.

'No, Grodnik, Trotsky has not returned to Moscow,' he said, each syllable cold and distinct. 'I have been informed that on arrival at Sviazhsk he uncoupled the engine of his military train and ordered that back to Moscow. He remains to lead the fighting in person. Trotsky's intention is clear. Either there will be victory or no one will remain alive, not even the Commander-in-Chief.'

Jorgashvili had been staring at Grodnik, black eyebrows drawn together thunderously.

'You're not calling our Trotsky a coward?' he demanded, levelling a thick forefinger like the barrel of a revolver.

'I was only making a remark in free speech!' the unfortunate man snarled.

The fiery Georgian pulled out a knife. 'If I slice off a bit of your tongue it won't wag so much.'

Frumkin gripped his arm and said sharply: 'Keep calm, Platon Stepanovich! There are more important things to do than quarrel among ourselves.'

'Deciding what part we can take in the counter-offensive, for example,' Lydia intervened dryly. An impatience for action stirred in her. On the run, in hiding and generally demoralized, it was no wonder tempers became so easily frayed. 'It's at least thirty versts to Sviazhsk, even if we can get through. Let's start our own offensive. Between us, scattered around, we have more than sixty men. We can attack supply columns and railroads. We can harass the enemy and make him divert forces that would otherwise be used in the battle for Kazan –'

'And make marbles out of moonshine,' cut in the slow faintly supercilious voice of Mikhail Norodsky, a young probationary doctor whose medical apprenticeship had been deferred for the duration of civil war. 'I've got sixteen rounds of ammunition and an old musket some Frenchmen must have chucked away at Borodino. Others are not so lucky. The state we're in we couldn't harass an army of old ladies, *babushkas*.'

There was a grin on his engaging freckled face. He was like the boys she'd known a century ago in Montparnasse, in that doomed summer of youthful conspiracy and easy love before the holocaust.

'I'll make you a promise, Misha,' she said, echoing the old levity, and her hand went up to her cropped hair in an unconsciously feminine gesture. 'You will be presented with the gift of a beautiful English P.14 rifle as soon as I can persuade a Czech legionnaire to part with one.'

'Exactly! The first thing we have to do is capture some weapons,' said Joseph.

Platon Jorgashvili was putting the blade of his knife to peaceful use, sharpening a stick with great concentration. 'How?' he asked, not looking up.

'Very simple.' Frumkin pointed in the direction of Kovali. 'There's an armoury in the village at the old police headquarters. Remember it, Lydia? We called in for a chat with Yasha Levitan, the commander, when it was still ours. There won't be much, a few rifles, grenades, maybe a couple of machine-guns and whatever we can pick up from the Whites we kill. It's our good luck the place is being held by Kolchak's bandits, not Czechs. The enemy is very strong in this area and we'd have to get out before reinforcements are rushed over, so it will be a hit and run operation.'

'When?' said Platon, plunging the pointed stick into the earth. 'Tomorrow?'

'What's wrong with tonight? One hour before dawn.'

Joseph had the knack of making it seem that he was merely summarizing decisions of the collective, after due discussion, but in reality everything was thought out in advance. He drew a rough diagram in the dirt. Platon and his Caucasian mountaineers would infiltrate from there, Lydia's group from here, while his own unit – the largest – crossed the river and opened a frontal assault on the village as a diversion to draw the garrison away and leave police headquarters lightly defended. Platon and Lydia would then storm the armoury, seize whatever weapons were there, and attack the Whites from the rear. Given the element of surprise, the battle should be brief and successful.

It was, as Joseph said, very simple.

3

She made the return journey alone. It was darker now, and colder. An early autumn had begun to rise out of the Siberian steppes, sweeping over the Urals towards central Russia like an insurgent army. Clouds obscured the moon, making it safe for her to move more quickly. Before long she was back in her own part of the forest.

Igor Ivanovich had got the men ready for instant departure. Despite his surliness, he was a good second-in-command with the qualities of a capable platoon sergeant. They were drinking the black unsweetened brew of roasted acorns that substituted for coffee and he handed her a mugful. It was scalding hot and noxiously astringent, but there was an illusion of nourishment in the warmth it brought to the stomach.

'Well,' Igor said gruffly, 'did you find out what's happening in the big outside?'

The big outside. It was a phrase that encapsulated an incomprehensible world where remote, momentous decisions were made that ordinary men could not alter. Was that how it seemed to them?

The wind swirled among the trees and leaves rustled plaintively. She looked round at her ragged band, eighteen survivors of more than forty. Some had died, others strayed off into the darkness like lost children, and for every single one – the living and the dead – she felt an appalling responsibility as if she'd led their peaceful lives into a deadly ambush. A few were peasants, most were workers. Her kind had incantated words of magic: socialism, freedom. And with an innocent excitement these young men had gone out to join the cheering, joy turning to bewilderment as the procession stampeded into chaotic slaughter. If even the great intelligences of revolution – Lenin, Martov, Plekhanov, Kautsky – quarrelled bitterly over the course of events, how could these boys facing death in a distant forest know if the sacrifice demanded of them were justified?

She told them all about Trotsky and the counter-offensive, conjuring up an image of the people rising in masses to defend their hard-won liberties, breathing more hope and ardour into her words than the situation justified. For if they had to fight an unequal battle it must be with a conviction of victory, but in their sombre faces she could only read one overpowering thought: 'Will I be alive tomorrow?'

'It's going to be tough,' Igor said.

She looked at him and said quietly: 'Yes, but we're going to win.'

Afterwards everyone swore that victory was won by Stepanchik and his wooden rattle. He was the smallest in the unit, Stepanchik, but only in height. Nature, the jokers said, had sold him short, putting the chubby legs of a four-year-old on a body of giant girth. He was good-natured enough about it if you didn't say it when he was drunk. Then it would take six men to stop him snapping your own legs off at the knees to bring you down to his own size.

On the outskirts of Kovali Lydia divided her force into two.

Igor Ivanovich was told to take his lot through a farmyard. The rest were to follow her across the cemetery. They would all meet up at the market square, where police headquarters was situated. Success, of course, depended on surprise. Their faces and hands were smeared with dirt so that all you could see was the whites of their teeth and eyes. Anything shiny got the same treatment. Not a sound must be made, not a shot fired, until Joseph Frumkin's men opened the attack south of the village to draw its garrison away. Stepanchik received instructions to keep close behind Lydia, being strong enough to strangle a man with his great hands which she could only do if she got the carotid artery first go off. And Stepanchik, of course, brought his wooden rattle.

'Good luck!' she said softly.

Igor Ivanovich's boys disappeared into the unpredictable darkness. Lydia nodded at the others. Mysterious shadows flew between gravestones as they crawled on hands and knees towards their fate. Except for creaking branches and the remote howl of forest wolves everything was quiet. A few small lights guttered against the black mass of wooden dwellings. There was a smell of damp earth, decay, night blossom, the excremental odour of rural squalor. War could be a thousand versts away.

Beyond the cemetery a dirt road led into the heart of the slumbering village. This was where danger really began. They lay flat, motionless, awaiting the signal to advance. Lydia scanned the silence. The loudest noises were Stepanchik's snoring breath at her side, the metronomic pulsing of blood in her eardrums. Nothing to see but the empty road, a procession of mean thatched cottages, the outline of a small church, its slender spire like an upraised finger.

Despite the wary excitement she always felt in such moments of tension, that curious sense of balancing like a tightrope walker over annihilating emptiness, her mind remained cool and practical. Only if their sortie was expected would an enemy lurking in the shadows remain so silent. Soldiers on routine guard duty were seldom inconspicuous, betraying their presence by some restless movement, a slight clearing of the throat, even a sigh of boredom. Yet the absence of sentries was disquieting. Were the Whites so incompetent as to leave an important route into the village undefended? Was there perhaps a mobile patrol somewhere in the area? Or were they indeed about to blunder into a fatal ambush? Well, there was only one way to find out . . .

She moved forward, swift and feline, beckoning the others to follow. As they did so, the moon broke free of a bank of cloud. It was a mistake not to have looked at the sky. Caught in its faint but revealing light, the men doubled up and began to run as if already under fire. She stopped them with a fierce, peremptory gesture, at the same time glancing sharply ahead. Moonglow threw elongated shadows across the rutted roadway. The glass of a window glittered. And there, in the doorway of the church some fifty metres ahead, a man's figure materialized.

His pale, vaguely defined face was turned towards them in an appearance of watchfulness but he remained strangely still. She advanced slowly, perplexed by the man's immobility, the heavy Colt .45 at her hips ready to fire. At fifty paces he could have been an effigy, at forty something lifeless, closer still the features seemed frozen in idiot laughter.

It was a soldier, fair-haired, with one of those typically open Russian faces, eyes widely spaced and a sprinkling of red pimples on his cheeks. He was perched on a stone ledge, head resting against the wall, fast asleep. The breath bubbled faintly from his wet open mouth. He cuddled a rifle in his folded arms like a girl, half-smiling. At most he was eighteen years old.

Stepanchik came up noiselessly. His eyes interrogated her.

In one instant her appalling decision was made. It was, of course, inevitable. At any moment the soldier could wake. There were probably others billeted in the church. Before her group had reached the end of the street, an alarm could be raised and that would be the finish of them all. She could not risk the lives of comrades by an act of mercy to a class enemy.

She nodded almost imperceptibly.

Stepanchik's enormous hands encircled the boy's thin throat, twisted and jerked. In the instant when the cord of life was snapped the soldier's eyes opened in terrified comprehension and, with a great shudder, his body surrendered its breath.

Stepanchik took the corpse's rifle as it slipped from the lifeless arms.

Pale and expressionless, Lydia hurried from that first pitiful casualty towards the battle to which it was the prelude. She'd learned to anaesthetize the horror of killing, if only in the midst of action, by a surgical excision of imagination. Nothing was allowed to enter the mind's taut web but tactical considerations of attack and defence. One aimed a rifle at an enemy target, not a human being. Forget about mothers, widows, orphaned children. To think otherwise would be to experience compassion, even guilt, and induce a fatal hesitation. To pity another and yet press the trigger was like shooting at one's own heart.

Once clear of the cemetery road, the village became more urbanized. Houses were closer together, built more solidly. There were shuttered shops, an inn, a whitewashed school with a belfry, the copper-domed mosque set in a small square surrounded by artisan workshops and, ahead of them, dominant, the square stone bulk of police headquarters. A light shone in a ground floor room. Parked in the forecourt was a motor-car. Everything was quiet.

Moving cautiously now from one doorway to another, they finally reached the market-place. It seemed utterly deserted. A cold breeze rattled the corrugated iron roof of an outbuilding, lifted eddies of dust from the beaten earth. Close up, police headquarters had a squat, sinister aspect. Shadows crossed and recrossed its single lighted window. It looked impregnable. An aromatic smell of burning birch bark came from a smoking chimney and, although there was no evidence of special vigilance, it was easy to imagine that hidden observers stood snugly in its darkened rooms waiting for them to expose their bodies to an annihilating hail of machine-gun fire. Opportunely, clouds abruptly extinguished the moon. The darkest and longest hour of night, the hour before dawn, was imminent.

A faint hiss made Lydia turn sharply. It was Igor Ivanovich, reassuringly in position with his men. She crawled over to confer with him. They had encountered no opposition, he reported in a hoarse whisper, but a heavily manned enemy post guarded the part of the village they'd traversed and, having the use of a lorry, it wouldn't take them two minutes to turn up on the scene once shooting began.

'It will start over by the river,' Lydia reminded him. 'If they go there, then we've got them.'

Igor rubbed his bandaged eye and grimaced. 'I don't mind telling you, I'm shit scared,' he muttered.

'Who isn't?' The blood in her pulse was effervescent with a mixture of fear and excitement. She shivered inside as if with fever. There was no dignity in war. An animal instinct for survival overwhelmed morale. The omnipresence of death, its idiot unpredictability, turned one into a quivering organism up to the very moment of battle. It was a case of the disease being its own cure.

Igor gazed at her, deceived by the brilliance of her dilated eyes, her white teeth gleaming between parted lips. 'You look as if you love it,' he said grudgingly. 'Don't get yourself killed.'

He could have bitten his tongue off. Though he prided himself as a true Bolshevik on being above superstition, it was an unlucky thing to say. He tried to think of something to neutralize it when the surrounding silence was broken by a solitary bird-call.

'Good!' Lydia said. 'That's Pasha.'

Igor blew out his lips and a prolonged vibrating whistle flew into the sky. Miraculously, birds in near-by trees sang in response. A pre-dawn chorus. 'I'm a country boy. I know their language,' he remarked, suddenly buoyant. 'Well, comrade, what now?'

'The hardest part,' she replied wryly. 'We wait. Check that everyone understands the orders. Nobody opens fire until I give the signal. When they start to leave the building it's going to be tempting.'

She watched him crawl away to do her bidding. Of all the unit, he most resented being under the command of a woman, treating her at first as though she was one of the girls in Kerensky's women's battalion who were said to have fallen for the good looks and charm of the February Revolution's ineffectual Prime Minister. Igor's grudging tolerance was won not by her unshirking acceptance of hardship, dirt and danger, nor by the fact that she was quick, decisive and her powers of endurance not less than anyone else's; it was simply, as he put it, that she could do anything a man could do except piss against the wind. An approximate truth, she reflected ruefully. War had unsexed her. She'd even stopped menstruating and experienced the loss of libido common among soldiers enduring the rigours of a hard campaign. The only hazard she risked additional to those faced by her fellow guerrillas was also bluntly summed up by Igor Ivanovich. 'If they ever capture us, comrade commander, you'll be raped first and shot last.' The fact that he was probably right did not make her less of a fighter.

Seconds ticked rapidly away on her wrist. The men were getting restless. Someone suppressed a cough, a rifle scraped audibly as its owner shifted position. Glancing out from the shelter of her doorway she noticed that a few more lights had sprung up in the village. People were beginning to awaken. The pressure of time built up, constricting her breathing. Surely Joseph should have already opened the attack? Darkness was their ally: it would be fatal if they were overtaken by dawn.

Across the market-place, a man appeared at the lighted window of police headquarters, stretched out his arms and yawned. A drooping moustache and black pomaded hair gave his plump face a foppish appearance. Someone else in the room must have said something, for he laughed soundlessly, moved his lips in rapid speech and turned away.

Suddenly it all began. A volley of rifle-fire came from the direction of the river in a series of small sharp explosions of pathetically limited duration, followed by another and another. The noise was scarcely threatening, barely sufficient to wake the sleeping village. The foppish face arrived back at the window together with several others. They peered out with surprise rather than alarm. More firing began, heavier now as the enemy post reacted to attack. A machine-gun opened up, rattling like hailstones on tin. Inside police headquarters a telephone bell jangled. The men at the window spun round. One went away, presumably to take the call, then the rest disappeared.

Lydia gave her entire attention to the building. Everything now depended on the reaction of its inmates. Joseph was gambling that the White garrison commander would interpret the attack as a major assault on the village and leave his headquarters lightly defended while he rushed reinforcements to the outskirts. So far it seemed he might be lucky. There was some hoarse yelling. Lights came on in upstairs rooms, followed by much banging and shouting. She tried to imagine the scene there: men startled from sleep, still bemused, getting in one another's way as they struggled into their clothes. Trouserless, sticky-eyed, fumbling for weapons – in other circumstances it would be an ideal moment to burst in on them.

It was torture to wait. She held herself under compression like a steel spring. A second machine-gun began firing in the distance, its menacing reverberations thudding against her heart. Could Joseph's group hold out? Something desperate and inarticulate rose up in her like prayer.

At last the heavy door of police headquarters swung open. A gush of light poured out. Lydia's men shrank further into the shadows, tensely gripping their rifles. A glum shock-headed soldier emerged into the forecourt in slow motion, ignoring the hubbub going on behind, spat on his palms, and cranked up the motor-car. He was followed by three officers, still buckling on their belts as they stepped into the vehicle. It moved off in a trail of smoke, headlamps unlit.

Inside the building orders were being shouted above the noise of blundering movements, stampeding feet. The open door exposed a drab institutional corridor, walls lined with wooden benches, official notices. Yes, Joseph's gamble was going to come off. The corridor was filling with men. As if pushed from the rear, they tumbled into the market-place, caps awry, tunics unbuttoned, turning uneasily towards the noise of gunfire. They seemed a little dazed with sleep and their eyes must still have been unaccustomed to the dark otherwise one, at least, might have observed something odd in the seemingly empty square: a slight movement in a doorway, a strange shape huddled in some dim corner like a bundle of rags. Instead the military voice of a sergeant barked out words of command and they were led off at the double.

Lydia still made no move. She watched the door of police headquarters close, abruptly returning the forecourt to darkness. Igor Ivanovich, Stepanchik, Dmitri and the rest were undergoing torments of impatience and anxiety. Timing must be impeccable. She counted its passing, second by second. One minute . . .

Close by but out of sight, Jorgashvili and his men waited

in excruciating suspense for the explosion of the first bullet before launching an attack from the rear. Two minutes ...

The sound made by the double-marching Whites mingled with the noise of machine-guns. Brief flashes lit the sky. There was a drifting smell of burning cordite. Three ...

'Now!' she called in a low, penetrating voice and raced for the building followed on scurrying little legs by Stepanchik. The rest of the boys leaped from their hiding places and ran after them, relief at the physical freedom of movement briefly overcoming fear.

She knew the layout of the building from a visit when the village was still in Bolshevik hands. Rooms led off on each side of the central corridor. Beyond the main office, right, was an armoury. A short flight of stone steps led to some basement prison cells. Igor's section were to clear the rooms on one side while her own group dealt with those on the other.

Stepanchik hurled his giant trunk at the door. It shuddered only. Others joined their weight to his and wood splintered at the lock. The morose interior suddenly opened up, harshly empty in the naked electric light. Chalked orders on a wall blackboard recalled a classroom deserted by its pupils. A shirt-sleeved man came out of a room. As Lydia fired, she received an instantaneous impression of small frightened eyes, thick dark stubble surrounding a gaping mouth. The boys began kicking doors open, firing blindly as they went. Smoke, obscenities and vivid explosions rioted in the air.

So far they were enjoying the short-lived advantage of surprise. The strength of the defence was unknown to them. Men died in arrested gestures of terror and amazement. Then as a Bolshevik stormed into one of the rooms the rapid stuttering of a machine-gun began and his chest was ripped open as if by the talons of an iron bird. The world disintegrated into nightmare images of confusion. Heavy furniture crashed to the floor. Some Whites began shooting over the balustrade of the upper floor and the electric bulb in the corridor, struck by a ricochet, flew into fragments. Screams were heard in the cells downstairs. It became difficult to distinguish who was shooting at whom.

Lydia had not forgotten their main objective – the armoury. She and Stepanchik took up positions on either side of the main office entrance. It had an upper flap, now closed, through which visitors were normally inspected. They pushed it open, fired rapidly and simultaneously into the room, then forced the door and sprang inside, still shooting.

An enormous figure reared up in the smoke, two others lay groaning behind an upturned table, blood was pumping in gouts of scarlet from the throat of a man slumped on the floor. The big man's gun spat flame at Lydia. Her left cheekbone reddened as if stung by a bee and the muzzle of her gun wavered as she pulled the trigger. Instead of piercing his heart the bullet struck his left arm. Blood trickled slowly down her face.

Stepanchik's eyes were as wild as if he'd drunk a litre of vodka. He worked his rifle-bolt but its magazine was empty. Seizing it by the barrel, he smashed the butt with all the force of his wide, powerful shoulders into the enemy soldier's teeth. The fellow reeled, put his hand over the mutilated cavity that had been his mouth, and gave an inhuman screech of agony. Stepanchik swung again and crushed his skull.

Too terrified to make a sound, the wounded men cringed behind the overturned table, lying in their own blood. They had been whiling away the night watch playing cards and the spilled pack lay strewn among a litter of broken glass. Stepanchik kicked the table aside and stood over them. He grinned. 'You've been having it soft, you bastards, smoking and drinking and ining your bellies to shit on our glorious Revolution!'

He lifted the rifle.

'No!' Lydia exclaimed involuntarily.

He looked round at her in blue-eyed amazement. 'They'd do it to us,' he said. 'No prisoners. That's our orders.'

'Not that way!' she yelled furiously.

Turning aside, she reloaded her pistol with a trembling hand then shot the men, deliberately, through their heads.

The entire building now resounded to the noise of battle but it reached her distantly. She was still trembling. Stepanchik gazed at her with tender concern.

'Are you all right, little comrade? Your face is bleeding.'

The incongruity of the remark brought her the nearest she came to tears.

'It's nothing,' she replied roughly, walking over to the big corpse and bending to pick up its gun. A taste of vomit came into her mouth. Nothing recognizably human was left of the face but its archaeological remnants: shreds of flesh, splinters of bone, raw pulp. She felt saturated in filth. One never got used to it. Precariously holding on to a thread of sanity, she said: 'Let's get on with the job.'

The armoury was locked. As Stepanchik stepped back several paces to charge the door a machine-gun opened up inside, drilling a neat pattern of holes through the black-panelled wood. In instant reflex, Lydia hit the floor. Stepanchik, miraculously upright, flattened himself against the wall. They remained in petrified attitudes as bullets in fusilades ripped through filing cabinets, shattered plaster, ricocheted from one object to another. Movement would be suicidal, yet inaction was unthinkable. Whoever was in the armoury had the means to hold out indefinitely.

The feeling of impotence was unbearable. That was how one got oneself killed. Pressure built up, found no release, exploded in an act of foolish or heroic self-destruction. It was something to avoid. But the entire operation hinged on speedily capturing police headquarters, seizing an effective supply of weapons and launching an immediate assault on the enemy's rear. If they failed, Joseph's ill-equipped group would be wiped out. And there was no time to lose, no time at all, she thought in trapped desperation.

A swift change of mood, characteristic of madness and battle-stress, abruptly overcame the nauseant horror she'd experienced during the previous moments of slaughter. Something between rage and panic took possession instead. Without volition she was on her feet, a gun in each hand. Expressionlessly, she blazed away at the intractable door. The lock blew apart.

To Stepanchik it was magnificent. Bullets flew everywhere and left her unharmed like a holy saint protected by an invincible halo. Pulling the stout wooden rattle from his belt, he whirled it round and round over his head to express the enthusiasm of his bursting heart. Perhaps it saved her life. It certainly brought them luck. Nothing in the world could sound more like a heavy machine-gun in full spate than the deafening clatter of that harmless toy.

Jorgashvili and two of his Caucasians suddenly rushed in, scowling fiercely and ready to kill on sight, three short tough men with a mountain wildness in their blackened faces. Astonished, they stared at Lydia; they stared at Stepanchik dancing up and down on his dwarfish legs and swinging his rattle; with casual disregard, their glances took in the blood and corpses.

Laughter wrinkles creased the corners of Jorgashvili's narrow eyes. He brushed past them and strode into the armoury. Stepanchik stopped his racketing. Lydia stood in an attitude of exhaustion, the empty revolvers hanging limply at her sides. She came to herself slowly, as someone surfaces from a drugged sleep.

There was a deathly silence. When she joined Jorgashvili in the armoury, spent cartridge cases littered the floor and sweet fresh air was blowing through an open window. Evidently the gunner had fled, alarmed by Stepanchik's wooden rattle. Not only that, but quiet had descended on the entire building.

They gazed at the racks of rifles and boxes of ammunition, the machine-guns propped up on spidery legs, everything oiled and nicely in order. The Georgian picked up a crowbar to lever the lid off a wooden crate bearing foreign markings. It was filled with English hand-grenades.

'Beautiful!' he said in a choking voice.

Tears ran down his grimy cheeks. He turned to Lydia and embraced her. Then he embraced Stepanchik and his fellow Caucasians, each in turn.

Everything went quickly after that. The Whites were demoralized even before Lydia and Jorgashvili regrouped and attacked their rear. As soon as the bitter fighting broke out at police headquarters, their commander assumed it was an assault by an overwhelmingly superior Bolshevik force of several battalions at least. News of the great Trotsky's arrival at the front had also reached him, embellished by rumours of brilliant, anarchic Red generals commanding divisions of pitiless assassins.

His men were enveloped in gloom. Imaginary bullets struck

between their shoulder-blades as they fought in darkness and terror against an unseen enemy. Then guns sounded from behind and grenades burst in their midst. They died easily. Some were little more than high-school boys who kissed their mothers goodbye and put on the white shoulder-tapes of loyalist volunteers in the adolescent delusion that war was a dream of girls and glory, and death a romantic wound in the breast.

The bloody night's work was over. Dawn came bringing ravens out of the forest. Only the reckoning remained to be done. Of their total force of sixty-three, forty-one guerrillas survived. Joseph alone had lost twelve, Lydia four. Igor Ivanovich was dead, his premonition fulfilled. Grisha Fedin, a quiet boy who wrote poems, had been instantly killed by a machine-gun. It had been the last night on earth for poor Dmitri and the Petersburg metal worker, Pyotr Agaryshev, who'd left behind a wife and four children. And among Joseph's twelve was numbered Vladimir Svirsky, of Novgorod, whose ancestors may have carved angels in the Cathedrals of St Sophia.

4

A young soldier lay on the makeshift operating table, his left leg shattered below the knee. He whimpered through chattering teeth and looked at them with a child's beseeching terror. Animal noises of suffering came from other wounded next door.

Mikhail Norodsky signalled to Lydia. She pressed an ether-soaked pad over the soldier's nose and mouth. His body became convulsed in its struggle for breath then the frightened, pain-filled eyes slid into unconsciousness.

Norodsky bit his lower lip in fierce concentration and amputated the limb at the joint. A sympathetic agony was imprinted on his face as he threw down the knife, tied blood-vessels and applied iodine dressings to the bleeding stump.

Lydia put the severed part of the leg into a zinc bucket and pushed it out of sight. An effort of will temporarily obliterated feeling but she knew the horror would leave yet another mutilation from which her mind would never completely recover.

She was reminded, haphazardly, of a woman she'd met whose husband was killed fighting in Moscow the previous autumn. 'I wish I could cross out my heart,' the widow had said.

'If I ever go back to medicine after this,' Norodsky said, gazing bitterly at his gory hands, 'I'll deserve a place in Ward Six with the other loonies.'

Outside it had begun to rain, a sullen, persistent downpour from a sky the colour of slate. The streets of Kovali were turning into mud. Gloom as relentless as the sea drowned them all. It was not Chekov's brutal portrait of the mental ward of a provincial hospital that occurred to her. She thought of the operating tent at Borodino in *War and Peace* when Kuragin was shown his amputated leg with the boot still on, an act of gratuitous cruelty somehow more chilling than the beastliness of war itself.

At least, she reflected bleakly, we must be grateful for modern anaesthesia and the fact that the Whites had left behind a decent store of medical supplies. In other respects their savagery had exceeded anything imagined by Tolstoy. One of the Georgians opened a cellar door below the building and discovered eight corpses, that of the former Bolshevik garrison commander, six other men and a girl. Large flies grazed on their blue and mutilated flesh and the stench was like a foul mist that left its putrid taste on the tongue. The outrages perpetrated upon their bodies were unbelievably shocking. Man in his inhumanity is always sexually perverse as if the one thing he is least able to contain is a bitter loathing of his victim's genitals. The garrison commander must have died slowly, slashed by a score of knives, his eyes cut from their sockets, ribbons of flayed skin hanging from his flesh.

Joseph was called. He stood in the doorway, a waxen pallor on his lean, cavernous face, staring at the scene in silence, turning away in silence, in silence beckoning to a group of guerrillas to follow him into the streets. They went from house to house searching for adult males and, having gathered thirty or more, brought them to the market square. Pale and trembling, in attitudes of furtive and uncomprehending guilt, the men waited for some dread punishment to be visited upon them. Joseph remained terrifyingly silent. Finally, he turned to one of his followers.

'Get them to bury the dead,' he said, and it was as though a corpse itself was speaking. 'Every single one of them. Not one body must be left above ground.' Stiff-legged, he walked back into the building.

Pity Joseph, she thought. Pity all who kill with revulsion and self-disgust fearing, more perhaps than defeat, the moral degeneracy that could be the price of victory.

'Now that we've patched up the others, Lydia, it's time to operate on you,' said Mikhail. He touched the encrusted blood on her cheek unprofessionally and smiled.

'I'll survive,' she said, grimacing.

'It would be wrong to let it fester,' he insisted, dabbing the slight flesh-wound with surgical spirit. 'We don't want you scarred for life, comrade commander, my dear. One day you'll have to go back to being a woman again.'

'Dear Mikhail,' she said, 'one day we must all go back to being human.'

When she arrived downstairs, Joseph stood in the wreckage of the main office with Platon Jorgashvili and several others. The last gruesome hours seemed to have left him stunned with fatigue but there was no trace of it once he began speaking. They had lived with death too much to cheapen it with rhetoric, he said. They all knew that a man had only one life. When it was lost something precious and unique went out of the world and mankind was poorer for the loss of it.

He recalled many things, sometimes with humour, about those who had died, their quirks and oddities, as one would of friends who were merely absent, and it brought tears and smiles to the survivors, easing them a little. Another political commissar would have used the whips of oratory, quoting Lenin and speaking of heroes, revolution, proletarian vengeance, invoking that demagogy of battle that made Trotsky proclaim: 'We have made a pact with death, therefore with victory.' Joseph remembered perhaps that people were best defended in sorrow and adversity by simple fellowship: that their darkest moments could sometimes be lit by laughter.

Having completed what was in fact a secular burial service, his manner became brisk and commanding. It was another day: life must go on: the future was making its demands.

They were to prepare the immediate withdrawal from Kovali. In addition to weapons, medicine and food, their booty included three lorries and a German staff-car. Mikhail Norodsky was to convert one lorry into an ambulance for the wounded; Jorgashvili's task was to load arms and supplies on the other vehicles, mount machine-guns ready to beat off enemy attacks and load up the men; Lydia and a party of six would search among the refugees sheltering in the village to make sure no White militiamen were hiding among them. Any found must, of course, be shot.

Suddenly a telephone rang.

It was an uncanny sound in the splintered room with its upturned desks and scattered files of bloodstained paper. They looked at one another uneasily.

The bell went on ringing. Joseph shifted some wreckage and stared at the black vulcanite instrument. After a moment's hesitation he unhooked the ear-piece. 'Yes, who is it?' he demanded tersely. A whispering and scratching, unrecognizable as a human voice, came through the wire decipherable only by Joseph. His expression became intent. They held their breath.

'Yes, Major, this is Ovschenko,' he said. 'Yes, everything is in order here. Our patrols are keeping an eye out for the Reds. We think there are some in the woods.'

The ear-piece crackled with rapid speech. Joseph listened carefully, nodding his head. 'Thank you, Major,' he said. 'We will do exactly what you say.'

Ringing the telephone down, he looked at the others and began to chuckle in malicious glee.

'That was Kazan, comrades. The Adjutant of White headquarters in person.' Laughter creased his grimy, unshaven face. 'There is bad news for us. Trotsky has reformed the Bolshevik forces, smashed an attempt to encircle Sviazhsk, set fire to the entire White flotilla on the Volga. We are warned that messages have gone out to all Red partisans ordering them to go over to the offensive. We must fight to the last man.'

Jorgashvili let out an alarming series of spasmodic gasps. 'That – that is too bad of Trot-Trotsky,' he spluttered, purple in the face.

'Trotsky is a devil,' someone remarked, grinning.

Joseph ripped the telephone cord from the wall. 'After such news it is only right that Kovali should be cut off from the world,' he said.

An apprehensive silence hung over the village. It seemed uninhabited, a no-man's-land abandoned to mud and desolation. Rain splashed in puddles, fell in great drops from the eaves of cottages, soaked through their tunics to the skin as they trudged along empty streets more like defeated stragglers than soldiers who had fought a bloody but successful engagement.

The search began in the schoolhouse and, as they entered, Russia's ragged population of ghosts looked up in dumb reproach. Even the children became silent, huddling closer to their emaciated mothers, afraid to cry. Nothing was more demoralizing than to see oneself monstrously reflected in the frightened eyes of children, and Lydia turned away in shame.

A bearded old man shuffled forward, slow and unsteady on rag-bound feet. He held his hands up to her, palms together in an attitude of supplication, sausage-like fingers swollen with the oedema of hunger. Shreds of dignity clung to his enfeebled frame as he stood in bowed meditation as if before an inscrutable authority.

'Please, your honour, give us bread,' he prayed in a voice of exhaustion.

Her throat was seized by constriction. That age-old, interminable cry of starving multitudes, and she had no answer. All she could do was shake her head.

'You are a Bolshevik, you promised to end poverty,' he intoned in a dry liturgical whisper. 'We have neither bread nor peace.'

With an effort, her voice as faint as his own, she said: 'We have not yet had time.'

'Listen, grandad, don't blame us,' one of the soldiers intervened gruffly. 'It's the scum of the counter-revolution has taken the food from your mouths. When we've done with the bastards everybody will eat.'

An accusing glare shone in the old man's fevered eyes and flickered out.

'Whoever wins, the people suffer,' he said and began to

tremble violently. Lachrymose moisture trickled out of his shrunken nostrils. He seemed about to fall. Lydia put out her arms to steady him. For a moment his head rested against her breast. Two fat lice crawled out of his matted hair and suddenly, with horror, she saw that an entire colony of vermin had settled on his body. Pity was drowned in an instinctive revulsion. She had learned to kill but could not overcome the fastidious disgust at filth drilled into her by childhood privilege and an English nanny.

'Let's go!' she ordered abruptly. 'There are no Whites hiding here.' And, steeling herself, she led her small party of guerrillas away to face other refugees sheltering in church and mosque and village hall. It took more courage to withstand their meek and bloodless ferocity than the lethal indifference of gunfire.

5

Travelling through enemy territory was a slow and cautious business. They navigated at night in close convoy, sending out patrols to scout the dark countryside, driving in low gear along rutted cart-tracks in the direction of Kazan. In the daytime they sheltered in forests, using leaves and branches to camouflage their precious vehicles. Two wounded died and were buried. Machine-guns were manned against surprise attack day and night. From the distant Volga, where it curved in a great loop towards Sviazhsk, winds carried disquieting reverberations of heavy guns into the dream-like autumnal peace through which they moved.

On the third day three men on patrol returned with a prisoner. He was a barefoot boy of about ten, tow-headed and as brown as a nut, clad in a patchwork of ragged clothes. They'd found him fishing in a woodland stream. More accurately, he had found them, for the soldiers were unaware of his silent presence until they'd incautiously exposed themselves. This posed an unwelcome problem. The boy endangered the entire group. If allowed to go free he could give them away to the enemy. On the other hand, he was just a kid, innocent. Unwilling to accept responsibility, they took him captive and left the decision of life or death to Comrade Frumkin, their commander.

Joseph looked down at the youngster in bitter exasperation. What shall I do with him? he wondered, flinching at the dilemma. Forty lives at risk, the proletarian republic fighting for survival, needing every one of them: and one small boy as unwitting an agent of peril as if he transmitted the germs of some fatal disease.

'Have you got a name, lad?' he asked gently.

'Vanya,' the child said. Eyes of guileless blue returned his gaze. His head was too large for its stunted body. He wiped a sleeve already shiny with snot across his snub nose and smiled.

'Where do you live?' The question was received in silence. 'Don't you know?'

Vanya's face clouded over. He scraped the earth with his toe as if reluctant to reply.

'Panovka,' he said eventually.

Joseph had heard of the place. It was at least forty kilometres to the east. What was the urchin doing so far from home? Could it be that he was a refugee who'd wandered away from his parents and got lost, or one of the many orphans of the civil war? If so, he thought with wry grief, one would have to adopt him as a son of the people.

He put an arm around the boy's frail shoulders and drew him close.

'Tell me about your dad, Vanya. Is he in Panovka?'

Vanya's expression became sullen and withdrawn.

'And your mum? You've got a mother, haven't you?'

Moisture trickled from the luminous blue eyes. The small mouth quivered but remained obdurately silent. To all questions about the whereabouts of his family, where he was staying, who looked after him, he returned no answer.

'Well, so you don't feel like talking, Vanya,' Joseph shrugged. He rolled a cigarette and smoked reflectively, tempted to send the little wretch away and gamble on the consequences. But it was not only prudence that restrained him. Something should be done for the boy. He could not be abandoned to wander unprotected from the random savagery of wolves in human shape.

'I bet you've never had a ride in a lorry,' he said. 'How would you like to stay with us for a while, eh? We'll look after you all right. Maybe take you all the way to Moscow. What do you say, lad?'

Vanya picked at his nose and gravely considered the proposition. 'Can I be a soldier?' he asked, glancing up with a peasant's bargaining shrewdness. 'Will you let me have a gun?'

Joseph playfully rubbed the boy's soft stubby hair.

'As long as you promise to shoot only bad people,' he conceded with a melancholy smile.

Soon after dark they made ready to leave again, another journey into danger. The men filed aboard their lorries with a minimum of noise. Petrol tanks were filled from carefully hoarded cans. Startled birds flew out of branches overhead as shuddering engines disrupted the nocturnal silence.

Having seen that his wounded charges were comfortably settled in the ambulance lorry, Mikhail Norodsky went forward to sit alongside the driver. Behind him a shadow parted from the trees. He turned, but before he could cry out someone clapped a hand over his mouth and jabbed a gun into his back.

'If you want to live,' a soft voice growled, 'just call your commander. And don't say why.'

Resistance was impractical and Mikhail wanted to live. All he could do was inject a note of warning into his cry.

Joseph detected it even above the throbbing of engines. He nudged Lydia. She was squeezed alongside him in the staff-car together with three other soldiers. They jumped out and drew their pistols, moving with deceptive casualness towards Norodosky and his unknown assailant.

'Stay where you are or he's dead!'

A hairy face appeared above Mikhail's right shoulder. Two eyes burned in the darkness.

'We've got you surrounded, so don't try any tricks,' said the stranger.

Intuitively, Joseph sensed that it was bluff. If they were really surrounded and the enemy had the strength he would have launched a devastating surprise attack, not stopped to parley. What was the point of this charade? To trick them into surrendering without a fight? Even in the most hopeless situation, it was no deal. Both sides were fighting a killing war. They would be butchered without mercy.

He lifted his arm as a signal to the drivers. One by one the engines cut out. Only the wind was heard, and branches rustling like birch-brooms sweeping dead leaves. But machine-gunners peered into the surrounding gloom ready to unleash instant fire.

'We dislike threats,' he said very quietly. 'Let our comrade go and tell us what you want.'

In answer, the man shifted his grip to Norodsky's throat and squeezed out a strangulated groan. It was not just a threat.

'If you don't answer to my satisfaction, this one will only be the first to go.' A harsh note of desperation entered his voice. 'You took my son. What have you done with him?'

Lydia looked at Joseph and said: 'He must be Vanya's father.'

'Yes, Vanya!' the man shouted. 'A kid like that! If you swine have harmed him –'

'We're Bolsheviks, not barbarians!' Joseph said sharply. 'We don't make war on children!'

'Bolsheviks?' was the stupefied response. His grasp of Norodsky slackened but immediately tightened again. 'Don't give me that shit!' he snarled. 'You're the same as slaughtered our folks in Panovka. Kolchak's butchers!'

'Lydia, go and bring the boy,' ordered Joseph.

Vanya was sleeping on a pile of sacks in one of the lorries. He responded drowsily when called and stumbled after her rubbing his eyes. Overcome with joy, the man ran to the child and seized him in a convulsive embrace.

'Jesus Christ! I could kill you,' he groaned, covering him with kisses. Sheepishly, he pocketed his revolver and turned to Joseph. 'His mother's out of her wits with fright. We thought he'd gone for ever.'

They belonged to a large group of workers and peasants who had taken to the woods with their families in flight from the Whites and formed a partisan band. On their way they'd encountered nothing but misfortune, living from day to day in fear of discovery, their ranks depleted by desertion and outbreaks of disease, hampered in effective action by the presence of women and children.

'Well, I congratulate you on your son,' was Joseph's dry

remark. 'A good little partisan. Rather than give you away, he let us think he was an orphan.'

The father grinned proudly. 'Vanya's all right. You can come out, boys, they're on our side,' he called.

A handful of ill-armed ragged men crawled from the undergrowth and edged nervously into the clearing. For a party bent on vengeance they may have been pathetic but were certainly not lacking in courage, Joseph thought. His heart was suddenly buoyant.

'Shall we join forces in our common struggle?' he asked.

Vanya's dad held out his hand and grinned.

Some hours later Joseph's guerrillas settled down to sleep in another part of the forest. The sun was beginning to rise. Mothers scolded their bickering children as if everything was normal again and distant gunfire nothing but the sound of receding storm.

Chapter Three

The first leaves drifted from the trees and the wind turned cold. Black clouds gathered. Rain slashed the forests in punishing fury. The northern sky was ripped apart by lightning. The partisans huddled over smouldering fires, trudged through mud, cursed the weather and their hard nomadic existence. Freedom was bitter.

One night, as they were about to move again, Lydia awoke with a wound in her head. She dragged herself up, puzzled by the pain in her limbs, her unbearable fatigue. A piece of burning lead was lodged in her brain. The earth rocked like the sea. Trees became an army of giants, closing in silently, and she could not stop shivering.

Joseph was saying something, his voice strangely remote: 'Kazan . . . railroad . . . supply train . . . sabotage . . .'

Dislocated fragments of the past floated through her clouded mind. Driving in St Petersburg past the stucco palaces of Nevsky, pink and green and white in the sunshine, spires of gold shimmering in the waters of canals . . . her father in court uniform leading her towards the enthroned Tsarina to make her rebellious curtsy, dear rejected father and his crumbling world . . . pain, pain . . . London now, the smell of fog and winter seeping into the drab room she'd shared with Peter, her unwanted lover . . . and months in the Kresty prison for disseminating seditious pamphlets, the slow, barbaric journey to sub-zero Siberian exile, all encapsulated in one hallucinatory moment . . . pain . . .

Joseph's voice again, gentle, exasperated. 'Lydochka, why don't you answer?' He looked at her, his grin fading, everything fading as she spun giddily with ever increasing momentum into . . . blackness . . . why? . . .

The echo spiralled with her into the abyss.

*

'Typhus,' Mikhail said, peering at the thermometer.

'Are you sure?'

'Absolutely.'

Norodsky undid her trousers, pulled them open, and pointed to some reddish spots on the naked abdomen. 'Mulberry rash,' he said. 'She has it all over her body. Face and eyes congested, characteristic stupor, violent trembling. It's typhus all right.'

He glanced up and saw anguish. Frumkin's concern was more than comradely. Mikhail experienced the chagrin he'd felt as a hospital intern in Moscow when all one could do to ease despair was offer the glib invocation of God and suppress one's disbelief. No anodyne for a Marxist. What else could be said? 'Have faith, she's in the hands of the historical imperative.' Poor suffering Frumkin. It could not have been easy for him, living side by side with her in platonic camaraderie, sending her into battle.

'How bad is it?' Joseph asked.

'It's hard to say.'

The reply was evasive. Professional instinct told him the disease was virulent. If hope there was, it lay only in the fact that the rash had not yet spread to her face. Should it do so then the prospects were that she would be dead within a fortnight of heart failure, possible gangrene. The medical dictionaries were, as usual, explicit in defining the fatal symptoms, but people stubbornly refused to conform. There was hope in that too.

A broken sound came from her. She woke up in a delirium, stared at them through a haze of non-recognition. The muscles of her taut stomach twitched convulsively and her limbs trembled. 'On fire,' she moaned. 'Burning alive.' She turned her cropped head from side to side in agony.

Mikhail buttoned up her slender nakedness and covered her with the blanket. Her fragility moved him: there were times when one forgot she was a girl, this determined Red guerrilla who fought harder than any of them, cultivating an imperviousness to fear and a tough endurance to prove she was as good as a man. 'One day,' he'd said to her, 'you'll have to go back to being a woman again.'

He smiled diffidently. 'You know her better than I do. Lydia's not one to give in easily. Disease is likc any other enemy. You only win by fighting back.'

'You can't do it alone,' said Joseph. He glanced out of the makeshift sickroom, a sheet of canvas supported by a wooden stake at each corner, gazing at their bleak encampment with puckered eyes. 'What chance does she have in these conditions – cold, mud, constant movement in overcrowded transport? What if we come under attack? Who is there to do the nursing?'

Norodsky shrugged. 'We must manage as best we can.'

'I know what you're thinking,' Joseph said with slow bitterness. 'She's only one among many. The collective is more important than the individual. When I have time I'll explain why this comrade is exceptional.' He looked at Norodsky as if he was an antagonist. 'Personal feelings have nothing to do with it, I tell you. Nothing!' There was an embarrassed silence. He gave a wincing smile. 'Well, you're right, Mikhail. It's not altogether true. Help me to carry her to the car. I'm going to take her to hospital.'

'Hospital? But where?'

'Wherever our army is. Kazan, Sviazhsk . . .'

'There's fighting all along the front. It's not practical.'

'We will get through.'

Love's madness: it was no use arguing. 'Good luck! Take care!' Norodsky called as the car jerked into blundering motion, heading towards the gunfire.

Joseph drove inexpertly through the sodden countryside, gripping the steering wheel as though clinging to the reins of a rebellious horse. The engine laboured in bronchial distress as he jammed his foot on the accelerator, fighting the machine's reluctance to keep pace with his own anxiety. Mud spurted from worn rubber tyres. Low-flying rooks, drifting like charred paper blown by the wind, took fright and darted into the dripping forest.

Waterlogged fields stretched down to a railroad and shreds of steam drifted on the horizon as an armoured train passed on its way to Kazan, some twenty kilometres away. The sight of it brought a stab of guilt. It should have been ambushed and attacked. He'd allowed personal feelings to interfere with his duty as a partisan commander. He deserved to be court-martialled: shot.

Sweat poured down his hollow face, stinging his eyes. He forced himself to think calmly. A fierce battle was raging around Kazan but the city was probably still in enemy hands. Best to keep south, cross the Volga somewhere near the township of Uslon and seek contact with units of the Fifth Army which operated in that sector. Lydia could then be taken to Sviazhsk and put aboard a train carrying wounded to Moscow. As Mikhail said, she did not give up easily. With all the medical skill and facilities available in the capital and her own vitality, she'd make a good recovery. In the twisted way things happened it might even turn out for the best. She'd be out of the war for a while. Safe. Only now could he admit the burden of anxiety he'd felt about her whenever they were in combat, how often he'd woken in terror from a dream that he'd fired a bullet into her heart with his own hand.

'Lydochka, darling, hold on! It's going to be all right!' he muttered, glancing at the limp form covered by a blanket on the passenger seat. She breathed through her open mouth as if the air hurt her lungs, breaking occasionally into delirious speech. Her closed eyes seemed withdrawn in contemplation of some absorbing interior mystery. White tapes were fastened to her shoulder-straps in the hope that she could be passed off, if necessary, as one of Kolchak's student volunteers. It was not improbable. The fever that blurred the bony contours of her face gave her an appearance of immaturity. She did not look so very different from the boys who had died for the old order at Kovali.

It occurred to him that never before had he seen her helpless. At their first meeting, almost ten years earlier, she was eighteen, spoiled and rich, standing in the early winter twilight of Warsaw's Marszalkowska wrapped in chinchilla like a luxurious doll, great sea-grey eyes sparkling with a youthful zest for conspiracy. In those days they were both anarchists, possessed by the romantic notion that Russian autocracy would capitulate to terror. In his own youthful arrogance, he'd judged her severely. They'd sat and talked under the jewelled lights of chandeliers in Café Ostrowski, adjourning later to watch a performance of *Petrushka* in the Teatr Wielki, and despite her irreverent wit and intelligence he'd diagnosed her as a thrill-seeker treating revolutionary activity as an exciting sport. This opinion was soon revised. Her cool aristocratic disdain concealed a formidable sense of purpose. From her base in Paris she helped to plan and execute a series of daring bank robberies for the movement, travelled to Madrid, Brussels, Rome, Berlin, Geneva and Warsaw on secret assignments and then, after three years of valuable work, became involved in a disastrous operation in London which resulted in the death of Poloski Murontzeff, one of her close associates, perhaps a lover. Two other comrades were also killed in the affair. She felt personally responsible for the entire fiasco. It changed her profoundly. Forced to flee from Poland himself to avoid arrest, he found her living in a tiny Paris attic, sombre, withdrawn, self-questioning. The boulevard cafés where she had consorted with emigré Russian poets and painters saw her scarcely at all. It was this Lydia with whom he'd fallen in love. Given a mattress on the floor, after a while he moved into her bed. On her part, it was unromantic. Sex, like food and tobacco, satisfied a need. Her passionate obsession was revolutionary justice. After making love, they lay in the shadowy room staring through the attic window at the bizarre geometry of jumbled roofs and sky, smoking and talking until dawn. Oh, that lyrical summer above the streets of Paris . . . They talked themselves out of anarchism and political naivete, joined Lenin's Bolsheviks, and then, suddenly, when it seemed to him that an indissoluble bond had formed in their blood, she announced that she was returning to Russia for underground political work. Alone. News reached him at second-hand of how she worked in textile factories, organized secret study groups, composed leaflets, was arrested and exiled to Siberia. By then he was in Switzerland, a fugitive from the imperialist war, and only after the March revolution broke out in Petrograd, where Lydia was already active in street-fighting and the soviets of soldiers, did they meet again.

The slight figure dressed in a stained military tunic and breeches had been leaning on the parapet of the Troitzky Bridge smoking and gazing at the Fortress of St Peter and St Paul. A cap rested negligently on the back of the Red Guard's untidily cropped head. The youthful profile had seemed vaguely familiar but it was not until he'd gone several paces that the shock detonated. He looked back.

In a characteristic gesture he had instantly recognized, the soldier took a last hungry puff of the cigarette and flicked the glowing end into the water.

'Lydia,' he said, retracing his steps.

Only just before, with a novel sense of triumph, he had been vividly aware of sunlight and river-craft on the broad sweep of the Nevsky, the bank crowded with afternoon strollers idly celebrating Petrograd's victorious revolution. Then, incredibly, overwhelmingly, she was there and all else was hallucination.

Lydia turned slowly, eyes dazed and ecstatic. In a voice husky with excitement, she said: 'Joseph, can you believe it? Is it all really happening?'

For one wild moment he thought she was referring to their miraculous encounter. But no man could be the cause of such transcendental joy, not in her, and his sudden appearance did not astonish her. Why should it? It was a time when everything at last seemed possible.

'It seems like a dream,' Lydia had said, the sun in her eyes, standing on the Troitzky Bridge in a city that freedom had made more beautiful than ever.

Then the dry rattle of machine-guns began and it was time to wake up . . .

Luck seldom favours the desperate, Joseph thought, but continued recklessly through the ravaged hinterland of fire-blackened hamlets, ruined farmsteads and peasants migrating in hopeless search of food and shelter. At any moment his path could be barred by an enemy patrol threatening summary execution if their papers were not in order. Yet the road unreeled kilometre after kilometre, small groups of soldiers walked by or sat smoking on the verge, and no one spared them more than an incurious glance. Then, suddenly, as they were rounding a bend male voices in loud boisterous song were heard above the noise of the engine. A large column of men, horses and light artillery appeared ahead.

The forest of bristling bayonets made his heart beat irregularly, but there was no turning back. Through Joseph's mind raced a recollection of Motke the Ganef, a disreputable character invented by his *alter ego*, the Yiddish writer Avram Frumkin. Trapped in a situation from which there was no escape, Motke relied on *chutzpah*, effrontery. Now it was up to Motke again. He reached out a hand and squeezed the bulb of the motor-horn peremptorily several times, simultaneously stamping hard on the accelerator. The car bounded forward.

A mounted White officer swivelled in the saddle and sharply scrutinized the fast-approaching vehicle. Perhaps he misread Joseph's grim expression as that of someone on an urgent mission to the battlefield, or the horn sounded with an intimidating authority. Whatever the reason, he saluted briskly and galloped the entire length of the column shouting at his troops to give way. They waved cheerfully as the car sped by, open-hearted Russian lads showing no trace of the ferocity with which they would soon seek to kill other, identical, Russian lads whom someone had said must be exterminated as Bolshevik scum. It was a situation that afforded Motke the thief sardonic amusement, even as his creator's Marxism sternly drew a class-moral and Joseph's heart still pounded at the thought of what would have happened had the ruse failed.

Kazan was less than ten kilometres away. At irregular intervals shells exploded with a noise as if great sheets of galvanized iron were being ripped apart. The sombre skyline flashed and darkened in abrupt eruptions of fire. Joseph swung off the road and entered a rutted cart track to detour the front-line city. The muddy path skirted fields and woodlands before disappearing into the folded landscape. There was no sign of habitation. The land had the wild and forlorn appearance of frontier country. Beyond the horizon he could sense the impalpable brooding Volga, the great brown river dividing Russia from the immensities of Asia that now, in his mind, had become the boundary between life and death.

Noises of suffering broke from Lydia as she struggled with her monstrous adversary. It was a war fought out in loneliness and terror and he found it unbearable that he could not reach her by voice or touch to offer at least a gesture of love. What made it worse was the sharpening sense of urgency, the fear that her condition was deteriorating.

A pool of rainwater appeared on the path, reflecting cloud and sky, deceptively shallow. The front wheels entered it and sank to the axles, churning deeper and deeper into the mud with the slow inevitability of nightmare. All his frantic efforts to get free were useless. It would require rope, manpower: but where to find them? . . . Torn between reluctance to leave Lydia unprotected and the need to obtain assistance, he climbed the crest of a low hill and scanned the surrounding countryside. A short distance away, in curious isolation at the edge of a wood, was a primitive stone structure that appeared to be a church. He began to run, his breath sharp and panting, sour with the taste of fear.

'The Monastery of St Nikita the Martyr,' proclaimed a notice on the heavy wooden door. His knock reverberated in uninhabited silence. At the back of the building was another door secured only by a latch. It led into a paved courtyard lined on one side with empty hen-coops. Heavy drops of water dripped from the mouth of a pump into a wooden tub. A peasant cart lacking one wheel leaned uselessly against the wall and a window looked into the monastery's stone-flagged kitchen. He rapped at the glass to attract attention.

'Is anybody here?' The echo of his voice returned hopelessly, yet he had an instinctive feeling that someone was keeping him under observation. The unknown enemy. No one trusted a stranger.

'Where are you hiding?' he shouted. 'I need help badly.'

A furtive sound, so slight he might have imagined it, came from somewhere near his feet. Some steps led down to the cellar and as he descended them a broad nose surrounded by hair showed behind a small metal grating.

'Go away, brother. We have no bread,' said a plaintive voice.

'I have not come for food,' said Joseph. 'Open the door.'

The reply was soft but obdurate. 'It is not permitted.'

The face vanished.

He returned to the yard and searched among some rubbish. Picking up a rusted piece of iron he went back down the steps, inserted it at the edge of the door and forced the lock. A dense, cloistered smell of mouldy straw, candle grease and human excrement was released, the rank piety of a hermit's cell.

'Brother, for the mercy of Christ, what do you want with us?' asked the soft voice.

Two pairs of eyes glimmered faintly in the mildewed gloom, one pair lower than the other. It was difficult to tell which belonged to the speaker.

'I have a sick friend. Our motor-car is stuck in the mud. My friend will die unless we reach a hospital soon. You must help me.'

There was a shuffle of padded feet. A black figure became detached from the darkness and loomed over him.

'We are forbidden by the rules of our monasticism,' it said in gruff tones of menace. 'Go in peace and God will help you.'

'God directed my footsteps here. Please come. It is very urgent.'

'I have told you. It is against our rules.'

Joseph pulled out his gun and the rules were changed.

'There'll always be the river,' the boatman said, an introspective melancholy etched on his elderly wrinkled face. It seemed his comment on the times. He rowed with practised ease, oars stroking the water, and the wooden villas, birches and neglected lawns drifted away. Other rivercraft quietly floated downstream trailing fishing nets. Only the red glare of distant gunfire flickering on the northern bend of the Volga contradicted the false autumnal peace.

Joseph's tension began to dissolve, replaced by a weak elation. For more than a month his group had been hiding in forests, moving only at night and after careful reconnaissance. It was the only way. The atrocities committed on captured Bolsheviks were limited only by the ingenuity of their torturers. Yet he had just driven forty kilometres in broad daylight through territory infested by Whites and bands of armed freebooters without once being challenged or made the target of a single shot. All thanks to Trotsky's great counter-offensive. And luck. It led them to the outskirts of a burnt-out village where an old fellow sat in his primitive shack at the water's edge obstinately waiting for things to settle down as though the civil war was just another spell of bad weather.

He was patching an old sheepskin coat with coarse sail-thread as Joseph stooped and entered the hut, hand resting on the butt of his revolver.

'Do you have a boat?' he demanded.

'Where d'you want to go?' the other replied without glancing up.

'Across the river.'

'The Reds are on that side.'

'There's no need to be afraid. They won't harm you, a worker.'

The boatman's shoulders twitched fatalistically. He stood up and stretched his small, wiry body. Something that could pass for a smile crinkled the leathery skin of his face.

'*Gospodin*, my wife and my sons are already in the ground so there's nothing more to lose. I'm not afraid of the devil and all his Jews.' He looked shrewdly at the gun in Joseph's belt. 'Either I take you or you'll pay me off with that, eh?'

Joseph shrugged. 'I have to get across.'

Without comment, the old man helped him to carry the insensible Lydia to the boat and lay her on a pile of sacks. Her inert form moved with the swell of the river as if it was already lifeless. In midstream she re-entered the twilight of delirium. Pitiful words bubbled from her swollen lips and burst without meaning, but like a child she said 'mama' and spoke the name of Christ.

'There's too many people in the world,' said the boatman, his voice dipping and rising to the rhythm of the oars. 'They push and shove for the little bit there is, and it all ends in slaughter.' He spat meditatively into the water. 'There's no understanding anything. A man gets kicked in the head by a horse and lives, yet chokes to death on a fishbone.'

When they reached the opposite bank he nodded his grey head in morose farewell, deftly turned the boat and rowed swiftly away.

Watching the departing boatman, valuing his surly humanity, Joseph shivered in the chill river-breeze and fought down a mounting apprehension. There was no reason for it: the worst was over. They had come through enemy lines unharmed and reached the safety of their own side. Up to that very minute he'd felt good about it. Now a paralysing uncertainty was creeping through his veins. Could it be the insidious beginning of typhus? At the very thought his body began to itch with the bite of infected vermin and he broke out in profuse sweating. They must hurry, hurry. With trembling fingers he undid the white tapes on Lydia's shoulder straps. Her eyes moved restlessly under their closed lids, as if struggling to awake from some vision of terror. Suddenly they opened but the horror, whatever it was, remained imprinted on them. She screamed. Joseph lifted her from the ground and held her tightly against his breast with a fierce, despairing tenderness. They had not yet eluded the enemy.

He climbed the steep bank. Shells were bursting in showers of stars in the northern sky and smoke obscured the horizon. A peasant cart passed some distance away but the driver did not hear his call or was reluctant to stop. Pushing through a dense thicket of bushes infested by clouds of gnats, he came across the decaying corpse of a horse colonized by armies of wasps, ants and huge buzzing flies. The narrow path petered out. Another opening led only to a slime-covered pond. He turned this way and that, the weight of Lydia dragging on his arms, his face scratched by sharp twigs, and each route ended in an impenetrable tangle of undergrowth. The scent of woodsmoke drifted up in the wind, evidence of human habitation. Navigating by smell, aching with tiredness, he broke through the thicket at last. And on the other side of a blessedly open field was a large timbered villa. The flag of the Revolution flapped at an upper window. Moved to tears, he stumbled towards it imagining food, succour, comradeship.

A sentry leaning against the wooden fence of the house straightened up and slowly levelled a rifle at his head.

'That's far enough,' came the terse warning. 'Where do you think you're going?'

Joseph looked at him with blurred eyes. The familiar pointed cap with its red star, the good blunt Russian face; he could have been one of his own lads.

'It's all right, we're comrades,' he said, smiling. 'We need help badly. My friend is desperately ill.'

Unimpressed, the sentry subjected him to an ill-natured scrutiny.

'What's illness got to do with it? This is a battalion of the people's Red Army, not a pill shop.'

'I'll explain to your commander.'

'Try explaining to me, uncle.'

The man was only doing his duty, Joseph reminded himself.

'I'm the commissar of a guerrilla group. We've been operating on the other side of the river. You can understand how things are, Kolchak's troops and the Czechs all around us, hiding in forests, no proper medical facilities.'

'Aha!' The sentry shoved his rifle forward and the look in his eyes remained mistrustful, that of a peasant watching a dishonest trader. 'You better have papers to prove that yarn,' he said. 'We don't waste time getting rid of snoopers and class enemies.'

A fevered palpitation throbbed against his ribs. He couldn't tell whether it was Lydia's heart or his own. She whimpered childishly again, and it lacerated him. Joseph's mood underwent a sudden reversal.

'What right' – he said, his voice shaking with rage – 'what right have you got to call us *class enemies*? We've been in action for weeks, and you stand there poking a bloody gun at us and spitting out insults! I demand to see the commander at once!'

'All right, all right! No need to bust your gut. We'll soon sort out the truth.'

The soldier put two fingers into his mouth and let out a shrill whistle. He was joined by an urchin-faced guard who grinned as he listened to his companion and, turning to Joseph, made a rocking motion with his cradled arms.

'Bring the *baba* along, mate. We'll get its arse wiped,' he said bursting into idiot laughter.

There's no point in letting it get under your skin, Joseph told himself angrily. They were the grandsons of serfs. Life had trampled on them, stunted their souls, brutalized their sensibilities. Under Tsarism they could expect to die before the age of forty with priestly promises of heaven and no escape from a brutish existence except in the fumes of vodka. It would take a generation of socialism to lift them out of the mire.

Inside the building soldiers lounged around smoking, oiling

weapons, exchanging barrack-room pleasantries as they lay on filthy blankets in unbuttoned ease.

'Hey, Farthole, who you got there?' one of them called.

The guard thrust two fingers into his face and smirked.

Without bothering to knock, he pushed open the door of an office that had apparently been a drawing room judging from its threadbare Turkestani carpet, mahogany table with ivory chess-board inlay deep scratched, plus *chaise longue* out of which stuffing protruded, and other ill-used relics requisitioned from the villa's 'former bourgeoisie'. An upright piano stood against a wall, and perched upon it like an organ-grinder's monkey was a man of twenty or so with close-cropped sandy hair and a face of freckled mischief. He picked at a typewriter in fierce concentration, one letter at a time.

'Don't interrupt for a minute. Got to finish this line', he said without looking up. A few more words were laboriously added before he gave them his attention.

'Wants to talk to the commander,' the guard explained laconically. 'Says he's a brave guerrilla and his pal's sick.'

The freckled youngster leaped acrobatically to the floor.

'Comrade Bloch is busy with his military duties. I'll see to it,' he said. He extended a negligent palm. 'Let's have your document.'

Joseph placed Lydia on the sofa and massaged his aching arms before handing it over. The sudden release of strain turned him dizzy. Bands of darkness floated before his eyes and he had the vertiginous sensation of falling. Again he wondered if it was typhus.

'Frumkin, Joseph Gershovitch,' said his interlocutor in tones of theatrical amazement, scratching his sandy head. 'Warrant as commissar commander of guerrilla detachment issued in Moscow 18 May 1918.' He put the document aside with a good-humoured shrug. 'Not a very good forgery, citizen.'

'Forgery? Are you serious? Can't you see it's stamped by the Commissariat for War?'

'It's still just a scrap of dirty paper. What's this scribble at the bottom?'

'That's the signature of Antonov-Ovseyenko. You must know who he is.'

'Of course, I'm not ignorant. Antonovsky-Pitipovsky. Everybody knows him.' He exchanged grins with the guard standing near by, then looked up slyly. 'All right, I believe you, thousands wouldn't. But what are you doing here instead of fighting with your own mob?'

The juvenile derision was becoming intolerable. 'I'll explain everything to your commander,' Joseph said dismissively.

The youngster jumped to attention, put up his arm in a stiff salute and recited: 'In the absence of the commander on duty, the deputy-commander, namely Petrovsky, Mitya, which is me, assumes full powers. Start talking, if you please.'

It was the worst of luck, falling in with such an indisciplined rabble. Sviazhsk was only about ten kilometres away. If the road was good Lydia could be taken there in half-an-hour, put aboard the hospital waggon of a train and be back in Moscow, on the road to recovery, by morning. But what sort of a man was in charge of this rogue battalion? An unreconstructed anarchist? An adventurer? A former Tsarist officer? The man could hardly be a principled Bolshevik.

'It's very simple,' Joseph said wearily. 'My comrade has typhus and must be taken to the rail junction at Sviazhsk –'

'Typhus!' Petrovsky appeared genuinely shocked. 'And you brought him here! That's sabotage. You could kill all of us.' He turned to the guard. 'How many did we shoot yesterday Vanya?'

'Three,' replied the guard, his urchin face split in an enormous grin.

'That was for stealing sunflower seeds, citizen Frumkin. Sabotage is worse.'

Joseph stared with horror into the freckled youngster's merry brown eyes. Sunflower seeds! Suddenly he was very cold. This was a psychopath who would kill whimsically, with enjoyment. There were madmen like that even in Bolshevik ranks.

'You want me to take them out and finish them off?' asked the guard. He unhitched the rifle from his shoulder, looking stern and important.

'Don't rush me, Vanya!' Petrovsky said, pacing up and down in frowning concentration.

They were retarded adolescents playing out a fantasy of power with real guns in their hands. He must humour them somehow, create a diversion. In the last resort . . . His hand moved stealthily towards his belt.

'I must remind you,' he said, 'of Decree Number 59 of the Sovnarcom. No one can be executed without formal trial by a field court-martial composed of two battalion commanders and a qualified political commissar.'

'Shit on that,' Vanya commented.

'Shut up!' Petrovsky stood over Lydia and peered closely into her face. 'There's something funny here,' he mused, and began to feel between her legs. His hand lingered. 'It's a filly,' he said, smiling.

Vanya hurried over in greedy excitement. A primitive force exploded in Joseph and his fist smashed full into the youth's face. He collapsed on the floor, dabbing at his bloody nose in dazed confusion. Petrovsky burst into laughter.

'You should have told me she was your sweetheart, Frumkin. We know how to behave. We don't shoot girls.'

Joseph said shakily: 'If you lay a finger on her again, I'll kill you.' The intense discharge of violence had burnt him out, leaving a cold smear of disgust. It was like racial humiliation. One always despised oneself for being forced into the role of victim, and the crude assault on Lydia would remain a shameful memory for a long time.

'Vanya, pick up your rifle and wipe your snotty nose,' said Petrovsky, quite unperturbed by the threat to his life. He vaulted on to the piano and gazed sulkily at Joseph as he swung his legs. 'I can't make head nor tail of your spouting about decrees and whatnot like some big boss.' The resentful tone implied that it would be much simpler to put a bullet through his head and be done with it.

'If you don't know what to do send him to old Bloch. He's the commander,' the young guard said sarcastically and spat out a mouthful of blood.

'I'm not asking your advice, Farthole. He put you on your arse, quick enough.'

'Well, I'm gonna tell him if you ain't.'

Vanya slouched out of the room.

'Hey, come back!' Petrovsky bellowed. He jumped down and ran off in pursuit.

The sudden quiet had an air of unreality. Was the hooligan game over or would it erupt again even more dangerously? It was an absurd and frightening predicament. This was clearly a case for the Cheka. Their military detachments were supposed to suppress such recalcitrants. In the vast shake-up going on not all the rubbish sifted to the side of the counter-revolution.

Joseph looked around for a telephone. None was in the room, and even if he succeeded in finding one it was improbable that assistance could arrive quickly enough. Nor could he leave the building with Lydia to seek aid outside and risk being shot by some gun-crazy sentry. He took out his own revolver to check that it was in good working order. There was the same cramped feeling in his stomach he experienced before going into battle.

The door opened abruptly and a man dressed in an ill-fitting military tunic buttoned up to the neck walked in with quick, nervous steps. A mild, reassuring, unsoldierly figure. The worried short-sighted eyes told Joseph all there was to know about Bloch as a commander. Intelligence and humanity, political acumen, too, no doubt: but these qualities were cancelled out by a crippling timidity. He looked like a schoolmaster driven to the verge of breakdown by rowdy pupils.

Brushing his sparse blond hair and standing in awkward readiness for instant retreat, Bloch spoke hurriedly, without preliminaries, as if to forestall contradiction.

'I'm sorry, what you ask is quite impossible. There are typhus cases everywhere. We have an epidemic in the village.' Bloch pointed through the window at a huddle of crooked one-storey dwellings crouching at the foot of a Byzantine church like peasant women kneeling for benediction. 'I don't have facilities, you see. Nor the authority. No,' he repeated, 'I'm afraid I don't have the authority.'

Joseph argued persuasively. An outstanding comrade. Of great value to the Party. Faced the rigours of guerrilla warfare as bravely as anyone. Personally known to Lenin himself. A special effort on her behalf must be made. The Central Executive would expect it.

'Women shouldn't be soldiers,' Bloch said, adding hastily: 'Please understand, I'm not opposed to the equality of the sexes.' He stared gloomily at Lydia, then placed the tips of his fingers on her wrist. 'Low pulse, extreme prostration, temperature at least 38. That's obvious even without a thermometer.'

'You're a doctor?' exclaimed Joseph.

'Dentist, actually, but I did my training in Vienna. They include a year's general medicine. When did the attack begin, yesterday?'

'During the night. We left camp early this morning.' An agonized note entered his voice. 'You must do something. It's a miracle I got her here alive.'

Bloch winced in sympathy and said: 'Oh, if you only knew how disorganized everything is.' He pressed the heel of his palm against his forehead as though trying to stifle a migraine and unexpectedly broke into Yiddish. '*Hob ich tsores!* Have I got trouble!' he groaned. The outbreak of revolution found him practising dentistry in Simbirsk. Then came the civil war and he joined the Red Army in the vague expectation of discharging his duty to the Republic by working on soldiers' teeth. Instead, because of the shortage of officers, he was given a fighting command. Things became more and more confusing. The Czechs. Refugees. Instructions to advance, retreat, fight to the last man. Half his unit vanished into thin air, some refused to obey orders unless they got more rations, others regarded the possession of a gun as a licence to terrorize the local population. 'And the decent fellows – there are those, too, you know – find it advisable to keep out of the way of trouble.'

'You should call in the Chekists,' Joseph said. 'They'll shoot one or two and the rest will behave.' He glanced anxiously at Lydia who had resumed her delirious soliloquy.

'You're from Warsaw. I can tell by your accent,' said Bloch, studiously ignoring the suggestion. 'Have you got a profession?'

'I studied piano at the Conservatoire but gave it up to do some scribbling.'

'Ah, a writer. I'm a Galicianer, son of a rabbi. My father could tell you stories better even than Sholem Aleichem. Life was hard in those days, but people knew how to laugh.' Bloch smiled timidly. 'I've jotted down a few of the tales. Who knows? Maybe there's something worthwhile there.'

The light imperceptibly turned lilac, hope fading from the day. What can I do to force this ineffectual man to take action? Joseph wondered in despair.

'Do you have any transport?' he asked. The other returned a harassed look. 'Bloch,' Joseph said harshly in Yiddish, 'I'm spilling out the bitterness of my heart! This girl must be in Sviazhsk by nightfall or she will die.'

The adam's apple in Bloch's throat worked painfully and he blinked with myopic distress. 'We have a lorry,' he gasped, 'but the driver – I'm not sure he is to be trusted.'

'Can you drive?'

'Yes, of course, but –'

'If you leave now you can be back here in less than two hours.'

'In two hours,' Bloch repeated dazedly. 'Well, perhaps . . .'

'Good, let's go immediately. Here are the comrade's papers.'

'But –'

'You will need to show them to the field hospital authorities.'

'Yes, indeed, of course.' Bloch collected his scattered wits and peered at the document in his hand. 'Lydia Alexandrova,' he read. His head nodded several times and he looked up shyly. 'Does she really know Lenin?'

Joseph thought of the short compulsive figure standing on the podium of a crowded hall, the voice whose iron logic hammered at the soul. And a different Lenin, shaking with sardonic laughter as they all drank tea in the Zinovievs' garden outside Paris. That summer afternoon seven long years ago, the sun vivid on her face. He lifted her gently. It was all locked away in the darkness of her mind. Impossible to think that she would not again be flooded with light and vigour.

'Yes,' he said, 'she knows him.'

Meeting the freckled Petrovsky in the corridor, Bloch said in an agitated whisper: 'I have to go to headquarters, Mitya. Important business. I'll be back within two hours, two hours.'

'Yes, comrade commander. All in good order, comrade commander,' was the grinning reply, and Petrovsky winked at Joseph mischievously.

The lorry drove off into the gathering dusk, trailing smoke.

Orange flashes ripped the skyline sending great rocks tumbling into an invisible canyon.

Joseph felt overwhelmingly tired and empty. There was nothing for him to do but go back to his unit, if he could find it.

Chapter Four

'What are you doing out of bed, Olyesha?'

The flaxen-haired nurse paused in her hurried journey through the crowded ward and approached a group of men smoking by the window. They shared a single cigarette, each taking a deep puff before passing it on to the next. There were four of them. One had an empty sleeve, another was minus a leg, a third had his face swathed in bandages like an Egyptian mummy and breathed through a hole left for his mouth. Olyesha, a deathly pale boy in his teens, pulled the front of his pyjama jacket together as if to conceal the dressing on his wounded stomach.

'I'm going back in a minute, Nina Grigorievna,' he said guiltily. 'We've just been discussing the shooting.'

'Is it true?' asked the one-legged man. 'There's a rumour it's all over.'

'All over?'

'They say he's dead.'

Nina Grigorievna looked appalled. 'No, Yury, thank heaven it's not. How can people say such things?' Her plump bosom heaved. 'Vladimir Ilyich is injured, but everything possible is being done and we must hope for the best.'

A dreadful thing, Lenin had nearly been assassinated! Semyon told her about it the previous evening when he came home from work. She had never known him so upset. 'A black day, Ninotchka, darling,' he'd said, hardly able to hold back the tears. Some demented creature, a girl, had shot Lenin with three bullets as he left the hall after addressing a labour rally. The woman came forward as if to ask him something and when Vladimir Ilyich turned she fired a pistol into his face. Everybody thought he'd been killed on the spot but he got up from the ground and was driven to his office in the Kremlin. Such heroism! Semyon said one bullet was lodged in his neck, the other hit his collar-bone. The doctors were very worried. A wonderful man, the hope of the workers of all the world.

'You're to get back into bed at once, Olyesha. And the rest of you, too. We want you to get well quickly, you know.'

She smiled tremulously, her heart full. One should smile as much as possible, she told herself, walking away and smiling, smiling with desperate concern at the shattered and the dying crammed side by side along the walls and down the centre of the long ward. The muscles of her face ached. The Sheremetyev Hospital was full to overflowing. Even the corridors were crowded. As soon as a bed came vacant, often before it could be made tidy, it was filled by one of those who had to make do with stretchers because of the shortage of accommodation. And yet they were lucky to be there. Thousands more lay on straw mattresses in former mansions of the rich, often screaming in pain for hours before an overworked doctor or medical orderly found time to attend to them. Not that one could spare the poor sufferers much time even here with dressings to change and medicines to administer; and emptying bed pans, sterilizing instruments, measuring out food in precious spoonfuls with everyone trying to wheedle another morsel. But at least a smile, a touch, a kind word . . .

A tall, bony woman, her cheeks flushed and hollow, came out of the bathroom carrying an enamel bucket of disinfectant. She was also a nursing volunteer, Galina Macgregor, daughter of a Scottish mining engineer and a schoolteacher by profession.

'Isn't it terrible?' she said, her long nose reddening distressfully.

'Yes, but it could have been even worse,' Nina replied. With a mild seizure of excitement, she confided that Semyon's chief at the People's Commissariat of Commerce and Industry had said another fraction of an inch and the bullet would have severed Lenin's jugular vein, and that Fanya Kaplan, the would-be assassin, was a cocaine addict hired by the British Consul, Bruce Lockhart (poor Galina flinched because he was her father's compatriot). Furthermore, it was all part of a big imperialist plot to put Kerensky back in power, because that very same day the Petrograd Cheka commander Uritsky was shot dead by a Socialist Revolutionary student.

Galina turned her horse-like profile and made whinnying noises of distress. 'I don't know why people can't be reasonable and settle their differences peacefully,' she said in bewilderment and hurried away after inquiring about the children, not without a trace of spinsterish envy.

Nina knocked at the tiny room which functioned as office and restplace for the hospital director, Professor Grigory Markov. His melancholy eyes, shaded by great tufted brows, looked patiently and absently right through her as she entered. A glass of tea, long grown cold, stood at his frayed elbow and the desk, which took up half the room, was untidily piled with old medical journals.

'Comrade Professor –' she began.

He swivelled in his chair and stood up, a small man with a bush of wild grey hair growing at the back of an otherwise bald cranium. 'I'll tell you exactly what I say to all my students, nurse,' he remarked abruptly as though continuing an interrupted discourse. 'Shock. That's the killer. As long as the vital organs are still functioning and there's not too much loss of blood the body can survive. Yet a perfectly healthy man in the prime of his years walks into the garden, is stung by a bee and phut! he's a goner. Shock. An upset in the delicate balance of the central nervous system. Warm blankets, hot tea. Can help, but not always.' He shook his head sorrowfully. 'The psychic damage of physical mutilation is beyond the reach of present medical knowledge. Sometimes all you can do is prescribe half-a-grain of morphine to ease them out.'

Nina was confused. The Professor seemed to be delivering a prognosis on the condition of Vladimir Ilyich and she felt ashamed to have come just to ask a personal favour. But the children must have food. There was only a cupful of carefully hoarded *kasha* left in the house and the herring heads had been used in yesterday's soup.

'Is there anything else?' inquired Professor Markov. He took his white coat from a hook on the wall and began to put it on. It made him look somehow more formidable.

'Please,' she burst out, 'I came to ask you if I could go early. My shift finishes in an hour but one of the other nurses has promised to help with my patients.'

'Yes, we are doing the best we can in difficult circumstances,' was the grave reply and, interpreting this as a positive answer, she thanked him and hurried to collect her coat from the staff room.

There was much confusion in the lobby. Orderlies tramped in and out carrying stretcher-cases from an improvised ambulance and placing them on the tiled floor under the supervision of Miller, a young American physician-volunteer who'd recently joined the hospital. Cries of agony echoed throughout the vaulted hall as if souls in torment screamed in every corner.

'Say, Nina, what are we going to do with them?' Miller asked helplessly in English. 'There's not an inch of room to spare in the whole goddam building.'

'Professoor Markov, he will push them in like . . . what do you call them?'

'Sardines?' Miller suggested. He made no secret of his exasperation at Russian inefficiency.

'It has to be that way. We can nothing do.'

She spoke in the level practical tones of a professional who had got used to the horror. In truth, no: it never went away. When she was younger, she'd have done anything not to have to go through this experience day after day. But nausea and terror were the price she felt she owed for the unexpected gift of private happiness when it had once seemed that her life had ended in bereavement and despair.

Involuntarily, she glanced down as two orderlies brushed by with a stretcher. There was a fleeting impression, dreamlike, of a familiar face. Miller motioned to the men, pointing at a vacant space in the mosaic of huddled bodies.

'It can't possibly be!' Nina thought incredulously.

'Hm! typhus,' the young doctor said, examining a tab fastened to the stretcher handle. 'There might be room in the fever ward. They don't usually last long there.' He looked up curiously. 'What is it, someone you know?'

'She's a very close friend.'

Miller said, 'She? My Russian isn't all that good. Did I understand you to say this kid is a girl? What is she doing among battle casualties from Sviazhsk?'

'If you knew her you wouldn't need to ask,' she replied wryly. 'Are you sure it's typhus?'

'I'm afraid so.'

Her bewildered glance went to a poster on the wall bearing the picture of a monstrous insect. 'Make War on the Louse.' She saw it every day when entering and leaving hospital. 'If the Soviet Republic does not defeat the lice, the lice will defeat the Republic.' And judging from the casualties of that war all over Russia, the lice appeared to be winning. Yet she'd still thought of it as something remote, like the plagues that ravaged dark-skinned anonymous multitudes of distant continents. A fastidious regard for cleanliness, even – in an obscure way – literacy, surely these conferred immunity?

She knelt by the stretcher and called in a low, urgent voice: 'Lydia, darling, can you hear me? It's Nina!'

The heavy eyelids fluttered and became still again.

'Afraid it's no use,' the American said. 'She's comatose. When they're like that they're lost to the world.'

Nina's tears which usually gushed with sentimental ease remained as a lump in her breast. At her lowest ebb she had drawn strength from Lydia, eased sorrow by sharing it with her. They had endured and survived a common misfortune in those remote days, eight years earlier, when both were romantic exiles of twenty, one addicted to clandestine exploits of political terror, the other experiencing the total and devastating love that comes but once in a lifetime. The Lydia of ice and fire, Poolka had called her in resentful admiration, with her great gull-grey eyes, her young arrogance, her casual disregard of danger. And thinking of that first meeting in a London tenement, it seemed the most bitter of ironies that that most privileged, beautiful, humorous and determined girl of whom she had been so furiously jealous should now be the defenceless victim of a hideous and lonely disease. 'Lost to the world . . .'

Miller clumsily patted her shoulder. 'You go home, Nina,' he said, sympathetic but brisk. 'I'll do my best for your friend. She could be feeling much better when you come on duty tomorrow.' She could be dead, too, but he refrained from saying so.

'If it weren't for the children –' Nina said, and her voice began to break.

'There is nothing you can do,' he insisted and propelled her away with a gentle push.

The early September evening descended like a fine rain of soot from the darkening sky as she crossed through the sparse traffic of Sukharev Square and passed under the high octagonal tower of the old reservoir into Myeshtchanskaya.

It was the hour when everybody seemed to be out catching a lungful of air before the unpredictable night invaded Moscow and it became too dangerous for all but the tough and adventurous to be on the streets. People stood in shabby clusters around a notice board reading the latest decrees, staring at posters admonishing them against hoarding, speculation and parasitic idleness, or argued with hungry bitterness about politics and the civil war. Others paraded out of habit alongside shuttered shops that once stocked imported luxuries for the guilty rich, dreaming perhaps that they would be reopened for the common people when things got better.

The city exuded a sour, defensive misery, but there were those who strode the ill-paved streets more purposively than ever in their lives, conscious of being citizens of the first workers' republic in the history of the world, proud to the point of arrogance that their square-set shoulders carried the burden of mankind's future. And it was these, often armed and in ill-fitting uniforms, whose rhetorical bearing sent slow eddies of apprehension and excitement through the drab throngs of the revolutionary capital.

Nina also walked purposively. Her thoughts, however, were not on history and mankind but on finding something with a scrap of nourishment to put into the pot. Meat was out of the question, especially in a communal kitchen. The merest smell of cooking flesh and someone would say you were an enemy of Soviet power feasting on the blood of the workers. *Pravda* called for such people to be shot. In reality, Semyon explained, there should be enough for all. The famine was created by speculators, profiteers and rich kulaks who ate their way through mountains of hoarded food because they regarded Soviet paper money as worthless and demanded payment in gold.

At the corner of Boulevard Spassky she boarded a crowded electric tram. A man pressed against her in the swaying vehicle.

‘So many people, eh, citizeness? Makes you go hot all over,’ he leered, exposing a double row of caried tobacco-stained teeth in a crooked smile. His breath stank, his pelvis jerked, one hand – as it were, accidentally – fondled her bosom. Seething with revulsion, she fought through to the open platform and, as the tram ground to a halt outside the old Nicholas station, alighted quickly, afraid of being followed. The outer circle of the city where she now found herself swarmed with Circassians, Tatars, Bokhari, Greeks, Persians, unkempt muzhiks from God knows where, and women dared not lift their eyes from the ground for fear that a stray glance might be interpreted as a lewd invitation.

The bagmen, entrepreneurs who scoured the countryside for peasants with a little of something to sell hidden away, operated in the maze of narrow, dark streets behind the railway. By rights, the wife of a responsible Soviet official should not be coming here. She dreaded to think what Semyon would do if he discovered the illicit source of the occasional vegetables that appeared in the greasy soup of herring heads.

And there they were, lounging in apparent aimlessness, their furtive eyes sharp as sharks’ teeth. Her heart palpitated as she felt them watching her. Several other women nervously ventured into the street: the bagmen watched them all. A signal was passed, one woman darted into a corner with a man, the shameful transaction was concluded.

‘Hey, missus, looking for something good?’ The speculator spoke softly, a cigarette smoking between his lips. He scrutinized her from head to toe examining the quality of her clothes, the two gold rings on her fingers, assessing her desperation. His glance lingered on her shopping basket as if X-raying its contents.

Obeying the abrupt inclination of his head, she followed him into the gateway of the goods yard. A raw wind blowing across empty railroad tracks penetrated through cracks in the wooden door.

‘How long since you tasted a good drop of *borscht*?’ the bagman asked. He was quite young, ruddy-faced from foraging around farms, and seemed good natured enough except for a certain cynical droop to his eyelids. Diving into a large sack, he produced a beetroot and held it enticingly under her nose.

'Can I have three?'

'Pay the price and you can take the lot.'

'Three will do. How much?'

She opened her purse and unfolded some crumpled roubles. It was a formal gesture, no more.

'I wipe my arse with those,' he said laconically. 'How about a pair of shoes. In leather. No? Well, I'll show you something special.' Swiftly looking up and down the street, he felt in his sack and brought out a greasy substance wrapped in newspaper. A rush of saliva came into her mouth. 'Pig's lard, missus. If that's real gold on your finger, it's yours.'

Shaking her head vehemently, she said: 'No, it's my wedding ring,' and took a woman's cardigan from her basket. 'I will give you this. Pure wool. If you have a wife . . .'

'A mother,' the bagman said, stroking the soft fabric. Then he pushed it away. 'No, not enough. Give me the other ring. Only a *boorzhvasy* needs two.'

The lard had an irresistible smell, evoking rich soups, *pirozhki*, gravies brown and nourishing, golden pastries. She must have it!

'Look how beautiful this is.' She held the cardigan enticingly against her rounded breasts and postured. 'It's pure Scotch wool. Nowhere in the world can you find such quality.'

'Scotch?' The man was puzzled.

'From England.'

'English, eh!' He laid his hand against her and an expression of lustful greed entered his face. 'The best in the world . . . For a mother nothing is too good.'

'Yes, you are right to think so.' She breathed with difficulty.

'Take it,' he said, holding out the greasy package.

The exchange made, he stuffed the cardigan into his sack and waited for her to leave. She stared tenaciously into his eyes. 'You have still to give me three beetroots,' she said.

'What a capitalist you are,' said the bagman in mock admiration, dipping into the sack again.

2

Home was a high-ceilinged room of a requisitioned mansion in Kozitzki Pereulok, close to the Church of Saint Sergius and opposite a small tree-filled garden that had been a cemetery until Moscow was set on fire by the retreating Napoleon. The great house now provided accommodation for government officials and their families. Those with a single room were fortunate. Many lodged in sections of once lordly chambers whose flimsy partitions trembled if someone sneezed.

It was dark when Nina arrived and a beehive buzz of activity resounded through the building as she hastened up the unlit staircase. The bathroom, now a communal laundry room, stood open to view. Two women, wives of functionaries at the Commissariat of Justice, were beating damp washing against the porcelain tub in an effort to drive out dirt without soap while muscular boys, an Apollonian obsession of some bygone Prince Volodarsky, nakedly disported in a mural of blue skies and Ionic temples. A stench of 'fish-glue', the irreverent description of the staple soup available, came from the kitchen where more women were congregated, and there was a flurry of polite greetings before Nina reached the privacy of her own room and with a heartfelt sigh of relief at last shut out the oppressive city and the daily struggle for existence.

Polina, the young student who looked after the children, left hurriedly for a Party youth meeting. Seven-year-old Poolka, who resented her absences, gave her a sulky kiss and became re-engrossed in a child's picture book of the life of Lenin. Baby Vova cried until she fed him the breast, mainly as a comforter for her milk was drying, and put him to sleep behind the curtained alcove. Soon Semyon would return from the office, she would cook delicious beetroot *borscht* and something extra-special with that precious savoury piece of lard, and the circle of her life would be complete. In contrast, poor Lydia lay among a thousand other sufferers in the Sheremetyev Hospital, utterly and desolately alone.

How lucky I am, she thought, sitting under a dim light suspended from the high ceiling among the simple furniture of her happiness. Yet happiness more than anything is vulnerable to the microbes of insecurity. Lydia's plight brought back the aching past: the shooting in Houndsditch eight years before, the shattering news of Poolka's death, trial at the Old Bailey as an accomplice in murder and attempted armed robbery (they had mistaken her for Lydia), months in Holloway women's prison when she told herself God was punishing her sinfulness and jealousy. How cruelly and suddenly life could be robbed of meaning!

Gripped by a premonitory fear, she gazed at little Poolka, child of her tragic love, growing more like his dead father every day. 'Come here!' she called and, seizing him in a close embrace, searched through his thick curly black hair, examined his underclothes, looked closely at the folds of his jacket. The enemy had crawled out from the poster. Lenin with a bullet in his neck: mutilated boys screaming in the dark: lechery, deformed and evil-smelling: an army of deadly lice crawling into the seams of Russia.

'Darling,' she said, 'promise me –'

She wanted to say keep safe; grow up in peace; let the future be gentle: but all she did was smother his eager, vulnerable face in kisses ...

Shulkin, a slight fair-haired man of thirty with a sparse reddish beard, listened tolerantly, clicked his tongue several times and made some appropriate comments.

'Very sad, darling ... Brought to your hospital, really! ... Yes, a remarkable coincidence ... How long since you'd last seen her? Eighteen months ago at our little marriage ceremony. Well, well ... Try not to be too upset. Who knows how it will turn out? ...'

It was like a distracting conversation taking place in another room, difficult to follow when one was preoccupied with the immensely absorbing problems of adjusting industry to the needs of war communism. Everything must be made subordinate to the requirements of the Red Army. Somehow the shortage of technical specialists and skilled management must be overcome, better use be made of available machinery, manpower wastage be stopped by firm emergency methods. His mind hummed like a high-powered dynamo, devising improved systems for centralized control, regrouping factories into more efficient conglomerates, converting the problems of steel production into precise formulae. Yes, all this and more could and must be done. Bolshevism + the Industrial Power of the Proletariat = Victory.

'Excuse me, my dear,' he said, and hurried away to write it down. Briefly disengaging from these momentous questions in deference to her concern, he added: 'Perhaps her family should be informed. Has she any relatives in Moscow?'

Nina watched him in affectionate exasperation. Outside his work, he was so absent-minded that it became embarrassing. He never remembered names, mixed up people and had even to be reminded to do up the buttons of his trousers. How often had she gone through the agonizing experience of being introduced to a colleague with: 'Comrade – er – excuse me one moment, I'm a bit confused – this is my wife – er – Nina. Yes, of course, Nina . . . Darling, may I present Comrade . . . Comrade – Good heavens! This is ridiculous, I know exactly who he is. We work in the same office.' Fortunately most of his friends regarded it as amusing.

'Semyon, you haven't forgotten who we're talking about, have you?'

'Of course not,' he replied indignantly. 'Lydia what's-her-name.'

'Alexandrova.'

'Exactly. A small blonde girl. Music teacher.'

'No, darling, not that one. Lydia is the tall girl you mistook for Inessa Armand, the friend of Lenin. She has no relatives in Moscow. Her father is the former Count Nikolai Alexandrov. The family are living in Switzerland or France.'

'How very unfortunate.' He stooped and brushed her cheek with his lips. 'We have a meeting of Sovnarkhoz. There are important decisions to be made. If I come in very late I'll try not to wake you.'

'Not too late, Semyon,' she pleaded.

'We shall see.' He kissed her again, a visionary look in his eyes, and muttered: 'Bolshevism plus the industrial power . . .' As he was about to leave he gripped her fiercely. 'Darling, tremendous things are going to happen.' He was a very happy man.

Nina cleared away the supper dishes, carefully wrapped the remains of the bread ration in a clean white cloth before placing it in the cupboard. (Both she and Semyon received rations under Category 2 – ordinary physical labour and intense intellectual labour – amounting together to four ounces a day.) She then tiptoed into the children's alcove to make sure they slept peacefully and had not kicked off the bed covers. She felt restless and vaguely frustrated. It was too early to go to bed herself and she'd only lie awake waiting for her husband to return. A copy of *Pravda* lay on the table. Semyon often told her she must improve her political education. The smudged print urged her to eradicate the bourgeoisie and mercilessly exterminate the vicious mad dogs of counter-revolution, admonishments that filled her with a depressing sense of inadequacy. Her head began to ache. Laying the newspaper aside, she went to the window and gazed across at the garden. Trees rustled, shedding their leaves. The usual couples sat in the dark, holding hands. Above the rooftops glowed a faint effulgence from the Gorodskaya Tchast, the inner city, and the Kremlin towers clustered darkly against the sky. 'There is nothing above Moscow except the Kremlin, and nothing above the Kremlin but heaven,' according to an old proverb. However intended, the words conveyed an immense loneliness, an image of the city as a great ship drifting on oceans no one had charted. She shivered and turned away.

Lydia . . . a sudden idea occurred to her. Leaving the room, she hurried along the corridor to a neighbouring apartment. Someone had scratched a gallows on the panel of the door. She knocked softly. There was no response and she was about to go when there were sounds of movement inside. Jacob Peters opened the door, barefoot, dressed only in trousers and vest, a broad leather belt with an empty pistol holster strapped around his waist. He was square, strongly built, Germanic in appearance. Damp blond hair curled on his chest.

'Yes, Nina, what is it?' His speech was slurred. There was a girl in the room.

'I'm disturbing you,' Nina said. 'I'm sorry.'

Privacy was a forgotten luxury. You couldn't even sit for five minutes on the communal lavatory without someone knocking and demanding that you hurry.

'Is anything wrong?' Peters asked reluctantly.

Bat-like shadows flew across the room as the girl moved through the rays of an oil-lamp and combed her hair before the looking-glass. Her dress had been hurriedly pulled on, the buttons awry. Nina felt horribly embarrassed at having intruded when they'd been making love. Like her furtive bargaining with bagmen for an extra morsel of food, it reminded her that so much of life was lived in the shadow of shame.

Peters made no attempt to disguise his impatience. Biting his lip with annoyance, he swung the door back and forward as if debating whether to close it in her face.

'It's Lydia Alexandrova,' she said in a low voice. 'She was brought into my hospital this evening. I'm very worried.'

'Lydia!' He seemed taken aback. 'But I thought she was – Don't tell me she's stopped a bullet!'

'No, it's typhus. She's very ill.'

'Christ! That's bad luck.'

A surge of tears came into her eyes. Suddenly death seemed very close, not only Lydia's but that of every one she held dear.

'Jacob, you've got influence,' she said intensely, 'can't you do something to help her?'

'Influence!' He glanced sardonically at the dishevelled bed, the shabby functional furniture and general dilapidation. 'I can arrest saboteurs. I can round up suspects and put them in prison. In some cases, I can order a man to be shot. But if I took an ounce of cheese I had no right to someone would denounce me as a criminal.' Abstractedly, he slipped his hand into the unbuttoned neck of his vest and scratched his chest.

'What can I possibly do? It's up to the doctors.'

Nina shook her head in frustration. 'That's the trouble. Our hospital is terribly overcrowded. Everybody – doctors and nurses – are exhausted. Do you know, she's lying on a stretcher with hundreds of other casualties. She hasn't even got a bed!'

Jacob Peters lifted his hands and slapped them helplessly against his thighs.

'Nina, Lydia's an old friend and if I could do something I would,' he said. 'But is there a single hospital in Moscow that is different? We've got battle casualties crammed into private houses. We're short of blankets, medicine and bandages. Everybody's starving. With all the influence in the world, you can't wangle a miracle. So tell me. Propose something!'

'Yes, I suppose you are right,' Nina said, defeated. Her voice broke. 'At least – at least, Peter Piatkov should be told. You know . . . how Peter feels about her.'

'Leave that to me. I'll tell him, I promise!' Jacob's eyes slid round to the girl in the room. She watched him through the mirror and passed her rough pink tongue over her lips like a cat. 'Do you know, I have to be back on duty in less than an hour,' he said to Nina in quiet desperation.

3

Peter Piatkov sat in his office on the third floor of No. 11 Bolshaya Lubianka, headquarters of the central Cheka, reading a three-day-old copy of the Petrograd newspaper *Krasnaya Gazeta*, a faint grimace of distaste wrinkling the corners of his eyes.

'Each drop of Lenin's blood must be paid for by the bourgeoisie and the Whites in hundreds of deaths,' he recited, irony in his pedantic enunciation of each separate word. 'Out of the way with the sentimentalists who are afraid to shed innocent blood . . . extermination . . . time to be pitiless . . . blood for blood.' Crumpling up the newspaper and dropping it into the waste basket, he glanced across at Latsis and said: 'Tell me, as a Latvian who has no special axe to grind can you explain why "European" Petrograd is so much more blood-thirsty than the Slav city of Moscow?'

Latsis, a heavy man, thirtyish, leaned back in his chair and rested his feet on the desk. The innuendo did not escape him. Chekist troops of Latvian origin had earned a reputation for zealously carrying out unpopular assignments. As one of their leading commanders, he'd used his pistol to snuff out quite a few political bandits himself. The thought gave him no pleasure: it was necessary, he had his orders and that was that.

'You find the style offensive?' He examined the closely-bitten nails of his right hand. 'It does not seem so different from the prose one reads in *Izvestia*. If you want elegance you must read Gorky's *Novaya Zhizn*. Good literature but poor politics.'

'Petrograd,' said Peter, 'is a perfect setting for melodrama. Those grandiose palaces, the great streets – Nevsky, Vosnesensky, Vladimirsky – that seem built for giants and are crowded with little people selling each other bunches of flowers, ice-cream, kvass, portions of cranberries, filling the stage like extras creating an atmosphere for the entrance of their heroic principals. I am referring to the old days, of course. Incidentally, I understand that Gorky's paper has been closed down.'

Latsis rocked gently to and fro on his tilted chair, thick lips thoughtfully pursed.

'It is easy to tell that you are an artist. I look forward to seeing the pictures you will paint of our own heroic times. But not the reprisals. You have your reservations there, I believe.' The Latvian looked up curiously and waited. There was no reply. '*Wir können nicht anders*, we cannot do otherwise,' he said soberly.

Piatkov gave a noncommittal nod. He was only too familiar with the justifications. The forces of intervention and counter-revolution were far more ruthless than Bolshevism whose aim, after all, was to wrest the nation free from centuries of servitude. An unprecedented tornado of violence raged over the old civilization and the whole of Europe was being torn apart. One day's casualties on any single sector of the Western front far outnumbered Chekist executions in all provinces controlled by the Republic. All of it was true, of course.

Yet he could not deny his misgivings. It was not, as some might call it, a moral twinge, the soft taint of petit-bourgeois liberal democracy or the sickness of Jesus. Lenin himself repeatedly and with remorseless logic urged exemplary ruthlessness in suppressing kulaks, priests and White Guards. Saint-Just was quoted: 'Those who half-make revolutions dig their own graves.' But reprisals recognized no degrees of responsibility. They were carried out against people seized as hostage for the conduct of others. To shoot a man because someone else resisted the confiscation of grain was stupid and ineffective. As for the murderous unreason of mass executions for a single act of terror, the multiplying categories of those regarded as unfit to live ... unless there was a swift return to sanity after the catharsis of indiscriminate revenge a Russian Robespierre might seize the Revolution, a preposterous but terrifying prospect.

'No, we cannot do otherwise,' Latsis resumed emphatically, engaging him in a cold duel of eyes. 'You are not inexperienced in conspiracy, so let me put it to you rather crudely.' Picking up a metal paper knife and pointing it deliberately at the centre of Piatkov's forehead, he pulled an imaginary trigger. (The imaginary bullet detonated a controlled explosion of anger in the victim, but he remained impassive.) 'Now if that shot was real our discussion would not interest you any longer, but ask yourself: is the finger alone guilty? The hand? The arm that raised the gun? The individual assassin is the finger, to destroy him solves nothing. He is the instrument of a conspiratorial group, the group is the instrument of an enemy class. Even those members of it who are sitting passively in their homes are objectively guilty and must be crushed.'

Piatkov abstained from smiling. 'I recognize the force of your argument,' he said. He looked at his watch and stood up. Ten minutes to midnight, time to go. 'The meeting is due to begin. Are you ready?'

They strapped on their gun belts. It was certain to be a grim occasion.

A score or so of leather-jacketed Chekists filled the conference room as they entered and took places in the front row with the more senior commanders. Most were still in their twenties yet vertical marks of power were already stamped on their faces and they moved with the defiant, almost swaggering, authority of men whose very reputation inspires fear. Piatkov briefly greeted acquaintances, noting signs of nervous exhaustion. The chandeliered light gave them a waxen tinge. One or two sparked with brittle vitality, their pupils enlarged and brilliant. Cocaine sniffers. The strain of the past few days had taken toll: killing wasn't easy.

At one minute to midnight precisely the door opened and the tall, untidy figure of Dzerzhinsky appeared followed by Jacob Peters. The noise in the room ceased as though cut by a knife. The sword of the revolution, his ascetic face honed by years of Siberian forced labour, went silently to the low platform and opened a folder. A cigarette burned in his hard, taciturn mouth and his light transparent eyes were narrowed against the drifting smoke. Suddenly he ground the smouldering butt under his heel and stood up under the twin pictures of Lenin and Trotsky.

'Comrades,' he began in a quiet Polish-accented voice, 'I have called you together to make a few simple announcements.'

Dzerzhinsky was a man who sought solitude, who shunned public occasions. He was a poor speaker. The building had been the headquarters of an insurance company and that very room must often have echoed to the dry tones of its chairman computing statistics and outlining commercial strategies. The head of the Cheka was also dry and statistical. The woman Kaplan had been executed by the commandant of the Kremlin. Kanegiesser, who murdered Moisei Solomonovitch Uritsky in Petrograd, had similarly paid the penalty. Hundreds of enemies of the Republic – 512 to be precise – were shot by the Petrograd Cheka in reprisal for the death of Uritsky and a similar number of fresh hostages had replaced them. The report droned on in these abstract terms, rendering the account of shootings unreal. They were paper deaths, mere entries in a ledger, nothing to get upset about. Perhaps conscious of a certain inadequacy, Dzerzhinsky spoke a bit louder and waved a hand in a half-hearted rhetorical gesture as he declared: 'We are serving notice that any further attempt on the life of our leaders will be followed by proletarian executions not only of hundreds but thousands of White hostages.'

'Hear, hear!' a voice broke from the back of the room as one of the younger Chekists was moved to enthusiasm. 'Serve the scum right!' he shouted. 'All power to the Soviets!'

The emotion was naive, the slogan out-of-date. Dzerzhinsky looked at the interrupter with unconcealed distaste and the blood was driven from the man's face as if he had been publicly slapped.

'I will not conceal from you that there are critics of our actions even in our own Party,' he continued. His lips twitched ironically and his eyes swept the rows of intent faces. (Peter Piatkov stiffened: was it his imagination, or had they rested on him a fraction longer than on others?) 'I sympathize with such critics. Terror lacks precision. There is no small cabal of plotters whose names can be crossed out of existence one by one without the need to shed a single drop of innocent blood. The counter-revolution is hydra-headed. Not enough paper and ink exists in the whole of Russia to list the names of all who hate

Soviet power. Therefore, I answer that terror is merciful. It compels fear, fear compels the class enemy to disarm, this disarming prevents the slaughter of hundreds of thousands of workers. Who then is most sparing of innocent lives, ourselves or our critics?'

Again, Peter imagined that Dzerzhinsky's eyes subjected him to a momentary interrogation. But why? A cold finger touched the base of his skull. He had been a secret service double-agent for too long to overlook the value of discretion. No one guarded his tongue more carefully, monitored his look, gestures, thoughts even, with more circumspection. He knew to a precise degree what it was politic to reveal. Latsis and others could suspect that his attitude to wholesale reprisals was disapproving, but they had no proof. Fortunately it was not part of his duties to join in the repressions. His concern in the foreign department of the Cheka was with the activities of Russian emigrés and conspiratorial elements abroad.

The speaker's voice buzzed in his ears like a loathsome insect. 'Decree . . . Central Committee . . . Cheka to be reinforced with Party members . . . concentration camps . . . shootings . . . executions . . .'

'Comrades,' Dzerzhinsky declared with icy clarity, 'this is the beginning of Red Terror.'

He disappeared in swift silence. Lenin and Trotsky stared down at the harsh emptiness of the platform. The leatherclad men pushed back their chairs and moved heavily to the door. Peter stretched his cramped limbs and turned as his name was called. He had no premonition of the blow that was about to descend on him.

'Lydia,' somebody said. 'Bad news. Typhus.'

Jacob Peters gazed at him, spectral, diminishing in waves of darkness. He had the dreamlike sensation of falling.

'Where is she?' he asked, his voice hollow and remote.

He was back in his office. A name had appeared on the writing pad. Sheremetyev Hospital. He sat in frozen stillness, staring at it.

At last he was able to leave. In a curious vacuum, a numbness of feeling, he had performed a number of necessary duties, dispatched orders, locked away files. As he emerged into the street, the wartime city was a huge hive of darkness sparsely scattered with the rectangular glow of dimly-lit windows, a hungry, desperate city wrapped in feverish slumber. Not that everybody slept. Restless insomniacs, kept awake by the craving for excitement, tramped the streets searching for violence as alcoholics seek the stimulation of raw spirits. The tips of their burning cigarettes wove firefly patterns in the soft charcoal density of night but veered sharply as the tall figure striding along the Bolshaya Lubianka became defined. His sheepskin hat enhanced his height. His leather jacket and Mauser pistol advertised his grim profession. Pyromaniacs have no desire to be scorched by the flames that draw them like frantic moths.

An interval of time had passed since he'd heard the news – an instant, an hour, an eternity? Shock paralyses the mind's chronometric cells. Images of the night returned charged with predestination. Latsis's insinuation, the pointing knife, Dzerzhinsky's narrative of terror, his piercing hangman's eyes – symmetrical forewarnings that the unseen adversary, the unshakable, relentless, pursuer, was somewhere close at hand and had made his move. He was wary of it always. Vigilance was ingrained, grown out of a childish discovery that God was neither benevolent protector nor the stern judge of wrongdoing but a cruel and arbitrary enemy. And when God was banished his malignity remained, not in the cruelties, greed and perversities of mankind, for which men alone must be held responsible, but in something totally mysterious, abrupt and inscrutably vindictive.

He did not value life for its own sake, he told himself. His instinct for self-preservation was healthy enough, but at the age of thirty-four existence became significant only in terms of social duties, personal responsibilities, the people one loved. His own loves were few, principally these: his work; his unique, precious and tormented Russia; Lydia. The adversary, like Dzerzhinsky, knew how to strike through hostages and now had seized the one person closer to him than anyone on the face of the earth.

Subdued lights burned in the hospital windows but the gate was locked. After ringing several times the rusty bell elicited a response. A bearded old man emerged from the brick lodge and shuffled across the courtyard. Sleep-bleared wrinkled eyes focused upon him with difficulty, with senile apprehension, as if Death itself had appeared on the threshold, a stern, upright figure in the uniform of retribution.

'We're closed, your honour,' he said reedily, clasping his hands to his breast and genuflecting.

'This is an emergency,' Peter said, repeating for emphasis: 'An emergency. You understand?'

The grizzled head nodded again and again. Snuffling sounds came from the tangled beard. Finally, the old man fumbled in the folds of his padded coat and, producing a large key, tremblingly unlocked the gate.

The small reception office at the lobby entrance was occupied by a man in a tattered military tunic, an empty sleeve pinned across his chest. He was fast asleep in a chair. Peter rapped on the glass. Haggard eyes were startled into suspicious alertness. The armless side of the man's body jerked as if reaching instinctively for a rifle.

'What is it, comrade?' he demanded.

'I've called to see one of the patients, Lydia Alexandrova.'

'Don't give me names. You shouldn't 've been let in. Come back in the morning and bring a permit.'

'I advise you not to be obstructive,' said Peter.

'Doing my duty,' the man said sourly. He tapped his empty sleeve. 'See this? Paid my dues to the workers' and peasants' republic. The Cheka don't frighten me. Is it official?'

He felt no rancour. The sturdy independence and refusal to be intimidated should, he supposed, be gratifying. More of it would save Russia. The spirit of October that stormed the Winter Palace. It was, in fact, a symptom of dissociation that his mind should run on such well-worn rails. And yet one more insolent remark and the hard lump of anxiety in his breast would explode. He held himself rigidly. The first article of faith: never lose control.

'Yes,' he said, 'it's official,' and the quiet inflexible tone, the stony gaze, sent a tremor through the ex-soldier. He rose hurriedly and went for the doctor in charge.

Another interval of waiting, a pulse throbbing in his temple like a tiny heart. Footsteps sounding down a far corridor. Faint stifled cries. An odour of disinfectant that carried the taint of disease. The empty lobby, its stained yellow walls plastered with grim posters and typewritten notices, recalled a deserted railway terminus in some forgotten city. That recurring image of separation.

At last a young doctor arrived, walking unsteadily. He seemed drunk but his white face indicated that it was only the effects of exhaustion. '*Moje nazwisko Miller*,' he said, wearily massaging his eyes. 'Oh, I'm sorry. That's Polish,' he added in English. 'God, I hope you can speak American. My brain's too tired to think in Russian.'

It was not one of Peter's more fluent languages despite, or perhaps because of, clandestine activities among revolutionaries in the garment district of New York and the East End of London but his clumsy accent communicated a more passionate concern than he would have revealed in his native tongue.

Dr Miller blinked and said: 'Yes, I know the girl. She's a friend of one of our nurses. They brought her in some hours ago. I suppose you'd like to see her. You know what typhus is like. She won't be able to communicate.'

And now it became a suffocating dream, his heart pumping fear, the crowded corridors of suffering, a walk through the wilderness of dread. He was nine years old and God in his divine malevolence led him forward to gaze at his dead mother.

'Here she is,' said the doctor.

A stretcher lay on the floor, one of many. Brownish light came from a dim bulb suspended from the ceiling. He saw her through blurred eyes, drowning, drifting, beyond reach, and simultaneously as a beloved face in a fading photograph, where all the hopefulness, the young and vivid promise, are made poignant beyond words because the brightness and the promise are doomed and irrecoverable. It was unthinkable that he should carry into an empty future that desolate image.

Miller said: 'There's not very much we can do, especially in these conditions. It's odd, though. Sometimes all the nursing in the world doesn't help. Yet others come through without a doctor in sight.'

'What chance –' His throat seized up: it could not even be

said, not in any language. Moistening his lips, he tried again. 'How . . . long to makc better?'

'I guess incubation has gone on for about six days. The crisis should come after another week, then if everything goes well her temperature will come down fairly quickly. It leaves them very weak. They need a long convalescence.'

'I want she should be put in bed. She is not to be on the floor.'

'What can I do?' Miller gestured helplessly at the densely packed ward. 'We don't have room. Not yet.'

'Doctor!' Peter gripped his arm and drew him close. There was a queer look in his eyes, something between menace and desperation. 'Doctor, she will have everything.' His voice broke. 'Everything. You understand me what I say? Everything!'

A fine, needle-sharp rain stung his face as he set out to walk home. Streets were deserted. The last enervating hours of darkness had driven away the relentless seekers after sensation. But as he began to cross the broad expanse of Rozhdestvensky Boulevard two trucks swept round from Lubianka and came to a grinding halt outside the Sryetensky Monastery. Soldiers armed with heavy revolvers jumped down. One of them drew a sheet of paper from his pocket and consulted it in the brief flare of a match. He spoke softly. The men moved off, entering houses two by two. They were searching for remnants of the bourgeoisie. It had already begun.

Although the birds in the Alexander Gardens were singing their dawn-chorus, it was still dark when he reached the narrow, four-storey house in which he lived. It was in a small street behind Znamenka. In the old days, cadets from the near-by Military Academy used to bring their girls to a café there where a gipsy played the fiddle. All, of course, gone: the girls, the music, the sprightly boys, now probably dead on the wrong side of the barricades, grooming incipient moustaches in imitation of Imperial Hussars. His room was an attic roofed with green copper. Its solitude suited him. The open window admitted a river smell and he could hear gull-cries and boat sirens on the Moskva.

It was in such a room beside another river that she had first come to him desperate for assistance, a girl terrorist of twenty who'd got involved in a foolish and bloody fiasco. Even the furniture was much the same: a camp-bed, a chair and table, a few books. But no paintings. The Revolution had cured him of that indulgence, at least. The only picture in the room was a framed sketch of her by the painter Feder dated April 1911, drawn one evening in the Rotonde in Paris. Feder sold it to him for twelve francs and it had been with him ever since, hanging on walls in Berlin, Geneva, New York, Stockholm, gazing down with its odd smile at the transient visitors who assuaged his intermittent lusts. However tender, witty, passionate or appealing, none of them stayed. They were for him the human equivalents of a stroll in sunshine along the Kurfürstendamm, the glittering reflection of Stockholm at night seen as the Hamburg ferry entered the waters of Saltsjön, a meal in a good French restaurant. One enjoyed them, but hunger was for home, for Lydia.

He boiled some water and prepared a black brew of adulterated coffee, bitter as remorse. Darkness ebbed from the window. Blue light began to fill the room, obliterating its shadows. He sipped his coffee and gazed broodingly at Feder's drawing on the wall above the bed. A fragment of verse floated through his mind. 'Poor soul, the centre of my sinful earth . . .' (There was, he suddenly recalled, a white scar on her cheek that had not been there before.) '. . . the centre of my sinful earth.' However the poet meant it, his earth was Russia and Russia was her voice, her smile, the depths in her eyes, her heartbreaking, self-destructive gallantry. He must not allow her to die, neither by war, nor by famine, nor by the virulent white army that ravaged her life's blood.

And the resolve hardened, became conviction. He would watch over her and all who touched her sickness, infuse drop by drop into her veins his own stubborn determination to bring her back to life.

Outside a grey September dawn washed over the rooftops. Moscow was waking to a new morning of terror. He could afford himself no more than two hours sleep. There were things to organize.

4

The long vertiginous spiral into blackness . . .
a mute, petrified horror of the void . . .
obliteration . . .
the quiver of a cell, bifurcating, pulsing, as if . . .
bits of her came together and . . . disin . . . teg . . . rated . . .
all . . . the . . .

she remembered (did she?) fleeing through a dry blizzard of heat, tortures of a multifarious hell, her skull on fire, flames burning the tissues of her eyes . . . and falling again and again falling into profound absences . . . huge worms tunnelling into her flesh . . . and glass cities shattering into geometrical patterns, exploding galaxies, labyrinthine corridors and . . . nothing . . . most of all . . . non-existence . . . nothing . . .

Then came dreams, the dream of all her restless years. A vast building swaying in the grip of some seismic upheaval, crowds scattering in panic and, as always, she has collected the children, calming them. 'Hush! This is only a dream. Presently we shall all awake.' But in this hideous vision walls, pillars and roof caved in upon the children and she lay like a crushed insect in the ruins with no awakening, only the swift transition from horror to horror . . .

The dream of the Stone Man. Colossal, sphinxlike, pharaonic, a blind all-seeing image towering above the desert or high above some phantom city. It does not move and yet comes closer, always closer, with terrifying stealth. She begins to run, stumbling through corridors of pain and shell-torn streets, faster, faster. Her heart is bursting. In panic, she glances back at the blind colossus. Its stone face bears a faint inscrutable smile. It is so near she can see the coarseness of its mineral pores, its cavernous nostrils. And the strength has gone out of her. There is nowhere else to run. Far below is the valley of dry bones. She stands on the edge of annihilation. A mindless frenzy takes possession of her. She swings her rifle and the butt smashes into the granite teeth. Blood spurts out in great shuddering gouts, but she keeps on striking one crushing blow after another. The lips of the Stone Man crumble, its mouth becomes a grinning hole, it bleeds rivers, it comes yet closer, monstrous, vengeful. It has the face of . . . the face of . . .

'Peter,' she said.

'What a greeting!' He touched the fleck of blood on his lip but did not relinquish her hand. His clasp was firm, reassuring. 'You're getting strong.'

'Peter,' she said, and there was the gladness of life in her weak voice.

The time was 4 a.m., the fourteenth day of her illness, although she was not aware of that. She was briefly conscious that it was a hospital, that she lay in clean white sheets on a crisp pillow, and that Peter was there: then she drifted back into sleep and hallucination.

Intermittently in the next few days she dreamed her whole existence. Odd, bewildering sequences appeared like living snapshots taken at random from a drawer. At one moment she was a small girl in a blue velvet frock and high-buttoned boots taking tea with her mother in Pivato Frères restaurant by Mariinskaya Square, and, before the orchestral music had faded, she was smuggling funds to the Barcelona anarchists and smiling with calculated coquetry at a Spanish frontier official to distract him from a too thorough scrutiny of her luggage. Clandestine leaflets fluttered through her dreams. She ate sour black bread again at her weaving machine in the Moscow suburb of Borogodsky, revisited the frozen Irtysh of her Siberian exile, where old grey-bearded Kostik carved saints in whalebone. From the house in Petersburg, its glitter of crystal lights on bare shoulder and braided uniforms, young Countess Alexandrova whose scornful image danced in a maze of mirrors abruptly rose with dirt-smeared face among her Red guerrillas, the gun in her hand spitting fire. And she dreamed of Montparnasse, the smoky twilight of the Place Denfert-Rochereau, the Boulevard St Michel, Rue Rivoli and the emigré Russian painters and poets drunk and nostalgic on cheap red wine in the Dôme Café, the forest Joseph younger by eight desperate years preaching Lenin's Bolshevism at her as they lay in bed in her high attic room, an immensity of stars over the Parisian roofs. Happy dreams, sad dreams, bitter and confusing dreams. The phantasmagoria of fog and dirt and blood one London winter, with

Poolka Murontzeff dead in a squalid bedroom, two doomed, fugitive comrades screaming hate at one another in a cellar hiding place, and in another bedroom Peter's hard thrusting body bearing down on her with its punishing weight . . .

Faces came and brooded over her, Nina's, Peter's, those of strangers, and Peter's repeatedly, but only dreams were vivid and they contained everything. It was as if all her past life, everything she had thought, felt and experienced, had been nothing but the dream of one restless night, and now, at last, it was over.

Early one morning Peter arrived at the hospital carrying an armful of clothes. There was so little strength in her that Nina had to dress her like a child. It seemed strange to be wearing women's clothes but suitable for her fragility. She greeted with weak laughter the sight of her sticklike arms and legs. Nina kissed her, eyes brimming with tears.

An *izvoshtchik* drawn by a horse almost as skinny as herself waited in the hospital courtyard. Peter lifted her inside, jumped aboard and they drove off. There didn't seem any point in asking him where they were going. It was sunny. The market stalls in Sukharev Square were selling autumn roses. The fresh air was miraculous. Nothing troubled her: things were as they were.

Peter had arranged everything. An hour after leaving the hospital they were nine kilometres outside Moscow in Davidko, a pretty little village beside the river Syetún. She remembered once having seen it after visiting Kúntzevo by carriage with her father to see in an old church the chalice cover embroidered by the mother of Peter the Great. It was in her fifteenth year when her father had entertained the notion that a young girl's rebellious inclinations could be subdued by inculcating an interest in traditional Russian art.

Davidko appeared unchanged. She was installed in a clean, simply furnished cottage room. The window overlooked a small garden and a centuries old wooden water-mill which splashed rhythmically to the flow of the river. An old woman and her twelve-year-old granddaughter helped look after her. It was an arrangement Peter made with the chairman of the village Soviet who called to say how honoured he was that a lady comrade of such proper revolutionary zeal should choose Davidko as a place of convalescence. He would not ask the former God who, thank God, had been abolished by science, to bring her speedy health, but he wished it for her in the name of Karl Marx and all the labouring proletarians in the entire Kúntzevo district. A beautiful speech.

With every passing day a little more strength returned. Peter brought butter, eggs, meat, fish, flour. He brought foreign books, magazines, honey and English marmalade. The famine seemed to have given way to abundance. Only later did she discover the source of it all. One restaurant in Moscow, the Praga in Arbatskaya Square, preserved for foreign diplomats and the most privileged *delegatzii*, was still sheltered from the harsh economic blizzard that had swept the country's larder bare of all but a few crumbs. What means of persuasion was used to have her elected to membership of this small elite she never found out. The Piatkov tenacity, no doubt. At the time she accepted everything without question, with the trusting innocence of someone new-born, content to be nourished and protected.

Of course, it could not last. The world began to whisper in her ear. Somehow after weeks of delay a letter reached her from Joseph. It gave off an acrid smell of cordite and spoke of brilliant, exhilarating victories. Trotsky's reorganization of the central front had worked miracles: Kazan swiftly recaptured, Tukhachevsky's First Army wresting Simbirsk from the Whites, the Volga crossed and the battle for the Urals being joined.

And the bad news, the low thunder of threatening artillery. Lenin's wonderful escape from assassination that should have been an occasion for rejoicing had unleashed a blind, vindictive rage that was still running its vengeful course. Red terror in Moscow and Leningrad: White terror and pogroms in the Ukraine. How bitter that the first anniversary of the Revolution, the marvellous October that promised universal liberation, should be greeted with these grim celebrations.

She had awakened from the fevered sleep of typhus to find Russia changed. Yet looking through her sheltered window at a Davidko peasant placidly fishing in the river, watching the sky change to the old, eternal seasons, she still retained the hope that in all that deeply mattered, in her intrinsic soul, the immense, mysterious land of Russia would always remain the same.

Part Two

'Terror cannot be dispensed with . . .'

V. I. LENIN

Chapter Five

Peter Piatkov opened the top half of the window slightly to clear the smoky atmosphere and was about to turn back to the seven men and one woman in the room when two policemen appeared from a side street and strolled in leisurely fashion along the opposite pavement of Camden Road. A bus trundled past, windswept passengers on the open upper deck shivering in the March cold. Peter also noted the arrival of a tramp who sat down outside some factory railings and laid a battered bowler hat on the ground. He stamped once hard on the floor.

Downstairs in the shop (S. Bender & Son, Gents Tailor. Cleaning, Sponging & Pressing. Suits Turned) Sam Bender took a box of matches from his waistcoat pocket and lit the dead stump of his cigarette, smoking thoughtfully. Then he filled his mouth with water from a cracked cup, sprayed it on to the ironing cloth and continued work in a cloud of steam. The policemen disappeared from sight among the throng of pedestrians. Sam's eyebrows twitched: he was a very observant young man who could press a suit with his eyes shut.

'There's no need for me to go over all the ground we covered in Moscow, comrades,' resumed Peter. 'You've all had invaluable experience in the pre-revolutionary underground movement and you'll need every bit of it. The Anglo-Soviet trade agreement is for us a vital breakthrough. They don't like us, but they have a feeling we've come to stay. That's good.' He nodded at their gruff murmur of assent. 'It's also, of course, the opening phase of a new game of espionage. We know it, the British know it. They're doing exactly what we are, infiltrating skilled secret agents into Moscow with their trade delegation. Never underestimate them. The British are good spies, some say the best in the world.' A slow grin spread over his face. 'Reserved, polite, hypocritical, more baffling than the Chinese to us simple-minded Russians.'

The group chuckled appreciatively as if at a family joke. Their faces were pallid and strained and they had nervous eyes. The woman, plain and heavy-breasted, straw-coloured hair pulled back in a tight bun, raised her hand hesitantly.

'It's my first time in this country,' she said. 'My experience was in the United States. The Americans are much more like us. Is it permitted to be friendly? If an Englishman invites us to his home as a guest, should we accept or not?'

'That must be left to your own judgement. Uncommunicative friendships are not uncommon here. Some people know one another for years yet have never exchanged anything beyond remarks about the weather, or sport. The British regard it as impolite to discuss politics and religion with acquaintances. Sex is, of course, never mentioned. They pity foreigners and treat them considerately as though they are rather feeble-minded, and foreigners tend to mistake that for friendship. On the other hand, you are here as Soviet businessmen and one does not trade well as enemies.' His tone sharpened. 'Naturally, you will approach all contacts with suspicion. They will have you followed. Your mail will be opened, your lodgings searched and your habits will be studied.'

Sitting astride a chair and staring at his subordinates one by one, Piatkov continued with severe authority: 'By our standards this is a country of rich living. Even the poorest manage to eat. You will have to resist many temptations. Our demands of you are unreasonable. You are short of men, money and technical resources yet we expect important results. It cannot be otherwise. We are a starving, suffering people bled white by seven years of world war, revolution and civil war. There is no peace. What the old world could not achieve by force and blockade it will try to bring about by subversion.'

He stood up and stamped twice on the floor. Sam Bender put down the hot iron and arranged the freshly pressed jacket on a wooden hanger. Then he passed a broom over the shop floor, sweeping snippets of cloth and dust into the gutter outside, glanced casually along the road and locked the door on his return into the shop. As he climbed the stairs his slouch disappeared and it was very much the disciplined Chekist who stood to attention before Piatkov to report: 'Everything in order, comrade.'

The group dispersed singly in different directions, leaving the building by a rear-exit that led to the canal bank where shaggy horses hauled barges of timber, coal and iron girders. Aksakov, deputy-leader of the Russian trade delegation, respectfully remained to await Piatkov's orders. Bender brought them cups of tea and withdrew.

'Keep them under tight control,' said Peter. 'London could go to their heads. It's like taking a strong drink after long abstinence. If there's any sign at all that a man can't keep his balance include it in your reports and we'll recall him.' The small, dark Aksakov listened attentively and nodded. Peter drank the last of his tea. Strong, sweet, stimulating: almost a forgotten taste. 'Come back to the hotel with me, there are still a few matters to discuss,' he said.

They went out through the yard, two men in heavy overcoats and low-brimmed hats, and boarded a tram, one travelling on the upper deck, the other on the lower, like complete strangers.

After Aksakov left, Peter returned to the window. Through the tangled branches of trees he could see the very bench in Russell Square where he'd once sat with Lydia. The hairs of his body bristled as at the touch of a ghostly hand, and when he turned away the empty room seemed unendurable. Coming to the Russell Hotel in the first place had been a sentimental indulgence. The foyer, the orchestra playing Strauss waltzes in the lounge, waiters of ancient vintage dispensing tea with trembling hands – only the absence of the young Lydia marked the passage of time since 1911. Now it could not be resisted. An overwhelming nostalgia had seized him and was sweeping him backwards. Leaving the hotel, he walked rapidly to Holborn and boarded a bus to Whitechapel.

In ten years nothing had changed. War cripples wearing medals on their tattered military coats sold matches and bootlaces or wound the handles of barrel-organs, otherwise the blasts of history had scarcely shifted the rubbish from Whitechapel gutters. The same grey, stagnant, ramshackle tenements and skirmishing wind whining over low slate roofs; the same ant-heap of writhing movement that once made him feel an unwelcome future was coming to birth in these ghettoes. Stirred by a lonely thrill, even the smell of squalor and industrial grime went to his heart. Incredibly, it was the smell of happiness, of falling in love. A fiery-eyed youth thrust a leaflet into his hand, crudely printed in Yiddish and English. *Workers of the World Unite*. That too was still going on.

Old Montague Street, like a faded photograph, brought a hard lump to his throat. Every stone was familiar, every face. Jews clustered on the corner of Black Lion Yard, the old synagogue, women shopping for groceries, more children than ever in strident play. Hoffman's bookshop, still peddling the same radical pamphlets, was only a little mustier. Portraits of Lenin and the Zionist Theodor Herzl offered the Jews a choice of rival messiahs, and tucked into a corner of the window, a shameful concession to commercialism, were some Jewish prayer books and phylacteries. The bell tinkled as Peter pushed open the door.

The first unsettling sign of change was the appearance from the back room of a sallow-faced female. He had expected Hoffman and she came as a shock. The old bookseller must be dead. He felt a curious sense of disorientation as though a familiar landmark had disappeared.

'Are you looking for anything special?' asked the woman, noting his hesitation. Behind her, propped up on a shelf, *The Communist Manifesto*, *Ten Days That Shook the World*, stations of a receding past.

'Mr Hoffman, he is not here any more?'

'You want to see my uncle? He doesn't see people.'

So he was not dead. 'I am an old friend,' said Peter, experiencing a rush of gladness as of something lost but found again. 'Does he still live in this house?'

She lifted her shoulders in an ironical shrug and replied: 'Where else? Upstairs like always. Are you sure you're a friend?' Her tone expressed scepticism, either at the idea that the old bookseller had friends or because she thought him not the type her uncle would know.

'For many years,' he assured her.

The woman looked queerly at him. Suddenly she began speaking in Russian so mutilated it required a moment or two to recognize the language. Peter was instantly alert. The British had learned a great deal about political intrigue and no longer looked upon it as mainly an exercise in foreign relations. Moscow knew of at least three prominent British communists who were undercover agents of Scotland Yard's Special Branch. Hoffman's bookshop had been kept under tolerant surveillance as a matter of routine for years, but the smugness had gone. Communist rumblings in Red Rhondda, on the Clyde, the slum-ridden cities had brought the spectre of Bolshevik world revolution to Britain's island. Only fools would underrate the toughness and professionalism with which this prospect was being countered.

Prudence called for a swift and tactful retreat. He was in London on a highly secret mission, travelling on a false passport as a citizen of the Weimar Republic of Germany. He had just warned Aksakov of the dire consequences that could result from a single blunder. Yet here he was, deliberately seeking a meeting with a man who knew his true identity in a place where every visitor must inevitably be an object of interest to British security. In his own terms, it was a cardinal act of folly.

And yet . . . Not for a long time had he been exposed to this kind of danger. It had its own tight exhilaration. After the grim texture of struggle in Russia, joylessly renewed every day, its victories bitter as gall, an old-fashioned skirmish with foreign security was a kind of recreation. Peter decided not to resist the indulgence.

'Madame, I do not understand you well,' he said, smiling faintly. 'You are asking if I come from Soviet Russia. Is it so?'

'I'm a member of the Party. I was just curious,' said Hoffman's niece, reverting to English. 'My uncle doesn't approve.'

'*Ach, so!* Very interesting.'

'And you?'

'Politics. So confusing.' He sketched a gesture of bewilderment.

Her black eyes flickered disbelief. 'Through here,' she said, beckoning him into the back room. It led into a dark passage reeking of mouldering books. 'You know the way,' said the woman pointing upstairs.

The querulous response to his knock was not inviting. Opening the door, he stepped into stifling tropical heat and a powerful combined odour of paraffin fumes, fungus and human decay. Hoffman was invisible. He had retreated from the world behind a bibliophilic barricade. It was like entering a labyrinth. Towering stacks of books, journals and bundles of old newspapers filled the space from floor to ceiling. Whichever way he turned his path seemed blocked but at last a narrow corridor was found. It led from Hoffman's steaming samovar to the cave where he sat at his huge cluttered desk.

The bookseller peered through thick layers of glass at an open book. 'I don't see people,' he said blindly. His obesity was now grotesque, clothes filthy, his print-worn eyes rubbed almost sightless. Of course he did not see people; the last strength of his dying eyes was reserved for books alone. 'Respect my privacy!' he snapped and returned to his reading.

'I wonder if you remember me,' murmured Peter. It was still not too late to retreat.

Hoffman slowly turned his shaggy head and sniffed the air like a bloodhound picking up the scent.

'Piatkov alias Schtern,' he said, his voice soft and malicious. 'Well, well! Have you joined the ranks of political refugees? There have been quite a few from the workers' paradise.'

'Tourists,' said Peter. 'They couldn't get on with the natives.'

'I suppose you're here as a journalist,' chuckled the old man. 'One of those who write stories in invisible ink.' Tears of laughter entered his dim eyes at this feeble joke.

'Still melodramatic, Hoffman.' Piatkov looked at him sardonically. 'And still a political refugee. Or are you now a neutralized Englishman?'

The bookseller remained unperturbed. 'What you are really saying,' he intoned talmudically, 'is that it is strange for a lifelong revolutionist who fought an underground battle against Tsarism not to return to the first socialist republic in the world.'

Peter drew a small stool up to the desk, careful to avoid dislodging a stack of books, and wormed his way into a sitting position. The reason Hoffman had not returned to Russia was obvious. When it finally came to it he'd been unable to tear himself away from his books and samovar. Conspiracy was his game and he'd played it brilliantly from his cosy nest in Old Montague Street. Soviet realities would kill such a man.

'You can be of better service here,' was his diplomatic reply.

'Ah, I see! You have come to recruit me.' Laboriously, Hoffman rose and shuffled down the corridor of books returning with two filthy glasses of tea. He felt the surface of the desk and found a bowl of sugar. Placing a lump between decayed teeth, he sipped lustfully. 'My dear former comrade,' he said. 'An old man has nothing to hang on to but his integrity. It is not politically fashionable but I am still an anarchist. You can keep your pseudo-revolution. It exchanged one gang of scoundrels for another. I despise you more even than the Romanovs. In the holy name of freedom you have robbed the people of freedom.'

Hoffman leaned forward until his nose almost rested on the younger man's face. Behind the high-powered lenses his eyes resembled marine organisms blindly searching for prey. He said:

'You have surrendered your mortal souls to the mass-murderers Lenin and Trotsky. Vladimir Ilyich, that great apostle of proletarian democracy, has abandoned reason for the iron logic of the bullet. His favourite expression has become, "You don't agree? Permit us to put you up against the wall".'

Peter undid his overcoat and suppressed a rising irritation. He had retained the notion that Hoffman's intellect was sharp, if not profound. Hoffman was just a bitter old man mouldering away in a book-lined tomb. It should not be necessary to explain to an old terrorist that revolution could not rest its case on reason and ignore the logical bullet.

'Say something for yourself. Give me an answer!' the old man taunted.

'Hoffman, I can only trade you my own platitudes. The bitterest feuds are between brothers. Freedom, like farting, is a full stomach enjoying the luxury of letting go. Or, to quote Marx, freedom is knowledge of necessity.'

'Yech! . . . Yech! . . . Yech! . . .' The fat body quaked with guttural laughter. 'Bolshevik pragmatism at its most cynical. Is that what you are going to tell the workers of the world about Kronstadt?'

Despite the overheated room, Piatkov felt a premonitory chill.

'I don't understand you,' he said, eyes riveted on Hoffman's blind, malicious face.

'You haven't heard?' the bookseller asked in feigned astonishment. 'Then it's my duty to tell you. The Red Army is wiping out the Red Navy with artillery, bombing from the air, prisoners being shot without trial. The Kronstadt sailors sent a radio message which was picked up in Finland. "The bloody Field Marshal Trotsky is standing waist-deep in the blood of workers," they said.'

In that disconnected moment it was the ugly invective against a Soviet leader that registered as shocking. The bloody Field Marshal. He had no particular liking or concern for Trotsky as a man yet the outrageous phrase remained like a jagged splinter in his mind.

'As you remarked so perceptively a moment ago, Piatkov, the bitterest enmities are between brothers. A blood-feud is going on. Lenin's butchery of fellow-socialists began it, Kronstadt continues it, and nothing can stop it unless Bolshevism is quickly swept into the rubbish bin of history. So it is written.'

'Not in the morning papers, Hoffman. There was not a word about Kronstadt.'

'Ah, but news flies through the air like a bird these days.' The bookseller opened a drawer and produced a wooden box. Attached to it were a pair of earphones and a trailing wire that followed a devious route towards the window. 'This is really a modern miracle,' he remarked happily, placing the earphones on his head and manipulating a small knob. Suddenly he smiled and waved his arm, conducting an invisible orchestra. 'Listen!' he commanded, passing the earphones to Piatkov. Faint music came through, fading, returning, fading again.

Peter said with bitterness: 'This miracle of yours only makes it possible for lies to travel faster.'

Hoffman tenderly replaced the toy and shook his venerable head.

'No, my friend, don't console yourself with hopes of capitalist propaganda. It feeds the public on such trivialities as Moscow's godlessness and sexual libertinism. Soviet barbarism does not have to be invented. Kronstadt is an atrocity. It will tear Russia apart and you will have to live with the consequences.'

The desk lamp cast shadows in the gloom-encircled room. Hoffman's glasses glinted with erudition and his face in chiaroscuro lost its bloated appearance. The rabbinical scholar immersed in timeless mysteries, or a painting by Rembrandt: the prophet Hoffman.

Peter stood up to go. He had a feeling of suffocation, an impulse to smash through the barriers of culture Hoffman had erected against the barbarities of the age. In Russia, in the past two years alone, there had been ten million civilian deaths. People were going up in flames and only those scorched by that fire had earned the right to criticize.

'Why in such a hurry? At least stay and finish your tea,' said the bookseller, but could not resist adding: 'It would be sensible not to go back at all.'

'Thank you for your advice, but it doesn't appeal to me.'

'One more thing, Piatkov.' The old anarchist gave a lopsided smile and stared blindly in his direction. 'We used to be on the same side, now I'm against you. What is to stop me picking up a telephone and calling the police? I doubt if they have forgotten Peter the Painter. They are also concerned about Communist conspiracy. I'm surprised you came here. It is uncharacteristically rash behaviour on your part.'

'There are two reasons why I will lose no sleep over it,' replied Peter, his fists clenched in the pockets of his overcoat. 'First, it is absurd to imagine that Hoffman, a life-long revolutionist, could become an informer in his old age.'

'And the other reason?' Hoffman asked gently.

'I'm not yet finished with the first. Absurd but not impossible. If Roman Malinowsky, one of Lenin's closest and most trusted friends, could turn out to be a Tsarist spy then a Polish-Russian emigré bookseller of radical literature can be the elaborate disguise of an Oxford University-trained British double agent. I admit it is rather too tortuous to be credible. What is more likely is that a man can turn informer out of embitterment.'

'Which brings you, of course, to the second reason why you will lose no sleep.'

'The second and more important is that Hoffman's experience has taught him an informer must live every moment of his life in constant fear of retribution. You wouldn't enjoy your lemon tea in such circumstances, I'm sure.'

There was a brief silence. The bookseller's chair creaked as he shifted his heavy body and returned his attention to the printed page.

'Call again, Piatkov.' His voice was charged with irony. 'I would like to discuss with you the well-known proposition that all men carry within themselves the seeds of their own destruction.'

Hoffman's niece stood at the door of the bookshop in the gathering dusk. 'Good-bye,' he said.

'*Tovarish*,' she called, 'give my regards to Moscow.'

2

The Citröen drew in to the kerb outside the Gare du Nord, its radiator steaming in the cold. Peter stood for a moment with one foot on the running board, ostensibly checking his watch against the station clock. Out of the corner of his eye he saw the man get out of a taxi and loiter over payment. Unmistakably the same man he'd observed checking the guest book at the *Hôtel des États Unis* – the close-set eyes and determined mouth, a bunched solidity about the shoulders, the cropped, abrasive nape of neck.

Lifting out his suitcase and nodding to the driver, he entered the station and bought some newspapers. People thrust against him: a war cripple offered lottery tickets, nude photographs: porters tried to disencumber him of his luggage: the man from the police department was never far away, making no attempt at concealment. A slow understanding formed in Peter Piatkov's mind which he decided to put to a simple test. Without haste, he entered the lavatory and took up a position at the urinal waiting for his pursuer to appear. Someone had vomited in the next stall but undeterred by the sour stench the police agent stood there, phlegmatically performing his duty.

'*Excusez-moi, m'sieu. Quelle heure est-il?*' Peter inquired.

The man carefully buttoned up his flies. '*Cinq heures et dix*,' he said, and the two of them rinsed their hands side by side, placed some *centimes* in the lavatory attendant's saucer and returned companiably to their respective roles.

Peter's intuition was confirmed by this episode. The men at the *Sûreté* were sending him a message. An approximate decoding would read as follows: 'We know who you are. Your presence in Paris is undesirable. We are shadowing you as a warning and to make sure you leave.' He rejected as unlikely the possibility that they knew his precise function in Soviet security. With French policy under Poincaré implacably hostile to the Soviet regime, it would be sufficient for them to have learned that he was a Russian travelling on a false passport. If more was known the temptation to detain him in the hope of squeezing out useful information might have been too much to resist. In fact, they were confessing uncertainty. The true message could be stated more simply: 'We have reason to suspect you are not the German citizen you pretend to be. In the absence of proof we are allowing you to leave.'

Closely followed by his attentive escort, he stopped at a tobacco kiosk for some packets of cigarettes, wondering uneasily if the reasoning was over-complacent.

'I have a few minutes before my train leaves, *m'sieu*,' he said to the Frenchman. 'As we seem to be going in the same direction would you care to join me in a cigarette?'

'Don't smoke,' the other replied. The two fingers of his right hand were stained with nicotine.

'Not when you are on duty, eh?' The man stared impassively, making no denial. 'Why are you shadowing me so heavily? Do you do it to all Germans? The war has been over a long time.'

'Which war?' The Frenchman's expression showed a trace of disapproval, as if to say: 'This is not the way to play the game. You are showing no respect for the rules.'

'I am beginning to wonder,' said Piatkov meditatively. Perhaps another policeman awaited him on the train. There could be orders to follow him right across Europe. Such obvious surveillance was sometimes used as psychological intimidation to demoralize the opponent by making him fear that his closest secrets had been exposed. Perhaps in this instance they had. He considered the disturbing possibility that a traitor existed inside his own department.

'Your companionship has been a pleasure, *m'sieu*,' he said.

'Now I must catch my train. Please tell your superiors I am innocent.'

Unsmilingly, the man followed him to the platform.

The Berlin express was on the point of departure. By the time he found the window seat in a first-class compartment reserved in the name of Schtern four people were already esconced, an elegant middle-aged woman with thin scarlet lips, a grey upright man who looked like a Junker ex-officer and seemed to be her husband, and two Frenchmen, one young with stiffly brilliantined black hair parted in the centre and cynically drooping eyelids, the other fat, elderly and, judging by the gross swelling of his exposed ankles, dropsical. Murmuring a polite greeting to these fellow-travellers, he took his seat and withdrew as firmly as if closing a door before turning to the newspapers.

Hoffman had not exaggerated the horror of Kronstadt. *Le Matin* spoke of thousands butchered, the *Berliner Tageblatt* reported orgies of slaughter, the *Chicago Tribune* described it as a Bolshevik blood-bath. Worst of all were the unctuous, moralizing editorials, obscene in the newspapers of countries which had sent an entire generation of young men to be massacred in a senseless imperialist war. And yet the news filled him with anger and shame. Starving Russia had struck itself a suicidal blow. Someone – Lenin, Trotsky, the Politbureau – must be to blame. No doubt the decision was agonizing, it may even have been necessary; perhaps if the responsibility had been his he'd have given the same order. But he had an irrational conviction that unless a hero came forward to take the sin on himself and accept crucifixion, guilt would fester in the soul of Russia. There would be no such easy salvation. No one would come forward. As Hoffman said, they'd have to live with the consequences.

Yesterday evening in Paris a Comintern agent insisted on concluding their meeting over dinner. A veil of cigar smoke hung over the comfortable restaurant. Spotless tablecloths, the glitter of glass and cutlery, mouths opening to receive rich soups, savoury meats, the great wines of Burgundy and the Rhine. Plump fingers crumbled the sacramental bread. The grossness was a mockery of famished Moscow and Kronstadt's dead, yet what was the point of indignation? The uselessness was enough to drive men out of their senses. They had to grit their teeth and hang on, the way the poor do, because the only way was to endure.

An hour had passed and the speeding train beat out its hypnotic rhythm, as remorseless a measurement of the passing of time as the loud ticking of a clock. He stared out of the window at the dark unreeling landscape, the lights of villages disappearing as swiftly as they came, and even the few days he'd just spent in Paris spun away into the remote past. He felt a loss of energy in himself. He was nearly thirty-seven, sixteen years older than the century and surfeited with the speed and violence of change.

A town rose out of the dark plain; factory chimneys, advertisement hoardings, people in dimly-glowing rooms arrested in mid-gesture, restaurants and bistros, traffic moving in the flare of street-lamps, then an abrupt transition to shadowy fields, trees silhouetted against the cold night sky. Sleep struck him soundlessly. The bustle of a station entered his disordered dreams and when he woke again, his brain cold and lethargic, the two Frenchmen had gone and other faces surrounded the grey Junker and his wife, incommunicably silent as they had been throughout the journey. A dining car attendant announced service of dinner. The compartment emptied. Taking advantage of his brief isolation, he took down his suitcase and methodically prepared for customs inspection at the frontier, placing his false documents of identity in his breast-pocket and sliding an envelope into the crevice at the window side of his seat. The precaution proved unnecessary. The frontier official flipped through his passport, asked some cursory questions and left with a stiff Teutonic bow. For all its speed, the train tunnelled into the German countryside like a slow relentless worm. They crossed the Main at Frankfurt, streaking the river with light. The weather turned bad, rain lashing the distant forest. He stared at his sombre reflection and sensed the East approaching.

Shortly after 3 a.m. he climbed the stairs to a room on the second floor of a small hotel near Berlin's Alexanderplatz and unlocked the door. Spichalsky, a prematurely bald, beetle-browed man of about thirty, leaped out of the chair in which he had been dozing and relieved him of his luggage.

'You must be tired after your long journey, comrade,' he

said. 'There's a *schinken* sandwich and a bottle of beer. You get off your boots and make yourself comfortable.'

A low-powered electric bulb hung down from the ceiling. Its frigid light exposed the flat inert planes of Spichalsky's face. His small eyes had something of the sluggish ferocity of a bull but were creased in the semblance of an ingratiating smile.

'Your orders were to be on hand when you came. Maybe you'd like to be left in peace to rest. I could come back in the morning.'

'No, I'd prefer you to make your report immediately,' replied Peter. 'I intend to leave for Moscow in three hours time.'

He hung his damp overcoat on a hook behind the door and glanced with distaste at his reflection in the spotted mirror of the washstand. Stretching tiredly on the bed and lighting a cigarette, he said: 'I'm listening.' Smoke swirled towards the murky ceiling. He had a brief, giddy sensation of the nocturnal city, the dark globe with its suffering multitudes swinging in perpetual orbit under the stars.

Spichalsky brought out a black notebook and began a gruff recital of events in Berlin's emigré colony of White Russians, their internecine rivalries, the fantasy of their 'death battalions' that would restore lost estates, imperial privileges, a vanished way of life. Spichalsky was a plodder, recording everything to the point of tedium: too many names, too much irrelevant detail. He lacked the talent for making significant connections.

Peter stifled an agonized yawn. The electric bulb became submerged in waves of drowsiness. 'Put all that in your written report,' he ordered and closed his eyes. 'Is there anything further before you go?'

Spichalsky smiled faintly. 'Only a rumour that a Romanov has appeared in Berlin. The Grand Duchess Anastasia, youngest daughter of the Tsar.'

'I know the genealogy,' Peter commented dryly. 'Any facts?'

'There's a mental hospital, Dalldorf.' Spichalsky's heavy face split into a narrow grin. 'They say a woman there, a patient, told one of the nurses in confidence that she was Anastasia. You know how things go here. Some people are ready to swear there's something in it.'

A woman in a lunatic asylum. Peter's tiny flicker of interest subsided. 'Get all the details,' he said. 'Doctors' reports. Names of everybody in whom the woman has confided. Physical details – age, height, colouring, birthmarks. And photographs. They are essential. I trust to your usual thoroughness.'

'Leave it to me, Comrade Schtern. Down to the last detail.' Spichalsky stood up and pulled a flat cloth cap well down on his low forehead for true proletarian effect. It made him look thuggish. He lifted his hand in a half-salute. 'Sleep, as they say, with a good conscience, comrade,' he said heartily, switching off the light as he left.

Conscience . . . A shadow passed across Peter's mind.

An instant later, as it seemed, it was time to begin travelling again.

3

As the train pulled into the village station of Pushkino, Mikhail Norodsky forced his way to the door of the compartment. A frenzied mass of refugees struggled for places on the open trucks. Clouds of steam rose from their gaping mouths. Hands clawed at him, voices screamed hoarsely. He stepped on to the platform and trod on something soft. It was the starved body of a young woman whose last strength had given way in the stampede. His foot felt unclean. A look of submission was imprinted on the woman's emaciated features and her wide-open eyes had the glazed incomprehension of a slaughtered animal. Mikhail pulled off his greasy cap and stood for a moment twisting it in his hands, head bowed in homage.

People were still trying to board the train as its iron wheels began to turn. He was swept aside in the rush. Wooden clogs trampled the lifeless woman and blood from her torn face mingled with the dirt.

'Get off, there's no fucking room!' yelled the uniformed guards, hitting out with rifle-butts at those clinging to the sides of the trucks, but some hung on with bleeding knuckles until the train disappeared from view.

Norodsky shrugged hopelessly and replaced the cap on his tousled head. There was too much death: a man couldn't take it in any more.

'Where do I find the Pokrovsky Nunnery?' he asked a refugee

huddling in a nest of rags against the timbered station-house wall. Tiny red eyes peered at him through swollen eyelids and the man pointed an uncertain, trembling finger towards the frozen lake and snow-brushed pines. The direction led nowhere. Norodsky turned up his coat-collar against the bitter March wind and limped away. Pushkino was not very large, he'd find the place on his own.

The famine sweeping across Russia had ravaged the village. Mourners pushing funeral handcarts to the cemetery. Bread queues outside the empty state bakery. Scarecrows squatting on sidewalks in apathetic expectation of death. In the market-place people bartering for their lives, offering tin kettles, children's shoes, patched trousers, books, feather bedding, brass candlesticks, ornamental trinkets – anything that could buy them a few more days survival. The bagmen, operating openly now under the licence of Lenin's New Economic Policy, watched everybody with the pitiless eyes of vultures. NEP authorized a return to private enterprise. It was going to pacify rebellious peasants, put food into hungry bellies, save the Revolution. Not immediately, of course, but later, for those who could find the strength to wait.

A crowd gathered around a small sallow man attracted Mikhail's attention. Excitement was intense. On a piece of dirty sacking at the man's feet lay a haunch of cooked meat. When an article of barter pleased him he cut a piece off the joint with a keen-bladed Circassian dagger and handed it to the lucky purchaser. Unable to postpone gratification, several were already chewing the meat with noisy pleasure.

'How about this?' asked one bystander, a woman, timidly holding out a fur jacket. A certain refinement of manner and ill-assurance betrayed a former bourgeoisie. Examining it critically inside and out, the trader nodded and pushed the fur into a bulging sack. He stooped to cut a wedge of meat, offering it to her on his grimy palm.

'For such a coat I should get a bigger piece,' the woman objected. In reply, he cunningly extended his hand further so that the smell of the food tantalized her. She grabbed the meat and began to wrap it in a cloth. Suddenly she hesitated. 'It's not human flesh, is it?' she asked, holding it close to her nose.

'It's dog,' the trader said laconically. His accent was Armenian. That and his lack of indignation increased her suspicion.

'Dog!' Her eyes became enlarged and she pointed a trembling finger at the cooked haunch. 'It's impossible, it's too big for a dog.'

'He was a big dog,' said the Armenian, shrugging.

'No, no! It's impossible!' screamed the woman.

'You want back the fur, I give it.'

The trader's surly independence confused her. Tormented by indecision, she turned to a neighbour and said imploringly: 'Look at it, what do you think? Does it come from an animal?'

'Don't look like anything that walked on four legs to me,' was the reply. 'Let him tell us where he got it.'

People pushed forward to sniff the suspect meat. They turned it over, poked it gingerly. There were murmurs of anger. Somebody cried: 'Murderer!' A man spat in the Armenian's face and several others began to jostle him. Terror entered his eyes, a recognition of martyrdom. Desperately he pleaded innocence as the crowd surged forward, treading the joint into the mud. It had become carrion, uneatable, and this seemed to enrage them further.

'Hey, soldier! Ain't you gonna do your duty?' a woman shouted at Norodsky. 'That murderer should be arrested and shot.'

'Nothing to do with me,' he shrugged.

Only a post-mortem could determine where the flesh came from, dog or horse, or man, or woman. People were eating rats in Russia. They were also eating people. One starving Ukrainian family consumed the corpse of its youngest child and, having thus overcome its horror of eating human meat, salted away the dismembered body of an orphan boy they kidnapped and slaughtered. The father and two sons over sixteen were shot, for murder not cannibalism. The morality of famine was not one Norodsky felt competent to adjudicate. There were worse things than eating the flesh of one's dead neighbours. He'd come from the carnage of Kronstadt and knew that his interference would not save the Armenian bagman. Guilty or not, it was all up for the poor bastard. They were going to kill him because they got some energy out of it to go on living. Adrenalin stimulation must have something to do with it. It was cannibalism too of a kind.

The screams of the mob pursued him as he continued his limping journey, troubled by an old wound in the thigh. Having circumambulated Pushkino he found the Pokrovsky Nunnery almost back where he started, on the far side of the railway station, a beautiful seventeenth-century piece of ecclesiastical architecture filled with starving women and children. Lydia stood at a trestle table wearing the cotton military tunic and breeches of a soldier, no gun in her belt but never more embattled in her life. Her hand rested on a frail old woman's shoulder.

'Where are you from, little mother?' she asked in her vibrant husky voice.

Norodsky unobtrusively watched her at her hopeless task. She brought to it the same obstinate gallantry he recalled from the days when they fought together as fellow guerrillas, the determination not to give in to frailty or exhaustion. Two young women relief workers assisted her, equally dedicated. That was what might save the country in the end: it had good women, the best in the world. They searched the refugees for lice, disinfected them, inspected their oedema-swollen joints, fed them a little soup, bedded them on straw mattresses, even made one or two laugh. The nunnery had never seen a greater miracle than that.

Lydia caught sight of him at last, spoke quietly to the small dark girl at her side and came over, too tired and depressed to smile.

'Mikhail, what a surprise!' she said. 'What brings you to Pushkino?'

Her hand was thin and feverish. He held it tightly.

'It's hell, isn't it?' he said.

'It's hell everywhere,' was her sombre reply. 'Let's go into my room and talk.' Generations of nuns had interrupted their cloistered meditations to sit with worldly visitors under the high narrow window. Its ancient walls gave off a musty smell of sanctity, but Lenin's picture now presided over the room. This was where she worked and slept, her needs stripped to the bone: desk, camp-bed, a chair, a few books. He shivered. The room was icy.

'Speaking as a doctor,' said Norodsky, gazing at her intently, 'I don't like the look of you.'

She laughed but it wasn't a good sound. 'Don't talk to me about doctors, Misha. There is one attached to this refugee centre. When I ask him if he can get medicines from Moscow, he answers that very soon we'll have everything we need. There is a new medical discovery, NEP. In time it will cure everyone. I also have a friend who is an economist. He assures me that Lenin's New Economic Policy is going to put meat into every Russian saucepan. NEP means bread, poultry and a great increase in pig production. NEP,' said Lydia, an ineffable bitterness in her eyes, 'is the name of the latest miracle. I can let my people have three spoonfuls of soup a day. Give me enough extra cabbages to make it four and I'll recite prayers of thanksgiving to NEP every night.'

'How many spoonfuls do you allow yourself? Two-and-a-half?'

'You've read too much Dostoevsky, my dear comrade Doctor Norodsky. I'm not planning to commit suicide.'

'I'm glad to hear it.'

'It's our duty as good Party members to keep up our strength,' she intoned, tilting the chair in parody of a self-satisfied bureaucrat and planting her clumsy felt boots on the desk. 'After all, we're the ones who have to groan under the load. Always keep a little something in the cupboard to warm the stomach, eh?'

'That's how it is, all right.' Mikhail grinned wryly. 'You can turn everything upside down but you can't change human nature. Someone manages to put a bit of class distinction on the belly.'

From outside came the wailing of children, bitter and inconsolable.

'God, how it tears at the nerves!' Lydia muttered, pressing her hand against her mouth as if to stifle a scream. 'Misha, do you ever get the feeling that this can't be happening, that we'll wake up to find it's all been a hideous nightmare?'

'The opposite feeling is worse,' he remarked. Sometimes it seemed that this was how it always would be, now and forever. More than once he'd drunk himself into insensibility on raw alcohol to escape that horror. Abruptly, he said: 'Lydia, I've just come from Kronstadt.'

'I don't want to hear about it!' Her voice shook. 'I'm sorry, but I'm a non-combatant now. Food's my concern, not fighting. The whole of Russia is starving to death. Its last piece of bread has been taken away. Isn't that bad enough without us killing one another?'

'I have to tell you. Joseph's in prison.'

'Where? In Kronstadt?'

'In Solovetsky Island. There's an old monastery there where the church used to shut up heretical priests. He was moved there four days ago.'

She was taking the news more calmly than he'd expected. Having experienced the lesser torment of Tsarist jails, she probably failed to realize how fearfully things had changed. Joseph's heresy was usually cured by the firing squad.

'You know Joseph when it comes to principles.' Mikhail shrugged in wry exasperation. 'He went to the brigade commander and asked to be relieved of his post. Couldn't order his men to fire on Red sailors because it was against his conscience. They placed him under arrest right away. I heard about it from Stepanchik. Remember Stepanchik?' Lydia sat in frozen immobility, her face bloodless and severe. The shock had got home. 'Poor sod, it's good-bye to one of those strong arms of his,' he chattered on desperately. 'They brought him in to the field hospital with the damn thing in shreds and he said, "What a to do, Doc! The fucking Whites never gave me a scratch and our own boys had to do this to me".'

'Poor Stepanchik!' Lydia said mechanically. 'Do you think he's – still alive?'

'Oh, old shortlegs is as strong as a bullock. He's in Moscow now at the Sheremetyev, where they had you for typhus. Go and see him. Make him feel good.'

'Mikhail, I'm talking about Joseph.'

Images of death splintered in his mind, arbitrary, sudden, always incongruous. To step out of a train on to a dead woman, lift a blanket and find a human being mangled by a random explosion. Death was the only certainty.

'I don't know,' he said wearily. 'I really don't know.'

With an abrupt violent movement she pushed back her chair and left the office. Mikhail followed more slowly. Side by side, they stood watching the queue of refugees lining up before the trestle table. They were terribly quiet, held in an agony of suspense lest the cauldron of soup should be empty by the time their own turn came. Those already fed lay on straw pallets staring glazedly at shifting shadows in the high raftered ceiling. Stained glass windows of Byzantine angels shed spectrums of coloured light on whimpering children.

'People are beautiful. One should never give up hope,' said Lydia. There were tears in her eyes.

She pointed at a stunted boy. He could have been nine or ten but the wizened face on the skinny stalk of his neck was that of an old man. Mimicking a monkey, he leered and gibbered in front of a group of apathetic youngsters. Undiscouraged by their indifference, the boy trailed his arms along the floor, loping from one to the other pretending to pick fleas from their hair and nibbling with relish. One swollen-bellied child began to laugh. Only one. A thin shaft of sunlight penetrating the cavern of despair.

'I'm going to Moscow,' said Lydia. There was a hard determination in her voice. 'Perhaps it's not too late.'

4

Dazed with travel and the confused, disembodied sensation of unreality that comes at the end of a long journey, the man who descended from the Berlin train into the noisy chaos of Moscow's Brest Station was no longer Schtern. For the time being the performance was over. He was like an actor who has wiped off the greasepaint and stares into the mirror at the wrinkles of anxieties that cannot be neatly resolved by the final curtain. Peter Piatkov was home and it was not a good feeling.

Moscow was still like a city at war. Homeless crowds camped with their bundles in the vast, sooty entrance hall, battle fatigue on the faces of Red Army men gazing hungrily at hungry girls, shabby buildings, people with empty eyes: an aimless, forlorn city, a city that smelled of defeat. Outside the station Victory, that monument of ridicule, rode its six-horse chariot above the Arch of Triumph. When he'd left, the streets were a white dazzle of frost, now snow in soiled heaps congealed on the pavements as dismal as frozen mud. Hurrying after a moving electric tram, he managed to get a foothold among the people grimly clinging to the outside rail, almost losing his suitcase in the process, and got off at Lubianskaya Square. The first thing to do was get to work. His empty apartment, a month's accumulation of dust on its furniture, offered a cheerless welcome and could wait until nightfall.

The department he headed, known as Bureau 3 – Western Europe, occupied a suite of rooms at the top of a house in Malaya Lubianka. Entrance was through a courtyard manned by a permanent sentry post. If the taciturn guard recognized him, he showed no sign of it as he checked his pass through the iron bars of the gate. Another check took place on entering the building but this time the soldier, a tall Siberian with scarred cheeks, showed his sharp white teeth in a smile and said: 'Good to see you back, comrade,' and as he ascended the wide staircase to his lofty quarters the greetings of those he encountered became increasingly obsequious.

News of his arrival preceded him mysteriously. A clerk relieved him of his case, carried it to the office and discreetly withdrew. Anatoly Lieberman, his principal assistant, came out of the cipher room with a sheaf of messages ready for perusal; a glass of bitter acorn coffee steamed on his desk and the elderly secretary, her grey hair mannishly cropped, busily arranged press-clippings from half-a-dozen countries in their various trays. A machine-gun clatter of clumsy, pre-1914 typewriters came from the main office. The message was clear: in his absence the security of the workers' republic had been vigilantly protected. He felt a chilling mistrust. Something was being concealed, an act of carelessness or indiscretion or worse. The man in the Gare du Nord.

Lieberman said: 'You must be tired after the journey. There's nothing that can't wait until tomorrow. Why not go home and rest?'

Piatkov re-appraised the tall, awkward young man through half-closed eyes. Untidy, restless, a multilinguist who acquired the essentials of a new language in a month and brought to his secret profession the skilful strategy of a good chess player. A Jewish intellectual, something of an idealist, he had the bright ingenuous expression of an eager student and slept with a

Bessarabian girl who wrote poetry. Idealists were fragile, easily disillusioned, but he detected no signs of cynicism in Lieberman's candid glance.

'I'll see you later, Tolya, after I've looked through this stuff,' he said, gesturing at the laden desk.

Yekaterina, the secretary, flicked open her notebook and sat down squarely on a chair, spine erect, knees modestly pressed together. A woman in her fifties, she had spent twelve years of exile as a Social Democrat in Vienna. Her only loves were Bolshevism and a sickly son of fifteen conceived in a brief affaire at Yalta one distant summer. Discretion was engraved in every line of her taciturn face.

'You too, Katya,' said Peter.

'Very good, comrade.' She rose obediently and smoothed the shiny seat of her serge skirt before stumping out of the room.

Concentration proved difficult. He leaned back in the leather-padded chair and closed his eyes. Fragmentary impressions of distant cities, foreign landscapes, floated through his mind awash with unease and he was haunted by a feeling of something misplaced. The memory of Hoffman returned to him, blind and oracular, possessed of a powerful malignity, and when he reopened his eyes the old man's face remained imprinted on the faded damask-covered wall of the timber magnate's bedroom that was now his office.

'You sit there thinking of treachery,' said Hoffman. 'You have begun to suspect your closest associates. But the one you mistrust is yourself. A worm is eating into your heart. You are asking: "Have we betrayed the sacrifice of a whole generation?" '

'Hoffman,' he said, his voice harsh and controlled, 'my answer to you is this. Bolshevism is the most significant event of our time, the greatest since the emergence of Christianity and, despite everything, *everything*, the most hopeful.'

The face turned into a stain on the wall and he was alone with the mute furniture, the pressure of silence on his eardrums, disconcerted to realize that he'd been speaking aloud. Settling back in the chair, he took up a file of reports and started work.

There was a great deal to get through. Bureau 3 had expanded like the Cheka itself, whose prisons and offices now extended over much of the Lubianka area. His staff was hand-picked for Party loyalty, intelligence, discretion and fluency in at least two foreign languages. If necessary, he could reach into a foreign city and destroy an enemy of the Soviet Union, but the circumstances would have to be exceptional and the execution arranged by an even more secret department, the principal arm of Soviet retribution.

Guile, not assassination, was the game he preferred. Get your men in the right places and political adversaries could save you a lot of trouble by cutting their own throats. The Okhrana had known how to do it. They planted their spy Roman Malinowsky in the party of Bolsheviks where he was elected to the Central Committee. Lenin wrote his speeches; he brought them to the Tsarist police chief Beletsky; Beletsky put in a word here and there, crossed out a paragraph, and the devil's work was done without leaving a footprint. For a time at least. The oldest trick in the world and still the best. Now the scope for initiative was enormous. In every country there were men who saw the October Revolution as the dawn of a messianic age. Intellectuals offered themselves as volunteers in the propaganda war. Would-be Mayakovskys dreamed of poems exploding like hand-grenades. The energy and enthusiasm only required directing into more useful channels.

Time passed quickly. His practised mind absorbed information, formed decisions. Cramp entered his limbs and he strode pensively up and down the room before plunging back into work. When he remembered to drink his coffee the brew had turned cold and scummy. The bitterness on his tongue reminded him of a rankling duty still to be performed. He rang for Lieberman.

'Sit down, Tolya. I have to talk to you about the Schtern itinerary,' he said, steel in his voice. 'Is it possible that it got into unauthorized hands?'

Lieberman looked startled. Reluctantly, like a sufferer from piles, he lowered himself on to the edge of a chair.

'Why do you say that?' he asked. 'Did something go wrong?'

'Please answer the question.'

'Well, no ... I don't see how. I could check the secrets register to see if anyone signed it out.'

'Do it immediately.'

He lit a cigarette and stared out of the window, smoking impatiently until his assistant returned.

'There's no record of the file being removed,' Lieberman said.

'I see. Tell me exactly who knew the details of Schtern's movements.'

Lieberman blinked worriedly behind his wire-framed spectacles and began to reckon up on his fingers. 'There's myself, Katya, Bogrov in the cipher room, Aksakov in London and Spichalsky in Berlin.'

'No one in Paris?'

'Of course not. Your instructions were that he would arrive there unannounced and make his own arrangements.'

'That was Schtern's intention.'

Peter Piatkov spoke of his *alter ego* as of an agent under his command. His subordinates might regard it as idiosyncratic but he'd learned from experience that a man must not merge too intimately with a false identity. He had seen Schtern many times, knew him better than he knew himself: but not for a single moment was Schtern permitted to usurp the mind, intelligence and emotions of his master. An undercover agent must be authentic. Masquerading as a watchmaker, he should be able to take the mechanism of a time-piece apart and skilfully reassemble it. Schtern's authenticity was created by splitting off a part of himself. Piatkov donated to Schtern his own cold, rational judgement, powers of concentration, misanthropic contempt for human weakness. Now, sitting in Moscow he thought of that lonely, severe, ambiguous figure journeying through Europe under his orders and was filled with dislike.

'The intention was frustrated,' he went on gloomily. 'Not only did someone in Paris expect him, they seemed to know by what train he'd come and where he was going to stay. Within ten minutes of his arrival at the *Hôtel des États Unis* the *Sûreté* sent a man to check his name in the hotel register.'

'It could be pure chance,' Lieberman ventured, plucking nervously at a loose thread on the frayed elbow of his jacket.

'Chance, Tolya, as a general rule, favours the prepared mind. I'm inclined to put it down to a lapse in security.' He gave a grim smile. 'I hope you don't talk in your sleep.'

'If I do I make sure that it's not in Russian,' said Lieberman, ruefully smiling in return. 'Shall we set up an inquiry?'

'It may not be necessary,' Peter replied, and his tone was ominous.

A short while later, on returning from the lavatory, he glanced searchingly into the cipher room. Of the four clerks, three men and a dark Jewish girl, only Bogrov interested him. The light shone on his assiduous profiled face and thinning hair as he worked on some papers in a small cubicle. A photograph of his wife and two children was tacked on the wall. Peter studied him for some moments, concealed by the half-opened door, then returned to his own desk.

Drawing out a blank sheet of paper, he wrote the following message: 'Immediate. Destroy list of Comintern contacts in naval bases Toulon, Marseilles, Oran. Operation Shark cancelled.' Reading it over, he added: 'Await fresh instructions,' and sent for Bogrov. 'Encode this and send it to Yegudin in Paris,' he said.

The cipher clerk read the message with a faint expression of perplexity and left. Yegudin would be even more puzzled. He had no list of contacts in French naval bases. Operation Shark did not exist. As an exercise in misinformation it stood little chance of success. But if Bogrov was a traitor and the random shot struck home Yegudin's apartment in the rue Peletiere would be mysteriously burgled. If so . . .

Peter thought of the family photo on the wall of Bogrov's cubicle and suppressed a sharp twinge of regret.

Half the day had already gone. He called in Yekaterina, rapidly dictated letters and memoranda, then left for a meeting of heads of departments in Dzerzhinsky's office. It was reached by a subterranean passage, part of a network of tunnels that made it possible to move from one section of the central Cheka to another without journeying through open streets. Those traversing this complex maze seemed under a curious constraint of silence broken only by echoing footsteps, an occasional rasping cough and the shuffle of sentries controlling admission to various buildings. Coming out of the underground corridors was like rising from a city of the dead. One suddenly felt able to breathe again.

Dzerzhinsky addressed his gathered chieftains in the conference room of his official suite. More cadaverous than ever and rumoured to be a sick man, he'd come straight from a meeting of the Vee Tsik, the Central Committee, and looked as if he'd neither slept nor washed for days. Curtains shut out the day like a suspected eavesdropper. He spoke in a fatigued voice, skin yellow under artificial light. A gloomy fanaticism looked out of his hooded eyes.

The famine had reached a point of such desperation, he told them, that Lenin had no alternative but to accept the humiliation of foreign aid. Feelers were being put out to the Red Cross and the American Relief Administration of Herbert Hoover. There was no doubt, he remarked bitterly, that the opportunity for espionage and subversion would prove irresistible to their capitalist enemies. The Cheka must defend the Revolution against this new, insidious threat. Once again, the message was vigilance.

'Vigilance,' hissed Dzerzhinsky. A spasm passed across his cold, incorruptible face and abruptly, without warning, he gave them the full reckoning of Kronstadt, holding none of the horror back. With appalled fascination, Peter realized that Dzerzhinsky was suffering. The mask had cracked, exposing the soul of a tormented idealist. His eyes jerked, his lips trembled, his voice was charged with agony, sweat glistened on the tight-drawn skin of his high forehead. It cost us our dearest blood, the thin blue lips said. We must absorb the grief, come to terms with it, assess its punishing consequences, ensure that it never happened again. Underneath self-justification throbbed the raw confession: *mea culpa.*

When it was over Peter descended into the underworld with a feeling that he would never emerge, that here he would suffocate of the generic guilt in which all the brotherhood with their Party cards and Chekist uniforms were implicated. Reluctantly, he climbed upstairs to face the accusation of daylight and shut himself in his office.

The telephone rang: he ignored it. It rang again insistently. Unhooking the earpiece, he said in cold, level tones: 'I am not to be disturbed,' replaced the receiver and resumed his meditation. Daylight faded: it grew dark. He remained motionless, withdrawing from thought, slowing the rhythm of his heart. Out of that silence he emerged with a conviction. Kronstadt had not only threatened the Soviet government, it could also have started the dismemberment of Russia in a new civil war. Georgia, Armenia, the Ukraine, Turkestan, the Don Cossack country, the Volga region, would have become Balkanized republics pillaged by rival Great Powers. There was no alternative, the rebellion had to be crushed.

He also concluded that an appalling blunder had been committed. The two notions were irreconcilable but it could not be helped. Man was trapped in the cruel metaphysics of ambiguity, doomed to error whatever his choices.

5

He walked home through the Alexander Gardens, still deep under snow. A sub-zero wind stung his face. It was long after midnight and apart from militia patrols and trams carrying night workers Moscow was shuttered and silent. A few lights burned behind the high stone wall of the Kremlin's inner city. Ashen moonlight filtered through broken curtains of cloud and the frozen trees stealthily emerged from shadow like an army in winter camouflage.

Except for a solitary passer-by engaged in an embittered quarrel with an invisible companion, the Gardens were empty. His own head, dizzied by the long exhausting journey from Paris and lack of sleep, was filled with a morose silence. Weighed down by his heavy suitcase, he crossed the broad roadway of Znamenka, stepping over piles of dirty snow in its gutter to turn into his own street. After the vast distances of travel, the house he lived in seemed small and shabby. Some bundled refugees sheltered in the entrance hall, their heads resting on the muddy floor in meek abandon. He scarcely noticed the spasmodic reflex of pity: one needed to forget everything. At the top of the fourth flight of stairs he almost stumbled over another figure stretched out on the landing in the dark. Cursing softly, he opened the door of the apartment as the intruder stood up unsteadily and followed him in.

'Where the devil –?' he started to say then hesitated, gripped by a queer intuition. Putting his case down, he struck a match and the flare confirmed it. 'Lydia!' Her white face was drowsy and defenceless. 'What is it? Are you ill?'

'I fell asleep waiting for you,' she said.

He felt his way past obstacles in the darkness and lit the paraffin lamp. An unsteady flame threw shadows on the wall. It lurched him into the vague menace of his familiar dream. Apprehensively, he said: 'How long have you been waiting? Why are you here?'

'I've been in Moscow since yesterday morning,' she said tonelessly. 'Nobody seemed to know where you were or when you were due back. I had to see you.' And then she told him about Joseph Frumkin.

Events of the past hours, the past days, reassembled themselves into a pattern of ill-omen. Hoffman's book-walled labyrinth, his eyes embalmed in glass, the shadow of pursuit in Paris and the clock at the Gare du Nord frozen on the time of departure; night-journeying trains, the two Junkers, male and female, lips sealed in bitter silence; Berlin, Spichalsky, mirrors, loneliness ... Russia bleeding from self-inflicted wounds in the northern snow.

Fatigue blurred his mind. There were intervals when he looked at the painfully thin girl in her shabby cotton uniform, her hair roughly cropped, and the dream seemed on the point of disintegration. She returned to him in many guises, each an aspect of recurring anxiety. Bitterly he reflected that in none of his dreams did she bring him happiness. For months they did not meet unless he travelled to Pushkino to snatch some time with her in competition with lice-infested refugees. Now she came to him on behalf of a former lover. Jealousy was also part of the dream.

Slowly, deliberately, as if to keep her in suspense, he struggled out of his heavy overcoat, stuffed his fur cap and gloves into the pockets and hung the coat on a hook. Wind shook the rickety window frame and he went across to draw the curtains. Moonlight gleamed on the frozen river. For an instant a vision came to him of men numbly writhing on the ice like flies in winter.

'You're tired, Lydia. Better lie down,' he said, lifting a blanket from the pile stacked with barrack-room neatness at the head of the bed and spreading it over the stripped mattress.

Obediently, she pulled off her muddy felt boots and stretched out on the bed. In her crumpled uniform, her boyish face tense, she looked like a battle-weary soldier.

'Peter, I've come for advice. Can anything be done?'

Anger stirred in him like a hot gust of wind. He wrenched open the straps of his suitcase and searched under a pile of carefully folded shirts until he found the bottle of cognac he'd brought from Paris. The water tap vindictively refused to run and he poured the precious liquid into two dirty glasses. What advice did she expect him to give? Wish the poor bastard a quick and easy death. He'd made his gesture, no doubt for all the right reasons, so better for him not to linger on. In his own case he'd have preferred to be shot on the spot while the glow of virtue was still warm. God knows, it was not a very durable feeling at the best of times. That was all it was worth: the price of a bullet.

'You can hope for the best, that's about all,' he shrugged, handing her a drink.

'I didn't ask you,' Lydia said with slow bitterness, 'for a death-bed pronouncement.'

'There's no point in deluding yourself,' he continued mercilessly. 'Frumkin is a soldier. Mutiny is a capital offence. In this particular case there's no grounds for mercy. That's the harsh but simple truth.'

Punishing her gave him a perverse satisfaction. At this moment he was her enemy, as he was his own, fulfilling a morbid need for self-laceration. This was how comrade killed comrade at Kronstadt, with a ferocious denial of pity, their love for one another turned inside out. They were all in the grip of madness, all of them.

'It may be the truth, but it's not justice,' she said. 'What has it all been worth if a man of principle, a Bolshevik, must blindly carry out orders to shoot down his own brothers-in-arms?'

'Christ! Lydia, I know!' he said angrily. 'It was bloody hard. They were the same boys who shelled the Winter Palace. Without them there might not have been an October Revolution. So it was a stinking rotten business to smash them to pieces. No one could have enjoyed giving the order. Frumkin's conscience is no more precious than the poor sod's who slogged across that ice and did the dirty work.' Or Dzerzhinsky's, torn between guilt and duty. *Or mine*, he thought, gulping down his drink to ease the ache in his breast.

'It's the shame of Russia,' Lydia said in a miserable voice. 'I'll try to see Lenin.' She stared at him in resentment at his ironic silence. 'Yes, I know that's silly, but I have to do something or I'd never forgive myself. Maybe the sensible thing would be to go to Solovetsky and speak to the prison commandant.'

'The sensible thing is to get too drunk to think.'

He brought the bottle to the bed and stretched out beside her. She turned and said: 'I'll need a travel warrant. Will you give me one? You know how important it is to me.'

Lamplight emphasized the hungry hollows in her cheeks and her breath smelled faintly sour. Their bodies touched without desire but his heart moved painfully at her nearness. Love was his sickness. Brandy was the medicine for that, too. Swallowing deeply from the bottle, he fumbled in his pocket and produced a blue carton of French cigarettes, the cheap pungent brand she'd always smoked in the old days. He'd bought several packs in the Gare du Nord for that very reason. He lit two and placed one between her lips. The intimate gesture flooded him with tenderness and brought a sudden onrush of lust.

'Frumkin is very important to you, isn't he?' he asked, jealousy constricting his throat.

'Caporal, beautiful!' She closed her eyes and inhaled sensuously. 'It takes me back to the Place Clichy and the Boulevard Montparnasse just as if it was yesterday. Sometimes it's impossible to believe that past ever existed. Can we have been as happy as it seems now?'

He let his own question die, overcome by despondency. The night was slipping away and there was no place for him in her nostalgic memories of Paris. Paris was Joseph Frumkin. For her it represented happiness, for him a remote summer of loss. Making a despairing bid for attention, he said: 'What about London, Whitechapel, that first time we met over tea in the Russell Hotel? Do you ever think of those days?'

Lydia answered slowly and reluctantly. 'For a long time I couldn't bear to,' she said. 'To be twenty and feel responsible for the death of your closest comrades – as if you'd betrayed them – is total nightmare. You know how I felt about it when we were together. I wanted to forget everything connected with London. I never wanted to see you again.' She blew out a stream of smoke and watched it disintegrate in the lamplight. 'I'm sorry, Peter. Am I hurting you too much?'

It was like scar tissue being ripped from an old wound yet, obscurely, he welcomed it. If there were poisons they would be better drained away. 'In an antiquarian way, yes,' he replied tightly. 'But I want you to go on.'

Lydia sat up and leaned for support against the wall, reaching for the cognac at last. She drank slowly in meditative silence. She avoided his intensely watchful eyes.

'It seemed as though I couldn't escape you,' her punishing voice resumed. 'Wherever I went your letters followed. Postmarked from everywhere, censored by scores of officials, getting through prison walls and barbed wire. They even reached me by dog-sledge across the midwinter Siberian tundras. I opened them with dread and destroyed them with loathing. Then a strange thing happened' – she looked at him in baffled wonder – 'I began to look forward to them. As I read the lines your voice seemed to be speaking. Sometimes no letter would arrive for months and I'd think with dismay that you'd stopped writing. Then a whole batch would come and I'd read them over and over. It's difficult to explain. You'd become indispensable to me.' There was a pause. 'You still are,' she added quietly. 'Just as important as Joseph.'

With an abrupt husky laugh she left the bed, retreating beyond the circle of light as if walking away from an indiscretion.

'This has been quite a confession. It must be this damned cigarette. I feel quite dizzy.' Grinding out the stub, she said: 'I've always wanted to be free, all my life. My father used to think I'd grow out of it once I became a woman and found a man to serve. But I knew I'd never belong to anybody, not even to those like you, Joseph, and others who mean a great deal to me. Perhaps I make so much of my responsibilities because I want to buy my right to freedom.'

Thanks for including me, he thought savagely. *Thanks for nothing.*

'Freedom,' he said, the taste sour on his tongue. A word that looked good on banners, Hoffman's rhetorical holy name, a swindler's slogan. Freedom was un-Russian. Not a bird, nor a star, nor anything in the universe was free. He felt an ironic pressure in the bladder. So much for freedom, he thought, going downstairs to the freezing communal lavatory. All her life she'd wanted the impossible. All he wanted was to protect what he loved and be indispensable to them and Lydia's confession had admitted her need of him. She would always need him, that was her unfreedom.

When he returned they went to bed, wrapped in army blankets and huddling together for warmth. Her thin body moved him unbearably as he held her close. She responded reluctantly at first to his caresses, then was stirred to a brief and violent passion. What he felt was no longer lust. The thought occurred to him that she made love as if sharing sex with a comrade, the way it must have been in her forest days as a Red guerrilla.

'Peter, give me another Caporal,' she said, sitting up and drawing the blanket round her naked shoulders.

He did so and turned out the lamp. The tip of the cigarette wove glowing arcs in the darkness. After a while, it dropped to the floor in a small shower of sparks.

Was she dreaming of Paris, he wondered, or of Joseph Frumkin in his icy Solovetsky prison cell?

His own dreams were fragmentary, wrapped in enigma. The air when he woke smelled of an acrid dawn. Lydia still slept. Moving stealthily to avoid disturbing her, he got up, swallowed a mixture of brandy and water and left a scribbled note on the table.

'The meteorology report from Archangel says the White Sea is frozen to a depth of three fathoms. Impassable to shipping but not to Piatkov. I will find out about Frumkin. You are ordered to do nothing without instructions. Disobedience will be severely punished. P.S. This letter may be destroyed – but not with loathing.'

On arrival at the office he dispatched an urgent message

informing the commandant of Solovetsky Prison that Cheka headquarters was interested in prisoner Joseph Frumkin. Notify immediately if alive or dead, it said. If alive await further instructions.

The message was an interference in the affairs of another department. He hoped that the vast bureaucratic muddle in service and government offices would allow it to go undetected. It was a cool calculation of risks but a gamble, nevertheless, and he knew he was a fool to take it.

Chapter Six

Fumbling under his shirt, Joseph Frumkin trapped a louse and crushed it against the wooden frame of his bunk. It was not much use, he decided indifferently, the vermin could eat him alive for all he cared. Far worse on the nerves was the slow suffocation of time. He'd given up trying to keep track of the hours or days he'd been in the cell. The effort was too exhausting. Like a swimmer at the end of his strength, it made him feel he was drowning. Better to drift, keep afloat, until they came for him. It couldn't be long delayed.

Krassin, the old Socialist Revolutionary, offered an object lesson in survival. Hugging his numbed fingers under his armpits, he completed six paces to the dungeon wall and said stoically: 'Everything must be given to the community. That, Izya, is fundamental.' His companion, the smaller, monkey-like Fuchs, a mandarin figure in a ragged frock-coat, retorted through chattering teeth: 'N-never! Utter n-nonsense! This is where I totally reject Rousseau and his entire theory of f-forcing to be free. A contradiction in terms.'

'You are confusing paradox with contradiction,' Krassin irritably but softly contended, his pace quickening under the spur of intellectual excitement.

Ever since breakfast they had been arguing over Rousseau's Social Contract, repetitively trudging six steps one way and six the other and flapping their arms to keep the blood in circulation.

Outside, beyond the high walls of the monastery prison, a limitless world of ice, snow, frozen seas and petrified forests was embedded in a silence as hard and crystal as diamond.

Everyone found his own way of not freezing to death in the Solovetsky dungeon except Yezhka, a Socialist Revolutionary in the third day of hunger strike, who seemed to be withdrawing with passive defiance from the intolerable suffering of the flesh.

The anti-Soviet Finn, Ekberg, lucky owner of a goatskin jacket, stripped down to his verminous underwear, worked up a furious sweat with exercise, then hastily piled on his clothing in a dubious effort to trap the heat. Two more SRs, locked in morose comradeship, constructed a shelter on one bunk with straw mattresses and coarse blankets and huddled together inside it. A young soldier named Gratchev had the healthy knack of sleeping through everything, noise, quarrels, cold, rousing himself only when food was brought or necessity drove him to the shit bucket.

Joseph tried to ignore the physical discomfort, slept fitfully and reviewed his whole life. It was, in a manner of speaking, his Day of Judgement for he already counted himself among the dead. He'd gone to Kirzanovsky, the brigade commander, and said: 'Sasha, I can't do it.' They were in Oranienbaum, the troops were preparing to advance across the ice under cover of darkness, heavy guns were limbered up ready to fire, the ultimatum expired. A claustrophobic sense of doom gripped the army as soldiers shivered in the glacial wind whipping across the frozen Gulf of Finland. Kronstadt was thought to be impregnable and the rebels were dourly intent on resistance: it was going to be a murderous undertaking.

Kirzanovsky had gathered his subordinate commanders in a hut on the long pier to receive last-minute instructions. They stood close to the *bourzhouika* stove storing up warmth for the cold crossing, looking like members of a mystic order in their hooded white camouflage. The brigade's task was to make the five kilometre crossing and launch a frontal assault on Fort Paul, west of the island, silence the naval batteries and move on to effect a landing at the Commercial Harbour. Kirzanovsky's lean young face was unnaturally rigid. 'Forget who they are,' he said. 'We've got to move in and kill fast or they'll do for us.'

Joseph waited until the others left. 'Sasha, I can't do it. It goes against the grain,' he said.

The brigade commander's jaws clamped together. 'Let's pretend I never heard that, Comrade Frumkin. Get back to your men,' he growled.

'Comrade Commander, I mean it. For me it's impossible.'

'Too soft-hearted, eh? Not a cut-throat like the rest of us.'

Kirzanovsky's sharp grey eyes narrowed to slits. 'How long is it since you've been with the Brigade?'

'About ten months.'

'We fought together at Novogrudok, right? Right. You were with me in that bloody shambles at Byeltsy when the Poles ambushed our ammunition wagons and we had nothing but spit left to fight the bastards. Right? You done your share in Prushkony, Kamenetz-Litowsk, and in retreat. That's the truth, eh?'

'Yes, comrade.'

The young Commander, ten years his junior, paced the floor angrily then came to a sudden decision.

'Frumkin, as God's my witness I'm giving you the last chance!' He spat on the hot stove. 'Get out there, take your place at the head of your unit and do your duty as a soldier and an honest Soviet man.'

Wind buffeted the timber walls. Iron clanked against iron as the machinery of war moved into position. Orders were being shouted and a vast murmur came from the grim multitude gathered along the shore. He looked at Kirzanovsky and did not stir. The sound of an aircraft engine passed overhead as a reconnaisance plane flew back to base.

Kirzanovsky drew out his heavy Mauser reluctantly. Lines of harshness appeared around his mouth. Ten months was a long time and they had been good friends.

'Get down on your knees, Yossi, and say a quick Jewish prayer,' he ground out. 'You're finished with this world.'

Afterwards Joseph could only recall the terror that flashed through him like a searing flame as he slumped down and clenched his eyelids. In that prolonged moment all else was obliterated.

The kick of a heavy boot sent him sprawling on his back.

'You disgusting pig, you've pissed yourself!' snarled Kirzanovsky, towering above him and beside himself with rage. He looked at the gun, uttered a string of obscenities and fired it through the roof. An orderly came running in. 'Ivan, send this man under escort to Petrograd for court-martial,' he yelled. 'Refusal to obey orders on the battlefield. I'll sign the charge sheet when this fucking business is over.'

As the train began the one hour's run from Oranienbaum to

the Baltic Station salvoes of great guns thundered across the frozen Gulf and jagged explosions lit up the night. Instead of reprieve Joseph felt a crushing grief. A great ship blazing with hope was foundering and in the scale of that catastrophe his own survival was meaningless.

And the time that followed was meaningless. He was put into a cell in the Peter and Paul Fortress but his true prison was the grey eternity of apathy and despair. It continued when he was sent the long journey north to Solovetsky Island with a group of other prisoners. On arrival the one-eyed commandant reviewed them with mordant irony and made a speech. Don't misbehave, don't moan, don't be put off by a bit of cold. Cold was bracing, it purified the air. They were better off than the poor famished bastards who had to put up with freedom, and he wished them a long and happy stay.

Joseph expected his own stay to be brief. Death's charge-sheet was on its way and he awoke each morning in the expectation that it would be his last. Periodically guards went from cell to cell calling out names from a prepared list. Men were led off and never seen again. Tomorrow, he thought, it will be my turn at last.

But in the passing days Joseph discovered that even if it meant living without hope he was not yet ready to die.

The squeaking wheels of a wooden trolley and hoarse voices raised in clamour announced feeding time. He got out his mess-tin and jostled to get near the door. Fuchs, skilfully using his sharp elbows, beat the tough little peasant Gratchev to first place and shouted indignantly: 'Stop pushing, everybody! What are we, men or animals?'

'Why don't you croak, you old bastard!' yelled Ekberg, the Finn, peeved at being near the back, and all of them squabbled as much to pass the time till the food arrived as out of rancour. Only Yezhka remained silent, his eyes glazed and faraway, connected to life by a feeble thread of will.

The dungeon door swung open and the guard dished out two ladles of fish soup into each outstretched mess-tin from a huge smoke-blackened tureen that looked as though it had been in use when the Monastery was built in the reign of Ivan the Terrible. 'What about him?' he asked, jerking his head towards Yezhka.

Krassin went over and spoke to the sick man who moistened his dry lips and said faintly: 'Not till I get justice.'

Fuchs held out an empty tin and grinned ingratiatingly. 'Put some in,' he said. 'I'll talk him round.'

Once the door was relocked everybody concentrated silently on the vital task of eating, each according to his temperament. One searched the muddy liquid in the hope of finding shreds of fishmeat before spooning it into his mouth. Another savoured each mouthful slowly on the tongue before letting it trickle down the throat. Quick eaters stared enviously at those who took their time, all licked the last drop of nourishment from mess-tin and spoon before stowing them away. And when the food was gone the still-empty belly felt cheated. It was then that men experienced the greatest despair for the hope of another meal seemed as distant as the prospect of freedom and hunger the only reality.

Lying on his bunk shivering under a thin blanket, Joseph struggled to obliterate physical discomfort by escaping from the rigid prison of time into the free landscape of imagination. An old friend released from a life-sentence in Tsarist captivity by the February Revolution had said that only fantasy saved him from cutting his throat. 'I depended on it for release like an opium-addict. After a while, I only had to close my eyes to summon dreams to my whim like an emperor. Beautiful women pleasured me. I feasted on nothing but the best food and drink. If I wanted sunshine it was as simple as turning on a hot-water tap.' The sun would not turn on for Joseph. He was left with the overpowering stench of the sanitary bucket, frozen darkness, a terrible sense of mutilation as if life had been amputated of all that brought hope.

'Let us walk a little, eh?' Krassin suggested, climbing off his bed and flexing thin shoulders against the cold. He was a dark Mephistophelian man with grey bushy eyebrows, a long bony face tinged yellow like old ivory and a grey-streaked black beard. As they fell into step, he peered up at Joseph through disintegrating spectacles, their rusty hinges tied with cotton, touched the stone wall before turning, and said: 'We could play a little chess, if you like?'

'Chess?' said Joseph.

'In the head, of course.'

'I don't think I could concentrate.'

Krassin nodded understandingly. 'You should try. It is not as difficult as it may appear. I will give you a Knight and two pawns.'

'Some other time,' Joseph said. 'Why is Yezhka on hunger-strike?'

'He is protesting because it is the third anniversary of his arrest and he has not yet been placed on trial. You are also expecting a trial. Learn from our experience. There is no justice. They will forget about you. One day someone will assassinate Lenin or Trotsky, or Sverdlov, or Stalin and to relieve their feelings a few of us will be taken out and shot.'

Krassin spoke calmly like a man long past bitterness, a man whose idealism and passion was burnt out, and yet his philosophical debates with Fuchs were often intense and acrimonious. 'One must keep the intellect alive,' he explained, shrugging. 'To be human it is necessary to remain rational. Our nature requires of us this last discipline. Everything else can be taken away – our wives, our children, our lovers, our health and freedom of action. If they could get inside our heads they would also deprive us of reason, the essence of humanity. How pleased they would be to do it! We are caged birds who can still fly and our jailers find it intolerable.'

Their fellow 'birds' followed each other to the bucket and noisily defecated as their stomachs digested the bad soup. Conversations began and died of cold and exhaustion. Men searched for lice, scratched themselves, absently stroked their genitals and sniffed their fingers. Muffled sounds like the dying reverberations of a brass gong entered the subterranean gloom. Joseph envied Krassin the heroic ability to soar beyond their glacial inferno.

He said: 'You were once a member of the Moscow Soviet. You played a part in making history. Instead of being rewarded you've spent years shut up in a prison cell. Have you no sense of outrage at all?'

'Outrage? Useless!' Krassin snorted. The vehemence gave something away. He trudged up and down the stone floor making windmill motions of his arms. It calmed as well as warmed him. 'I do not wish to appear mystical,' hc said, 'but I've long come to the conclusion that we are all participants in an inescapable tragedy, we Russians. A nation's history is a consequent narrative. You and your Jews are still enacting the dramatic sequence that began with your exodus from Egypt, and in that respect it is Zionism not socialism that must complete the pattern. Russia was born in confusion and violence. Our veins seethe with the blood of a score of warlike tribes. The Mongol conquest brought an autocracy and serfdom that five centuries have not shaken off. Ivan the Great imposed unity, Ivan the Terrible fear, Peter the Great dealt with his rebels by roasting them alive. These are the currents of our history. These determine its flow. We are doomed to ancestral savagery. In 1917 a Russian convulsion of violence took place and we called it Revolution, but it soon became autocracy with a Bolshevik mask. We who helped it to power have no right to feel outrage.' He walked on in silence for a while, then resumed: 'Our Revolution had the defects of millenarianism. It expected social injustice to be instantly transformed by a miraculous apocalypse. We imagined that in one stroke the guilt and anxieties of a nation would be converted to the high energy of constructive purpose.'

'You have given me history according to Krassin,' Joseph remarked. 'It has no relevance to the dialectical materialism of Marx and Lenin.'

Krassin gave a twisted smile. 'If Marx could see what Lenin has done to Marxism he would tear out the hairs of his Jewish beard,' he retorted.

They returned to their separate bunks. The conversation with the old Socialist Revolutionary, despite its pessimism, left a faint glow of warmth in Joseph's heart. They had talked to one another like free men. There was something to Krassin's philosophy of survival, after all. A window opened in his shuttered mind. Tomorrow he'd try a game of chess.

Darkness solidified, became night. Burying his head in the blanket, he drifted slowly into hibernating slumber, and suddenly he was a boy in Warsaw carrying his music case to the Conservatoire. Warm sunshine flooded from the sky. An orchestra played the liberating chords of a Bach concerto. The stippled pattern of summer leaves on the grass of the Saxon Garden brought a resilient happiness . . .

The abrupt and noisy opening of the cell-door startled him awake. Groans and exclamations of alarm came from the prisoners as their dreams were snatched away. In strode three shadowy figures. The dazzling beam of a torch flashed in their eyes.

'Attention! Which is Frumkin?' The peremptory voice belonged to the one-eyed commandant, a huge dark shape stretching to the ceiling. Joseph forced a sound through his constricted throat, heart palpitating in the gross clay of his body.

'Get up! Jump to it, you bastard! Bring your things!' the commandant yelled.

Blinded, legs trembling, he climbed from the bunk and gathered his belongings. Someone hustled him to the door and, as he passed, a fellow prisoner stealthily gave his arm an encouraging squeeze. Krassin murmured: 'Courage!'

Still drugged by sleep, moving through geometrical corridors of nightmare, he was vaguely aware of homesickness for the claustrophobic cell. They were tearing him from his friends. There was too much space: unknown, treacherous.

The footsteps of his escort rang in his ears, multiplied by echoes to those of an army on the march, and suddenly he knew he was being led to death. The knowledge brought a stunned disbelief. For years he'd lived with the simple and appalling fact of death, thought about it, prepared for it, became reconciled to it: but it was always tomorrow.

Tomorrow!

Sanity slipped away. The bullet would strike between the eyes. Consciousness, the entire universe, would pour out of the hole in his head in one blinding instant. Non-existence . . . the only certainty. And he was prepared. But *tomorrow*. Please! . . .

Shock paralysed his brain to its roots and his limbs refused to function. He was seized by the arms and dragged along. Then, mysteriously, something disconnected in Joseph Frumkin. He lost all sense of time and place. He walked to his death like an automaton.

The footsteps halted. A door swung open on darkness and he was pushed inside. 'Examine him, doc,' said the commandant.

He held the torch levelled like a gun, a gleam of light refracted in his single eye.

One of the men stepped forward, gazed keenly into Joseph's rigid face and pulled open his shirt. The icy metal tip of a stethoscope probed his bony chest as the doctor listened intently to the drum beat of his empty heart.

'Fit,' the doctor said tersely.

They left him alone in the cell and locked the door. After a while the mind brought back its pain. He experienced the reprieve of living discomfort. Sub-zero air flowed through a small grating high on the wall with a bitter purity. When his eyes adjusted to the gloom he saw a straw palette on the floor covered by a blanket.

Joseph could not sleep. They had spared him until tomorrow, but his last night on earth was not to be merciful.

2

Shyness contorted Stepanchik's broad ruddy face into a grin of idiocy as he caught sight of Lydia coming towards him through the crowded ward. She waved and smiled, but her eyes were strained. Nothing seemed changed in the three years since she'd walked among the wounded in this very hospital. The sick, maimed and dying, still occupied every inch of space.

She turned to Nina and said: 'That's my friend over there.'

'I'll leave you then. They need me in the operating theatre,' said Nina. 'Come and see us soon. Poolka misses you. He likes you to tell him about his father.' She added softly: 'I hope everything will be all right with Joseph.'

Stepanchik sat on the side of his bed, his famous short legs not quite reaching the floor, and exclaimed shyly: 'Well, would you believe it? Look who's here?' The stump of his bandaged right arm jerked as it offered a phantom handshake.

'How are you, Petrushka, my dear?' asked Lydia, pressing his good hand.

'As you can see, Comrade Lydia, the sons of bitches made a hero of me at last.' Despite the gruffness, a plaintive, almost childish note in his voice made her flinch. 'Blew me up with the blast of a twelve-incher when I wasn't looking, the bastards.'

She nodded sympathetically and sat down beside him.

'It knocked me out for a bit and when I come to I found I'd lost my nose-scratcher.' He grinned ruefully. 'The old saw-bones says it won't grow back again.'

'You'll soon get used to it and be as good as new,' she said with forced cheerfulness.

'Yeah, sure, but how will the girls take to a one-armed cuddle?'

He looked at her anxiously, the grin fading. Lydia gathered that he expected an expert opinion. She was female as well as a soldier. Back in the old guerrilla days she'd heard him talk a lot about girls. Coarsely explicit about his tastes, he liked them big and healthy with plenty to squeeze.

'Petrushka, take my word, they'll love you all the more for it. Nothing wrong with the rest of the equipment, I bet.'

A dirty laugh gurgled in Stepanchik's throat and his eyes brightened. 'First class there,' he boasted. 'There's a black-eyed nurse I'd like to try it on. Eighteen, built like a mare and ready to be saddled.'

'Does she give you any encouragement?'

'Comrade, darling,' he said yearningly, 'she bends over and rubs my face with them two beauties, it's all I can do to stop myself taking a grab.'

'So there, you've got nothing to worry about.' Lydia winked and brought out a packet of Peter's French cigarettes. 'Give her one of these and tell her all the girls in Paris are smoking them.'

'Never on your life. Only tarts smoke,' Stepanchik retorted with a disapproving shake of his head, then he went fiery red. 'Oh, I didn't mean you, Lydia. You're different. You're one of us.'

'I'm just ruined. Too far gone,' was Lydia's laughing reply. She broke open the carton and lit a cigarette, passing it to him after taking a few puffs. He did the same and they continued to share the smoke like old comrades.

'Those were good times,' said Stepanchik, crinkling up his eyes reminiscently. 'Nothing like being with a bunch of partisans. You fight together, you laugh together, everything's shared out fair and square. I mean, we was a band of brothers. A comrade would give his right arm –' For a moment he was unable to continue, but before she could think of something to fill the painful silence, he shrugged and resumed enthusiastically: 'Yeah, great days all right. Remember when you went berserk attacking that armoury and the machine-guns blazing and you firing off two revolvers like an angel of vengeance?'

'And you with your wooden rattle.'

'And those mad Georgians. Real wild men, those fellows.' A sad regret for the diminishing past shadowed Stepanchik's limpid eyes. 'It wasn't bad in Poland, neither, in the beginning. You should've been with the unit then. They dished out good rations and anything short you could get from the Yids. If they didn't like it, you singed a bit off their beards and they soon changed their tune,' he said with innocent brutality. 'At least, in the beginning, before Comrade Frumkin told us it was against Marxist Leninism and he'd shoot the balls off the first bastard what did it again.' Taking a deep puff of the cigarette and holding it out to her, he snorted smoke through thick nostrils and asked: 'Did you hear how Frumkin got the shits up and was disobedient of the lawful command of Brigade Commander Kirzanovsky?'

'Piotr Ivanovich,' Lydia said reprovingly, 'it's not right to say that. You know Comrade Frumkin isn't a coward. He didn't think we should fight our own Red sailors.'

'That's easy to say,' argued Stepanchik. 'We was all pissed off about it, but orders is orders and they must of done something for the Imperialists against our Workers' and Peasants' Republic or we wouldn't be told to shoot the guts out of them.' A frowning conviction settled on his stubborn face. It had cost him his arm after all. 'Frumkin wasn't the only one. There was whole units laid down their guns. The Chekists pulled one in every five from the ranks and blew his brains out on the spot. That got the fuckers moving, I'll tell you.'

Lydia sent up a silent vehement prayer to be spared further grisly details, but Stepanchik drove on with mutilated bitterness.

'The question didn't have nothing to do with Comrade Frumkin's kindness to any Red sailors or he wouldn't of been seen grovelling on the floor begging Brigade Commander Kirzanovsky not to shoot him. And it don't seem right that he got away with his yellowness when the rest of us went into that terrible battle for the common cause.'

'Get well and be happy, Petrushka,' said Lydia sadly. 'Let's hope in the end we'll all see the sense of it and it will be good for everybody.'

She pressed the carton of cigarettes into his hand and slowly left the hospital. Savage gusts of wind swept into Sukharev Square along the grimy Myeshchanskaya with a prolonged howl like white Siberian wolves baying for blood. She felt depleted and discouraged by Stepanchik's bitterness against the martyrs of Kronstadt. No wonder he looked back nostalgically to the forest comradeship of guerrilla warfare. Despite everything – the hunger, the fear, the moments of despair – there had been a whole-hearted innocence and idealism about those days which seemed to have gone for ever.

Yet the visit had yielded one piece of information Peter told her was vital. The news he'd received from Solovetsky was that prisoner Frumkin was alive and being held for an unspecified military offence. An examination by the prison doctor found him fit. But Peter warned her not to be hopeful: an inexorable judgement awaited Joseph. It was not a case in which he himself would be permitted to intervene, he'd already gone beyond his powers by sending a message in the name of the Cheka without obtaining higher authority. In the whole of Russia only one man could save Joseph from death, the commander whose order was disobeyed. Who was he? Had he already set in motion the crushing machinery of military justice? If not, could he be reached in time to be persuaded to be merciful? These were problematic chances, unlikely of solution. Lydia could not accept that. She promptly took brief leave of absence from the refugee centre and set out to find the man. Mikhail Norodsky could have helped but there was no way of knowing where he'd gone after he left her in Pushkino. Now Stepanchik had provided the Brigade Commander's name. Kirzanovsky.

Crowds jostled around market stalls in Sukharev Square in a pandemonium of huckstering, cursing and bargaining. The first rewards of NEP were in evidence – rissoles of millet mixed with herring frying on hot braziers, dried-up Polish turnips, sunflower seeds – and people were ready to tear the shirts off their backs for barter. A gang of *bezprizorny*, derelict orphans of civil war, scampered round the stallholders like scavenging dogs. The entire population of Moscow, swelled by soldiers from a dozen Soviet races idling away the first weeks of an unfamiliar peace, seemed to be on the streets. The people were coming out to breathe. Lydia thrust through the milling market-place with a sense of urgency. Somewhere in the immense geography of Russia was the solitary Kirzanovsky. She must lose no time.

In the course of the next twenty-four hours Lydia progressively descended to the lowest levels of the military bureaucracy. The resplendent authority of the Supreme War Council, as vested in a hook-nosed official with gloomy, suspicious eyes, sneezed continually into a grubby handkerchief and would say nothing except that location of Red Army personnel was a state secret. Central Bureau sent her to the Records Department. Records Department requested an application in writing stating full details of information required and purpose of inquiry. An approach to Northern Command, mentioning Kronstadt, elicited that the matter concerned came under the jurisdiction of the Petrograd military district. In every office identical portraits of Lenin and Trotsky stared at her, combining severe and masterful dedication to historical necessity with hovering smiles of fatherly benevolence. Armed guards sealed off forbidden corridors. There were rooms too secret to enter. Each abortive interview involved tedious delay until clerks could find time from the pressing business of the Republic to listen to her. As the late winter evening deepened into night, the last of her interlocutors, yawning and rubbing sleep from his eyes, offered the advice that information about a relative could be obtained from an address in Tverskaya near the Pushkin monument.

By the time she reached the shabby colonnaded building, its stone balconies spread with victory slogans on red streamers, it was locked for the day and a homeless family encamped on sacking in the shelter of the recessed doorway. An old man, a skeleton wrapped in rags, had gathered into the protection of his skinny arms a kerchiefed young woman and her two small children. They crouched closer together as Lydia approached, fearing she'd come in her soldierly garb to evict them. Defensively, with old-fashioned servility, the aged man explained that they were only waiting for the office to be reopened as they'd not heard from his son, the girl's husband and a soldier in the Sixth Army, since a letter written on the Feast of Saint Nicholas. They'd travelled from Yaroslavl to find out, God willing, if the boy was in good health and how soon he'd return to his own folks. Guilt inherited from her privileged upbringing stirred in Lydia as she wished them luck. With a bed waiting for her in Peter's apartment, she was as far from the extremes of hardship as when her father sent her up to bed without supper for an act of rebellion. Fortunately, the weather had turned less cold. Instead of snow, chill rain drizzled from the overcast sky. With the incredible humility of all Russia's poor, they would share their small portion of bread and endure the discomfort, grateful at least to be dry.

Next morning she found the information bureau in a state of siege. Elderly people, women and children stampeded around the entrance while two militiamen yelled vainly at them to form an orderly queue. Either her uniform earned her special treatment or she was mistaken for an employee of the department, for a path into the building was forcibly opened for her. A harassed official in the foyer sought to regulate the crush of relatives struggling to enter an already overfull waiting room where clerks sat behind small windows, received inquiries, closed shutters while they departed to consult records and reopened them to impart their findings. It was a slow, laborious process. Children wailed, women quarrelled, nerve-wracked functionaries pounded ledges in impotent rage. People were as bothersome as flies, reclustering as fast as they were driven away. Unwilling to wait interminably only to risk being swatted by a petty bureaucrat's scorn, Lydia ascended a flight of stairs to the higher echelon of the first floor. The din receded: the atmosphere was sedative, drowsy with the sound of muffled voices and the leisurely tapping of typewriters. A girl crossed the far corridor with a tray of steaming cups.

Choosing one of several closed doors at random, Lydia knocked lightly and entered without pausing for an invitation to do so. The man behind the desk, his tunic unbuttoned to expose a youthful throat, hastily pushed a blotting paper over the sheet on which he'd been writing. He had startled amber eyes, abundant chestnut hair and delicate features. Clasping his hands nervously, he gazed at her in puzzled interrogation, smooth eyebrows flying to meet the hairline above his pale forehead. An air of dust and neglect in the room, an accumulation of yellowing papers on the cramped surface of the desk, gave Lydia the impression that urgency was not a factor in the occupant's duties.

'Good morning, comrade,' she said crisply, in a manner that seemed to increase his uneasiness. 'Alexandrova, from the Pushkino Refugee Centre for Women and Children.'

The man limply shook her hand and relinquished it quickly. 'Please take a seat,' he said. 'One of the chair legs is shaky, but I think it's quite safe if you don't sit too far back.'

He managed his pleasant baritone voice like an actor, and it crossed her mind that something vaguely familiar about him would define itself before the encounter was over. Perching precariously on the edge of the infirm, cane-seated chair, she said: 'I'm trying to locate an officer, Brigade Commander Kirzanovsky. The Supreme War Council advised me to come to you.'

'The Supreme War Council!' Amazement and perturbation threw his harmonious features into confusion. He seemed a little frightened. 'Forgive me,' he protested with a small laugh, 'but I'm surprised they know I even exist.'

'The senior official I spoke to most certainly did,' Lydia assured him disingenuously. 'You are in charge of this department?'

'This isn't exactly a *department*. There's only Kuznetsov and myself. We're sort of attached to Welfare.' The vague way he spoke suggested that the connection was slender and he himself was not sure quite how it worked. 'Are you inquiring on behalf of the officer's wife?'

'Why, does it make a difference if I am?'

'Well, of course! We trace missing soldiers who are not really missing. It's usually wives who are trying to find them when they don't want to be found. Generally they've taken up with another woman. Sometimes they've got a taste for freedom or they've contracted some kind of wound and are ashamed of it. That's very peculiar, comrade, but it's not uncommon.'

Lydia recalled Stepanchik's rueful anxiety about his one-armed cuddle. Her own experiences of fighting side-by-side with men had taught her that more even than the dread of death was the fear of an emasculating wound, or of some hideous disfigurement they thought would make them repulsive to girls. 'I'm not suggesting that Kirzanovsky is missing,' she said. 'Brigade Commanders don't vanish into thin air. I just want to find out where he is now.'

'Oh, then I'm afraid you've come to the wrong place.' The young man, vastly relieved, unconsciously smoothed his neatly barbered hair as though he'd safely come through a sharp physical struggle. 'Perhaps they can help you downstairs.'

Lydia looked coldly at him. 'I have no time to waste, comrade,' she replied curtly. 'Imagine I am an anguished wife, if that will help.'

'Well . . . are you?'

He had the shy eyes of a boy afraid of women, and at last she recognized him. The summer of 1917 when crowds danced in the streets of Petersburg and poets nightly hymned the first free dawn of centuries in the Little Theatre in Fontanka.

'Innokenty Breit,' she said, 'I've heard you recite your poems. With all sincerity, I can tell you I'm very anxious.'

'That's gratifying,' he responded with enthusiasm. 'Although I don't get much chance to read in public now I'm still writing a lot.' As if by accident, he shifted the blotting paper and several irregular lines of verse were exposed. The title seemed to be 'Butterflies Among the Bullets.'

Lydia hurriedly forestalled a possible recitation. 'You are going to help me? It's very urgent.'

'I'll do my best, of course.' Regretfully the poet covered up his work and applied his mind to duty. 'What is the name again?'

'Kirzanovsky.'

He wrote it down, dipped the nib of his pen into the inkwell, and asked: 'Where was he when you last heard of him?'

Quietly, she replied: 'Kronstadt.'

An ink-blot dropped on to the paper from the poised nib. 'That's quite recent,' he said without looking at her. 'If he's not with the troops occupying the fortress, he'll probably be in Petrograd. A letter could be on its way. The post is so irregular.'

'Please find out for sure. I have to see him.'

The intensity of her manner troubled him. Fingertips restlessly drumming on the desk, he pointed out that their records were not necessarily complete or accurate; that the best thing she could do was to leave the matter in his hands for a few days and leave him to get in touch with her. She insisted on him doing something immediately.

'Very well,' he said, spreading his hands in surrender. 'I'll have to ask you to wait. It may take a little while.'

He was gone about twenty minutes and returned carrying a sheet of foolscap blurringly duplicated. His eyes met hers and slid away. It was a few moments before he spoke.

'Are you the next-of-kin, comrade?'

'No,' said Lydia. Her skin prickled.

The man spread the sheet of paper on his desk and read out the following: 'Kirzanovsky, Alexander Fedorovich, age 25, Brigade Commander Ninth Army, Order of the Red Banner. Died in battle, 9th of March, 1921.' Slowly, he lifted his head. 'I'm truly sorry,' he said.

Peter listened in silence, displeasure in the set of his jaw and his severe averted profile. When she finished speaking, he said in a cold, grating voice: 'You must be relieved.'

'You make it sound as though I'm responsible.' Lydia stared miserably at him across the lamplit table. 'Do I have to tell you how I felt when I heard the boy had been killed?'

'No,' he said. 'You don't have to tell me.'

An ambiguity she did not wish to penetrate was concealed in the reply. There were depths in Peter as mysterious and forbidding as the dark side of the moon. She took the kettle off the spirit-stove and poured boiling water into a jug containing ground coffee, filling the room with the rich, dark brown smell that brought a whole vanished era instantly to mind.

'You ought to arrange to go to Paris more often,' she said lightly. 'Real coffee and French cigarettes. It seems incredible such things still exist.'

The remark was meant to alleviate the atmosphere but he treated it with sour mockery, asking: 'Are you still a Francophile?'

'Of course. Isn't everybody?'

He thought of Bogrov, the cipher clerk, and the secret investigation being conducted into his friendships and affairs. Yesterday was Bogrov's free day. He had taken a walk in Petrovsky Park carrying skates. But the ice on the lake had begun to thaw and after discussing its safety with another would-be skater Bogrov and his chance companion wandered for a short while through the trees. When they separated, the cipher-clerk's coat pocket was weighed down by a liquor bottle. The other man, when followed, proved to be a member of the French Communist delegation staying at the Metropole Hotel, the left-wing faction favoured by the Comintern, naturally. Francophilia? Or treachery? He sipped his coffee in brooding silence.

Lydia was equally silent and preoccupied. She felt a curious involvement in Kirzanovsky's death. When the news was imparted to her she was stabbed by a sharp pang of grief as though she'd truly been his next-of-kin. She wished she'd known him. The intuition came to her that perhaps he'd wanted to be killed. It sometimes happened to a soldier that way in battle. There were times when it was not death but survival that appeared intolerable.

'What will they do now?' she asked suddenly. 'I'm talking about Joseph. Surely if there's no charge . . .'

The expression in Peter's eyes, savage and contemptuous, froze her.

'He will have to sit in jail until someone remembers to release him,' he said. 'It may take a long time. There's a price to pay for everything. It's justice, of a kind.'

He wants me to be punished, too, Lydia told herself. At this moment, he is filled with bitterness for loving me.

In Solovetsky Prison, returning to his solitary cell from a half-hour's exercise in the frosty courtyard, Joseph laid out the chess-pieces in his mind and imagined that Krassin was his opponent. By dint of intense concentration he fixed the board clearly with his inner eye and opened for white with the Knight's gambit . . .

Chapter Seven

'It's good to be going home, eh, Bogrov?' Peter said, falling into step with the cipher clerk. Out of the corner of his eye he saw the man in a ragged overcoat and workman's flat cap studiously look the other way. Day and night surveillance had turned up nothing suspicious in Bogrov's behaviour except for the meeting with a Comintern delegate in Petrovsky Park. He would, following his usual practice, enter his communal dwelling house, draw the curtains of his room and not leave until it was time to go to work in the morning, picking up a copy of *Pravda* to read on the tram.

They were among the last to depart from the office. Only the small night staff under Tolya Lieberman remained when Bogrov cleared his desk and brought his files to be locked in the secrets cupboard so that nothing remained, only those he carried in his possibly treacherous head.

A dim light from a window shone on the cipher clerk's pale inoffensive face and he clutched the lapels of his jacket to protect his chest from the cold wind.

'Yes, comrade, a long day,' he said, bobbing respectfully, and hastened to add: 'But it passes very quickly.'

'You find the work interesting?'

'Indeed, I do. And valuable. It's good to feel one is doing one's share.'

Peter's mistrust was confirmed. The tone – that of a traditionally servile minor official speaking to his superior – was a bit too close to satire; Bogrov was not the type. And yet events might prove him innocent. If every sly parodist concealed a traitor half the scribblers in Russia merited hanging.

'This is my tram-car,' said the cipher clerk, smiling awkwardly. 'See you tomorrow morning, comrade.'

Bogrov hurried to join the jostling queue as if glad to escape and Peter walked off, huddling into the collar of his overcoat. He didn't have a good feeling. Bolts, guards, walls, nothing was impervious to treachery. It wasn't a good feeling at all, attacking the mind, groping in the stomach like a spreading cancer.

A man lurched against him in the dark. 'Look where you're going,' he snarled, fighting an impulse to smash his fist into the stranger's face. An irregular rhythm beat in his chest: he felt shrunken in stature. The symptoms were familiar. No need to ask what was wrong. Alarm signals had been ringing in his ears ever since he left London.

His attic room was cold, damp and depressingly empty. Attacked by the infantile disease of self-pity, he brewed a bit of his French coffee on the paraffin stove and livened it up with some brandy, drinking the mixture in brooding silence as he stared at the oily Moskva through a gap in neighbouring roofs. Down below a late party was in progress, other people's laughter – mindless and egotistical – rising through the floor. It kept him awake for a while, and when at last he drifted into a shallow sleep only a moment seemed to pass before the telephone startled him awake again.

Lieberman's voice crackled over the wire. 'Peter, can you come at once? I'm afraid it's serious otherwise I wouldn't –' Cutting into the apologies, he said; 'Yes, yes! Send the car. I'll be ready immediately.'

Security patrols roamed the uneasy streets. They stopped to interrogate the vagrants sheltering in doorways as if sifting through bundles of rags. Solitary pedestrians stood with their arms upheld while their pockets were searched for weapons or illicit property. Here and there lorries waited at corners collecting suspects. The civil war might be over but peace was precarious, wormeaten with mistrust. Strange noises creaked in the silence of night. The great hungry city seemed to be turning restlessly over and over in its sleep.

When Peter arrived he found Lieberman crouched under a single light in the deserted general office, his nail-bitten hands smoothing the crumpled pages of a closely written document. He looked like a student in the grip of examination nerves, wild-eyed, dishevelled, contemplating the ruins of a promising future. One stork-leg wound round the other, he swivelled in his chair and held out the sheets of paper.

'Bad news from Paris!' he said lugubriously. 'It was brought by special courier.'

'I've been expecting it.' Peter spoke with leaden calm. 'Let's go to my office.'

Still in his overcoat, he stood in the centre of the room and read the document in morose silence, handing each page back to Lieberman as it was completed.

The report, as anticipated, came from Yegudin, one of the most experienced Bolshevik secret agents in Paris. At 7.30 p.m. the previous Sunday he locked the door of his small flat in the rue Peletiere and left for a social evening with a group of White Russians he'd been instructed to infiltrate. Punctiliously, he noted the time of his return as 11.53 p.m. In his absence, as he discovered later, the place had been visited by intruders. Yegudin's cover was that of a professional translator. Having made some strong coffee to clear the fumes of wine from his brain, he settled down to complete the translation of a short memoir on the civil war in the Ukraine that depicted as heroic the deeds of the bloodthirsty anarchist brigand, Nestor Makhno. He then made the disconcerting discovery that the paperweight he used to keep the manuscript open lay in the precise position in which he'd left it but on the wrong page. Another disturbing fact came to his attention. Somebody had deliberately changed the date on his desk calendar from Sunday 3 April to Monday 4.

Yegudin then began a meticulous examination of the apartment. Although nothing appeared missing and there were no obvious signs of disorder, objects and furniture in the two small rooms had been slightly displaced, an ashtray on a shelf exchanged for one on a table, a chair moved, books rearranged into an unfamiliar sequence. Baedeker's *Paris* had a spill of paper inserted and, when opened, Yegudin saw that a ring had been pencilled around the name of La Coupole, the café where he often met emigré intellectuals. There was no evidence of forcible entry: both windows were fastened: the door had been securely locked. Not being a believer in poltergeists, Yegudin concluded that the flat had been thoroughly ransacked by experts who, for some mysterious reason, chose to plant tell-tale clues of their intrusion. It seemed evident that his cover had been penetrated by *Sûreté* counter-espionage. He, therefore, left the apartment, followed the emergency procedure and now awaited instructions.

'The French have an arrogant sense of humour,' Peter remarked, looking at Lieberman with a dry meditative smile, and heard the echo of contemptuous laughter. Someone in Paris knew him a little too well.

Lieberman said: 'We'll have to recall Yegudin. I hate to think of the mess this makes of our operations in France.'

Peter walked to the window and drummed irritably on the glass. It was still dark but the sound of gulls screaming over the river announced an unwelcome dawn. He looked into himself and diagnosed the infirmity of failure.

'At least we now know who our traitor is,' he said tightly. 'Have Bogrov arrested immediately.'

'I can't tell you where my husband is,' Bogrov's wife said in quiet desperation, clutching one child in her arms while the other held on to her skirt. In the passage of the communal apartment, the housing committee chairman was yelling for order. 'Don't be nosey, comrades! Take the youngsters away and get on with your own affairs! You are preventing the comrade Chekists from carrying out their duty.'

'Put a stop to that disturbance,' Peter Piatkov told one of his men.

The fellow stepped outside. 'Go on! Off!' he ordered laconically and the excited women flurried like leaves in a gusty wind and settled again further from the door.

Two big Chekists, their faces blank and expressionless, were methodically creating chaos. They emptied cupboards; upended the contents of boxes and drawers, examining letters and photographs; shook out books and suspiciously peered into their hollow spines; searched under the worn linoleum; opened up the sofa that converted into a family bed and ripped open the canvas to sift through its horsehair stuffing. One of the searchers unscrewed the back of an alarm clock and probed its mechanism with clumsy curiosity. The other licked the point of a pencil ready to record items placed under arrest.

Peter turned away with an air of bitter distaste, glancing out of the window at lines of ragged washing strung across the yard and, beyond, at the unpaved streets of wooden dwellings. Faded lettering over an empty stable spelled out the name 'Fomich' and offered cartage for hire. It could have been a village in the middle of nowhere instead of a Moscow suburb. Perhaps that mattered a great deal to the absent Bogrov. His certificate of graduation in law hung framed on the wall and he may have considered that a man of education deserved better than a cramped room in a squalid district.

'They will put everything back in place,' he told the frightened woman. 'You say you didn't see your husband leave. How is that possible?'

'I was asleep,' she replied, looking hopelessly at the floor as if she expected not to be believed. The little girl at her side stopped sucking a thumb and said, pointing at his gun: 'Bang-bang dead.'

Peter's smile was strained: he lacked the knack of being at ease with children.

'He said nothing at all to you about going away?'

'No. When I woke up he was gone.'

'Did he give you the impression of being worried?'

'Comrade,' the woman replied, and her lips trembled, 'show me a human being who does not have worries.'

'It is in your interest to answer frankly,' Peter said with official severity. 'Has your husband shown signs of being under strain? Has he spoken about problems at work or in his private life? Have you heard him express dissatisfaction with the political situation? Was there anything at all unusual in his manner recently?'

'Why do you ask me all these questions?' The woman stared in terror. 'What has he done, my Kostya? Please don't torture me! Tell me what is wrong.'

He could offer only the meagre explanation that a full investigation was necessary when a worker of state security unaccountably went absent. The rest was ruled by secrecy.

She nodded at everything he said but scarcely took in a word.

'I can't understand it, I can't!' she murmured repetitively, and plucked at his sleeve as he turned to go. 'I swear to you, comrade, my husband is a good man, honest, a man of principle.'

'Let us hope so,' he said, avoiding her eyes because there was no hope. The Party and State did not overvalue principle. It was subjective, individualistic, difficult to define. The suppression of the Kronstadt rebellion had affirmed in blood what Bolshevism held as self-evident. Loyalty, not principle, was the essential requirement. By sinning against that commandment Bogrov had condemned himself to death and imposed a punishing future even on the innocent child his wife held in her arms.

2

Treason was an intimate disease that spread its poison throughout the whole system. The Party Control Commission ordered a drastic cleansing. Loyalty checks were instituted, codes were changed, revised procedures initiated. In France, the network must be completely reorganized. On occasions Peter strayed no farther from his desk than the office sofa for two or three hours sleep from which he awakened with temples throbbing. Like a climber afflicted by vertigo he kept his gaze grimly fastened to the rock-face, refusing to acknowledge fear of the abyss.

Meanwhile the traitor was reported arrested many times: on the frontier, seeking to board foreign ships, in food queues, railway stations, hiding in cellars, creeping out of back doors from some romantic escapade – an average little man with thinning fair hair, victim of an accidental resemblance to a typewritten description that could fit half a score of people in any crowd gathered on a Russian street. Bogrov was as ordinary as grass: that was his protection; but as long as he remained at liberty the menace to Peter's work persisted. There were questions he alone could answer.

Undermined by self-doubt, experiencing a profound mistrust of his own capacities, Peter's mental briskness deserted him. His mind revolved in circular orbits of futility. It was a lonely feeling. In a moment of weakness he lifted the telephone receiver and asked to be connected with the refugee centre in Pushkino. Lydia's voice reached him through an electric storm and there was nothing to say. An oath of silence inhibited him: the act of confession was forbidden even to the one he loved. He thought of Bogrov, dreamed of Bogrov, imagined he caught glimpses of him everywhere. It was more pernicious than the obsession of love. Bogrov squatted in his skull and won every argument.

Then came a breakthrough. Some poor fellow riding a train to Smolensk fell in with a gang of vagabonds who robbed him, kicked him around a bit and threw him out of a moving truck. Picked up insensible and taken to a militia post, he hadn't a scrap of paper to show his identity and, as a consequence of this irregularity, was kicked around a bit more with a sort of provincial roughness and taken to the local Cheka. There he received some extra kicking for telling a lot of lies until something about his appearance caused one official to check him against the file copy of Bogrov's particulars, after which he was treated with great respect as an important prisoner and transferred to Moscow showing little sign of wear and tear except for a ruptured kidney. The thought of the damage that might have been inflicted on one possessed of such vital information filled Peter Piatkov with a cold fury and he issued instructions that no investigation should be instituted until Bogrov was restored to approximate health.

The Chief Investigator, a nervous man with the dark melancholy face of a Spanish inquisitor, paced distractingly to and fro as Peter Piatkov read the long-winded transcript of interrogation.

The man's body blocked out the light. He tossed his smouldering cigarette-end out of the open window with incendiary violence and remarked: 'He's playing with us. It's obvious.'

'Is it all like this?' Peter flipped through the thick sheaf of paper, selected a passage at random, and read aloud: 'In my opinion it is impossible to answer your question without an agreed definition of the meaning of loyalty . . . and what do you mean by Russia? . . . and, another thing, the legitimacy of State power . . .'

'Well, he's a clever little bastard,' the Chief Investigator said defensively. 'It seems to be making sense when you're writing it down, but it all disappears like steam on a mirror.' He threw himself into a chair, propped his booted legs on the trestle table and discontentedly flicked at a dribble of ash on his skinny thigh. 'He's the type that thinks they're smarter than you. You can always tell, it's a sly look in their eyes. I instructed my men to play up to it. Let them think you're simple-minded and their tongues get a bit too clever. The trouble is,' he said, scowling, 'Bogrov's got nothing to lose. He knows we'll have his neck whatever he says.'

'Everybody's got something to lose,' Peter said. Lenin gazed ironically at him from an old photograph on the wall, the shrewd optimistic Lenin who still retained laboratory certainties of scientific change. But he'd seen him crossing the former Square of the Tsars in the Kremlin a few days earlier, a small crumpled figure waving a tired, impatient hand at Sverdlov, two men exhausted by history.

'I like to keep decent standards,' gloomily ruminated the Chief Investigator. 'Treat a man like a man, with respect, even if he is a prisoner. I can twist his arm easy as anything by threatening his family, but that's not my way.'

He was speaking, of course, for the record. Hypocritical sentiments dripped from the fangs of the most monstrous officials in conformity with the latest Party insistence on legality. Brotherly leadership, impeccable behaviour, reconciliation, no more Kronstadts. Those hardened by the politics of terror were made uneasy by it and overdid the sanctimony. Unconvincing as butchers preaching the virtues of vegetarianism.

'At least it's not a question of establishing guilt. We won't screw repentance out of this specimen, but he doesn't deny what he's done,' the man continued. His narrow lips parted in a smile like the flash of a knife blade. 'I'll make up the documents for summary court-martial, then he can get the bullet.'

'Not yet,' said Peter.

'Why not? What is there to wait for?'

'Traitors are more valuable alive than dead. You shoot them only when they've got nothing more to tell. We still don't know how Bogrov was recruited, what instructions he received, whether he acted alone or as a member of a group, what information he disclosed and how he transmitted it. He's blown a hole through our security but we don't know how big it is. Keep working on him.'

The Chief Investigator plucked at a loose fold of skin on his seamed forehead and sank lower into his chair with a long-suffering sigh. 'Very well, comrade, I'm here to do the best I can. Only it's my opinion, speaking from experience, that this is a very difficult fellow who'd have the tongue pulled from his head – in a manner of speaking – before he'd cooperate.'

'Comrade,' said Peter, 'there's an old saying in Pskov, where I was born, that a man is born with a tongue to praise God and confess his sins. It's my opinion that Bogrov shares that secret craving with the rest of us.'

Later that night, to the tune of Ukrainian folk songs from the fluted horn of a phonograph, Semyon Shulkin, the economist, expounded to Peter the theory that much was to be learned from capitalism that could profitably be integrated into a socialist economy. Nina listened proudly to every word and kept glancing at him to see if he was suitably impressed.

It was the fourth anniversary of the Shulkins' wedding. The cramped two-roomed apartment was bright and polished, brass candlesticks shone, a vivid Bokharan rug turned the bedstead into an Oriental couch, red winter berries and dark evergreen formed a decorative table centrepiece, and Nina had conjured up a miraculous feast of beetroot soup, pirozhki and a bottle of Georgian wine that could only have been got together by assiduous barter in the Moscow street-markets.

Pert and flushed, her flaxen hair shining, and wearing an embroidered peasant blouse that enhanced the soft curve of her breast, she was more like a country girl of seventeen than a mature woman lapped by warm domesticity. Ten-year-old Poolka, orphan of her first love, nibbled sunflower seeds as his print-hungry eyes greedily scanned an English copy of *Robinson Crusoe* fast losing its threadbare covers. The younger child slept peacefully in the adjoining room. Her father-in-law, a gaunt man wearing a Jewish skull-cap, who listened in bemused silence to the discourse of his erudite son, got up quietly and removed the wax record as the voice of the Ukrainians came to an abrupt and grinding halt.

'You see what I'm driving at, Piatkov?' Shulkin said earnestly in the silence that followed, his eyes blazing with pure intelligence behind the lenses of his spectacles. 'We would be applying the manufacturing and marketing skills without the exploitative elements. In what way is it inconsistent with our principles?'

'We are simply learning from our mistakes,' explained Nina, looking fondly from her husband to Peter at the inopportune moment when he was in the act of surreptitiously consulting his watch.

'I quite see that,' he agreed hastily, adding: 'I wonder what's keeping Lydia? Are you sure she's coming?'

'You haven't heard a thing,' pouted Nina. 'Of course she'll come. Did you ever know Lydia not to keep a promise? If she's late there must be a good reason for it.'

Her impatience was scarcely less than his. Lydia's arrival would make him more human and she so wanted this special evening to be a success. Peter alone – so polite and uncommunicative – was an uncomfortable presence. She'd only asked him to the celebration because of Lydia, but as long as he was in her house she must entertain him.

'I'm afraid our guest is bored with our subject, Semyon.' She crinkled up her snub little nose and laughed. 'We must find something more exciting to talk about or he won't stay.'

A flicker of amusement broke the surface of Peter's taciturnity and it vexed her. Why should the idea that she shared Semyon's interests seem so silly to people? She was an intelligent person, a senior hospital worker, not limited in her abilities to the simple arithmetic of keeping house.

'You are bored, aren't you?' she was driven to insist.

'Not at all,' Peter murmured politely. 'I find your subject fascinating.'

'No, Nina is quite right. A host should not monopolize the conversation. It is inexcusable.' Smiling diffidently, Shulkin moistened his fingertip to pick up a breadcrumb and placed it carefully on his tongue. He did not find it easy to alight on a suitable topic and his smile wandered in amiable helplessness from face to face.

'Of course, your work must be interesting just now, but I suppose you're not permitted to discuss it,' said Nina, looking at Peter provocatively.

Scrupulously non-committal, he admitted that his work was indeed interesting but much too technical to be understood by anyone but specialists. This reticence added the force of mystery to his role in their eyes. The little they knew about him did not extend to his function in the powerful secret organization he served. It could, for all they knew, be concerned with executions and the hunting down of saboteurs and political opponents, with acts of swift retribution. They sensed in his reluctant speech the compression of a gloomy will. His infrequent appearances in their lives, his watchful silences and abrupt departures, did nothing to dispel the uneasiness.

'As long as our country is surrounded by enemies there will be plenty of work for the Cheka,' said Shulkin in tones of despondency not untouched by bitterness.

Peter did not fail to detect it. Wrenching himself away from his preoccupation with the case of Bogrov, or perhaps because of it, he remarked: 'In that respect I count myself among the Slavophiles. We have our own dynamic of development. It is not only enemies we must guard against. The Russian soul should be protected from the sweet corruption of foreign friends.'

Although this was uttered quietly his voice had a cold authority that captured the attention of everybody in the room. The old man, Shulkin's father, glanced up warily as though suspecting a racial innuendo. Young Poolka brushed a lock of hair from his eyes and stared at him as a strange creature who had invaded his island adventure. 'I was born in England, in the city of London,' he asserted with a rebellious expression so much like the dead Polovski Murontzeff that Nina's heart was rocked by it. 'But you are still a Russian,' Peter said, his gaze sombre.

Nina was again reminded of that first distant encounter when he materialized out of a Whitechapel winter fog, wrapped in ambiguity, to announce quietly: 'My name is Schtern.' And afterwards it seemed that he had come as a destroyer, an angel of death. The memory fell like a shadow across the feast.

'Shall I put on some more music on the phonograph?' asked her father-in-law in a heavy Yiddish accent.

'No, Papa,' she replied mechanically, 'we must save the needle.'

The old man gave an afflicted shrug and patted away a yawn. 'Excuse me, I go to bed. Good night!' He left them and shuffled slowly into the darkness next door.

Laughter penetrated the matchboard wall from an adjoining apartment. Snatches of conversation drifted up from the street. Footsteps approached, receded. The snuffle and groan of sparse traffic laboured along Kozitzki Pereulok past the bare trees of Saint Sophia. More footsteps, hasty ones this time, and Peter listened intently. A wry smile entered his face. 'That,' he said with affectionate irony, 'is the belated Lydia.'

She came in like a brisk wind, generous with her precious store of energy, and renewed them all.

'Darling, happy anniversary!' she cried, embracing Nina. 'I couldn't get a train from Pushkino. The usual shortages of fuel. Semyon, stop looking like a smug family man and use your brilliant brain to solve the national transport problem. Hey, Poolka!' She looked at the boy indignantly. 'Do you think you're too big to kiss your favourite aunt?'

He grinned with delight and retorted: 'You're not my aunt and you didn't come to see us for weeks and weeks.'

'I know, and it was very wicked of me.' She kissed him, nevertheless, with a loud smacking noise. 'I've brought you a present,' she said, pulling a book out of her tunic pocket. 'Lovely poems by Lermontov, all about angels and summer cornfields and dashing Cossacks on their beautiful horses . . .'

'Oh, thanks!' Poolka said excitedly. 'He's the one who was killed in a duel.'

'That's what poets are like, my dear one. Either they die of a broken heart or fight duels for the love of beautiful ladies.' She smirked at Peter and said: 'Dreadful reactionary nonsense, but I believe every word of it.'

'When you say it, we all do,' he answered.

Her glance dwelt on him interrogatively, noting signs of strain around his eyes, then she turned to Nina and handed her a small package. 'Not to be opened until you're alone,' she said. 'It's such a miserable gift I'd be ashamed.'

Nina hugged her and cried, then rushed away to bring the food she'd been saving for her.

When they left the Shulkins' apartment Lydia slipped her arm into Peter's and said: 'What's the trouble, Petya? You sounded very strange on the telephone the other day. I had the impression you wanted to tell me something.'

He continued walking in silence for a while. The warmth and pressure of her linked arm, the husky concern in her voice, dissolved that ache of loneliness: but the rush of emotion that followed found him unprepared.

'You're not ill, are you?' she asked.

'Ill!' He gave a short harsh laugh, hardening himself. 'For some peculiar reason it's all I can do to hold myself together.'

She looked at him in dismay. Not the self-disciplined Peter whose every thought seemed deliberate and every act willed, whose spartan severity was incorruptible, the man who contrived order in the midst of chaos and never publicly admitted to human frailty! Of all people, surely he would be the last to break!

'And you can't forgive yourself for it, I suppose.'

'It's a pathetic, detestable condition. A man needs to have a good opinion of himself,' he said. A grimace of distaste twisted his mouth and he added brusquely: 'Forgive me, I shouldn't have spoken. The last thing I want is pity.'

'Oh, Peter!' she protested. 'What's the trouble? If you can't tell me, you can't tell anybody.'

'That's it exactly. I can't tell anybody. Forbidden.'

Lydia raised one eyebrow. 'I see, a state secret.'

'A small one. Too bad it finds me the worse for wear.'

They began to cross Krasnaya Square, dwarf sentries in shadow under the Kremlin wall, tiny people scurrying before a marauding wind under the black and timeless sky, and she said with a derisive laugh: 'Will it matter a hundred years from now if you whispered your little state secret into my shell-like ear?'

Peter turned up his collar as a shield against the cold. 'In my profession,' he said with mock severity, 'that is a blasphemous question and I am a devout believer. The God I serve is very quick with the thunderbolts of wrath.'

'I know, and he's been far too active lately.' Lydia seized his hand and began to run across the windswept tundra of the vast Square. Laughing, she paused for breath when they reached the shelter of the street behind St Basil's Cathedral. Suddenly she became serious.

'Be indestructable, Peter,' she said. 'For my sake.'

They set off down the sloping streets towards the river and, somehow, he felt that the crisis was beginning to pass.

Framed in the spyhole of his solitary cell, Bogrov's existence was simplified into an image of despair. It showed him immured in a cement box that admitted no ray of daylight, only the muffled sounds of captivity. He sat in dejection on the edge of his plank bed, lips moving soundlessly, and a dim globe on the ceiling exposed the defenceless dead-white scalp beneath his sparse fair hair. If he was aware of being watched he gave no sign of it but stared hopelessly into space with the apathy of a caged animal.

Peter motioned to the prison guard. The jangling of the heavy bunch of keys disrupted the curious humming silence. As the iron door swung open Bogrov looked up warily and with an air of defiance but immediately reverted to indifference. The door closed again, leaving them alone.

'I hope you're not offended that I didn't visit you earlier,' said Peter ironically polite. 'You've given me so much work to do, I haven't had time.'

He spoke without rancour, approaching the analysis of treason impersonally, as a scientist will examine the germs of a loathsome disease under the lens of a microscope.

Bogrov had acquired the spy's ability to convert his flesh and bone into a mask. The thin nose with its small neat nostrils, the prim mouth and pale-lashed eyes of bleached blue were drained of expression. Lacking the talent to be anything but himself, he sought concealment in becoming nobody.

'I thought the interrogation was over,' he said in a colourless voice.

'Abandoned would be more accurate. You achieved a stalemate by not telling us anything we hadn't already discovered by ourselves.'

Bogrov permitted himself a faint smile.

'So all that remains is my crucifixion. When is it to be?'

'Are you in a hurry to die?' asked Peter, ignoring the aspiration to divinity.

'No, but this' – Bogrov gestured at his surroundings – 'can hardly be called living.'

'It's possible to adjust to everything after the shock is over. That's the worst, isn't it? When you're torn away from the busy world and the clock stops – no tram to catch in the morning, no people to talk to, or newspapers to read, nothing to mark one day from another, your entire existence reduced to grey irrelevance.'

The former cipher clerk lowered his eyelids and remained silent. Peter paced the cell as if he himself was a prisoner, finally leaning against the wall under the ventilator grille and pursuing a sombre monologue.

'You're alone, immobilized, hideously aware of the shifting sensations of your own body. There is nothing to do. Going to the bucket to shit is an event. Thoughts scurry through your mind like rats in a cage. You try to think of the last time you made love to your wife, of walking in the park with your children. The recollection is already becoming ghostly. An hour of solitude in a cell and it seems that life is rushing into emptiness, all that you love left behind like a forlorn group on an empty railway platform. You have a desperate need to look into a mirror to confirm your own reality. There is no mirror. You begin to forget your own face.'

Bogrov said apathetically: 'You've described it well.' He stood up, shuffled to the sanitary pail, urinated with difficulty and threw himself full length on the bed. It was a gesture of dismissal.

'The strange thing is,' Peter continued carefully, refusing to acknowledge the signal, 'that we are prepared to put up with the utmost misery rather than die. All our instincts insist on survival.'

He was reminded of an Okhrana interrogator he'd known in Tsarist times who successfully wheedled confessions out of suspects exhausted by their ordeals with the beguiling catch-phrase: 'Life is sweet, my friend. The rest is rhetoric.' It was not, however, in his power to promise Bogrov life in return for cooperation, although it would be a good bargain. Bogrov had made no attempt to profess innocence, expressed no repentance, asked no mercy. Instead, he claimed that his treason was an act of pure patriotism, perpetrated to save Russia from a power-hungry tyranny. In his case, the sweetness lay in the rhetoric not in the living.

'Yet man is the one animal able to transcend the instinctive fear of death,' he mused. 'He will die for a cause with more passion than he gives it in life. Has it occurred to you, Bogrov, that this is often a perverse attempt to escape from death altogether into some vicarious immortality?'

The cipher clerk, without making reply, clasped his hands against his crotch, drew up his legs and meekly invited sleep. His silence was no less formidable for being unassertive. Simply and humbly, it withdrew from participation.

An electric shock of rage tore through Peter. 'Get up on your feet!' he spat out.

Bogrov's eyes snapped open. Slowly, he stood up and stared rigidly into space. His pallor was that of excitement, not fear. A striking disparity existed between his appearance and manner. The once neat clothes were soiled and crumpled; black grease had collected on his shirt collar; his skin suffered from a vitamin deficiency that caused it to flake and dried mucus clung to the corners of his meagre lips. Yet dignity remained like a rod of steel at the core of his immoderate humanity. If violence was to be offered, he was clearly ready to withstand it.

'I'll decide when this interview is over,' said Peter jerkily. He leaned against the wall waiting for the agitation to subside. The infirmity shocked him. Nothing could be more humiliating than loss of control and he fought against it grimly, with self-contempt. The prisoner bent on martyrdom, who referred to his execution as crucifixion, rejoiced in degree to the intensity of persecution. Nothing would more confirm the nobility of his sacrifice than to be scourged on the road to Golgotha. Before anything could be got out of Bogrov he must be brought down to the dirt-level of common humanity.

His heart slowed to its normal rhythm. Walking over to Bogrov, he stared coldly into his eyes and said: 'I'll be coming to see you again. Let me warn you against one thing, the sin of pride. Judas is your precursor, not Jesus. You've sold out your country and nobody ever made a worse bargain. Prepare yourself for a shock because next time I'll explain how you've been cheated.'

Without recollection of having made the return journey, he

found himself back in his office. Lights burned in empty rooms. Objects of furniture seemed possessed of an independent authority, and in a disconnected moment he glanced at the black vulcanite telephone and saw it as a weird erectile insect with one round malignant eye. Interpenetrated by a pervasive unreality, his mind continued the one-sided dialogue with Bogrov, interpreting contradictory meanings into his silences. It occurred to him that the *Sûreté* in Paris were engineering a brilliant strategy. They were putting Bogrov to deadly use. The spy was a weapon in their hands and the weapon was meant to destroy him. For the first time in his life Peter felt enmeshed in a gladiatoral net, uncertain that he would be able to struggle free.

For an hour or so he read official papers, drafted memoranda, surrendering to the drug of work until the letters blurred on the page. He stood at the window, smoking a final cigarette and staring gloomily at the sky, then, with a last word to the night staff, pulled on his heavy overcoat and left. As he entered the street a figure stepped out of a doorway. It was a woman. Her head was bound in a kerchief and her body bundled into shapeless clothes, but there was something timid and young in the way she moved. She stood directly in his path, determined to waylay him: probably a girl ready to sell herself for bread, he thought, and the familiar reflex of pity for the plight of women stirred. He felt in his pocket for some paper roubles: they were of little value except as a donation of sympathy.

'I'm sorry –' he began to say, then stopped: it was Bogrov's wife.

She said something about her husband. Peter shook his head violently and pushed past, hearing her footsteps in faltering pursuit. As he turned the corner he saw her standing irresolutely on the pavement staring after him.

From then on he became a haunted man. She was waiting again the next day and again he rebuffed her. The third time it was past midnight and her eyes were circled with fatigue. She must have been standing in the doorway for hours.

'Go away! You have no business here!' he muttered.

'Please!' she said. 'For my children's sake.'

Abruptly rounding on her, he said intensely: 'Stay with your children! This will not help them at all. You will be informed at the proper time.'

He continued walking, his heart pumping unevenly as if he ascended a steep slope. When he went to bed the woman's face appeared just as he was on the point of sleep and jerked him horribly awake.

The following night he hurried past her without a glance. Her soft voice persecuted him. He began to see her in crowded streets, as a dark shape on the gloomy landing when he climbed the stairs to his apartment, staring with empty eyes from the window of a passing tram. She became an archetype: Moscow was filled with her resemblances. Her meek and obdurate presence, so like Bogrov's, entered his dreams.

When at last he decided that the time had come to see the spy again and left for the Lubianka he noticed with relief that the street was deserted. A prison van turned the corner and disappeared into the chill, smoke-blue dusk. Then he saw her. She stood in a doorway and did not try to approach him, but her eyes looked at him with a piercing, terrible awareness as though she recognized in him her husband's executioner.

'I'll interrogate him in here,' he told the Chief Investigator.

'Very sensible,' the other agreed. 'He's too much at home in that cell. The man's a natural recluse. When we put a stool-pigeon in with him he just carried on as if the fellow didn't exist. Our man talked himself blue in the face, tried to pick quarrels by upsetting Bogrov's stew, woke up screaming in the night pretending to be sick, and all he got for his pains was "good morning", "good night", "ask the guard to bring the doctor".' The Chief Investigator extended his bony face across the table and spoke in a confidential whisper. A strong taint of stale tobacco and halitosis hung on his breath. 'May I,' he murmured, 'make a suggestion?'

'Of course,' answered Peter, leaning away.

The movement was ineffective, serving only to encourage his companion to edge closer. 'Mind you, I wouldn't even mention it, but this is an abnormal case.' He cleared an obstruction from his throat. 'We've tried everything and it's been no good, right?'

'Quite right.'

'And it's a question – a vital question – of the security of the State, yes?'

'Espionage,' agreed Peter, nostrils twitching, 'is precisely that.'

'Why not give him a fright?' breathed the Chief Investigator.

'Torture? But, surely, nowadays . . .'

'Not exactly torture. Put a gun against the back of his neck and march him into the yard. Just to see the effect. It's a serious business, I know' – the Chief Investigator bared his yellow teeth in an embarrassed grin – 'but circumstances justify it. Once they crack, they talk.'

'Let us talk frankly, comrade,' said Peter unpleasantly. 'Tickle a man's spine with a gun to make him think he's taking his last walk on earth and he'll probably dirty his pants. But a loose sphincter doesn't always loosen the tongue. We will not get the information we want out of Bogrov without his willing cooperation.'

'He'll tell you what he told us,' his colleague declared lugubriously. The long bony fingers flipped through the transcript of interrogation and he quoted: 'You ask me to tell you the truth. My answer is that every man's truth is different . . . Language imposes the disguise of meaning on the incommunicable . . . I expect to be misunderstood.' Slapping the document in exasperation, he got up and said in parting: 'Have a nice chat.'

The door slammed shut and Peter was alone, entombed again in the prison of his thoughts. Time passed in slow soundless moments like drifting snowflakes. He walked briskly and nervously up and down the room as if the physical activity would restore circulation to his numbed mind. It did not help: the channels of inspiration were blocked and when the guard's knock came he answered it irritably, with an expectation of inevitable failure.

Bogrov entered and stood with lowered head before the table. He looked dazed and fatigued, eyes smudged by lack of sleep.

'Sit down,' said Peter. He dismissed the guard and stared at the prisoner in brooding concentration. Once again he received the impression of a baffling anonymity. From his knowledge of Bogrov's biography, the solitary child of elderly parents, orphaned at an early age, he inferred that it derived from the need to remain inoffensive and unnoticed, as a stick insect, deficient in the armoury of aggression, will simulate a dry twig to deceive its predators. Not by chance was such a man led to the profession of a cryptogrammarian, a practitioner of language as a means of concealment. 'I expect to be misunderstood.' On reflection, the statement was peremptory. The misunderstanding was skilfully calculated so that whatever his appearance the true Bogrov remained unfathomable, a master of deceit. Yet on the rare occasions when he did speak plainly his tone was forthright and arrogant. Peter recalled a passage in the interrogation.

Question: 'Supposing you had the opportunity to address the Central Committee of the Party, what would you say?'

Answer: 'I would say, gentlemen, you have betrayed the idealism of our Russian people.'

Question: 'But isn't it too soon to tell? Four years is no time at all in the scale of history. We are still at the stage of demolition of the old society, including its so-called idealism. Do you really expect socialism to spring up overnight?'

Answer: 'You have brought us the socialism of ruffians.'

There was really nothing more to add to the brief exchange. The political motivation was all there. But rebellion sprang from the hidden passions and sufferings of men, from moments of private agony which twisted the metal of the soul, and Bogrov must have had more than his share of humiliation. It was at this point that Peter chose to begin.

'I doubt if you've ever made a more momentous decision in your life than the choice of treason,' he said. 'Would you care to explain what led you to it?'

A sad vacancy overcame Bogrov and he answered wearily: 'Treason is not the right word. I no longer recognize the legitimacy of the Bolshevik regime. It is a government of usurpers.'

'You haven't always thought so. You joined the Party, served as a Chekist on field intelligence with the Red militia, enlisted in the cipher department. According to service records, the very model of loyalty. Yet at some time – we don't know when – you began systematically to pass secret information to a foreign power. What happened? Did you wake up in the middle of the night a changed man, or were you always an anti-Bolshevik who chose to infiltrate the Party in hope of destroying it from within?'

'Perhaps in my heart I was always against you, but I revere Marx and believed in Lenin, his false prophet.'

'Until? . . .' probed Peter.

'Until the scales fell from my eyes.' Bogrov gave him an apologetic smile. 'You'd be wasting your time if you try to find out exactly when this came about. You need the information. It would help you to find out how long I've been in contact with the French and how much I've told them. I can't possibly let you know that. You understand my position,' he said in his soft voice. 'From my point of view, *that* would be treason.'

Once again the cul-de-sac. A relay of interrogators, one taking over as the other flagged, had all run up against that soft implacable obstacle. Anxiety and frustration constricted Peter's throat. He reached for the carafe and poured a glass of water. Hatred momentarily overcame him, succeeded by a cold, impersonal dislike that found its way into his narrowed eyes.

Bogrov remained indifferent. Perhaps he was too tired to care. His hands hung limply between his bony knees and he had difficulty in supporting the weight of his head. Untidy strands of hair straggled down the nape of his scrawny neck. Peter stifled the temptation to spray him with a mouthful of water. 'Pay attention!' he rapped out. The spy sighed laboriously and shifted on the hard seat of the chair. The faintest of ironical smiles touched the corners of his lips.

'Make the most of your amusement because I'm about to show that you're the hero of a black comedy,' continued Peter. A look of curiosity rewarded this opening. 'As is usual in this *genre*, the central character had no idea that he is a ridiculous figure. On the contrary, he believes passionately in his own nobility and the purity of his sentiments. He is the lover enduring unspeakable torments to protect the honour of a whore under the impression that she is an unspotted virgin. You know the sort of thing. Take your own case. Here you are, sitting in prison waiting to be shot. Do you know why?'

'Because in your judgement I'm a traitor.'

'Yes . . . but also because in the judgement of the French you're a loyal Communist. Does that strike you as macabre?'

Bogrov's drowsiness vanished. His smile turned hesitant. 'Are you saying they betrayed me? Why should they, even if they mistrusted me?'

'A good question,' said Peter. 'It puzzled me at first. But let us take this step by step. Who recruited you?'

'I refuse to answer that.'

'Well, I'll tell you. No one. You found a way to volunteer your services.'

'Pure speculation. You have no –'

'Be good enough to listen!' Peter interrupted him in quiet, ominous tones. 'We will see where this speculation leads. So your eager offer is received in the Quai d'Orsai. How? Let's say with caution. Intelligence officers are cynical about human nature. Men sell their country out of greed, or because they transfer their loyalties, or from motives of ideology. They can also be blackmailed into treachery. These are crude but effective categories. One possibility is never overlooked: deception.'

He leaned back in his chair concealing the relish he was beginning to feel under a chilling aloofness. A spell was being woven. It could be detected in the atmosphere of the room like a change of temperature.

'Could it be, the gentlemen of the Quai d'Orsai ask themselves, that this Bogrov is being planted on us by the Cheka as a double agent?' he resumed. '*Quelle chose*, we must investigate. An emissary arrives in Moscow with the Comintern delegation, a secret meeting is arranged and the two of you have a little talk. He discovers that you are offering yourself very cheaply, a few francs for expenses, perhaps a bottle of cognac to seal the bargain. Nothing more. Political motivation? You do not want to restore the Romanovs or establish a right-wing dictatorship. Instead you speak about the betrayal of Russian idealism, socialism contaminated by terror. There is a coarse expression in our business. "It comes out of the mouth but it smells like a fart".' Suddenly he recalled the noisome breath of the Chief Investigator and laughed. 'I'm sure they have a similar vulgarity in French. They sniff your Russian idealism and it doesn't smell good to them at all.'

Bogrov was no longer looking at him. His body was twisted sideways in the attitude of a reluctant listener. The defensive posture gave something away. However impassive his expression there was a visceral reaction. The man was, in his way, a true innocent but not a mediocrity. He recognized the force of these conjectures. However stoical he remained about death, the thought that his sacrifice may have been useless must appal him. His throat moved convulsively: he was beginning to suffer.

'We've suspected you for longer than you think,' added Peter untruthfully. 'False information was concocted and you passed it on. The *Sûreté* found themselves chasing non-existent agents and investigating improbable conspiracies. This discredited you entirely. It's a familiar technique but the old tricks are often the best. Are you beginning to see how it all works out?'

A curious choking sound came from Bogrov and drops of sweat trickled down his greying face. Suddenly he put his hand up to his mouth and a thin yellowish vomit escaped through his fingers. Shuddering uncontrollably, he gave up all resistance and allowed the sour and meagre contents of his stomach to spill over his lap and feet. This physical incapacity seemed to fill him with shame. He looked up guiltily and gasped: 'I – I'm – sorry, but I . . . please, let me go – back to the cell.'

'We're not finished yet,' Peter said coldly. He held out his handkerchief. 'Wipe yourself down. I warned you that this would be uncomfortable.'

Striding to the window, he pulled it open to disperse the reek of vomit and stood for some moments while Bogrov ineffectually dabbed at his soiled trousers. To drive the moral advantage home, he remained standing, gazing at the sick man with an air of distaste as he took up the narrative again.

'You'll recall my visit to Paris a short while ago,' he said. 'You notified your contacts of my expected arrival, the fact that I would be carrying documents in the name of Schtern and that I'd stay at the *Hôtel des États Unis*. They reacted in a most peculiar way. Instead of keeping me under discreet surveillance, someone is sent to tread on my heels. I cannot read a newspaper without the fellow looking over my shoulder. Why? Our friends in the *Sûreté* are clever and logical. When they do something like that it's for a purpose. And then, to make their intentions plain, they behave strangely again. You supply them with information that the Bolshevik secret agent Yegudin has a highly valuable list of names connected with naval espionage. They promptly ransack Yegudin's home, put everything neatly back in place except for one significant detail. In other words, a "visiting card" was elegantly left so that Yegudin should know they had paid him a call.'

Bogrov stared at him dully. 'Visiting card?' he asked in a failing voice.

'Yes, a witty gesture.' Peter permitted himself a bleak smile. 'I won't bore you with the details. Of course, there was no list of names, nor did they expect to find one. They were now convinced you were a double agent, Bogrov, and with Gallic politeness they returned you to us. The message read: not wanted.'

He allowed the silence to thicken, watching his victim closely. Bogrov gave every indication of being crushed, sitting in his own vomit with body slumped, gazing wretchedly towards the window as if contemplating a bid for suicide. He rubbed his eyes and drew his palms down the length of his face. Several times he seemed about to say something but shook his head hopelessly and remained speechless.

Eventually, Peter said: 'You will want to think about all this. I'm sure you'll come to the conclusion that you've made a tragic and terrible mistake. You are going to pay with your life. That is our law and nothing can alter it. But there is still one service you can do for your country and it will ease things for your wife and children. Make a full confession: tell us everything. Or, if you prefer, ask for pen and paper and write it all down.'

He went to the door to summon the guard.

'We all have to die, Bogrov. Perhaps all we can hope for is that it will be quick and merciful. Do your duty and I promise you that.'

Jacob Peters had just turned to the chunky, drably dressed American trades union leader and said: 'Comrade Sullivan, I'd like you to meet Comrade Schtern, one of our most active workers in fraternal relations with the international proletariat, who has spent some time in your country,' when a crippling pain shot through Peter's chest and his left arm went numb.

The great St George Room of the Kremlin spun in a vertiginous haze of white and gold and the huge candelabra with its thousand electric lights soared away like a receding galaxy.

Jacob and the American looked at him queerly. A cluster of black and yellow faces behind them stared with fixed smiles.

'I once heard you speak in Chicago,' said Peter in a faint voice. 'I ...' Giddiness and pain overcame him again. 'Yes, a meeting ... of longshoremen.'

The palace chamber rocked in disequilibrium; marble columns, victory shields commemorating Muscovite conquests, the great ceiling, arches, pilasters, the princely statues gazing in blank rigidity at the shabby throng of foreign trades unionists, all the incongruous, awe-inspiring Kremlin splendour, bobbed soundlessly in waves of darkness.

Jacob Peters steered him into the anteroom. 'You're ill, you shouldn't have come,' he said severely, making him sit on a couch.

'No, it will pass!' He struggled to his feet. Jacob grinned and pushed him down again. 'They'll think you're drunk and it will be bad for international solidarity, because none of them can get a drink until after the speeches. Go home and get to bed.'

Jacob returned to the reception. Reflected in a huge baroque mirror was a collarless man in an ill-fitting suit sitting on an ornate gilt and velvet couch under a painting of Lenin. The man looked like a sick, overburdened minor official; Lenin's picture replaced the well-known painting by Ryepin of Alexander III receiving the homage of his parents. Peter managed a flicker of amusement and felt a little better. A perfect propaganda poster of the new Russia. The weary proletarian official was his own disguise for the occasion as one fitting the popular foreign image of a cloth-capped, tieless, down-to-earth representative of the 'socialist sixth of the world'.

Still shaken but perceptibly stronger, he carefully negotiated the five stone flights of the immense granite staircase that led to the vestibule and called on the commander of the Kremlin Cheka who arranged for him to be driven home. He woke up that night with a burning sensation in his head. Terror had infiltrated his defences, bringing nightmare visions of pursuit by agents of a vengeful God. Bogrov's wife stood in all the corners of his dreams. His heart seemed bruised beyond repair.

Next day he submitted his naked body to the probing instruments of a young doctor. The thoroughness of the examination made it seem that more was at stake than a search for causes of some temporary incapacity. His very fitness for continued service appeared in question and he did not know what he would do with his life if the verdict was unfavourable. The medico went about his work whistling cheerfully between his teeth. His antiseptic hands smelled like those of an embalmer. He engaged in bright relentless gossip as if determined to divert a doomed patient from morbid meditation. Peter's anxiety increased.

'Well?' he asked heavily as he put on his clothes.

The doctor recorded his findings, head bent over the case-history sheet. Looking up briefly, he said: 'Nothing fatal,' and continued writing. The tone was humorous.

'No heart disease?' Peter persisted, unreassured. 'I had all the signs.'

Laying his pen aside, the other said: 'I'd wager that you were once a medical student. Pain in the chest, left arm numb, headache: diagnosis, heart attack.' He pushed his hands into the pockets of his white coat and projected a mocking lower-lip. 'Phantom symptoms, comrade. Apart from slightly high blood-pressure, I'd say your trouble is nervous exhaustion. How old are you? Thirty-eight?'

'Yes.'

'Well, there you are, you're not getting any younger,' the doctor said, uttering the platitude with the supercilious arrogance of a man on the right side of thirty. 'I suppose you work sixteen hours a day building socialism like the rest of us, take your worries to bed and sleep badly. It won't do,' he warned briskly. 'I'm recommending a complete break for at least a month. Immediately.'

'Not immediately,' said Peter.

He was waiting for a confession: only that would cure him. And the latest report from the Lubianka was that prisoner Bogrov had called for writing materials. Hope, like a narrow shaft of light, penetrated his interior gloom.

*

Bogrov wrote steadily for a day and a night. A folding table had been installed in his cell and strict orders issued that he was not to be disturbed. He covered page after page in minute handwriting, occasionally pausing for meditation before plunging back into his task. The only interruption was when food was brought by the guard. He consumed it absently but ravenously, cleaning the mess-tin with his tongue, and there was something equally ravenous in the way he wrote, as though through it he tasted his life to the last drop.

Restlessness drove Peter to the prison to watch him through the peephole. Bogrov's face was flushed. Like a poet seized by inspiration, he seemed totally oblivious of his surroundings, lips moving as he silently read a paragraph over, deleting an unsatisfactory word and replacing it with another, gazing into space now and then with dazed, excited eyes.

Peter could scarcely contain his impatience for the document to be finished. He wrote his own hopes into it: it would tell him all he needed to know, abolish the ignorance that was his greatest peril, free him from the obsessive fear that every move he made was being followed with sardonic amusement by a powerful and secret enemy whose agents might at that very moment be engaged in further betrayals. Bogrov's treachery had nullified all codes, rendered locks insecure, aroused the spectre of hidden accomplices. Now, watching him assiduously commit his revelations to paper, he felt an odd kind of gratitude, akin to affection. With regret, he reflected that it was a last act of contrition. Before the peace it brought could be fully savoured Bogrov's life would swiftly be terminated.

'Give him these,' he told the prison commandant, handing over some cigarettes. 'A smoke may sweeten his last hours.'

At nightfall on the second day, when only the echoing footsteps of guards pacing the stone corridors disturbed the prison silence, the spy was seen to have vacated his writing table. The commandant had the cell unlocked. 'Have you finished?' he asked. Bogrov shook his head. 'I'm too tired. I must sleep tonight,' he replied apathetically. With an understanding nod (orders were to be sympathetic) the commandant gave him the cigarettes, lit one for him and remained until it was safely extinguished. 'Pleasant dreams,' he said as he left. Just before the guard went off duty he peeped into the cell and reported to the relief officer that the prisoner was asleep, his hands, according to regulations, resting on top of the blanket.

The following morning the telephone rang in Peter's office as he dictated messages to his secretary. 'Bogrov is dead,' said the caller. Curtly, with a wry movement of his lips, Peter said: 'I'll come immediately.' The secretary noticed nothing unusual in his manner when he dismissed her.

He lay exactly as he'd been found, stretched out on the blood-soaked mattress, his face grey and bitter under the dim electric light. Fibres of cloth were caught under his blue fingernails, showing that he'd clawed at the blanket in his last paroxysm. He had died agonizingly, by his own hand. The instrument of suicide, congealed in blood, stuck out of his neck. It was the steel nib of the pen with which he'd written his confession. Bogrov had used it to rip open his right jugular vein. Then he'd laid his hands on top of the blanket to avoid arousing the suspicions of the guard and choked in the welter of his blood; for so slight a corpse there was a lot of it.

'Who'd imagine he'd do himself in like that?' the prison commandant remarked disgustedly, adding in self-defence: 'You said he was to have writing materials as long as needed and he insisted on pen and ink.'

Peter shrugged with indifference. 'It's out of my hands now,' he said, rejecting responsibility both for Bogrov's death and the manner of it. Each had had his role to play and neither of them had questioned the rules of the game. He glanced at the corpse with grudging respect. A rusty pen-nib. It must have taken a great deal of determination to get it to do the job. Well, good luck to him. To kill oneself was the choice of a free man.

Gathering up the pages of confession, he hurried back to his room. Tolya Lieberman, moving his long thin legs as delicately as a crane, met him in the corridor. With farcical solemnity, he asked: 'Is it true? About Bogrov?' His eyes blinked earnestly behind the foggy lenses of his glasses. 'Did we get the information out of him?'

Parodying an official spokesman, Peter replied dryly: 'The Soviet Government has no knowledge of the existence of such an individual and no further comment will be made.' Before closing his door, he said: 'See that I'm not disturbed.'

Rain was falling on the city from a dark and funereal sky. Rooftops glistened black beyond the window. The sky shed an ecclesiastical gloom like the shadows that gather in old monasteries, a suitable atmosphere in which to read a message from a dead man. He switched on the light, settled into his chair and turned eagerly to the manuscript. Like a student's paper, it was neatly headed 'Konstantin Fedorovich Bogrov, Lubianka Prison,' followed by the date, and opened with an arresting paragraph.

'No man can know the truth about himself. He can only guess at the source of his feelings or the origin of the thoughts that arise in his mind. Put together every biographical fact and the sum does not add up to a life. A man exists in himself as a fish swims in the mystery of an ocean.'

Having thus dismissed the utility of facts, Bogrov then briefly set out the circumstances of his childhood, commenting assertively: 'After my parents died I was taken in by a bachelor uncle. I had no friends of my own age, nor did I need them. A child playing alone creates his own world so completely that it comes as a shock when others intrude. The beautiful world of the imagination is shattered. He is told to wash his face, tie his shoelaces, eat food he dislikes, perform tiresome duties. He is punished for breaking rules he does not understand and so is introduced to the tyranny that will oppress him all his years and instil in him the desire to oppress others in return. I freely admit that I chose to study law out of a perverse ambition to one day sit in judgement over my fellows and exercise upon them powers of life and death.'

A morbid, guilt-ridden personality rose out of the pages. The inoffensive Bogrov had detected in himself a monstrous capacity for evil and fled from it in fugitive terror. He married, he said, for sanctuary, in the hope that the normality of family life would shelter him from his pursuing demons. Soon he came to believe that the deformities in his nature were a product of the social environment, and that abnormal sensitivity to influences had caused him to internalize the cruelties of life in Imperial Russia, whose 'angel of evil' in latter days was embodied in Rasputin. The destruction of this imperium had become synonymous with his own exorcism. He'd joined the 'Party of Avengers', as he called the Bolsheviks, in preference to its rivals because it promised a drastic rearrangement of society that would liberate the people and exclude injustice for ever. Bitter was his disillusion as he witnessed the crushing of Socialism's enemies turn to the extermination of its friends. The people's freedom was snatched away and replaced by famine and terror. Lenin, 'the new angel of evil', had erected a pyramid of privilege more absolute than its predecessor and now demonstrated his cynicism by introducing the New Economic Policy that brought the greedy morality of the market-place back into public life. And so on, and so on.

Bogrov meditated assassination but frankly admitted his temperament was unequal to an act so blatant and self-advertising. He also believed that Lenin's autocracy would find reincarnation in someone no less severe and that the Party would seek reprisal in a wave of vengeful terror. As had been shown at Kronstadt, where even peaceful opposition led to the furious slaughter of thousands, his misgivings were justified. But long before this event he had decided to undermine Soviet rule from within by passing its secrets to a foreign state. France, as the most antagonistic of the Great Powers to Bolshevism, became his choice.

The tone so far was not one of repentance. Peter smoked nervously and read on, his hopes dwindling as the information he sought failed to appear. The character of the writing changed: it became less orderly, the even letters formed with thick impetuous strokes as though to give an added, declarative emphasis to the writer's statements.

'I regard myself as a prisoner of war,' Bogrov had written, 'bound by honour not to disclose anything that may be of use to the enemy. I came very close to breaking point when you described so convincingly how the *Sûreté* itself betrayed me. Your guesswork had the neatness of mathematical logic, and it almost destroyed me. There is nothing more annihilating than total despair. One more twist of the knife and I might have told you everything, pouring out my bitterness as my body emptied itself of vomit. I thank God for giving me the strength to hang on to a thread of resolve. For the truth or otherwise of your speculation is immaterial. The government of Poincaré is almost as loathsome to me as my own. I used the hatred of France for Bolshevism for my own purposes, and a plague on both your houses. You do not know the extent of the damage I've caused. It is greater than you may think and its effects will long outlive me. In the terror of my death, this knowledge sustains me. There is nothing more I have to say to you. (Signed) K. F. Bogrov.'

A separate sheet of paper was headed: 'A Last Message To My Wife.' 'Dearest Elena,' it said, 'perhaps they will not permit this to reach your eyes. If not, the burden of my silence will be hard for you to bear. You know nothing of the cause I served, only that one morning you awoke and the place at your side was empty. When I stood in the darkness of our room looking down at you and our sleeping children, that act of necessary cruelty was the hardest thing I had ever done in my life. Since then there has not been a moment when I have been free of the pain of my love for you. You are innocent and I have made you suffer. Russia is full of grieving, innocent women. Kiss the children good-bye for me and forgive me every day of your life, Kostya.'

Peter screwed up the page and threw it into the waste-basket. Failure spread its numb paralysis through his mind. From the adjoining office the clicking of typewriters tapped out a message of futility. Bogrov's secret was still intact and as long as it remained so his department would be a hazard to the security of the state instead of an asset. The idea disabled him: it threatened his very survival: he fought against it with all the dwindled resources of his will. What the dead man refused to divulge must be discovered. Doggedly, he began the process of elimination. Everything Bogrov had done during his service as a cipher clerk, every message he'd handled, all the information to which he'd had access, must be sifted. Again and again, if necessary.

Fatigue eventually ground him to a halt. It was after midnight. Stumbling to his feet, he shrugged on his coat and was about to leave the office when something occurred to him. He went slowly back to his desk, hesitated, then stooped to search through the waste-basket for Bogrov's last message to his wife.

Wryly, he smoothed out the crumpled page, folded it neatly and put it into his pocket.

The woman stood in the rain, alone in an otherwise empty street. He stopped and looked at her in silence for a moment.

'I have something for you,' he said.

She took the sheet of paper from him and began to unfold it.

'Don't read it here,' he said. 'Wait until you get home,' and walked rapidly away, his lame heart knocking, afraid to look back.

3

Jacob Peters had sent a note. It said: 'Come to my place tonight. There will be a little something to drown our sorrows.'

The formula suggested a party and when he arrived at the rooms Jacob now occupied in a mansion near the Bolshoi Theatre ('Commissars live in palaces') a blast of conviviality struck him as he entered. Peters liked to get a crowd together occasionally, and judging by the flushed faces and inebriate merriment sorrows were already liberally awash.

'Holla, Piatkov!' somebody yelled. 'Good to see you. Chuck off your coat and have some fun!'

A thickset Chekist officer plunged out of the crowd and encircled his neck in boozy affection, at the same time retaining hold of a blonde partner. The girl was painfully thin and seemed dazed by the gaiety that surrounded her. She was dressed in blue velvet rubbed bare under the arms and on the seat. Her feet were encased in soldier's boots. She smiled nervously with bad teeth.

Peter removed his colleague's embracing arm. 'I will do my best,' he said, unsmiling. They disliked one another.

'What's the matter with you? It's a short life.' The fellow punched him amiably in the chest and lurched away.

The overcrowded room generated an uncomfortable heat. Discarding his sheepskin jacket and fur hat, Peter began a scrutiny of the party guests. Some were laughing and talking loudly, some tried to dance in the restricted space available, others gathered convivially around a battered upright piano. A Red Army officer hammered at the keys. Like the tipsy Chekist, those surrounding him were gaily pessimistic. In rousing voices, they sang:

Lice in our overcoats and yet
Faith in our hearts . . . the wagons sway.
Whether by shot or bayonet
Death's sure to take us on its way.

Jacob Peters approached waving a half-filled glass. He had grown a Lenin moustache and pointed beard but, lacking the narrow Asiatic eyes and high broad cheekbones of the leader, they gave the impression of having been comically fastened to his square Germanic face.

'It's no good looking. She's not here,' he said, grinning.

Peter glanced round ironically. 'Who isn't? Everybody else is.'

'You know very well. Your dearest comrade. I telephoned Pushkino and practically threatened to bring her under armed escort. She refused. Too busy with the widows and orphans.'

'You promised me something to drink,' Peter said, looking away.

'That little something you'll get. Grub, no. We had some Baltic herring but these hungry bastards haven't left a tail.' Jacob filled a glass to the brim from a Georgian *hillada*, a brown earthenware jug used for storing wine, but the stuff looked more like raw spirit. 'What are you screwing your eyes up for?' he asked in injured tones. 'It may not be the best, but it's not rotgut, either.'

'*Na zdrovie!*' said Peter, swallowing the tumblerful in one huge gulp. Tears streamed from his eyes and liquid fire scorched his gullet. The drink was *pertsovka*, vodka flavoured with red pepper. It felt damned good: he needed it. 'More,' he ordered, holding out the glass. The second thawed his heart, the third anaesthetized Kronstadt, Bogrov's wife, failure. It effervesced in his bloodstream. With the fourth in his fist, he ploughed through the crowd towards a group surrounding the Shulkins.

'A pity Lydia couldn't come,' said Nina, gazing at him, as she usually did, in guarded fascination.

'Sweetheart,' he said, peering intensely at her snug and shapely bosom, 'let us speak of the madness of love. What does the poem say? "I dream of nocturnal feasts and young women garlanded with flowers", or something of the sort.'

'Peter, you are a little drunk,' Nina remarked, laughing

uneasily. She glanced at Semyon but he was addressing an earnest lecture on Lenin's new economic policy, NEP, to a stupefied audience of three and did not notice.

Peter drained the *pertsovka* and absently placed the empty glass in Shulkin's hand, who absently received it.

'Your blue, blue eyes,' he said emphatically. A morbid expression had come over his face. He stared at her chillingly as if she were an intrusive stranger. Yet in reality it had nothing to do with her. He was his own stranger. It was not only that Jacob's apartment, the people, Nina, himself, had suddenly become remote, the noise they all made reduced to an abrupt diminuendo. A stunning awareness of time as a tangible dimension had overtaken him, as travelling by train across Europe he had glanced up from his newspaper and watched the actual countryside of space fly swiftly past the window. He could see them all, he could see himself, the room they inhabited a lighted cell in one of the earth's great cities, and their brief lives hurtled through time so fast the dark wind brushed his face. He again experienced the bewilderment of the traveller who has outdistanced all he holds precious – his life's luggage mislaid at a station whose name cannot be recalled, to which there can be no return . . .

'You've got frightening eyes,' said the girl. 'You terrify me.'

Another drink was in his hand. He screwed up his frightening eyes and tried to focus the face behind the voice. Perhaps it was another party. Another time? Well, why not?

'I come from a family line of nineteenth-century men,' he confessed gravely. 'That's a shameful burden but you can't just dig a hole and bury it.'

'I'm an actress,' said the girl. 'We're bringing revolution to the theatre. The bourgeois theatre is a corpse sitting on a stage speaking dead words. The new theatre must be a machine for building Socialism. We're Constructivists.' She said it as if reciting something committed to memory, a catechism, and then she said: 'You're cruel. See how cruel your mouth is. I bet you like to beat girls black and blue. It would terrify me to be alone in a room with you.'

She accompanied him home. He walked with rigid steadiness along rocking pavements until a rare *istvoshtchik* picked them up. The emaciated horse had to be stirred by the whip to keep it moving.

As they climbed the stairs to his apartment the girl breathlessly told him that her group was rehearsing a play about a brick factory. The jerky narrative communicated a powerful tension and when they entered his room she stared at him with glittering eyes and exclaimed: 'Why have you brought me here? Don't dare to touch me!'

'Take off your clothes,' he said, going in search of a drink. He returned with a bottle of cognac, two glasses and one of the blue cartons of French cigarettes. The girl was already naked.

'What's your name?' he asked, handing her a drink and slowly sipping his own as his gaze traversed the curves of her slender body. She was beautiful. Her head was a mass of black curls and a bush of black pubic hair contrasted dramatically with the smooth white skin of her belly.

The girl was shivering. She put up a hand to cover her breasts.

'Galya,' she said. Pressing herself against the wall, she watched him narrowly and added: 'I'm a virgin.'

'Get into bed if you're cold.'

'No,' she said, 'not even if you force me.'

Undressing leisurely and watching her through the haze of his smouldering cigarette, he thought she could be the daughter of Modigliani's 'The Italian Woman'. There was a southern sturdiness about the pelvis and her thighs were slightly too heavy in proportion to the delicate shoulders and young conical breasts. Caucasian probably. Nineteen or twenty. He stubbed out the cigarette and slowly stood up.

Without clothes his body had a menacing power. It was hard, sinewy and disciplined to the needs of violence. Its nakedness seemed curiously blatant. Although his head hair was dark brown a coarse reddish growth grew round his genitals and the nipples of his hairless chest were pink and protuberant as in certain species of gorilla.

Galya watched him round-eyed, her lips full and parted. 'No!' she screamed, turning her face to the wall as he approached. For a moment or two he still looked at her with the eyes of a painter – the superb line of neck and shoulders, the narrow back tapering into a small waist, hips curved like the bowl of a stemmed vase and the buttocks, plump and firm as two white melons on slender legs.

She peered over her shoulder, a black curl obscuring a wicked eye and wriggled. Lust flared in him and he pulled her close. The sensation of his hard, trunklike penis against her cleft drove her wild. She turned and fought with primitive savagery, with teeth and claws and fists and butting head, yelling obscenities. Her eyes were brilliant and enormous. It was a war of exultant bitterness. They staggered about the room, collided with furniture, rolled on the floor. Slippery with the lust and sweat, they grappled mercilessly on the hard, soldierly bed. Galya laughed, sobbed, shrieked, and when he entered her she bit his lips and shoulders, shuddering against him with tears of abnegation, triumph and rejoicing.

The desperate night of love was resumed again and yet again when what began in seeming earnest was reacted in playfulness but with no less vigour. She defeated him at last. His blood felt weak and clear, and when he awoke from a profound, exhausted sleep she was up and about, singing, a smell of coffee in the air.

'Shall I come again tonight?' she asked.

'Not tonight,' he said, touching his sore lips.

'When then?'

He drank his coffee thoughtfully. In the morning light she looked like a capricious child.

'Don't you have to act in your brick factory at night?'

'Oh, really!' she exclaimed, exasperated. 'I told you, we're only rehearsing.'

'Write down your address.'

'I will do nothing of the sort,' Galya said petulantly. Pouting at Lydia's portrait drawing, she declared: 'Is she the reason?'

He smiled wearily. 'Write down that address, then go and make your bricks like a good little Constructivist.'

'I'll go, but I won't write down anything.' Nevertheless, before she left she scribbled on a piece of paper, screwed it up and flung it in his face.

He lay a little while longer thinking calmly of nothing much, then got up and walked naked to the window. Oblique rays of morning sunshine glinted on the river. A cargo boat thrustfully drew a wide swathe through the dark green water. He felt good and confident and glad to be alive in a time when the flow of history was tidal and immense.

Part Three

BERLIN

Chapter Eight

Walking in early afternoon sunshine through the tree-rustling Unter den Linden, not entirely in possession of her own reality, Lydia found that Berlin had worked its first surprise. Something repressed in the years of famine and civil war had begun to stir: life was taking on a kind of irresponsibility. The sour, hopeless stench of human misery she could do so little to alleviate was left behind. Berlin's own savage contrasts of fat-bellied gluttony, war cripples and hunger were somebody else's problem. It gave her a bonus she'd not expected, a sense of liberation.

Newsboys dodged along the crowded boulevard shouting headlines from the latest edition of 'BZ'. Sensations were the order of the day and no one took much notice. They turned instead to the financial columns to read the noon stock reports on the falling value of the mark. The pillars of capitalism crashed soundlessly in the bright afternoon and she felt an absurd, gaseous elation which made everything seem possible. It was not unlike an excursion into her youthful anarchic past when she stepped out of the train at the Gare du Nord with a marvellous conviction that whatever she demanded of the future would be forthcoming. But in the Paris of her nineteenth year the happiness of wine, bread, cheese and strong tobacco could be bought by the poor for pennies. Here and now money speculators thronged the Linden enclaves of luxury snapping up whatever was going on the cheap while ordinary Berliners ate frost-bitten potatoes and smoked cigars made of cabbage leaves. The sunshine mirage of the past faded. There was work to be done.

She stopped outside Bister's dress shop and gazed critically at the spectral, unsmiling woman in ill-fitting clothes reflected in the window of simpering dummies. The dress belonged to Nina, her shoes were scuffed, darned cotton stockings wrinkled her ankles. The hurricane of revolution had stripped her of personal belongings and clothes she'd been offered in Moscow, modish enough in 1917, would scarcely suit an aristocratic emigré living in 1920s Berlin off the proceeds of jewels salvaged from Bolshevik expropriation. 'How much can I spend?' she'd asked Peter. 'Whatever's necessary,' he said in reply. The money was now in her purse. It could have come from a Fabergé oval emerald in diamond setting she'd inherited from her grandmother. The idea was amusing. She was already entering into her new role.

But crossing the threshold of the shop she hesitated, suddenly unnerved by an opulence of gleaming mirrors, soft carpets and warm scented air. A fat Pekinese ambled the length of its lead and sniffed her feet. Fashionable ladies stared in remote disdain at her intrusion. It was a world she'd not visited for more than ten years, that she'd almost forgotten existed. A neat, middle-aged assistant in black came forward and, making an instant assessment, inquired patronizingly: '*Was darf es sein, Madame? Kann ich Ihnen helfen?*'

Lydia's eyes narrowed. '*Vielleicht*, perhaps,' she replied in the old cool manner that had commanded subservience in the far more exclusive salons of the Faubourg St Honoré. 'I want to choose some dresses. What have you got to show me?'

The assistant again inspected her shabby attire and gave a pursed smile. 'How much are you prepared to pay, Madame? If you say what you can afford I will see if we have something suitable.'

'Bring out the best you have and kindly leave it to me to decide if it's suitable.' Lydia sat on a spindly gilt chair and turned the pages of a book of fashion-plates with an air of boredom.

Excitement spread among the other customers as they sniffed drama. Surely a policeman would be summoned to eject this evidently unhinged, half-starved creature who, from her appearance, could hardly have two *groschen* in her pocket. The assistant was undecided, recognizing authority in Lydia's firm, controlled voice. Finally, a flush on her sallow cheeks, she pulled a number of Bister's choicest creations from their hangers and spread them on the counter. Lydia rejected, selected and called for more, then disappeared into the fitting room with several of her choice. Some fifteen minutes later she emerged carrying one over her arm and handed the rest to the woman.

'Send these to the Hotel Bristol,' she said, ignoring the fact that she'd become the centre of interest. 'Now I should like to choose some accessories.'

Hats, underwear, silk stockings, scarves and shoes were added to the pile before she rose and walked with military stride to the fitting room with a complete change of wardrobe. Business was entirely suspended as the other ladies waited for her to re-emerge. The thick velvet curtains parted. An involuntary murmur of astonishment arose at Lydia's transformation. 'Is it an advertisement?' someone asked, puzzled.

Herr Bister himself had been brought from his office and was less impressed. He hurried forward and waved a soft, peremptory hand at the costly purchases.

'How would you like to pay for these, Madame?' he demanded, cuttingly polite.

Lydia looked down at his short, plump figure. She opened her bag and rustled some crisp banknotes.

'Will English sterling be satisfactory?'

A mercantile gleam shone in the costumier's eyes at the sight of the splendidly sound currency of the Bank of England.

'Madame, of course! Most certainly!' He shot a severe glance at his cringing assistant as if she had sacrilegiously questioned the financial solvency of the British Empire itself. 'Did you say you are staying at the Bristol? I shall send everything over immediately, by special delivery, without a moment's delay. May I inquire Madame's name?'

'Countess Alexandrova,' said Lydia.

Herr Bister followed her all the way to the door.

In the next leisurely hours she went into Friedlander's, the goldsmith, and selected two brooches, visited Lohse's perfumery to pick up some crystal bottles of scent and had her hair dressed in the *salon des dames* of the Hotel Adlon. A cosmopolitan chatter in the thronged foyer stilled momentarily as she left the salon and paused before a large mirror. The dream impression became intensified.

Watching her with a hint of amusement was a slender young

woman elegantly costumed in black except for a green chiffon scarf fastened at the throat by a brooch. A cloche hat of green velvet fitted closely on her shining dark shingled head. The face was that of a vaguely familiar stranger: high oblique cheekbones, small classical nose, large grey eyes of a singular light colour, an astringency about the firm compressed lips.

Lydia looked at the young woman judiciously, decided she would do quite well, and walked quickly out of the hotel to keep an appointment at Bauer's Café a short distance down the Unter den Linden at the corner of Friedrichstrasse. A wry anticipatory smile touched the corners of her mouth. Passing boulevardiers subjected her to favourable appraisal. Her smile broadened. They were ogling the ankles of a soldier of security about to begin a secret assignment.

The summons to the Cheka, a week earlier, had taken her by surprise in the middle of an argument with the Pushkino food commissary for extra rations. Harsh words had been exchanged and an angry, red-faced official threatened to report her to the Party Control Commission for anti-Soviet phrasemongering. When the telephone rang in the Refugee Centre and a curt voice ordered her to appear before a Commissioner of Security it was natural to assume that the idiot had carried out his threat. A car was sent for her. 'Am I under arrest?' she flippantly demanded of the chauffeur, glancing at the pistol on his belt. 'Orders to bring you to Moscow,' he grunted and said not another word before handing her over to the guard at the Central Cheka.

An escort marched her to the administrative section through a machine-gun clatter of bureaucracy as military clerks jabbed stiffly at the keyboards of massive typewriters. The atmosphere was that of a staff HQ in the midst of major operations. Filing cabinets slammed shut, telephones jangled, voices spoke with quiet urgency. What could this busy organization want with her?

They went through a door and the noise suddenly ceased.

'Good, the Chief is waiting for you,' said a pleasant young officer, springing to his feet. 'I'll take you to him right away.'

'Am I in trouble?' she asked.

'Why, have you got a guilty conscience?' He grinned disarmingly. 'If so, you're in the wrong department.' He rapped softly at the door of the inner office, put his head inside and said: 'Comrade Alexandrova's arrived.'

'Come in, please!' a voice called.

A solitary lamp illumined the desk and the room was heavily curtained to exclude daylight. Half in shadow, the Chief's face was further concealed by the hand that propped up his forehead as he bent over some papers.

'Close the door and sit down,' he said without glancing up. 'We have a lot to discuss.'

Her perplexity increased: the voice was Jacob Peters's but the tone, quiet and impersonal, made no concession to their long acquaintance. He was not alone. The erect uniformed figure of Peter Piatkov stepped into the circle of light and greeted her gravely. The two men were indicating that this was an official confrontation. It was as though she were on trial.

Jacob leaned back in his commissar's leather chair and stroked his neat blond beard. His eyes were sharp.

'I'm going to put you a question. Think carefully before you answer.' Pausing to underline the effect of his words with silence, he said: 'Have you ever considered enlistment in the Cheka?'

She stared at him in astonishment while her mind reviewed the manifold activities of Dzherzhinsky's Extraordinary Commission Against Counter-Revolution and Sabotage. It could be stern but brotherly, cold and retributive, selfless or corrupt; however it functioned, the element of fear was never absent.

'No, it's never occurred to me,' she replied warily.

'Why not? You've got the right qualifications. Party member in good standing, fluent in foreign languages, former partisan commander . . . and, not least, service as an undercover agent.'

'Undercover agent! If you're referring to the old days in Paris, the truth is less romantic. All I did was carry messages to scattered groups of anarchists.'

Jacob lowered his eyelids ironically. 'Your adventurism, as we remember, also included bank robbery, currency smuggling and terrorist activities.'

'Surely,' she said, 'I don't have to remind you and Peter what a mess I made of that.'

'Just growing pains, Lydia. After all, how old were you – nineteen, twenty? Now you're a seasoned Bolshevik, politically and emotionally mature. Why not join us?'

She looked at Peter, puzzled by his silence. The glance he returned remained noncommittal. This was something she'd have to decide on her own. There was a gulf between her experience and theirs. Whereas the revolution had brought her into the bosom of the people, made her one with its suffering, they'd become the praetorian guard of State and Party, vigilant policemen of hard-won Soviet security. It had turned out to be a dirtier job than expected, more tarnish than lustre. Someone must do it but it had no appeal for her. She had a fastidious preference for clear moral choices: fighting an avowed enemy, feeding the hungry.

She groped in her tunic pocket and extracted a half-smoked handrolled cigarette. Jacob Peters quickly produced a well-filled case and held it out. 'Try Virginian tobacco,' he suggested. 'A present from foreign comrades.'

'Thanks, I've got used to these.' She lit the stub and breathed out a lungful of acrid smoke.

The meaning of the gesture was not lost on Peters. 'Our offer doesn't appeal to you,' he said without affability.

'Not just now.'

'Why, are you thinking of your refugees?'

'Yes,' she said. 'I'm thinking of the famine.'

'It's no longer a valid excuse,' Jacob Peters argued. 'Ships are now on the way from America with food, medical supplies and teams of relief workers. It hasn't been an easy decision for us but we've allowed them in. This leaves you free for other duties.' He came round the desk and loomed over her. 'I've not brought you here for a Marxist analysis of the struggle between world capitalism and the workers' state. Shooting may be over but not the war. The other side will stop at nothing – the knife in the back, the kick in the groin, the poisoned handshake.' With bristling beard and flashing eye, he continued to harangue her on revolution, *partiinost* and her duty to history in flagrant imitation of Leo Trotsky.

'I'm happy to be made redundant by American bully beef and milk powder,' she said. 'What do you have in mind for me?'

'One thing at a time.' Jacob miraculously returned to his normal, dapper self and smiled with sly triumph. He rang a bell to summon his aide. 'Comrade Alexandrova is ready to fill in the questionnaire,' he said.

The young officer led her to a small room, empty except for a table and chair. His manner was grave and ceremonious. Paper, pen and ink were provided. 'Write down everything – social origin, education, membership of organizations, details of relatives living abroad, the history of your life.'

'Everything? Alpha and omega?'

'No,' he said, 'not omega. The end is written only when the file is closed.'

The solemn, irrevocable process, initiation into a secret order, was sealed by the swearing of an oath to guard all information acquired during the course of her duties with her life and to accept death as the penalty for failing to do so. She wrote it out and signed it.

'Now choose a code-name for yourself,' said Jacob.

Noting her indecision, Peter intervened with a suggestion. 'How about Selena?'

Lydia tasted it on her tongue. 'Selena.' Greek for the moon. 'Why not?' she shrugged.

'It was my mother's name,' said Peter, and the message in his eyes was that the last barrier between them had gone.

Jacob produced a bottle and some glasses. 'Another gift from foreign comrades,' he said, baring his teeth in a challenging grin as he poured the three drinks. Short body held stiffly erect, he lifted his glass and announced: 'Welcome to Selena . . . and to the return of Countess Alexandrova!'

'May she make a triumphal entry into Berlin,' added Peter.

'You amaze me,' Lydia said, sipping her drink thoughtfully.

The next day, closeted alone with Peter, a story of Byzantine intrigue and her part in it was unfolded. It involved secret negotiations in three capitals – Helsinki, Berlin and Moscow – known to only a handful of people. Irreconcilable enemies were engaged in forming a pragmatic alliance by means of deceit, betrayal and double-dealing.

'Under the Versailles Treaty Germany is forbidden to maintain a general staff or manufacture weapons of war,' explained

Peter. Dry and matter-of-fact as his tone remained, joy of the enthusiast shone in his eyes. 'At the beginning of this year *Sondergruppe R*, a secret department of the German War Ministry, approached Kopp, our representative in Berlin, with an interesting proposition. They will rebuild our armament industry on condition that Russian factories under German technical management produce airplanes, submarines, guns and shells for the *Reichswehr*. For this purpose they are prepared to overlook the fact that we are Bolshevik devils who eat babies for breakfast. Kopp reported to Trotsky and received instructions to explore the offer further. We received instructions to smell out *Sondergruppe R*.'

'And I'm one of the bloodhounds?' Lydia laughed. 'Even with a false beard I doubt if I could pass for a German general. Or am I supposed to be very feminine and friendly?'

'In some cases,' said Peter, 'you'd do better as a good looking boy.' He looked at her with some misgiving. 'Don't think I'm not jealous. Jacob chose you for this assignment. I was not happy about it.'

She leaned back, hands thrust into her pockets, and whimsically gazed at her clumsy felt boots. Peter had nothing to fear. The idea of sexual adventure with some stout Prussian officer was ridiculous. The only affair she craved was gastronomic, to fill her empty stomach with sausages, sauerkraut and good German pastries.

'I'll try to justify Jacob's confidence,' she said, maintaining a light tone. 'My one self-indulgence will be over-eating.'

'That is not reckoned in the Cheka as disloyalty,' said Peter. Becoming businesslike again, he explained the advantages of the German offer and the suspicions Soviet intelligence had formed that there were those in *Sondergruppe R* who regarded the strengthening of Russia as too big a price to pay even to build up their own arsenals.

'Here is a dossier on one man we particularly suspect.' He passed her a blue folder. 'Herr Professor von Huberhof.'

Lydia opened the dossier and was confronted by a photograph. The face was not that of a fat Prussian. Von Huberhof looked lean, quizzical, irreverent. His eyes were sharp and mocking as if observing the discomfiture of an opponent. He smiled

with his mouth shut. He looked intensely and silently alive. Above all, he looked dangerous.

Peter watched her closely, but her expression remained non-committal. She could be a commander in the field reading a map to determine the lay of the land.

'I'd like to study this file,' she said. 'Is there an empty room somewhere?'

'Next door,' he replied. 'I'll see that you're not interrupted.'

'By the way, how do we reconcile our negotiations with the war lords with the call to German workers to start a revolution?' she asked on her way out.

'The *Reichswehr* does not believe in a German revolution. Nor, I suspect, does Lenin, not after the failure of last month's Communist rising in Upper Silesia. The harsh fact is we need the generals and their technicians more than German slogans of proletarian solidarity. Don't be shocked, Lydia,' he said, cynically spreading his hands, 'that's the way history is made.'

She looked at him down the length of her nose, tilting her head in a characteristic pose of disdain, and said: 'Next you'll be telling me that Machiavelli was a Marxist.'

When she left the building the blue haze of spring filled the dusky streets and scent of lilies of the valley filtered into Moscow from woods surrounding the city. Lydia breathed in deeply, possessed by a sense of excitement she'd not felt for a long time. Soldiers noting her stained uniform gave her comradely greetings, imagining that like themselves her war was now over. She pressed on eagerly, returning to the Pushkino refugees for the last time.

The dark, compact figure of Peter rose from behind the screen of an ornamental rubber plant as he monitored her progress through the café. Bending over her hand and grazing it with his lips, he murmured: 'Life repeats itself.'

Zigeuner music. The smell of coffee and sweet cakes. Black-coated waiters waltzing with their trays among the crowded tables. Smart women wearing blood red lips and laughing in shrill soprano. It could be ladies' afternoon in Reiter's on Nevsky Prospekt in doomed pre-war St Petersburg. Some were talking loudly in Russian: the gossip was unchanged.

‘Unbelievable,’ Peter said, staring at her.

‘Yes, it’s very peculiar.’ She gave a husky, bewildered laugh. ‘I’m not absolutely certain who I am.’

He said: ‘I pinched myself when you came through the door. In came the shocking girl I first met in London. But the look in the eyes. The battle-scars show. Did you know that’s how to tell a great painter? Rembrandt could convey the experience of a lifetime in the way he painted eyes.’

Coffee was brought. She talked and smiled and listened. A swarthy fiddler leaned over her and scraped a yearning melody. Then he vanished. It was all meaningless, without reality. Perhaps that’s how it was, a series of arbitrary appearances flaring up in impenetrable darkness. No past, no present, no future, only a useless attempt to impose logical progression on formlessness and call it time, call it history.

‘... through the window. Do you see him?’ asked Peter.

‘Who?’ she queried vaguely, staring at him like a somnambulist.

‘The one by the lamp post.’

With an effort she brought herself into focus and followed the direction of his gaze. A thickset man with powerful shoulders stood on the pavement outside impassively watching the passing crowd.

‘Spichalsky,’ said Peter. ‘Services available in emergency.’

She nodded. ‘Code name Pochhammer. Contact by pneumatic post at Linstrasse 47. Allow two hours for delivery then rendezvous at the destination board of Bahnhof Alexanderplatz. In dire necessity only.’

‘It doesn’t have to be dire. Spichalsky knows the pitfalls of Berlin. He can be very useful.’

‘I’ll try to avoid the pitfalls unaided.’

‘I see you’re recovering from the shock of arrival,’ he said, a shade ruefully.

‘Slowly.’

‘Good. Don’t rush things. Find an apartment, settle in, cultivate White Russian friends. It’s necessary to get used to the water before starting to swim.’

‘I’ll do my best, Peter, I promise.’ She watched as Spichalsky looked towards the window, stared briefly as if signalling through the glass, then walked away.

'Pity I can't stay until you've got properly organized. I have to leave in an hour.' A bleak look entered his face. 'For once it won't feel like going home.'

'We'll meet again . . . soon,' she said, touched by the chill of that solitude that surrounded him and from which he sent out his signals of love like an insistent S.O.S.

They left the café together.

'*Do svidanye*, Lydochka. And good luck,' he said when they arrived at her hotel, and strode abruptly away.

2

Brushing an invisible speck of dirt from the green plush curtains, Frau Flügel said: 'The princess Sophia was very happy in this apartment. She hated to leave, only her sister's husband, Count Chebyshev, opened a restaurant in Paris. May I ask if you are acquainted with the princess? She moved in the very best circles.'

'No,' said Lydia.

Frau Flügel nodded and released a prolonged 'Ah . . .' It was difficult to decide if it was intended as confirmation of a deep suspicion or of an equally profound disappointment. She was thickset, fortyish and highly curious. Streaks of grey sprang from the centre parting of her dyed black hair, the trace of a bleached moustache showed at the corners of her long upper lip.

'I pride myself on my beds,' she said, her experienced eye continuing its frank scrutiny of the new Russian tenant. 'A good old-fashioned German *Federbett*, the kind in the old days a whole family would sleep in. You don't have a husband, Countess?'

'No,' said Lydia.

'Ah, those dreadful wars! You have a very nice neighbour, Herr Doktor Konrad Neubert. Beautifully preserved for his age. Not that he's old, really. The princess thought him charming. Well, I musn't chatter on so. You look very tired, pale. Recovering from an illness, perhaps?'

'No,' said Lydia.

'Believe me, I understand. We, too, have been defeated. It's always the very best people, the cream of society, you might say, who suffer in such times. What can we do? We're too civilized. And everything is so dear it costs a fortune to have a bath. How can I manage with this inflation? The price of coal, you have no idea!' Frau Flügel looked at Lydia indignantly and said: 'I'm sorry, I really can't stay and talk any longer. I have my work to do.'

It was difficult to know what had offended her as she stumped out of the room, but Lydia saw her go with relief. Perhaps it was the price of coal. She sat in an ancient armchair, lit a cigarette and tried to adjust to her new surroundings. The huge old-fashioned apartment had been split into three self-contained units, each of two rooms, kitchen and bath. She could have put twenty refugees into the bedroom alone without overcrowding. The wardrobe, like Frau Flügel's *Federbett*, was spacious enough to accommodate a family and other massive articles of furniture stood around in gloomy, untenanted silence. The vanished princess Sophia had left some mementoes – a broken celluloid comb, a frayed whalebone corset, wool slippers with holes in the toes. Lydia switched on the light to exorcise her ghost.

A small balcony protruded from her window over Sachsischestrasse, four floors below. Outside Becker's *Bierkeller*, on the corner of the twilit street, a stout bald man emptied a bucket of water on the pavement and brushed it with a stiff broom. The roofs of Berlin-Wilmersdorf made patterns on the skyline like the letters of an unfamiliar language. She had visited the city many times in the past yet now its very ordinariness seemed incredible. How could the world have been going on in much the same way when Russia had been shaken to its foundations?

A gentle knock came at the door. It was the Herr Doktor, clean and shabby black suit bagging at the knees, high celluloid collar, humble but not unassertive eyes set close to a long thin nose. His smile exposed a gleaming set of artificial teeth as he welcomed his charming new neighbour and offered a selection of chivalrous services that, he delicately hinted, could alleviate the bachelor loneliness of both of them.

'Very kind, Doktor Neubert. It's good to know that if I need help I can call on you, but you must not put yourself to inconvenience,' she murmured, edging him out of the doorway with some difficulty. Back in his own apartment, he played the bitter sentimental song '*Wie weit es ist nach Paradis*' on the phonograph and the sound came through the wall like a reproach.

Suddenly, she was tired, tired with a crushing accumulation of fatigue. She threw herself on the bed and fell asleep. An hour or so later her eyes opened to a terrifying ambiguity. She was in an unknown room of an unknown city. She seemed to have dreamed decades of violence, and now someone in that dream was dreaming her.

Chapter Nine

Each day that passed awoke in her responses that had lain dormant the entire turbulent decade since her twenty-first year. Whereas in Russia life had been reduced to stark simplicities, Berlin was paradoxical, confusing, tainted with a seductive corruption. She would lie in the expensive warmth of Frau Flügel's big old-fashioned bath soaping herself in scented lather then breakfast off eggs, rye-bread, honey and other delicacies. She watched the sunshine promenade of rogues and speculators while sipping coffee at a window table of Bauer's Café in Unter den Linden, or sat among the Bohemian fringe of writers, painters and artists' models who frequented the Romanisches Café near the Kaiser Wilhelm Gedächtniskirche. Uprooted Russians were everywhere. Balalaika music and the smell of borsch drifting from doorways of Russian restaurants induced forgetfulness of the famine she'd left behind in fumes of nostalgia. She listened to blazing arguments between protagonists of old political parties – Mensheviks and Kadets, Monarchists, Black Hundreds shrilly proclaiming that Russia had fallen to the Jews – with mute incredulity that so much heat could still be stirred from burnt-out embers.

Berlin amazed and appalled her. It was a city of war cripples and glossy profiteers, hunger and riot, luxury and excess. In the very same street bone-gnawing poverty existed beside clubs pandering to every variety of sexual appetite. George Grosz cartooned the age as a monstrous festival of greed, lust and cruelty. Neo-expressionist painters turned canvases into a frenzied assault against all that the stiff-backed German bourgeoisie held sacred, cinematographers projected images of gross perversity and evangelists proclaimed that the world was coming to an end in orgies of damnation.

In this steaming compost absurd legends took root among

those who still nourished dreams that the simple, misguided Russian people would send the Bolsheviks packing and put everything back the way it was. On the briefest acquaintance someone would tell her, in strictest confidence and as a fact that could be attested on the best authority, that the Western Allies were secretly gathering a new army of intervention. 'By the end of the summer it will be all over.' She also heard of peasants impaling commissars on sharpened pitchforks, suicide battalions still fighting in the Ukraine, and the Tsar and his family mysteriously surfaced somewhere every other day – in Pilsudski's Warsaw, in a remote Scottish castle, arriving in Tibet disguised as Buddhist pilgrims. Familiar rumours were shuffled and rearranged like worn Tarot cards. Some of the ghastly atrocities retailed may well have been true – she and her friends had been shocked and humiliated by similar outbreaks of brutality – but she listened to them with angry scepticism. They were the enemy. Bitter was their weeping by the Spree: if I forget thee O Imperial St Petersburg. And though they grieved for Russia with an exorbitant and hopeless sense of loss, she could not forgive them the mounds of corpses, the bitter price they'd exacted for the surrender of their misused power.

Idleness soon became irksome. Getting used to the water didn't suit her temperament. She wanted to strike out, to take initiatives. The problem was one of direction. For reasons of secrecy she must work independently of the Soviet network in Berlin. Even Spichalsky did not know precisely what she was up to. Moscow relied on her to use her ingenuity. The orders were to penetrate *Sondergruppe R* as a lone agent. How? The intelligence group did not officially exist, although she knew the names of some of its members. Neither instinct nor reason recommended a direct approach. It would probably not be difficult to scrape up an acquaintance with Ernst von Huberhof or one of his friends, but ideally von Huberhof or one of his friends should be led to think he had discovered her.

The café in Kurfürstendamm was very noisy at the morning coffee hour and the man at her side, another brief acquaintance, rustled his newspaper furiously.

'Read that!' he muttered. 'They're not fit to be called human beings.'

He thrust the paper at her – *Vozrozhdeniye* – 'Rebirth', a gutter-sheet belonging to the monarchists. It was the story of brothels for sex-crazed Soviet workers supplied with nationalized women from sixteen to sixty. That, and orgies in the Kremlin, came up every other day of the week.

Neutrally, her voice hard-edged, she said: 'I've already seen it,' and was about to hand it back when a name caught her eye. General Fyodor Yegorovich Nikolaev. In equally bold print was another name, Frau General von Seeckt. An interesting juxtaposition, particularly as one had heard of F. Y. Nikolaev. More than that, the name belonged somewhere among her archaic memories. She looked at the paragraph again, a display announcement of a piano recital in aid of needy Russians.

'Very interesting,' she said, and stared with abstract intensity at the blur of traffic outside the café window, tuning in to the past. Generals passed in cavalry procession, bowed affably across dinner tables, clanked their swords at royal investitures. Too vague. Suddenly, as vivid as yesterday, her mind recalled a vanished afternoon.

The palace gardens of Peterhof, summer 1905, four months into her sixteenth year, the year that men, women and children were massacred outside the Winter Palace. She stood by the Bronze Samson fountain, hating her father because he served as an aide to the murderous Tsar. Water splashed from the lion's throat into a basin of pink marble. The three little Grand Duchesses walked with their English governess along the pebbly shore of the Gulf of Finland under the watchful eyes of a regiment of armed guards strategically posted to prevent kidnapping or assassination. Tea awaited their return. Precociously rebellious, she awaited the revolution.

Stomping on to the terrace came the side-whiskered, bemedalled old gentleman she knew as General Nikolaev muttering soldierly imprecations. She distinctly heard him threaten to shoot the Minister of the Interior and hang the General Staff. In her innocence, she imagined a palace revolt was imminent, but the old man was merely letting off steam. Eyeing her hopefully, he inquired if she ever had reason to visit the Saratov district. It appeared that he'd been banished there for some misdemeanour to become the military governor. 'There's a Tatar in you somewhere,' he remarked, twirling his grizzled whiskers and rolling his bloodshot eyeballs. 'Handsome lot.'

In retrospect, the incident had an old-fashioned charm. Now the old butcher sponsored charity concerts and seemed to have the right connections. The outlines of a strategy began to form in her mind. One had to begin somewhere and that distant acquaintance could be a start.

The recital took place in a house of faded elegance on Friedrichstrasse. Faded lady volunteers dispensed tickets with smiles of charitable sweetness. 'How kind of you to come,' they murmured, handing out cyclostyled programmes.

One half of the large music salon was occupied by a phalanx of silent, stiff-backed Germans with bristling napes and attendant womenfolk, obediently on parade, no doubt, at the orders of the Frau General. In contrast, the Russians were feverishly animated, twisting in their chairs to chatter snobbishly in French and giggling with their neighbours. Closed windows excluded the competition of birds in the tree-filled garden as the sounds of Liszt filled the airless room. A *valse*, a nocturne, musings on religion and solitude: in deference to the needy beneficiaries of the occasion the mood was one of plangent melancholy.

In the front row, blonde hair plaited on the crown of her head like an ageing Rhinemaiden, Madame von Seeckt set her features into a suitable expression of cultural piety. An overweight man beside her polished his monocle and screwed it into his rigid eye. As far as Lydia could make out, the erstwhile military governor of Saratov, Fyodor Nikolaev, who occupied the other flank of the patroness, was having difficulty in keeping awake. Slumped at the level of her shoulder, only his ancient head, tufts of wiry hair sprouting from large ears and gaping nostrils, was visible. 'Bravo!' he cried at the end of each piece, nodding vigorously and clapping his hands but relapsing into somnolence once the music resumed.

'How are you, Fyodor Yegorovich?' she asked, accosting him when the audience began to disperse.

Rheumy eyes blinked, watering with the effort of recognition. 'My dear er –' he began valiantly, seizing her hand.

'Lydia Nikolaievna Alexandrova,' Lydia said. 'You visited

us at Peterhof. My father was attached to the Royal Household.'

'Of course, of course! *Enchanté de vous revoir, Madame*. And how is Prince Nikolai?'

'Count,' she corrected gently. 'He is well. My father will be delighted to hear that I've met you. He will want to know all about it.'

'Excellent! Fine fellow! My best regards!' The General kept hold of her hand and gazed round distractedly. 'Don't leave just yet, my dear. Must say good-bye to Madame Seeckt.'

He hurried over to the Frau General who stood among her officers' wives, sinewy neck proudly extended, and engaged in a competition of flattery ending in a truce when he administered a whiskery kiss to the back of her hand. Returning slightly winded, he said jerkily: 'Insist you have supper with me. An old friend, Prince Nikolai. Must talk. Ever been to *Der Blaue Vogel*?'

'Not yet. I'm new to Berlin.'

'Russian cabaret, my dear Lydia Nikolaievna. Worst performers you ever saw. Frightful! You must come.'

The invitation was, of course, irresistible.

Blue birds would have suffocated in the smoky candle-lit gloom of *Der Blaue Vogel* but Lydia's septuagenarian escort found the atmosphere rejuvenating. He polished off a vast quantity of *Rheinische weisswurst* washed down by hock and brandy. An off-key piano thumped out the song 'Yes, we have no bananas' popular in inflation-ridden Berlin. Tipsy couples revolved on the dance floor. The General laid a trembling hand on her thigh and declared: 'A bit more flesh and you'd be a beauty, my dear.' The gesture was merely nostalgic for he quickly withdrew it and added regretfully: 'Ah, you should have known me in my prime.' There was a short mournful silence before he rallied sufficiently to ask some fretfully suspicious questions about her family, palace officials, protocol and members of the former nobility.

'Fyodor Yegorovich, I do believe you think I'm an impostor,' she said with cool amusement, but his mood had by now improved.

'Just interested, my child, just interested,' was the unruffled reply and, excusing himself, he plodded to the lavatory. He must have been thinking things over there, for on his return he levelled a roguish forefinger and said: 'Got you placed at last, Lydia Nikolaievna. The fellow in Kislovodsk who got a bullet right in his manhood, some police chief, you're the minx who did it.' Sweeping aside protests that this remote episode had been exaggerated, the General growled: 'Just what the scoundrel deserved. Ran off to Paris afterwards, didn't you? Tell me about it. I'm a nosey old man. Like to hear everything.'

Lydia looked across the table at his bloated, hairy face. The eyes were sharp, alive with cunning under the wrinkled lids. She didn't believe a word of the buffoonery. It was clownish greasepaint, a melancholy defiance of the grotesque indignities of old age. There could be no doubt about it: Nikolaev was putting her to the test. She'd better be convincing.

'I went to Paris when I was eighteen,' she said. 'For the usual reasons, and some that were unusual. The family's choices didn't suit me. I hated being rich and spoilt and useless. I was a militant feminist. I still am.'

Her cover story had been well rehearsed. On Peter's advice she'd built it as far as possible out of certain truths. Re-arrange rather than invent, exploit one's ambiguities, remain as true to yourself as is consistent with your purpose: these were his rules. The young Lydia Alexandrova had attained a certain notoriety and the chances of encountering someone who would remember it were high. She had the feeling that such a person was sitting opposite her at the moment.

Pausing to light a cigarette from the guttering candle-flame, she grinned and said: 'You can imagine what an embarrassment it was for my father. I did everything a well-born girl was not supposed to do.'

The General's wet lips parted avidly and he gave her an encouraging nod.

'Politically, too, Fyodor Yegorovich,' she went on disappointingly. 'Father's principles were firm and simple. Love Russia, be loyal to the Tsar and treat your peasants like human beings. Yet there was his only daughter in Paris consorting with wild students who read Proudhon, Bakunin, Marx and Kropotkin. It was fun.'

The old soldier could not restrain himself. Spluttering out a mouthful of brandy, he roared: 'Fun! I'd have warmed your seat with a stick if I'd been Alexandrov.' The idea tickled his senile lechery and he repeated it with variations, several times.

Lydia extended her arm and flicked ash on the floor. 'I wonder,' she mused, 'what mischief you got up to as a young subaltern?'

'I dare say you know a little about that, young woman. Junior officers did what was expected of them. Gambling, carousing, that sort of thing. Some of our young officers also got troublesome ideas.' He glared at her. 'We're not all wooden-heads, my girl. Knew your friend Kropotkin when he wore the uniform of Alexander II's Imperial Guard. Not above reading a book or two myself, either.'

'There, you see. We've all been foolish in our youth.'

'Point taken,' he conceded gruffly, but whether this referred to the irony or endorsed the sentiment remained unclear. 'Have another brandy and tell me more about your adventures in Paris.'

Instinct warned that she was in danger of becoming glib. Too much brandy already. The piano pounded an unrecognizable tune. At a near-by table, a party of Germans linked arms and sang with inebriate sentimentality. 'I have a slight headache,' she said, covering her empty glass. 'What else is there to say? We were all mad about making the world a better place. Reckless and silly, of course, but always for the best of motives. I got into a few scrapes and in one of them a friend of mine was killed, somebody I loved very much.' An unrehearsed catch came into her throat: she felt an absurd prickle of tears. It hurt to think of the past, like wounds incurred in the desperate playground of the nursery. Even the recollection of brief happiness hurt. Life had had a doomed effervescence: when the sparkle went an aftertaste of bitterness remained. 'It sobered me up very suddenly and, typically Russian, I thought I must make atonement. A few twilight years of poverty and obedience. No,' she said, intercepting his gargoyle look of astonishment, 'I didn't run to the Church. You remember what happened in Russia in the 1870s? The students went to the people. Young girls from the best families became mill hands working fifteen hours a day in cotton factories. Boys became woodcutters, blacksmiths and labourers.'

'Saw it with my own eyes,' Fyodor Yegorovich averred, shaking his shaggy head. 'They went off to preach the holiness of labour to *muzhiks*. Came back with spit all over their spectacles. And you – did it purge your guilt?'

'It left me too tired to think about it.' Not, she omitted to add, the shuttling racket of looms in the long sheds but preaching socialism to exhausted women who never had enough to eat. That belonged to the part she could not disclose, her return to Russia to work in the underground movement; exile to Siberia; revolution and civil war. Instead, by carefully transcribing the circumstances, political agitation became social work in Paris slums, Siberia its antithesis, America. It was a journey she might well have taken had her life turned a different corner.

General Nikolaev tugged thoughtfully at his whiskers. His idea of America was naive. Gold prospectors, savage Indians, cowboys and skyscrapers. Why hadn't she remained? Homesick?

'Homesick,' said Lydia.

He stood up unsteadily and steered the wreckage of his obese flesh towards the dim light of *die Herren Toilette*. She took the opportunity to pay a similar visit. A white-faced girl who seemed scarcely sixteen hung over the washbasin in shuddering nausea. The noise outside, masked by the rush of water down wastepipes, resembled the squawking of hilarious parakeets. Face powder and pieces of dirty cottonwool littered the floor. On her return, Lydia mistook the direction of her table and, looking round, caught sight of a man sitting alone in a dark corner. His cigarette glowed, briefly revealing the square heavy face. Comrade Spichalsky. He discreetly gave no sign of recognition. No doubt, he'd come for the cabaret and its Russian artistes, drawn by the same homesickness as the White Russian general. But when she regained her table and looked back Spichalsky had vanished. His abrupt departure lodged in her mind, a small focus of disquiet.

At midnight the pianist played a fanfare and dancers left the floor. A white beam of light fell from the ceiling to reveal the dazzling figure of a man in full Circassian rig of tight-fitting black *tcherkaska*, soft red leather boots, jewelled dagger and rows of cartridges in the tiny pockets of his tunic. He stood, slender and motionless, staring ahead with the remote indifferent gaze of an arrogant mountaineer. A balalaika began playing from the outer darkness and the tightly coiled springs of the dancer abruptly unwound, flinging him into a whirling stamping *Lazatzka.* His blond handsome face sweated and turned scarlet with the effort at virility. Bared lips and clenched teeth remained fixed in an artificial smile.

There was a snuffle at her elbow. Old Nikolaev, returned after a prolonged absence, was quietly weeping into his brandy.

'Our Russia!' he said chokingly, groping for her hand.

Not hers: not even the Russia of her father – bourgeois, stuffy, haunted by insecurity, clinging to its liveried house-servants, crumbling country estates and other remnants of feudalism as the tide of unrest began to sweep it all away. Russia. Women and children starving in the Pokrovsky Nunnery. The drab May Day multitudes in Red Square restless under the whiplash of oratory, hungrily reaching out to the future. Black frosts, grain-starved fields, villages where the dead outnumbered the living: a country tormented beyond endurance but huge with hope.

Yesterday's children of privilege clapped in frenzied nostalgia for the picture book Russia of their prancing puppet. It was fitting. They had emigrated from reality long before 1917, a century before, when it was already being said that one word of truth hurled into Russia would be like a spark landing in a keg of gunpowder. The explosion had shattered them and they still failed to understand why.

When the dancer vacated the spotlight a pair of extremely ragged comedians backed into view and collided. With elaborate apologies they brushed each other down, addressing one another as prince and count almost in parody of Lydia's conversation with Nikolaev after the piano recital. This provoked hilarity among the audience, intensified when the ragged count stooped to pick up what he thought was a coin, examined his fingertips and wiped them resignedly on his grubby trousers. The prince undid the string that supported his baggy pantaloons and, fishing around rather obscenely inside, produced an enormous rubber sausage. 'Please do me the honour of dining with me, my dear Count,' he insisted as he brought out salt, pepper, mustard, eating implements and a fly-whisk from various oddly placed pockets. His pantaloons kept on falling down until he pulled the front of them up and tucked it into the collar of his shirt like a bib. The count replied lugubriously: 'Dear Antosha, Prince Antosha, whom I love like a brother, enough of this Count nonsense. It's taxi-driver Russki, my good German gentleman. Humbly at your service, sir.'

Later in the programme the two comics were joined by a third. One wore a large hooked nose, another's features were those of a sinister Oriental, the last had lines of cruelty painted on his face. All spoke Russian with atrocious accents and their hands were daubed with red. The sketch lampooned a meeting of Lenin, Trotsky and Dzerzhinsky who postured like rival fighting cocks, signed endless death decrees and squabbled over the share-out of loot. With a certain crude vigour it represented Russia in the bloodstained grasp of Jews, Asiatics and renegade Poles.

Fyodor Yegorovich missed this act entirely. He snored against Lydia's shoulder with a noise like the low grumble of a dying volcano. Coarse whiskers tickled her ear and his open mouth stank of brandy and decay. She patiently endured the weight of his shaggy head. He was a sad old villain and she rather liked him.

2

Peter stumbled in the fog of uneasy dreams. A labyrinthine pursuit through blank corridors of menace. Schtern overtook him. 'Who do you think you are?' mocked an echoing voice. At the far end of a library of tombstones stood Hoffman, the ultimate Interrogator. He woke up sweating.

'Who the devil are you?' he demanded, groping for his gun belt. The chair where it hung was missing. Everything was in the wrong place.

Naked from the waist up, the intruder stared briefly and turned away. 'Looking for some kerosene,' he said, rummaging in the cupboard. 'She keeps it somewhere. You wouldn't know where, I suppose?'

'No,' said Peter. His eyes were painful as though sand had got under the lids.

'Expect I'll manage without,' said the man, shrugging.

He went out, leaving the door open, and entered a room on the other side of the passage. He left that door open too.

Galya slept through the interruption, breathing lustfully against the pillow in a tangle of black curls. Livid teethmarks showed on her soft white neck where he'd bitten her. Not so much passion as self-defence, Peter reflected wryly. Her leg still straddled his stomach and her hand lay like a small tenacious crab on his groin. She protested drowsily as he disentangled himself. 'Nice pig! Come back.'

Sounds of market huckstering, the clatter of small workshops, children's voices, filtered through the noise of morning traffic from the surrounding slum streets of Zaradye. In the heat of summer, the squalid atmosphere seemed sultry, Neopolitan. Their clothes had been discarded in haste over the floor. A cockroach, shaken out of his trousers, scuttled into a crack in the wall.

Galya kicked off the bedsheet, wriggling voluptuously in shameless pleasure at being naked and replete. 'You were very wicked last night,' she sighed, passing the pink tip of her tongue over her upper lip. 'Very cruel! I'm bruised all over.'

'Who is the man who came in looking for kerosene?'

'Kerosene! Some fat chance!' Galya snorted, raising a leg and admiring its shape.

Peter splashed some water from an enamel jug into a basin and rinsed his face.

'Does he walk in here whenever he feels like it?'

'Antosha? He's always on the scrounge. You should read his short stories. He's brilliant.'

'All your friends are brilliant,' he said dryly.

Galya threw up both her shapely legs and vigorously bicycled. The bed springs twanged and groaned. 'We see life and art in a new way. A slap in the face for old-fogey taste. Antosha says Tolstoy, Chekhov, Dostoevski and all that gang must be chucked overboard. We're original.'

'Yes,' said Peter. It made him feel very old.

'D'you like my place?'

'Yes, it's very original,' he said.

The tiny room was plastered with a collage of theatrical posters and weird bits of verse painted in large bold letters. Drying his face on a tattered piece of towelling, his eyes were drawn to a legend above the blotched mirror.

> Kryuchkov chopped Germans into little bits
> Because they smoked Asmolov's cigarettes.

Bounding out of bed Galya twined herself around him as closely as tropical liana binds the trunk of a tree.

'I was good last night, wasn't I?' she said in a coaxing voice.

'Magnificent. You didn't give in until you drew blood.'

Pounding his chest, she screeched: 'Pig, pig, pig! That's not what I mean at all. I'm talking about my art.'

'Oh, your art?' Trapping her wrists to prevent her doing more damage, he said: 'An astonishing performance. Astonishing!'

He'd gone to the Korsh Theatre in Petrovka to see her. The place was packed to the doors. People hungered for imaginative drama. Even something about a brick factory, staged behind glowing footlights, induced forgetfulness of the famished present. Too stridently propagandist for his taste, the play-actors made speeches about bayonets dipped in proletarian blood and cemented the foundations of socialism with their own. It was, of course, a symbolic brick factory. Galya strutted about in tight overalls that showed off her figure. She died on the barricades wrapped in a red flag but revived to take him back to her room for a ferocious bout of love. Energy, youth, ambition: the combination exhausted him.

'I shall burn myself out,' said Galya intensely. 'I shall die young. But I shall be the greatest actress in the world.'

The sun, swollen with fire, blazed over the hazy city. Moscow steamed like a tropical swamp. Walking through the desultory streets, his shirt stuck to his back, he longed for the shade of cool birch forests, a swim in the deep waters of a woodland lake. Work was going to be not purgatory, the purifier, but inferno, punishment. Press-cuttings, reports, coded messages, jangling telephones, conferences: a full diary awaited him.

The first thing he saw when he sat down at his desk was the

Berlin mail, one square thick envelope addressed in the characteristically impulsive handwriting of Lydia. An obscure reluctance to open it made him deal with other business first. For weeks there'd been no word from her. Every day a letter had been expected, but nothing, not the briefest message. Jacob Peters had asked: 'What news from Selena?' He'd answered: 'She won't write until there's something definite to report.' Now it lay on his desk and, because of the impatience with which he'd awaited it, he left it there.

In any case, there were more pressing matters. A breakthrough had come in the laborious task of rebuilding the French network after Bogrov's treachery. An agent of the *Sûreté*, linked with the international arms dealer Basil Zaharoff, had succumbed to a shrewd combination of blackmail and bribery and was sending invaluable material, every line of which had to be sifted, checked, assessed and acted upon. Already the man had disclosed the identities of three White Russians recruited by French Intelligence for missions in Bolshevik Russia. They were arrested by the Special Section on arrival and so far the *Sûreté* had no inkling that all messages from these spies were coming from Peter's own department of the Cheka. Peter felt a special satisfaction in outwitting the *Sûreté*: the memory of being insultingly escorted to the Berlin train had not ceased to rankle.

In other respects, too, he had cause for satisfaction. Industrial and scientific espionage had begun to produce limited results. Excellent information was coming from England and good progress was being made in setting up pro-Soviet committees among foreign intellectuals. The soporific morning passed more quickly than he'd feared. It required the sharp interruption of the telephone to remind him that he was due at a meeting of senior Chekists and high officers of GRU, the intelligence section of the Red Army, in the Kremlin Barracks.

The sentry at the Nikolskiya Gate took his pass and telephoned its details through to an invisible authority. Security at the Barracks also remained stringent, checks being made both at the entrance and outside the conference room. An impregnable sense of occasion draped him as he joined the group assembled at its long polished table. It was still difficult to believe it was real. He felt like a figure in an historical pageant. Boris Godunov, the Mongol Tsar, had built his palace on the site where now they sat and the great Tsar Cannon that could hurl a ball weighing two tons to crush an enemy still stood outside, an obsolete symbol of power. 'We, the people ...' he thought, and dark laughter came from somewhere in his depths.

They all performed their roles. Adjusting his *pince-nez* and gripping the lapels of his jacket, an official of the Commissariat of Foreign Affairs, deputy of Krassin, the Negotiator, spoke as if every word was being enscrolled in the eternal archives of time instead of a stenographer's notebook. Secret discussions with the German War Ministry had reached an important stage. For Russia it meant an immense programme of arms manufacture that could change the power balance of the world – Krupps guns, Blöhm and Voss submarines, Albatrosswerke aeroplanes, all pouring out from Soviet factories. At the same time secret military academies to train German officers alongside Russians were to be established. A technical mission headed by high *Reichswehr* officers would shortly arrive to discuss final details.

Clenching his fist for emphasis, and pausing to ensure that the shorthand writer was suitably attentive, the voice of history declared: 'Comrades of the security services! This will turn the imperialist Versailles *Diktat* into a mere scrap of paper! This spells doom to the military supremacy of the Western interventionists! Forward to a new crisis of world capitalism and Victory of the Proletariat!'

Peter got back to the Lubianka shortly after two. History showed its drab undersurface in the shuffling queue of the staff canteen. He exchanged his ration coupons for some cabbage soup and a grey hunk of bread before returning to his desk to tackle the Berlin mail.

No professional agent had ever turned in such a report. They would list places visited, contacts, conversations, documents purloined, everything that contributed to an impression of drudgery and devotion to duty. She made no attempt to conceal her enjoyment. It was a very long time since she'd been so cheerful. The abrupt, sombre Lydia battling with fierce loyalty for her refugees, her guerrillas, her small group of friends, the Lydia whose gaiety had hardened and turned sceptical, the resolute, shabby, soldierly Lydia with her tense impatience for action was a different woman entirely from the one who enclosed a scribbled personal note that said: 'Peter, some of the things here are so crazy it can't be happening. I've rediscovered amazement.'

As he continued reading his own amazement grew. Why did she go on at such length about the decrepit Nikolaev, a military failure who made bellicose speeches at counter-revolutionary rallies? Nikolaev had been investigated and written off as a windbag, the one question not cleared up being the source of money for his free-spending habits. Lydia now provided the answer.

'The General's apartment in Charlottenburg is the fund-raising headquarters for various White Russian charities. Contributions come from London, New York, Paris, Vienna and so on. A good deal of it goes into Fyodor Yegorovich's own pockets.'

Vulnerable to blackmail, Peter automatically noted.

'At our first meeting I had the awkward problem of getting him undressed and put to bed. The caretaker, a one-armed war veteran, helped push him up three flights of stairs. The General sleeps with two loaded Lugers under his pillow to repel Bolshevik assassins. He must be subject to nightmares for the wall opposite the bed is riddled with bullets. He's also convinced we are out to poison him and eats nothing at home unless it's first tried on the dog. The dog is very fat, as is the General, so the arrangement suits them both.'

In similar light vein Lydia described her swiftly ripening friendship with the former Governor of Saratov. They dined together, strolled in the Tiergarten and visited curious night-clubs which allowed the old man to express his fiery disapproval of moral degeneracy, a thing he enjoyed doing. At last her courtship paid off. The General took her with him to a reception given at the residence of the *Reichswehr* commander-in-chief, von Seeckt, and introduced her to General von Hasse, principal negotiator for *Sondergruppe R*, among others. Conversation remained disappointingly trivial, much concerned with food, inflation and deteriorating discipline among the young. Yet the first part of her plan, penetration of the opponent's first line of defence, had been achieved.

'So far,' she wrote, 'Nikolaev had been merely a visiting card that opened the right doors. He seemed too aged, too eccentric, for any serious mischief. Two days later something happened that made me change my mind. He telephoned to cancel an arrangement we'd made for tea as he felt slightly unwell. I decided to drop in and see what ailed him. My arrival seemed a disagreeable shock.

' "Lydia, I'm expecting a visitor. Please go," he said.

' "Who, the doctor?"

' "Yes, yes, the doctor."

' "Then I'll stay. I'd like to hear what he says."

'Fyodor Yegorovich became positively abusive in his agitation. He gave the impression of panic. Leaving the apartment I almost collided with a small dark man who hesitated, looked closely at me and continued up to the next floor. I had an odd feeling about him. He reminded me of those *flics* in Paris who hung around the anarchist cafés in workman's overalls watching everyone out of the corner of their eyes. Glancing up through the banisters I saw him creeping down the stairs. He remained on the third floor. He was certainly no doctor. I took up a position across the street and waited.'

Terseness, sharp and breath-quickening, had taken over. Peter tensed in his chair. His cigarette smouldered in the ash-tray, unnoticed. He saw the street in Berlin, its sunshine and shadow, the big, square, ugly houses. Be careful, he thought. Don't stand on the pavement. An attractive woman loitering alone arouses curiosity. Make sure you can't be seen from Nikolaev's window, he wanted to say, and immediately parted the curtains of a room he'd never visited, watching with anxious vigilance the vulnerable Lydia of his imagination.

'They came out separately after about ten minutes, the other man first. He got into the driver's seat of a black Mercedes parked a short distance away. Early thirties, Breton face, pop-eyes under thick black eyebrows. A man below medium height wearing a broad-brimmed felt hat. The General followed a minute later. They drove off. The only cab available was a *droshky*, the horse in no hurry. Luckily they were held up by heavy traffic in Kaiserdamm and I changed to a motor taxi. The Mercedes turned into the courtyard of Bayerisherplatz 15.

Other men entered the building and the gate was locked. Whatever was going on, it didn't look like a tea-party. There is a fountain with some benches in the centre of the square. I strolled over and sat down. Glancing up at Number 15, I saw that the curtains of an apartment on the first floor were drawn. At that moment a young man joined me on the bench, began to read a book, put it away and opened a conversation. It seemed advisable to leave.

'The meeting lasted just short of an hour. I had a taxi waiting round the corner. The men dispersed one by one, going in different directions. Fyodor Yegorovich, very cheerful and smoking a large cigar, hurried along as briskly as a youngster. As soon as the black Mercedes appeared we swung into the stream of traffic and followed. It stopped outside Mätthaikirchstrasse 3b, just west of the Tiergarten, and little Breton-face entered the house. Mätthaikirchstrasse 3b is the address of the French Consulate. I am now trying to find out the name, rank and function of Nikolaev's visitor. It goes without saying that it will not be his real name, nor his real function. I fear that the General is working for French Intelligence and the small dark *flic* is his control.'

The red sun shifted westward, huge and feverish in its slow decline. Flies zipped distractingly through the heated air and grazed among the papers on his desk. Peter laid aside Lydia's report, not his anxieties. She'd acted with initiative, run risks, stumbled on some secret meeting place. But whose? The regular German secret service's? *Sondergruppe R*'s? The *Sûreté*'s? . . . It was by no means clear that Nikolaev worked for French Intelligence and improbable that Breton-face, as she called him, was the General's control. A control avoided being seen with an operational agent, would be foolish to visit him in his home, and in no circumstances accompanied him to a meeting. Whatever her early adventures, Lydia was too inexperienced to understand the enigmas, the devious complexities, of professional espionage. Nikolaev could be acting for the French, or the Germans, or the British. He could be a double agent employed by more than one master. Certain mysteries were never elucidated. The only thing that could be said with certainty was that he was not connected with Soviet intelligence. Better re-examine his dossier: something, some small detail that took on significance in the light of Lydia's disclosures, may just possibly have been overlooked.

He rang for his secretary. She hurried in, crumpled, middle-aged, reliable. Not for him one of those Moscow University graduates eager to put her brilliance at the service of Socialism in a career of travel and adventure. Staidness had its own good grey merit.

'Katya, bring me the file on Nikolaev, Fyodor Yegorovich,' he said. 'And make a note of the date it was last checked.'

Katya flapped her notebook at an aggressive fly. Patches of sweat showed under the armpits of her cotton blouse. 'Yes, comrade. Right away,' she said. A strong female odour remained when she left the office.

Peter's mind, still analysing and assessing the information received, dwelt briefly and pessimistically on the young man with the book who'd shared Lydia's bench in Bayerisherplatz. Her report was insufficiently explicit. How many benches? Were the others occupied? Was it her impression that he sat beside her because the seat happened to be available or to begin a flirtation? Had he detected her interest in the curtained apartment? 'It seemed advisable to leave,' she wrote. If merely to avoid a pick-up, all very well. But if she thought the man was there to keep observation then her departure served no useful purpose. It was already too late. Her full description would now be in the hands of a hostile network. If it suited their purpose, Nikolaev would hear that his charming protegée had seen fit to spy on him. The logical conclusions would very quickly be drawn.

Too quickly . . . His heart took on an irregular rhythm. Given these hypothetical circumstances, imagining that Nikolaev worked for him and some other Lydia for the enemy, he'd turn the problem over to Special Section. An expertly planned disappearance would follow. He had no illusions that others were less ruthless. It was the only way the game could be played. He hoped to goodness she'd been lucky this time, the book-reader just a student out to get a pretty woman.

The telephone rang. Jacob Peters spoke with clipped urgency: 'They arrive on the 17th. Mid-morning.'

'I'm not with you,' he said blankly. 'Who arrives where?'

'The German technical mission. Here. They're going to inspect some derelict armament factories in the Petrograd area. We have eleven days. Get your people on the mark in Berlin. Can't have accidents. What news from Lydia?'

'Oh,' he said. 'Good. She's making contacts.'

'Still making contacts!' Jacob gave a mocking laugh. 'What's happened to the famous panache?'

Peter clamped the receiver on its hook. The famous panache was what frightened him. Lydia still had too much of the old galloping boyar spirit. It needed curbing. A bit of Spichalskyism was necessary. The swiftness of the hare, the sureness of the tortoise. Spichalsky was dull but sound, an unobtrusive plodder with a tough hide. Drawing up a sheet of paper, he wrote: 'Chief to Pochhammer. Immediately contact Selena. Discuss joint action to deal with Breton-face emergency and send report for approval. Utmost urgency.'

Katya returned with the file. 'It hasn't been looked at for a long time,' she said, placing it on the desk. 'It hasn't been signed out since January 1919.'

'I'm not surprised,' commented Peter gloomily, handing her the message. 'Have this encoded and sent right away.' The secretary went out. 'Just a minute!' he called. Anxiety still gnawed: Spichalsky might take a week to get off his arse.

'Yes, comrade?' Katya waited obediently for her commander to come to a decision.

'Make arrangements for Schtern on the first available train to Berlin. Ask Comrade Lieberman to come in. I want him to take over for a few days.'

There'd still be time enough to comb through Nikolaev's dossier, he decided, blowing off a layer of dust and opening the faded cover.

'Shall I cancel this message?' asked Katya.

'No.' Spichalsky would still be needed. He had the notion that a situation in which he'd need all the help he could get was developing.

It was developing faster than he knew. An interval of two days had passed between the time Lydia wrote her report and his receipt of it. The information was already out-of-date.

3

General Nikolaev spoke emphatically. 'Liver,' he growled over the telephone wire. 'The doctor said liver. Nothing to worry about, m'dear. He gave me a good dose of salts. Sorry I was short with you yesterday. Hate being fussed when I'm out-of-sorts. I say, can you hear me?'

'Yes,' said Lydia.

'Hope I didn't send you off in a huff.'

'You can't help your liver,' she said. 'I'm pleased it's not serious. You should be better quite soon.'

'Fit already. Only needed a good night's rest,' the old liar boasted.

'I'm glad to hear it.'

'Don't go away,' yelled the General. 'Something I want to ask you.'

Herr Doktor Neubert entered the hall from his room carrying a straw shopping bag. The half-open door exposed his tidy bachelor bed, the gas-ring, sparse objects arranged in obsessively orderly patterns – a glimpse of neat, soul-withering loneliness: the room of a suicide. He came towards her, exposing his artificial teeth in a hopeful smile.

'*Guten Morgen*, Countess. Would you care to join me for a pleasant walk? Such a beautiful morning. We could perhaps stop for coffee later.'

'I'm sorry, Herr Doktor, I have something to do,' she replied, her hand blocking the telephone, avoiding his meek, resentful eyes.

'So, too busy! I am also sorry. Never mind.'

He took his leave with a cold nod. The earpiece buzzed impatiently. 'Well, what do you say? You'll come, of course.'

'Fyodor Yegorovich, there was an interruption. What did you ask me?'

The General explained once more. He required her this morning to accompany him somewhere. To a madhouse. A madhouse? Yes, yes! of course, he said irritably as if no request could be more reasonable. A large establishment out at Dalldorf. About once a month he regarded it as necessary to go there and offer cheer to those of his afflicted countrymen who were inmates.

They were, after all, casualties of the revolution. Talking with the men was bad enough but the females were inclined to pull off their clothes and make a nuisance of themselves. She'd oblige him if she'd relieve him of that ordeal.

Lydia said yes, she'd gladly do it and would come over right away.

For a very particular reason she wanted to go. By coincidence, Dalldorf happened to be the hospital where von Huberhof practised, the same von Huberhof whose connection with *Sondergruppe R* she'd been asked to investigate. Then, again, perhaps it was not such a coincidence.

The nurse, abrupt and matter-of-fact, provided a brisk tourist guide to hell.

'We get every type, the whole human race one way and another. Mostly melancholia these days. A lot of war widows, of course, but in my opinion inflation gets them worse. It's much harder on the women than on men. For years they've been buying bread at twenty pfennigs a loaf and suddenly its the price of a fur coat. Flesh and blood can't bear it. Their brains just snap. The craziness is too much. The old ones give a lot of trouble. Some get spiteful, or they can't control their bowels, or their minds are so worn out you can't do a thing with them.'

She led the way down blank corridors talking non-stop.

'We try to keep them amused. There's gardening, books, handicrafts, all that. The trouble is they're all really begging for attention. Who's got the time? Visitors are a nuisance, too. I don't mean ladies like you, of course. Relatives and friends. People expect lunatics to be funny, playing Mary Magdalene or Cleopatra – we have those too, of course. There's a girl here thinks she's queen of the Russians, Grand Duchess Anastasia. Very quiet person actually. Most are like that, sad. You wouldn't know they weren't as sensible as you or me until you started to talk to them. It upsets you, doesn't it? I can tell by the look on your face.'

Lydia kept silent. She watched women sewing, weaving baskets, knitting, making soft toys. She saw others who stared in blank despair with eyes that had wept themselves empty. She stopped to speak to two Russians. One showed no disposition to be friendly, replying briefly and with studied contempt to her inquiries. ('A bitch, that one,' said the nurse.) The other, a dark intense girl who'd been a piano teacher, displayed some healed scars on her wrists where she'd tried to kill herself, explaining in rational tones that the magnetism that made music had drained out of her fingers.

'The doctor will soon get that put right,' said the nurse, hurrying Lydia away. Outside, walking ahead of their elongated shadows, she pointed to a glass porthole and said: 'Have a look in there.'

A demented woman, hair spiky with sweat, sat in a padded cell exhaustingly struggling to free her bound arms. 'We don't like strait-jackets,' volunteered the guide, 'but there are times when the only thing to do is strap them up.' She lectured on patients who fouled their beds, ate their excreta or smeared it over themselves, tore off every stitch of clothing, screamed constant obscenities, could be restrained from savage self-mutilation only by the exercise of brute force. Out of deference to the lady visitor's refined susceptibilities, she abstained from exposing her to actual contact with these poor wretches. 'You'd be shocked out of your wits,' she said. 'I'm used to it but they even make me puke, the things they get up to.'

Again Lydia kept silent. If anything it was too hideously familiar. The world was a place of famine, pestilence, madness and she belonged to a generation that had seen it all.

'Let's slip in here and have a smoke, eh?' the woman suggested, entering a lavatory. A strong smell of lysol came from open water closets. Sitting on an upturned bucket, a smouldering cigarette stuck in her mouth, she pointed to the graffiti on the drably painted walls. 'Filthy minds they've got, eh? Not that it bothers me as long as they don't draw it with their own shit. It's funny when you come to think of it. We wouldn't allow ourselves to think of things like that. They let themselves go. We'd all be mad if we let ourselves go.'

'Yes,' said Lydia, 'we would,' and she thought suddenly of Stepanchik rearing up on his short legs to gleefully smash a man's skull with his rifle butt, of her own thin thread of sanity stretched and snapping at the sight of tortured flesh that had once been living men. She thought of ashen-faced children with stick-like limbs and the terrible luminescence in their huge starved eyes, and she pushed these thoughts away because they brought a disabling, utterly futile, sense of guilt. Because, even in the midst of it, when you had a job to do you cursed softly and carried on. You even occasionally managed to laugh.

'I think I've seen enough for one visit,' she said.

The nurse threw her cigarette end into a lavatory pan and flushed it away. 'You can't go without having a look at Anastasia. Just as a matter of interest. Some people think she's real. Not all the lunatics are inside.'

They entered a small crowded ward. Patients read, lay on beds, chatted. Elderly women played cards. A fat girl gazed up out of childishly unhappy eyes and then hid her face in a book. One woman with bobbed grey hair sat cross-legged on the floor like a sturdy peasant beside a pale girl reading a magazine.

'*Achtung!*' called the nurse, clapping her hands. 'This nice lady is from the Russian Society for Social Aid, so be on your best behaviour.' Nudging Lydia and signalling with her eyes, she said: 'That's the kid, reading the mag.'

The bobbed-haired woman jumped up athletically, tightened the cord of her dressing gown like a prize fighter preparing for ring combat, and demanded offensively: 'What are you doing, giving away bibles?'

'I'll send you one if you wish,' said Lydia mildly.

'Me? I know it backwards. Also the Koran, the Baghavad Gita and the Egyptian Book of the Dead. You don't look like a fully evolved spiritual being. I'm a very ancient soul. You interrupted my meditation.'

'Then I apologize,' said Lydia.

The square face with its thickening masculine jaw remained truculent. 'I should think you would. Just because I'm here don't get the idea I'm not right in the head. I speak my mind, that's all.' She stared round challenging anybody to deny it and, with an unexpected change of manner, drew Lydia aside. 'That girl there,' she said pointing an emphatic finger, 'has got royal blood. Three hundred years of Imperial breeding runs in her veins.'

Lydia looked at the pale, sad girl and asked in Russian:

'Are you really Anastasia? I knew her when she was a small child.'

The legend that a daughter of the Tsar had miraculously survived the slaughter of Ekaterinburg was the most persistent of all and, despite herself, she felt a flicker of curiosity, even imagined a faint Romanov resemblance.

But the 'Grand Duchess Anastasia' turned away. Either she'd not understood or she refused to answer.

'In one of my many incarnations I was a priest of Osiris, God of the Sun,' said the woman with bobbed hair following them to the door.

The nurse rounded on her crossly. 'Go away, Klara! And tidy up the crumbs under your bed. You know you're forbidden to eat in the ward.'

'*Hereinkommen!*' someone called.

The rumble of laughter in the consulting room stopped abruptly as she pushed open the door into a dense-texture atmosphere of dark wood, leather-bound books and nicotine. The three men turned, arrested at a moment of masculine amiability like figures in a group picture by Franz Hals. They looked at her with the hard predatory gaze that enters the faces of men at first sight of a pretty woman. Their mouths had a smirking lewdness as if they'd been exchanging coarse jests. Still under the influence of her tour of the demented, the effect was threatening.

General Nikolaev, hairy nostrils quivering, hugged her shoulder and said (the revolting old humbug): 'Our dear sister of mercy. Come in, come in! I've been boasting about you.' She was introduced to a dark, saturnine Egon Otto Schmidt, high-bridged nose and eyes on each side of his long pointed head. And to Hugo von Huberhof, the face in the Moscow dossier, smiling with shut mouth as he smoothed greying wings of hair, eyes coldly amused, silently warning that appearances didn't fool him; who almost imperceptibly pressed his thumb into the centre of her palm as he stooped for the ritual hand kissing; whom she instantly assessed as insolent and dangerous.

Schmidt and Nikolaev left the room to talk over something

or other. Von Huberhof seated her in a padded leather chair. His manner was that of a considerate physician: the eyes said one thing, the voice another. She now realized that the General had not brought her to Dalldorf to visit the tormented members of her sex, nor for the pleasure of her company. She was there to be looked over, examined. The knowledge of being manipulated aroused resentment and she reacted by subtly parodying femininity, crossing her shapely silk-clad legs and leaning back with the artificial grace the pose required.

Von Huberhof stared and smiled. '*Let's see what we can find out about you,*' the blue diagnostic eyes said. '*I have my own system of making judgements. Clothes, mannerisms and other such superficialities count for little. Your silences interest me, your unconsidered remarks, the involuntary movements of eyes, lips, hands that betray thoughts and feelings you try to conceal.*'

'It's splendid of you and General Nikolaev to take the trouble to come here,' he said. 'Our Russian patients get very few visitors. Most of them have no relatives in Berlin and lack of friendship is part of their trouble.'

'You really think it helps?'

'Certainly. I'm not, of course, at liberty to discuss patients in specific terms but there's one man I shall call X . . .' He went into the neuroses of X at tedious length, apparently in order to keep her under close observation, and concluded: 'So you see, in that case the response has been quite remarkable.'

'You make it sound very simple,' Lydia said to keep the conversation going. The conclusions he drew did not depend on her superficial responses.

Von Huberhof's glance briefly settled on her neatly-turned ankle. 'Nothing about insanity is simple, Countess. The mind is *terra incognita.* Psychoanalysis is merely a tool, a crude compass. We're still explorers in a dark continent whatever that clever Viennese Hebrew chooses to tell us.'

The instinctive hardening of her gaze did not go undetected.

'I do believe I've shocked you,' he remarked with cool amusement. 'Perhaps I should have said Professor Freud. You mustn't think me an ignorant anti-Semite. I quite admire the gentleman. He has just given the world an ingenious new theory. As far as my simple mind can make sense of it, it has to do with the self-punishing instincts of the ego. A typically Jewish concept. The Old Testament is full of murderous exasperation with Jewish failure to fulfil the exacting requirements of their jealous, vindictive God. The Jews are not like other men. They see their entire history as punishment for cosmic transgressions. Everywhere they spread a contaminating awareness of evil. They are . . .' he hesitated for a suitable word – 'very mysterious. They have a long memory, they never forgive old injuries. Jewish children who have scarcely learned the alphabet know the names of Babylonian kings. They curse men who have been dead three thousand years. They grieve bitterly for people slain by ancient Romans as if it was yesterday.'

It was quite astonishing what had happened to von Huberhof's calculating eyes, Lydia thought. The pupils had undergone a definite contraction, the lids were narrowed: they no longer looked in the slightest amused. For the first time since she had been left alone with him von Huberhof's eyes and lips spoke the same language. He continued to stare with meditative intensity through her, beyond her, as though she and the world were images springing from the dark recesses of his mind. It lasted no longer perhaps than a few seconds but von Huberhof seemed to come back from a long mental journey.

'My dear Countess, I mustn't bore you,' he said and laughed deprecatingly. 'I shall send for some coffee and you will tell me all about yourself.'

Returning to Berlin, Fyodor Yegorovich slid the glass shutter across so that the chauffeur should not overhear and took her gloved hand, fondling her fingers one by one. '*Lubimy*, my love, you made a good impression. A very good impression.' Phlegm gurgled in his throat as he chuckled. 'Not really touchy about Yids, are you? You got Huberhof puzzled. He even thought there might be a bit of the Semitic in your racial background. These Germans have no sense of humour. You don't know the Russian aristocracy, I told him. Tatar blood in all of us. We're a lot of bloody Turks.'

As soon as she arrived home she ran for the second time that day a bathful of Frau Flügel's expensive hot water, flung off her clothes and soaked the tension out of her body. That was the easy part: one soaped it away leisurely, cleansed one's pores, relaxed in the steaming air. What could not be eliminated was the ingestion of horror and filth, the uncomprehending panic of a nameless woman imprisoned in a padded cell, the corroding obsession that surfaced in the handsome blue eyes of the cynically intelligent von Huberhof.

Horror connected with horror. Her thoughts helplessly drifted back to the civil war and the monster famine it gave birth to. People in Russia were still being crushed in its giant teeth. A parasitic army of typhus-bearing lice crawled in its wake pullulating in the wasted flesh of living and dead alike. The Kronstadt of women and children, of the old, the weak, the defenceless, someone had called it. She thought suddenly of Joseph Frumkin who had dropped out of sight with a brief letter that reached her in the Pokrovsky Nunnery saying he was alive; and at the time, struggling hopelessly to keep death from her charges even for a day, it seemed as much as anyone could ask for. When she listened to von Huberhof's diatribe of hate it was Joseph that came to her mind, a battle commander who killed with nausea and self-loathing, and, linked to the memory of Joseph, his dead cousin Yoshka Brenner in faraway, remote London speaking with impassioned bitterness of Easter pogroms and the meek submission of the victims. How little she had then understood: how necessary the loss of that ignorance. It left no illusions. Sitting in that soft comfortable chair facing von Huberhof she knew that his kind offered her no choice. They aspired to be the lords of life and death, they were the famine-makers. She was ready if necessary to kill von Huberhof, and von Huberhof was ready to kill her. Provided he judged it convenient. What followed now? . . .

Chapter Ten

Frau Flügel brought her a letter. In the top left-hand corner it bore the stamped impression '*Rohrpost*'. A *pneumatique*. Opening the envelope with the knife that had decapitated her breakfast egg, she drew out a single sheet of paper. 'Friends have been asking about you. Why not meet?' signed 'Pochhammer'. Unhurriedly, she drank down her black coffee, smoked a cigarette and looked out of the window to consult the sky before deciding what to wear. The day promised to be very warm. She put on a cream-coloured linen suit and some light, fresh make-up, brushed her shingled hair and listened at the door before leaving. She was not eager to bump into the Herr Doktor en route for his morning constitutional. The only sound was that of a cooing voice. '*Liebchen! Süsser!* You break my heart when you look at me like that. Here's your icky-licky milk.' Frau Flügel was talking to her big marmalade cat. Lydia left and locked the door.

Thoughtfully sucking a sweet, Spichalsky stood behind a strategic pillar at Bahnhof Alexanderplatz, a copy of the *Berliner Zeitung* spread across his face. He saw Lydia before she saw him. By his reckoning Piatkov's lady spy was ten minutes later than she should have been. Two hours for delivery of the letter, say twenty minutes to the rendezvous, half-an-hour at the outside. A novice obviously. Spichalsky prided himself on being as dead on time as a bullet hitting the centre of a moving target. Indeed, it was with a marksman's careful eye that he watched the tall young woman arrive at the station's Königstrasse entrance and stand for a moment to orient herself before strolling through the crowd to the destination board. Too many people looked at her. Men. Not good to be so conspicuous. Slowly folding his newspaper, he walked over and jolted her slightly.

'*Verzeihung*, *Fräulein*, I am sorry,' he said.

'*Ganz und gar nicht*,' was her urbane reply. Deliberately exaggerating her Russian accent and looking slightly distrait, very much the kind of impractical creature who would need masculine guidance, she asked: 'Can you tell me, please, from which platform leaves the train for Magdeburg?'

'I shall be happy to show you. It's on my way,' said Spichalsky.

They emerged from the station at the crowded Central Market.

'The Central Market,' said Spichalsky. 'Really? Where they sell things?' Her tone conveyed astonishment. He looked at her humourlessly. 'For the right price nothing is impossible to buy in Berlin.'

Most of the people she saw lacked the right price. They moved from stall to stall staring at frost-bitten potatoes and wilting cabbages and reckoning up the dwindling value of their marks. It was a tidy, disciplined poverty. None of the jostling confusion and raucous altercations of market places back home where the drama of each transaction became the passionate concern of bystanders. Here even the poor quality fruit and vegetables were clean and on parade. The German respect for *ordnung*. In Moscow there were jokes about the way German communists demonstrated. Everything meticulously organized, clenched fists upraised at the correct angle, militant slogans threatening revolutionary cataclysm. Then, punctually at dinner-time, banners were folded and everybody trooped home to eat. Only now there was little to eat. Perhaps the banners would remain unfurled and the sporadic fighting in the streets turn into full-scale insurrection. Wouldn't it, she wondered heretically, be better to do business with German Bolshevism than *Sondergruppe R*?

'Would you tell me what this meeting is for?' she asked after they'd walked in silence, an arm's length apart, along the wide curved sweep of Neue Friedrichstrasse, an oddly-matched pair reflected in glittering shop windows.

Spichalsky moved his shadow closer. 'Breton-face,' he said and turned laconically towards the screech of tramcars, the multiple confusion of traffic, as if having said that much his interest in the matter was ended. Lydia sensed more than contempt in his manner. Under the gruffness was an awkward resentment. Spichalsky disliked women: he especially disliked a woman doing a man's job. His blunt averted profile was reticent about everything but that.

The surge of the street caught her up, an adrenalin stimulation of crowds, noise, movement. No *ordnung* here. The city jittered like a great machine in need of lubrication. A gang of youths, obviously unemployed, slouched past, mean-eyed and sullen. Horses reared and slithered in fumes of petrol. Tattered posters for beer, cigarettes, gargantuan sausages; for furniture, clothes, theatres, miracle remedies; eat this, take that, buy, buy, buy. And the posters grew dingy, became unstuck, were ripped away in rage, for who could buy but speculators and profiteers? News placards proclaimed a whirlwind of strikes, riots, inflation, crime, and a score of newspapers offered rival panaceas: socialism, democracy, the red star of communism; blood and destiny, bring back the Kaiser, eliminate the Jews, God save the mark. Morning drunks reeled through the deafening streets. A blinded war veteran squeezed his accordion. 'Yes, we have no bananas.' Pigeons in gutters, scavenging mongrels (they were not yet reduced to eating dogs), sharp-featured urchins racing death across the turbulent roads. No *ordnung* in this sun-warmed, brutal, overcrowded metropolis. Ex-soldiers in shabby clothes, recovered from shell-shock, walked by with furious eyes. Lydia was reminded of the last summer before Russia's revolution. Violence was building up like flood water.

They crossed the Friedrichstrasse Bridge into the sudden peace of Museum Island. Spichalsky led her to the riverbank. The sense of crisis vanished. It was as though they had regressed in time to an earlier, more leisurely city of muted traffic, quiet lawns and flower-beds, of spacious and dignified buildings filled with the art treasures of a labelled and orderly history, the mellow cultured Berlin of Bismarkian optimism. Nursemaids wheeled pampered infants beside the beautiful River Spree. Gulls settled on the water's edge and flew off crying hoarsely; river boats spread lazy iridescent ripples like slowly opening peacock fans.

'Let us sit.' Sweating in blue serge suit, tight collar and thick-soled polished boots, Spichalsky undid his jacket and pushed back his grey cloth cap. He lowered his broad buttocks carefully on to the grass, loosened his tie a centimetre or two, stretched his chafed neck and sighed. The warm breeze ruffled his cropped thinning fair hair. He looked like a factory foreman in Sunday clothes on a day's outing.

'A bon-bon, comrade? No?' The big shoulders shrugged as he unwrapped the sweet and slipped it into his mouth. The obstruction muffled his voice. 'So tell me, what is the emergency?'

Sun glittered on the water, plane trees rustled in the light wind, nothing could be more deceptively peaceful.

'I was not aware that there was one,' Lydia replied.

'In Moscow they have a different opinion.' Spichalsky's short-lashed eyes were both shrewd and naive but otherwise lacking in expression. He took a slip of paper from a waistcoat pocket and read out Peter's message then struck a match and set fire to it. 'Let us not waste time. I have another meeting in an hour. Berlin is a centre of counter-revolution and we are very short of man-power.'

The rebuke was supposed to emphasize the authority he wielded as chief of the local network. No doubt he resented the fact that for reasons not divulged she did not come under his orders but was directly responsible to Central Cheka.

'I'll be very brief,' Lydia said. 'First, Breton-face.'

The little *flic* slipped away like an elusive figure in a dream as she talked, but Spichalsky pressed for details and more details: height, build, colouring, approximate age, shape of features, manner of dress. He drove a Mercedes? What colour, year of manufacture, licence number, distinguishing marks, general condition? How many men had attended the secret meeting place? Was there more than one exit to the building? Did it have a fire-escape? Under what name was the apartment held? Had she taken note of the names of other residents? . . .

Many of these questions, much to Spichalsky's satisfaction, Lydia could not answer. He was teaching this *elegante*, this beginner, an elementary lesson in the profession of espionage, showing her that she was talking to an experienced agent who knew his business inside out.

'Now we come to the question of Nikolaev,' he said.

'There was nothing in the message about Nikolaev.'

Spichalsky waved dismissively. 'It is taken for granted. We

must see what we can find in his apartment. Daytime is best. It arouses less suspicion and we have the light.' He narrowed his eyes suggestively. 'Could you keep the old fellow busy for a few hours? Say tomorrow afternoon? In your own place perhaps.'

Lydia clasped her knees and watched the passage of a river steamer with great interest. It would be very boring to get angry, she told herself. They generally enjoy it when you do. It's what they hope for – feminine hysteria, loss of self-control. Anger in a woman always seems to them ridiculous.

'No, that is not a good idea,' she said, her voice quieter than usual, each word as cold and separate as a splinter of ice. 'You will look after the Frenchman. I will deal with General Nikolaev in my own way.'

Someone else might have been warned by the crispness of tone that he had underestimated his adversary, but Spichalsky was inclined to be heavy-footed with the female sex, his experiences of women being mainly limited to paying one of them a visit when he had the need of a bit of tenderness.

'That's just what I said,' he grinned. 'You deal with him in your own way, we'll deal with him in ours.' Blundering on, he said: 'I saw you both in *Der Blaue Vogel* the other night. You get on very well together.'

'Was that your assignment, to keep me under observation?'

He stared disingenuously. 'Why should I do that?'

'There is no good reason why you should,' said Lydia, looking straight into his cold marksman's eyes. 'Nor why you should have left so quickly when I saw you. You missed the cabaret.'

'I go there strictly for business,' he protested stiffly. 'Much goes on in *Der Blaue Vogel* that interests us. Well, now, is it arranged for tomorrow afternoon?'

'No,' she said. 'We are making no arrangements about that.'

'I insist on it. The apartment must be searched. Comrade, you are only a woman. The job needs men. Two at least.'

'Comrade Pochhammer, let me put it this way,' said Lydia. 'If Moscow had thought this was a job for furniture removers they would not have sent me.'

Spichalsky's face became somewhat puffed and his neck bulged over his shirt collar. He stripped the wrapping from another bon-bon and sucked voraciously. It brought no comfort. Slowly, he stood up and brushed the seat of his trousers.

'I will report your refusal to cooperate,' he declared ominously.

'Do whatever you think is necessary,' she said.

'The consequences may be serious,' Spichalsky said. There was much more he could have said had it been possible to speak out frankly and honestly. If he hadn't bitten it back it would have jumped off his tongue. Spichalsky did not trust Piatkov's lady spy. She might have *protektsia* but he knew her type, nothing better than a high-class police whore. Once a real aristocrat, they said. He did not believe the former class-enemy could change their spots. Spichalsky had a nose for treason, he'd like to tell her. Spichalsky had his eye on her. Let her keep to the job of picking up information by getting men drunk and opening her legs. Whore! Filth! Stuck-up bitch!

'Thank you for the discussion, madam colleague,' he said with what he judged to be deadly irony. And, crunching the remainder of the sweet between his teeth, added: 'For me now the problem is clear. The one thing left is to decide how to dispose of it.'

Lydia watched him walk stiffly away, heavy-shouldered, a bulge under the left arm where he kept his gun. Some grass remained stuck to his backside. He would care disproportionately about that if he knew. It would not suit his idea of dignity. Spichalsky did not like his dignity slighted. The enemies are not all on the other side, she thought. But the thought was hardly new. The depressing thing was that those on your own side were the most dangerous of all.

Passing the colonnaded entrance of the Egyptian Museum she had a sudden impulse to become immersed in its cool antiquities. An obelisk of Rameses II and his sacred monkeys stood in the huge vestibule. Tombs of emperors dead 5,000 years; painted earthenware; flutes, strings and cymbals whose music had been lost for ever; the jewelled toilet case of a crumbled beauty . . . She recalled the woman of many lives in Dalldorf, priest of Osiris, God of the Sun. Was she so mad, after all?

The sun dazzled her when she left the Museum. Through the rainbow of her watering eyes she glimpsed the short compact figure of a man hurrying towards the Lustgarten. Her heart stopped: for a moment she thought it was Breton-face. The figure retreated rapidly, merged with the anonymous crowd. Just imagination, she told herself. A thousand people looked like that. The buffeting of the teeming streets resumed. She was back in the twentieth century.

2

Spichalsky boarded a Grosser Ring electric tramcar at Alexanderplatz to keep an important rendezvous in the working class suburb of Wedding. He felt thoroughly put out. The woman had stirred him up with her nonsense, the bitch. He didn't like to be ruffled: it upset the order of things in his head. Bad enough to have to work with incompetents who got into a mess and expected Spichalsky to straighten it out. All right, he was prepared to take all that shit, but let's have some cooperation for fuck's sake. Such a fuss about giving the old man's place a going over. It was simple routine. He'd done her a favour even to mention it. Spichalsky didn't have to ask permission of anybody, not even Piatkov, to turn over an apartment in the course of duty.

The heat in the crowded tram was insufferable. Andreastrasse, Kottbuserplatz, Gneisenau. More and more passengers got on, pushing and shoving for standing space, the sweat poured out of every pore, making him itch, and the more he thought of it the angrier he got.

'All right, give a bit of elbow-room!' he snarled as somebody pushed him in the back. Nollendorf, Lützowplatz. More got on than got off. He stood pressed against the tits of a fat woman and felt his face turn red with what was going on down in his trousers. Knows no conscience, the old soldier down there. The tram swayed, jolted. Bloody . . . awkward . . . like a gun barrel . . . He risked an embarrassed smile. The fat woman looked as though her mind was stuck on the price of groceries. Women . . .

. . . They never got rid of their class arrogance and the females were the worst. She came along, painted up and stinking of scent, as if he was some ignorant peasant called in to clean the muck out of a stable. Furniture removers. A man like him who'd fought as a platoon sergeant at Tannenberg, escaped from prisoner-of-war camp and got back to Russia in time to storm the Winter Palace.

He'd got around to storming Lydia's Winter Palace when they reached Bahnhof Wedding. Spichalsky bought a ticket and descended the grimy steps to the underground. Fritz Erkner in oil-stained overalls, waited on the platform, dead on the dot. One of his most reliable men, Fritz. A Soviet citizen of Volga German stock, he'd built up cast-iron cover as a metal worker from Düsseldorf who settled in Berlin and joined a Freikorps *Sturmbattaillon*. When Chancellor Ebert dissolved these units Fritz became a member of an underground right-wing group of German nationalists. The stuff he turned in was always good. Merely seeing his tough good-natured face improved Spichalsky's mood. He felt he was back in business.

Fritz Erkner trod out his cigarette butt and slouched to the far end of the platform, showing no sign of recognition. They entered the last compartment of a Ringbahn train and moved to a seat at the end as it swept into the tunnel. Only now did Spichalsky notice that Fritz showed signs of tension. His eyes were haggard, his mouth taut and severe. He got out a crumpled pack of cigarettes and lit one, staring blankly at his own reflection as it travelled along the black tunnel wall.

'Anything wrong?' asked Spichalsky, almost tenderly.

Erkner took a folded sheet of paper from his overall pocket and silently passed it over. Under cover of his newspaper Spichalsky opened it and saw a number of names. The first was that of Walter Rathenau, German Foreign Minister. 'Another assassination list?' Erkner gave a cursory nod. Drawing up such lists was a favourite pastime of right-wing German fanatics and Rathenau, chief advocate of *Erfüllungspolitik*, the policy of accepting the Versailles Treaty, always appeared at the top.

Pointing a nicotine-stained forefinger at one of the names, Erkner said: 'They want me to kill this man. Three of us are to do it.'

'Kaufman. Who is he, a politician?'

'No, a Hamburg banker.'

'Any reason?'

'Socialist inclined, maybe. Most of the list are Jews.' Erkner gave a low agonized laugh. 'The names are picked like in a lottery.'

Spichalsky carefully refolded the paper and placed it in his wallet. 'It's not serious, Fritz. They love to play the assassination game. You can forget it.'

'This time, it's serious. A decision has been made. They are talking about a national revolution of the right. It will begin with a big campaign of terror.'

The train ran into a station and they became strangers again. As it restarted Erkner bent towards Spichalsky and hissed in his ear: 'I won't do it. I don't even know him. I can't kill someone I've got nothing against.'

Imperturbably, Spichalsky said from behind his newspaper: 'How long have you got?'

'Until the 28th of June, the anniversary of Versailles.'

'Over a month. We'll ask for instructions.'

'I won't murder an innocent man,' said Erkner through gritted teeth.

'What happens if you refuse?'

'I'm out, finished as far as they're concerned. I'd have to go into hiding.'

This was a real emergency. Spichalsky glanced around to make sure he was unobserved, laid a friendly palm on the other's knee, and said softly: 'Fritz, listen to me. I know just how you feel. Who enjoys killing? But be realistic. They think very highly of you at home. You're badly needed, one of our best agents. Sometimes we have to put our feelings on one side. Let Moscow make the decision, eh?'

'It isn't right,' Erkner muttered.

'Dear, dear, comrade, what business is it of yours or mine? They want to shoot one another? It's their politics, not ours. You won't save the man's life. If not you, someone else's finger will be on the trigger. We have our Soviet work to do, isn't it so?'

They travelled through a couple more stations and Spichalsky could see that Fritz was still down in the mouth. A bright idea came. Nudging him with his elbow, he said: 'How about a bit of fun tonight? Feel in the mood?'

Erkner shrugged. 'No, Boris. That sort of thing doesn't appeal to me. I've got a decent girl I see a lot of.'

'I'm talking about fun, not debauchery,' Spichalsky declared a trifle indignantly. 'We'll visit someone's apartment, look around a bit and afterwards go to a quiet beerhouse I know for a drink and a chat.'

'That,' said Erkner gloomily, 'sounds like work.'

'All right, it's also in the line of duty.' Spichalsky saw no contradiction. He was a man who enjoyed his work. 'Come on, take your mind off things.'

'Are you sure there are no problems?'

'No problems. I've given the place a good look-over. You can get in with a bent nail. Of course, if the old man stays in tonight . . .'

As twilight deepened the lights in Nikolaev's came on. Fritz Erkner said: 'Maybe he's not going out.' A queer idea of fun, he thought, fishing out a cigarette and turning into the doorway to strike the match.

The hiatus between day's end and the beginning of Berlin's feverish night found the street deserted. 'Give him a chance,' Spichalsky grunted, focusing his binoculars on the window. Owing to the angle of vision, little could be seen through the gauze curtains – a plaster frieze, ceiling shadows, the gilt-framed corner of a picture. The heavy drapes were drawn, shutting off the view completely.

Time passed. Five minutes, fifteen, an interminable half-hour. The pulse of the city imperceptibly quickened. Taxi-cabs drew up; people arrived and left; music came out of houses. Stars floated up as the indigo sky turned black.

'Boris, we might as well go, we're wasting our time,' said Erkner, and as soon as he finished speaking General Nikolaev stumped out of the building and waved his stick at a passing horse-cab.

Spichalsky hurried into action. Normally a cautious man, he might have had a qualm or two about his impetuous initiative in this case but Piatkov's message said utmost urgency, the stuck-up Selena wouldn't cooperate, and it was so easy it was going to be a pleasure. He'd studied the layout. Quietly into the courtyard, past the one-armed janitor's room, three floors up the service stairs, and a mortice lock on Nikolaev's back door that would give no trouble to a practical-minded schoolboy.

They were in the apartment, as the saying goes, in the twinkling of an eye. Spichalsky took stock, his nose twitching. The General left a smell like an old dog. Working with electric torches, they examined correspondence, photographs, documents, and rubbish of a lifetime. Faded love-letters, old-fashioned pictures of pretty girls who must since have become grannies, formal invitations to soirées held when Alexander III sat on the Imperial throne. Nothing of what Spichalsky would call espionage turned up – no one left such stuff lying in a drawer – but Nikolaev was obviously a dangerous plotter, maintaining contact with counter-revolutionary former bourgeoisie in many countries. All the details – names, addresses, financial contributions to so-called charitable societies that surely acted as cover for subversion – had to be recorded, and Spichalsky worked zealously. Turning the pages of a diary he came across an interesting entry. It was scribbled under a reference to some piano-recital. 'Met Countess Lydia Nikolaievna Alexandrova. Father old friend (?). Good-looking girl. Amusing.'

Spichalsky felt the slow burn of an explosive excitement as he followed the development of this first reference through subsequent pages. Nikolaev was much taken with his new acquaintance. After their third meeting he wrote cryptically: 'Check Paris.' Was that a clue to the involvement of Bretonface? They dined together, visited places of entertainment, then another intriguing entry, tacked on to a note about a night-club visit. 'Spirited girl, Lydia. Sense of adventure. Maybe just what we're looking for. Discuss with H.'

There was a good smell of conspiracy there. Humming cheerfully, Spichalsky faithfully copied down every word and replaced the diary in the desk drawer.

'Fritz,' he said, 'let's have a look in the bedroom.'

Sure enough there was a safe, stuck behind a picture on a bullet-scarred wall.

Erkner stared in astonishment. 'What does he use it for? Target practice?'

Concentration on essentials left no room for idle curiosity. Having carefully examined the safe, Spichalsky said: 'It's too difficult. This will have to be left for another time.'

The key grated in the front door-lock.

'*Um Gottes Willen!*' prayed Erkner, abruptly switching off his torch. They collided in the darkness.

'He's come back early,' whispered Spichalsky in a shocked voice.

The door slammed and a shaft of light penetrated from the hall. A heavy body in a state of disequilibrium stumbled about the apartment using terrible language.

The two intruders edged into the hall as Nikolaev appeared from the drawing room and blundered past them into the bathroom with swimming movements of his arms.

'Too drunk even to see us,' muttered Erkner with relief as they reached the back door. When they were almost down to street-level Spichalsky made a dreadful discovery. He'd left his cap behind.

'I've left my cap,' he said, aghast.

'Forget it, Boris. It's too risky to go back.'

Spichalsky hesitated, but there could be no question of leaving it. Nikolaev must have no suspicion that his apartment had been searched. 'I'll meet you in the street,' he said. Creeping upstairs again, he listened outside the door until the silence told him that Nikolaev was asleep. . . .

The General was having one of those damned nightmares. Feeling rather seedy, he lay on the bed fully dressed, boots and all, and there were these two thugs standing in the hall as he went off to puke in the bathroom.

Cunningly, he opened one bleary eye. The devils didn't know he could do that in his sleep. There they were, still lurking about. He fumbled under the pillow and pulled out the Luger. Always kept one handy.

'Bolshevik assassins!' he yelled, firing wildly, and the pig squealed. Took care of him that time, all right.

With a contented grin, General Nikolaev turned over and settled into alcoholic oblivion. By the morning he wouldn't remember a thing about the dream.

3

Early the next morning when Lydia sat at the dressing-table mirror critically arranging her face for the day, she heard the telephone ring in the hall. Someone answered it, then tapped on her door.

'Countess Alexandrova!'

'Just a moment,' she called.

'It's the telephone.'

'Yes.' She opened the door to be confronted by Herr Doktor Neubert, gaunt blue-veined ankles bare, a dusting of dandruff on the shoulders of his threadbare dressing gown. His eyes were red from insomniac fatigue.

'A man for you,' he said reproachfully. 'He was quite impolite when I asked his name. Excuse me, I am not a messenger, I told him.'

'Quite right,' said Lydia. 'Whoever it is, I shall let him wait.'

In fact she wanted the Herr Doktor out of the way before taking the call. A chronic eavesdropper, he looked thoroughly disappointed as he stalked back to his room.

'Ernst Huberhof,' said the voice, battling with a storm of static that gave her the puzzled impression that he was telephoning to inform her of a change of government.

'Whose cabinet?' she asked. 'I'm sorry, would you mind repeating that. I can't hear very well.'

'Caligari,' von Huberhof distantly boomed.

'Oh, I see! Has there been another political crisis in Rome?' She spoke tentatively, not having heard of an Italian politician of that name and puzzled why von Huberhof should think his career had any interest for her.

'No, no!' Faint laughter came through the wire. A famous film of that name was being revived in the Berlin Marmorhaus cinema after scoring a brilliant success in New York, Paris and London. Von Huberhof thought it would be interesting to see as the story was set in a lunatic asylum and proposed that they visit it together and have dinner afterwards.

'Are you free? This evening? I would be honoured,' he asked, his voice richly coaxing even on a bad line.

'I'll be glad to come,' she said. 'Will you call for me?'

Von Huberhof hesitated. Sounding very embarrassed and not at all convincing, he replied: 'No, if you'll forgive me, I would prefer that we meet at the cinema. It's not convenient to leave the hospital early. It would be better if we met at 7.30 in the foyer.' He gave her the address and rang off.

It might be considered odd, she thought, that a man who

treated mental illness all the time should choose to use his leisure watching actors simulating madness. Then, again, von Huberhof was a pretty odd man according to information available in Moscow. Something of a pre-war explorer, a wartime Fokker pilot, now a psychologist and certainly a mystery. Instinct told her that it was going to be a strange but interesting evening. Perhaps he calculated that the film would put her into a suitable state of mind for it.

Chapter Eleven

Just before seven she left the house and walked towards the Kurfürstendamm to get a taxi-cab. Almost simultaneously the small car parked outside Becker's *Bierkeller* swung in a wide semi-circle and followed. Its boxlike body rattled and the noisy engine left a trail of oily smoke. As it passed her the driver slowed and stopped. It was not an uncommon nuisance although the cars were usually more impressive. She turned quickly into Zahringerstrasse but the persistent driver followed, pulling up a short distance ahead. He got out, leaving the engine running. A crowd of people coming in the opposite direction obscured the man and she could see only that he was tall, wearing a soft felt hat and a grey flannel suit.

The man waited until she drew level then seized her arm and pulled open the passenger door. 'Get in, Lydia,' he ordered and she was so taken aback that a moment or two passed before it registered with her that it was Peter.

'What a stupid thing to do!' she said furiously. 'That gave me a shock.'

Peter returned to the driver's seat and struggled with clumsy gears. 'If it was someone else it would have been worse,' he said as the car jerked into motion. 'I did try to telephone you from the *Bierkeller* but whoever it was who answered insisted on knowing my name.'

'And naturally,' she said, beginning to smile, 'you refused to tell him.'

'Naturally. Who is the watchdog?'

'Just a neighbour. He lives across the hall and is our self-appointed telephone-answerer-in-chief. I'm afraid he dislikes anonymous callers. You're the second today.'

'Oh, really! May I know who was the first?'

'In due course,' she said and laughed. 'First I have to get over my surprise. Couldn't you have let me know you were coming to Berlin?'

'No time. Something you wrote made me leave in a hurry. You've upset quite a few of my arrangements. How does my secretary explain to fussy officials of the Foreign Affairs Commissariat that I've vanished into thin air when they've crowded me into their busy diaries?'

'I don't think there was anything that alarming in my report, Peter,' Lydia remarked mildly.

'Then,' he said, 'you haven't seen Spichalsky yet.'

'I have. It wasn't a pleasant meeting. We didn't get on well at all.'

Peter listened in silence as she explained, displeasure in every grim line of his face. 'That's going to make things difficult,' he said. 'I'm relying on Spichalsky to stop you getting yourself killed.'

'I take it you're joking.' In fact she was sure he was but it still annoyed her. 'I feel much safer without his protection.'

Peter took his eyes off the road to stare at her briefly and bitterly. 'I'm not joking,' he said. 'Just to watch you walk down the street frightens me. You take yourself too much for granted, as though survival requires no effort. Luck has kept you alive more than once. Spichalsky's more reliable than luck. He knows every twist and turn of Berlin. He needs to. There's a high mortality rate in our business here. This is the danger-zone. In comparison the rest of Europe's a playground.'

'You're forgetting something,' she said, her voice hard. 'More people die of starvation in little Pushkino in one day than all the spies done to death in Berlin in a year. I'm not at all unaware that staying alive is difficult.'

He had certainly not forgotten and it worried him that she put it that way. Because people die by thousands in famine, she was saying, one's own life is cheap. The logic was bad, the attitude suicidal.

'You're here to do a job, not to pay penance for the troubles at home. I wish I could get it into your obstinate head that it's better to play safe in this war than to take chances. There's no romance in it. A good agent doesn't stir up any dust. He thinks three times before he moves. Sometimes, having thought it over, he makes no move at all. A rash step and he'll either end up dead or be dragged off to jail where they'll make him talk or crack him like a louse between their fingernails.'

'Peter, I'm not as reckless as you make out,' Lydia remonstrated. 'I have no intention of committing suicide or allowing myself to be murdered, and the idea that I shall be cracked like any kind of loathsome insect is frankly a very offensive suggestion.' She leaned over and pressed his hand. 'Now, stop feeling so responsible.'

They exchanged a glance of amused exasperation. Peter reluctantly switched his attention back to the problems of city traffic. It was the last golden light before dusk, shadows of buildings already turning blue, the tables of pavement cafés emptying of late afternoon idlers, that brief interval of time when a summer's day takes on a reflective melancholy.

'I'm not in the mood for being responsible at all,' he said. 'Do you realize this is the first time I've seen you in weeks and you've never looked more beautiful?'

'Bread, honey and real eggs for breakfast.' Her husky laugh concealed a momentary awkwardness at his unexpected sentimentality. His intensity usually produced more reticence.

'You make me hungry.' Peter glanced around and took his bearings. 'There's a place near here where they do a very good sawdust *bockwurst*. Let's go.'

Lydia glanced at her wristwatch. 'I can't. In ten minutes I have to meet von Huberhof at a cinema.'

He steered the car into the kerb and clamped on the brake. 'You're going to the cinema with von Huberhof?'

'Yes, and then to dinner.'

It was not often that Peter looked at her with such chilling impersonality, all expression drained from his face. She knew him too well to mistake the reason. He felt rejected, terribly hurt, and could not bear her to witness his humiliation. Peter had withdrawn. The man who confronted her was his doppelgänger, Schtern.

'Just over twenty-four hours ago I read your report in Moscow,' he said with the judicial severity of a prosecutor. 'You had not even made the man's acquaintance. You gave no indication that any meeting had been arranged. How is it possible that you are now so friendly?'

She spelled out how it was possible in equally concise terms.

'Today is Friday. The report was written early Tuesday morning. On Wednesday morning Fyodor Nikolaev asked me to go with him to the Dalldorf lunatic asylum. Von Huberhof and I were introduced. I can't give you a full account now because it will make me late. The Cheka should surely approve because infiltrating *Sondergruppe R* and getting to know von Huberhof were the assignments I was given.'

'The Cheka congratulates you on your zeal,' said Schtern at his most sardonic, 'but is slightly concerned that events appear to be moving with suspicious rapidity.'

'I'm keeping pace with developments, not arranging them and I'll bear the suspicions in mind.'

His fingernails tapped the steering wheel, clicking like an abacus. His manner was utterly business-like.

'I shall have to detain you another few minutes to explain certain essentials. Before leaving Moscow you said you saw the problem here as one of opening the right doors? By chance you've opened one door our Berlin network completely overlooked. General Nikolaev. We re-examined his dossier. It contained a detail that had been dismissed as unimportant. In 1918 when Nikolaev first came to live in Berlin he became friendly with a rich businessman named Berendt and spent some weeks in Paris on business for him. On the face of it this had no special significance. Berendt speaks Russian fluently and has many acquaintances among White emigrés. You know his name, of course?'

'Is he the same Berendt who now directs the Eastern Division of the German Foreign Ministry?'

'Yes, he took over the post in 1919 and is well-known for his anti-Soviet views. He believes Germany's best interests lie in closer relations with the Western Allies. We have no reason to love Herr Berendt. A cross-check of his file produced an interesting discovery. At the very time Nikolaev was in Paris acting as his business representative, Berendt was busily engaged as an intermediary between the provisional German socialist government of Ebert, Scheidemann and Landsberg and certain French government ministers. It is a reasonable assumption that

Nikolaev's commercial transactions in Paris were merely a cover and his real function was as a secret political agent.'

Schtern's eyes suddenly focused on the projecting rear mirror. It reflected a uniformed policeman standing some distance away. The officer seemed to be paying them an uncomfortable interest. Schtern restarted the car and drove a devious route through various streets before pulling up again.

'This throws an entirely new light on General Nikolaev,' he resumed as if there had been no interruption. 'It probably explains the role of Breton-face. The General must have formed contacts with the *Sûreté* and your little *flic* is the go-between.' The sardonic tone returned. 'The Cheka must also congratulate you on the unmasking of Nikolaev. We wrote him off as a foolish nuisance. We may have been right to judge him a fool, but we should not have written him off.' He glanced at his watch. 'You now have only five minutes to keep your appointment, but I'm sure von Huberhof will wait.'

Lydia opened the car door. He closed it again and said: 'Telephone me from a public call-box when your meeting is over. No matter how late.' He gave her the number and instructed her to memorize it. 'Ask for me by the name of Schtern.'

She looked into his eyes. They remained cold, exact. 'Yes,' she said, 'I know.'

At the corner of the next street she hailed a passing taxi-cab.

2

Spichalsky sat up in bed very respectfully and winced whenever he moved his bandaged shoulder. 'You see, comrade –' he began again.

'You left your cap behind and you had to remove the incriminating evidence,' said Peter, nodding in exaggerated understanding.

Another train went by with a terrific clatter; a caterpillar of lights streaked across the window and the small room shook like an invalid with Parkinson's disease. Spichalsky's tidily folded trousers slipped off the brass rail of the bed. Peter picked them up, considerately dusted them and put them back in place. Everything else withstood the convulsion in good order.

'Thank you, thank you. Very kind,' said Spichalsky, bobbing his head and wincing.

'What I don't quite understand,' said Peter, resuming his measured pacing of the room, 'is' – he twisted sideways to look at the titles of the wounded man's books neatly arranged along with old illustrated magazines; apart from the correct political literature, Spichalsky's taste ran exclusively to sentimental German fiction – 'how a man of your great experience could have got into such a mess in the first place.'

'Exactly, comrade. You see, as a man of experience –'

'Let us look at this thing in an orderly fashion,' said Peter, pausing at the washing stand to note that Spichalsky's toothbrush, dental powder, piece of soap, razor, shaving brush and nail-scissors were all properly lined up and ready for inspection. 'In the first place, considering it in an orderly fashion, should it be done. Next, is it agreed. Further, how to do it and when. In addition, who is to carry it out. Penultimately, proceed to fulfil the task. Last but not least, do it efficiently and well and leave everything ship-shape. Do you agree?'

'With every word,' Spichalsky fervently assured him, 'but –'

'The other party did not agree. That is what you are going to tell me, eh?'

Spichalsky gave a vigorous nod and poignantly touched his injured left shoulder. 'Not only so,' he said, 'but she also –'

Turning at the foot of the bed and silencing him with an upraised palm, Peter continued thoughtfully: 'On point Number Two, no agreement. Then the rest is clear. Until consultation with higher authority, points three, four, five and six must be postponed.' He looked up severely. 'You did wrong, comrade. A serious error of judgement. It was bound to end badly and we have to be thankful that the outcome was not worse.' Pointing to the centre of his forehead, between the eyes, he said: 'Imagine if the bullet went in there. Instead of a torn shoulder muscle, the body of a Soviet intelligence officer on the carpet, out of which our enemies could concoct a serious international incident.'

With the roar of an enraged lion, a train tore through the night on the adjacent railway line. The window-panes rattled like a dry skeleton shaken by a tornado and every object in the room jittered and danced. The trousers slipped off the rail once more. Peter dusted and hung them again.

'The nine o'clock express to Schoneberg,' said Spichalsky dolefully. He launched into a laboured account of his conference with agent Selena, the superhuman patience with which he'd tried to bring her to a reasonable point of view, her woeful ignorance in comparison to his own immense experience as a soldier of the revolution and a Chekist, and his opinion that perhaps, in view of, purely because of past experience, and suchlike considerations as entries in a certain Nikolaev diary, the said agent Selena should be kept under observation from top to bottom, so to say.

This time Peter heard him out with no interruption and, up to the last point at least, not without a certain sympathy. He had a reluctant respect for the unprepossessing Spichalsky and valued his work. For a Russian, his thoroughness was positively Teutonic. The relentless accumulation of detail might be boring and indiscriminate but nothing of use was left out – fact, fiction and idle gossip were interspersed with accurate observation and the texts of official documents. Spichalsky's skill in obtaining access to confidential filing cabinets verged on the brilliant. And he did it on the cheap. No costly bribes or expensive entertainment. A female German party member introduced into the right office, a beer and *bratwurst* for a plain, lonely secretary, bed too if it became necessary, and the copy of an interesting memorandum or letter passed through the usual channels to Moscow. For bread and butter intelligence gathering there was no one better.

The blundering idiocy over Nikolaev was, therefore, totally out-of-character and explicable only in terms of a mental seizure provoked by the self-possessed, overpoweringly elegant Berlin-Lydia. Poor Spichalsky had set out to prove his superiority and made a mess of it. That could be overlooked. The sly but ponderous hints that Lydia might be up to no good and could not as a former aristocrat be trusted was, however, bad for morale and, far worse, dangerous for Lydia. On the principle that innocence could never be proven, and in the grim knowledge that many good people had been shot by certain of his bloodthirsty colleagues on far less suspicion.

A harsh rage suddenly swept Peter. He paced the scuffed linoleum up and down, up and down, with the sullen fury of a caged tiger.

'Spichalsky,' he began so abruptly that his subordinate became rigid with alarm. 'Spichalsky, you've given me food for thought about slander and lies. I have in mind the Comrade Selena whose great revolutionary record under her real name of Lydia Nikolaievna Alexandrova is known in the highest circles of our Soviet Government.' Approaching the bed and cruelly gazing into Spichalsky's startled eyes, he asked menacingly: 'Where were you in 1911 and what were you doing?'

'In 1911? Where? ... At home, comrade. In Simferopol ... I was working,' said Spichalsky, his voice trailing off, 'in the fruit market.'

'In the nice warm Crimea, eh! And Comrade Alexandrova, who could eat off gold plate and had coachmen and servants to carry out her slightest command, left everything to join the labouring women in cotton mills and bring them the immortal sayings of Karl Marx and Vladimir Ilyich Lenin. Did you know that, Spichalsky? Did you know what she was doing when you were a soldier of the imperialist war? Freezing in black Siberian winters as punishment for struggling to bring justice to the suffering workers. Tell me, Spichalsky,' said Peter, bringing his face to within an inch of his unhappy subordinate's, 'where were you in 1918 and 1919 and 1920?'

Spichalsky opened his mouth several times before he could manage to speak. 'Naturally, comrade, doing ... my duty. Here ...'

'And all the time you were living off the fat here in Berlin this traitor, this renegade, this sly snake of the former bourgeoisie,' said Peter in a tone of drawling and contemptuous irony, 'was fighting and killing counter-revolutionaries as a commander of heroic partisans. Fighting for our starving, suffering Russian workers and peasants, Spichalsky. Blood and death, Spichalsky. That's the loyalty we're talking of.'

Another train racketed past, shaking the room, and Spichalsky's trousers slid once more off the rail. This time Peter left them on the floor.

'Blood and death and loyalty, Spichalsky,' he said. 'Never mind the class question. If there's rot in the root, the fruit tastes sour.'

'Yes, comrade. Very true, very true. All I was saying is that a man –'

'A man is a man, yes,' interrupted Peter sternly. 'But one last word on the question of the female gender. Brains and guts, Spichalsky, are not carried in the balls. From whose lips does a man learn to be a human being? From a mother, Spichalsky, a mother. A man who forgets the courage of his mother is insulting the bravery of Russian womankind.'

A decent shame settled on the blunt, homely features of Boris Spichalsky and the muscles in his bare throat quivered in the effort to control an honest emotion. He had a mother. Moisture filled his eyes.

'Comrade Piatkov,' he said after a silence, 'thank you for the frankness of your words.'

Only when he was left alone did the hate return, as bruised and nagging as the pain in his mangled shoulder.

3

Ernst von Huberhof said: 'Most remarkable,' his voice resonating in the confined space of the cab. He took off the broad-brimmed black hat that gave him an artistic look and rested it on his knees. His handsome, distinguished head turned towards her. 'Did you not think so?'

'Yes.' Lydia looked away. The power of cinematic images was unfamiliar to her. Nightmare interpenetrated reality. Von Huberhof's hat, his dense physical presence, a ring gleaming on the little finger of his hand, the vibrant voice trained to soothe, pacify, disarm and dominate. In her whole life she'd seen motion pictures perhaps ten times, flickering comedies, absurd romances, crude propaganda moralities. But the film they had just left had taken her unawares. She felt as though it had driven her closer to her own insanity. Through Caligari's hypnotic spectacles the world became an autistic conflict, images of one's own disordered imagination. And it was, in a sense, true, she thought. One invents one's own horrors. The high-explosive disintegration of a man can be less terrifying because less imagined than a child's appalled reaction to a deformed shadow.

'From the professional point of view,' said von Huberhof, 'it is like staring into a sick mind with a microscope. I am referring to the mind of the one who made that picture. He is of course a very disturbed and dangerous man.' White teeth showed in a smile. 'We are dining in my home. Much pleasanter than a noisy restaurant. My housekeeper has everything prepared.'

A sultry humidity permeated the glittering night. The fairground lights of Berlin streaked past the window, a city interiorized into dream. Pictures of nudes grotesquely displayed outside *Nachtlokal*; fox-trotting couples moving rhythmically through boredom and eroticism in mauve-lit dance halls; diners guzzling flesh, fruit and wine while vagrants methodically sifted the leavings in swill-bins. Before morning someone would die violently in time to make the afternoon newspaper editions. The murdered ghosts of Rosa Luxemburg and Karl Liebknecht still haunted the streets. And tall glasses foamed with beer, paunches swelled with it, it oiled the merry-go-round.

'Do you think such a film could have been made anywhere but in Germany?' Lydia wondered aloud.

'Perhaps not,' von Huberhof replied after careful consideration. 'Without approving of the picture, I must admit it is talented. We are a highly creative people. Our genius for poetry, philosophy and drama is not sufficiently appreciated. German civilization has more to offer the world than music. Schiller, Goethe, Rilke, Kleist, Nietzsche, Schopenhauer. The list is endless.' He placed his hand on her arm in the darkness of the cab and shifted musingly to the soft flesh above the elbow. 'By the way, I wish you would call me Ernst. May I use your first name?'

No Heinrich Heine, no Gottfried Lessing, she noted. Naturally, no Karl Marx and not only because he was a Jew.

They spoke to one another on first name terms about nothing very much. His touch disturbed her and, despite the antipathy, she felt an unwelcome stirring of desire.

The taxi deposited them outside a low-timbered villa in the

Grunewald. Von Huberhof unlocked the door and stood for a moment listening in the hall before leading her into a long oak-beamed room. Ancestral portraits hung on the walls, the mounted head of a great stag, group photographs of young men in virile poses. Despite the warm evening, logs smouldered in the open fireplace. The table was laid for two, a pink and perfec rose in a slender silver vase beside one place, and candles set in silver completed the intimate atmosphere.

'I noticed you looking at my *Bruderschaften* photographs,' von Huberhof said smiling. 'I'm always meaning to get rid of them.' They had had the ritual sherry and were being served dinner by a woman in black so self-effacing that only the rustle of a starched apron betrayed her existence. 'The good old days, the good old comrades, every few weeks another reunion. One drinks gallons of beer and fellows slap you on the back and say, "Christ! do I remember you at that bloody mess in Cambrin. Mud, blood and rain, eh? Pissed down for a week." At another reunion a great big chap with a red moustache pummels you black and blue shouting, "What a day that was when Herr Flautermeyer gave you six scorchers for sticking a tin-tack on his chair," and you realize you were nine years old and he's the spotty boy who sat at the next desk in school. You are right to consider us a sentimental people, but these are really tribal rites. When it comes to the point, I can no more take them off the wall than throw out my great-grandfather's picture.'

He talked very freely about himself while they were at table, drinking a good deal of wine and laughing a lot. Lydia was not deceived: these were merely preliminaries.

'I decided to be a flyer partly because I got fed up with the filth of the trenches but more because I disliked the idea that at thirty-four I was already an old man. They were right, of course. The real knights of the air were blue-eyed boys of eighteen or twenty, although the best of them, Baron Richthofen, was an elderly twenty-five or so.'

'Why did you decide to become a psychiatrist?' she asked.

He looked at her with hard, smiling, wide-open eyes. 'That is the most difficult question you could ask me. Not for the same reason as Dr Caligari, of course. But I'm not sure I really know the answer. As soon as I qualified in medicine I rushed off to Africa to escape the boredom of tinkering with bodily disease. All those ulcerated stomachs and messy plumbing systems. Maybe it was a little like getting out of the trenches into the sky. Whatever madness is, it's not earthbound. Then I got excited by it, as flying excited me. The sense of living at the very limit of reality, of seeing everything in strange perspective. The first man who tried to become a bird and killed himself . . .' his voice altered in tone, becoming oddly quiet and reflective, 'was the madman of his time.'

Von Huberhof continued to smile across the length of the table and his gaze remained fixed on her. Fixed, and not seeing. The reflected flame of candles set his eyes on fire, and in his altered voice he spoke of men who died finely, stepping across safe frontiers of knowledge into the unknown, committing their density to the experiment of air. He spoke like a visionary about war. The warm scent of night stock drifted in from the garden and von Huberhof spoke of death and the nation. With bitter pride he told of young students in patched civilian clothes fighting anonymously to the last drop of blood to prevent Silesia being detached from a crumbling Germany. Future engineers, magistrates, dentists, university professors, who'd left their studies for the secret war against the Poles, he brought them vividly to mind, thin and battle-scarred and magnificently selfless. Red drops of wine stained the tablecloth, the ancestral portraits nodded with stiff dignity on the walls, sweet air from the garden bent the candleflames, and von Huberhof talked of the *heilige Bruderschaft* of young men dying finely in Upper Silesia. And some years hence, thought Lydia, those who survived, the lawyers and professors and dentists and politicians, would slap one another's backs, eyes swollen with drunken tears, and say: 'Remember Langemarck, old friend? What a shitty do that was.'

Why is it, she asked herself, that seen from across the frontiers of one's own country and ideology, all this seems mawkish and grotesque? Did she not have her own *Bruderschaft* who wept much the same tears when they met, remembering Kovali, Kazan, Simbirsk with the coarse, ironic deflation that all old soldiers use to tame unbearable experiences? Von Huberhof spoke with visionary intensity about war and Germany the way she herself sometimes spoke about revolution and Russia. If it was madness she shared it. To hate one's enemy was, in her belief, necessary: to recognize and respect his sincerity hard but also necessary. It often exercised a morbid fascination. One had to guard against that. She looked down at her hands, hands that had killed. She had held men in the sights of a rifle and stifled curiosity, suppressed pity. It was an atrocious thing, deliberately to destroy a human being. At the moment of kill the mind reduced the enemy to an abstract target, for a momentary hesitation of the trigger finger and the life of a comrade, a crucial battle, could be lost. But afterwards the corpse's humanity asserted recognition. You turned it over, went through its pockets. The bent photograph of a smiling girl, 'To Grisha with love,' a carefully folded letter almost worn through with reading and re-reading, the key of a door, an acorn carried for luck. You were perfunctory about it. Someone made a joke. Otherwise it would feel like murder.

The housekeeper glided in with a starched rustle bringing coffee and broke von Huberhof's mood.

'It's impolite of me to be so self-indulgent,' he said, suddenly crisp. 'I didn't bring you here to talk about myself. Let us have our coffee and brandy in comfort on the couch.'

He stood up, a man who moved with a certain compact grace, and drew dark blue heavy curtains across the window, sealing off the garden. Fireglow, candleflame and the diffused light of hooded lamps threw velvety shadows, softly glittered on gilt portraits and polished furniture, creating an isolation in the room as if it existed on an island in a sea of night.

'This has been a curious evening,' he began, joining her by the fire and lighting a thin Dutch cigar. His expression was quizzical. 'I have the distinct impression that you've been carefully observing me, waiting to see what move I'll make. Am I right? I'm sorry, do you smoke?'

'Yes.' Lydia took a cigarette from the proffered silver box. It was an answer to both questions.

'The obvious explanation will have occurred to you.' Von Huberhof gave a relaxed smile. 'I am fond of women. I'm especially attracted to women like you. With a fine-edged, borderline, rather dangerous beauty that I'd describe – if you won't misunderstand me – as unfeminine. There's an air of independence about you. You give the impression of being very controlled and, at the same time, adventurous. I find that challenging. If you took to the air you'd be a superb aviatrix.'

'Even at the ripe old age of thirty?'

'Have you never wanted to fly?' von Huberhof asked, amused and incredulous.

Lydia looked thoughtful. 'I've often thought it would be wonderful to ride a motorcycle.'

'At tremendous speed?'

'Naturally,' she said, and they both laughed. Lydia took a sip of brandy and blew out a reflective stream of smoke. 'The obvious explanation might have occurred to me had it not been even more obvious that General Nikolaev did not take me to Dalldorf just to see those unhappy women patients.'

'The General hasn't been the same since he met you. He's in love. He wishes he'd known you in his prime.'

'Fyodor Yegorovich is an old dear,' said Lydia, 'but bringing me to Dalldorf had nothing to do with love.'

'Why, then, do you think you were brought?'

'I've no idea but it makes me very curious.'

Von Huberhof's smile became enigmatic and he spent a moment or two observing the ash on his cigar. 'He talked a great deal about you. He remembers your father as an equerry of the late Tsar –'

'Not exactly an equerry,' she murmured.

He waved, dismissing it as of no importance. 'The General also spoke about certain youthful political extravagances, not altogether uncharacteristic of your rebellious generation, and all sorts of other things like social work among the poor and a long trip to America.'

'I had no idea he was so obsessed with my experiences,' said Lydia coldly, 'nor what business he had discussing it with you.' She stared at him. 'You're not, by any chance, connected with the secret police?'

Had Peter heard he might have been appalled, but instinct told her the reaction was sound. It was too much like a police interrogation of a privileged suspect whose status required a little wining and dining.

'*Grüss Gott!*' Von Huberhof's laugh was unnaturally loud. 'Why do you think they'd be interested in you?'

Speaking with bitter emphasis, she replied: 'It's clear you've never had to live the life of an exile.'

'My dear Lydia . . .' He pressed her hand sympathetically.

'Fyodor Yegorovich,' she went on, 'said I'd made a good impression. Why should it matter what kind of impression I made on a perfect stranger?'

'I will answer that very soon, but at the risk of making you angry I have to say that something about you puzzles me.'

'What do you mean?'

'Behind everything Nikolaev has said there is a strange vacuum. You did this, you went there, some years ago you lost someone you loved. The profile is unfinished. A person experiences friendship, passion, grief, failure, happiness, disappointment. You appear to be a woman without an inner life.'

Lydia's eyes became very wintry, very bleak. 'This conversation has gone far enough. Is it possible to telephone for a taxi-cab?'

'Please be patient. I realize it seems impertinent, but there's a very good reason why I need to know as much as possible about you.'

'No,' she said, swept by a genuine gust of anger. 'There's nothing you can say that would persuade me to tell you one single thing about what you call my inner life. It does not, and cannot, concern you.'

With an air of finality, she stood up and moved to the door. Von Huberhof intercepted her. Placing his hands on her shoulders, he looked deeply and searchingly into her eyes. Speaking with solemn vehemence, he said: 'I want to trust you! I do trust you! But it has to be so completely that I'd be prepared to have my right arm cut off on your behalf.'

The warmth of his touch again affected her unwillingly, a sullen irresistible stirring of desire, and her brain, clear a moment before, felt drugged and clouded by wine. She forced a husky laugh. 'You sound as though you're inviting me to join some secret *Bruderschaft*.'

He continued to gaze into her, his hands on her shoulders, and the sudden silence grew charged. 'Perhaps,' he said, 'I am,' and led her back into the intimacy of the warm and dusky room.

They sat closer together. The ring on von Huberhof's little finger gleamed in the firelight. The blond hairs on his strong, clever hands shone gold. He turned to her, a network of concerned wrinkles around fine luminous eyes as blue and intense as the colour of the curtains that shut off the garden.

'Your family lost everything in the Revolution,' he said softly.

'Not everything. We lost our wealth.'

'And your country,' said von Huberhof in tones of deep compassion. 'That is the worst of all.'

'It is terrible to lose one's country,' said Lydia.

'People whose country has been torn from them,' said von Huberhof, 'are like ghosts whose bodies were killed with unspeakable violence.' He opened the silver box and offered her another cigarette, a token of sympathy. For a moment he seemed on the point of slipping an arm around her, then chose instead to offer a different consolation. 'There is no need to despair, Lydia. I have reason to believe it won't be long before Russia is rid of the Bolsheviks.'

His quiet assurance held such authority that it gave her a sharp stab of alarm. Coming from a man connected with *Sondergruppe R* the remark had an ominous resonance. The politics of conspiracy made everything possible. Could it be that the elaborate secret negotiations of the German War Ministry with Soviet representatives cloaked a devious plan to destroy the Revolution? That all the talk of armament factories and clandestine military academies was designed to create means to smuggle into the heart of Russia the nucleus of a conquering army?

'Why do you say that?' she asked, trying to sound hopeful rather than apprehensive.

'Because only Lenin holds the murderous thieves together. He has never recovered from the 1918 assassination attempt by the Jewess Kaplan. I have it on reliable authority that one bullet remains in his neck and causes violent seizures. He has a year or two at the most and the minute he's dead the rest will be sticking knives in each other's backs.'

She felt a reassuring rush of contempt. If that was the quality of von Huberhof's intelligence information there was nothing to fear. It could have been one of the White Russian rowdies, commanders of the imaginary death battalions, holding forth in a backstreet bar. Lenin's illness and impending death was another of the miracles that would have them waking up one morning to find that the clock still stood at a quarter-to-yesterday and history hadn't happened at all.

'Unfortunately,' von Huberhof said austerely, 'some of the best men in Germany, our own people, are more pessimistic. They are convinced that Russian Bolshevism is here to stay and advantages can be gained by coming to terms with it.' He shook his head in bitter frustration. 'I wish I could speak more freely, but . . .'

'I would first have to tell you about my lovers,' smiled Lydia.

He shrugged and grinned. 'Perhaps not even then.'

The burden of an onerous and unwanted secrecy sank into a lake of silence. Von Huberhof lit another slender Dutch cigar and stared reflectively into the fire. A log collapsed in a small shower of sparks.

'Ah, Germania, lost between its easterners and westerners!' he sighed. 'I have dear friends on both sides. Fine fellows playing at being Metternichs, Bismarcks and Prince Machiavellis without a decent card in their hands. The one will end up making Bolshevism impregnable, the other will turn us into a vassal of English kings, French vintners and American-Jewish millionaires. I have nightmares of Germans falling before the walls of Communist Moscow or dying as hired Legionnaires to preserve the colonial empire of France.'

'But, Ernst, far from Bolshevism becoming impregnable you said that in two or three years Russia will have got rid of it,' said Lydia, puzzled.

'That does matter to you, doesn't it?'

'Very much,' she said.

Von Huberhof took hold of both her hands and said impulsively, like a boy making a reckless declaration of love: 'I believe in you, Lydia, and I want you to believe in me. Do you?'

She looked sombrely at him and replied: 'I believe in the sincerity of your love for Germany.' And in the virulence of your hatred for most of what I value, she added in silent safeguard of her own integrity.

'Thank you,' he said. 'And will you promise to respect what I tell you now as a sacred confidence?'

'Of course,' she said.

Apparently much moved, he lifted her hands and bent his head to kiss them. Speaking in a low, confiding voice as though an invisible listener were present, he said: 'There is a group of us, Germans and Russians. We are united by devotion to the lands of our birth and detestation of the Communist evil. This is our cause and we serve it on the basis of three principles – loyalty, silence, obedience. I want you to join us.'

Der Bruderschaft. Gently Lydia withdrew her hands. *Der heilige Bruderschaft*. She went through the motions of indecision.

'What would I have to do?'

The mordant expression returned to mask von Huberhof's face. 'Well, there's no blood-mingling rite so we won't have to cut our veins,' he said. 'Nor would it be appropriate to expect you to carry out acts of terror.'

'Brrh! I hope not. Perhaps I'll ride a motorcycle and carry messages.'

'No, I intend to give you flying lessons and send you over Moscow to drop pamphlets on the doorstep of the Kremlin.'

'Delicious thought,' Lydia said.

Becoming serious again, von Huberhof explained that he was not sure at that moment what she'd be asked to do. Everything would be discussed in greater detail at another meeting, perhaps the next day. They might want her to travel, make contacts, transmit funds. Whatever it was, she must disclose it to nobody. Were these conditions acceptable?

'In principle, yes,' she replied. 'I suppose I'm mad to say so. I have the sort of slightly sick, swooping excitement one gets from travelling fast down a steep ski-slope.'

'That is a good feeling,' commented von Huberhof and smiled.

'How soon,' asked Lydia, 'will I be given my first task?'

He considered the matter carefully. 'Probably very soon. But let us not think of it now. The circumstances call for a toast.' He twisted the wire from a bottle still dusty from the cellar, the cork flew out and freshly poured champagne foamed in tulip-shaped glasses when a creaking was heard and the door-knob stealthily turned.

The shaft of yellow light from the hall outlined an immensely tall woman in a trailing white nightdress leaning for support on a stick. Grey hair streaked with faded henna straggled almost to her waist, and great blank eyes stared out of her white emaciated face like holes cut in a mask.

Paying them no attention, the tall woman wandered about the room with a kind of ruined dignity carrying on a muttered monologue.

Von Huberhof slowly set down the champagne bottle and unobtrusively pulled a bellrope by the fireplace. Quietly and patiently, he said: 'Mother, what are you doing out of your room?'

'Don't bother me, Ernst,' was the flustered reply. 'Can't you see how worried I am? I've lost my animal. Argus! Argus!'

'Her wolfhound,' von Huberhof confided to Lydia. 'He has been dead for ten years. Come, mother,' he said, taking her arm, 'please go back to bed.'

'I will not, not, not go to that dreadful room. Those dreadful people keep tapping at the window and the servants never come when I ring. Your father would have had them instantly flogged. The servants loved your father, Ernst. He was very kind to them.'

'I will ask Martha to bring you a nice warm glass of milk,' said von Huberhof. 'You know how much you need your beauty sleep.' He tried to lead her away but she wrenched herself free and pointed imperiously at Lydia. '*Who is that girl?*'

His manner became brusque. 'She is a friend, mother. Now do come.'

'A friend! Always a friend!' The woman laughed with shrill sarcasm. 'Wine and candles and female friends. *Quite disgusting!*'

'Mother!' The flesh around von Huberhof's nose had gone white. 'You are being very tiresome. I must insist that you go immediately to your room.'

'Don't dare lay a finger on me, Ernst!' She tossed back her long disordered hair and glared tragically. 'I am the Gräfin Elfreda von Huberhof. I really cannot understand why decency and nobility no longer command respect in this world.'

A starched rustle announced the hurried arrival of the black-clad housekeeper. 'Very sorry, Herr Professor, I gave Madame her sleeping medicine. She must have spat it out when my back was turned.' Firmly grasping von Huberhof's mother round the waist and holding one of her arms captive, she declared as if speaking to a child: 'Now, Madame, we're going to wish everybody good night and go nicely to bed. Good night, everybody!'

The housekeeper began hustling her away but the old woman wedged herself against the door-frame and screamed: 'Don't sleep with him! He's filthy! He wears rubber things! I gave birth to an unnatural son!'

Von Huberhof drew in a hissing breath. The woman could still be heard screaming as she was dragged up the stairs. 'My mother is not a Gräfin,' he said, staring bleakly into the dwindling fire. 'Our rank is modest, a family of landowners from Schleswig-Holstein. Although there are two other sons and five grandchildren she has got it into her sick head that we are a dying dynasty.' Involuntarily, his glance lifted to the eighteenth-century portrait of an ancestor, lingered and turned away. 'I am sorry you witnessed this embarrassment,' he said. 'Shall we drink our champagne?'

Lydia avoided looking at him. Whatever antagonistic force his personality had exerted was broken by his mother's madness. Like the smudged letter and creased family photo in the pocket of a dead enemy, it turned her hatred into a grudging pity. The blue-eyed dangerous von Huberhof was a bachelor in his forties shackled to a mad mother who could not be escaped by taking to the skies or travelling to a remote country. Madness is of the air, he'd said, but for him it was rooted in the very earth he grew from. The madness of his mother turned the world into an insane asylum. It explained Dalldorf. It could explain the *heilige Bruderschaft* that sought to protect the motherland by gallantry and terror, purge her of phantom enemies and bring back the purity of health.

Von Huberhof gazed at Lydia with melancholy intensity. Her mouth was filled with the bitter-sweet sparkle of champagne and a vision of the electric city spun like a carousel in the fairground of her mind. He lifted his hand and slowly passed the back of it over her face. Blond hairs brushed over her flushed cheek like the legs of tiny spiders.

She would never, never quite understand why, but Lydia knew that she wanted von Huberhof to make love to her.

Chapter Twelve

Three flights down in the lobby the telephone begins its faint, high-pitched ring. In Room 37 Herr Schtern, journalist from Basle, Switzerland, strikes a match and sees it is ten past five. The flare dies out, plunging him again into darkness. Dawn glimmers through a rent in the curtain. He lies back on the pillow and the telephone goes on ringing, its sound travelling hopelessly through the dingy hotel.

He tries not to listen. Every time it rings he thinks it must be her at last, but it never is and his mind plunges into another waking nightmare. She arrives at the cinema, spends a pleasant couple of hours there with the sociable von Huberhof, steps confidently into a waiting motor-car. Instead of being taken to a restaurant she is brought to a secluded apartment where some astute, relentless men have been assembled. Tell us who you really are? Who employs you? What are your instructions? After the initial shock, she treats them, of course, with scorn. But the process is just beginning. They are professionals and the methods will be varied, skilful, prolonged and, if necessary, cruel.

He gets off the bed, eyes gritty with fatigue, and pulls the curtain aside. Pigeons stir as night drains from the sky. Dim lights burn in padlocked shops; windows remain shuttered; zinc bins stuffed with garbage stand on pavements; streetlamps still shine in the wan, deserted dawn street. His throat is parched and he turns from the window to get a drink. The tepid water tastes of loneliness.

Another scenario: jealousy. She enjoys her evening. She drinks far too much over dinner. He can see her flushed and hilarious, compliant to obscene fumblings: she is naked, lustful. He recoils in disgust at the bitter and envious voyeurism he has aroused in himself.

Prowling the room in stockinged feet, he lights a cigarette

and listens to the unanswered telephone. After a while the ringing stops. He smokes nervously and waits. Someone in an adjacent room breaks into a rasping fit of coughing. He has given up hope again when there is a knock at the door.

'*Telefon*, Herr Schtern,' says a drowsy voice.

'*Jawohl, danke*.'

Now that the long-awaited call has come, anxiety is replaced by a dull anger. It is her turn to wait. He stubs out the cigarette, puts on his shoes and buttons his shirt, slops water over his face and slowly dries it before descending the stairs. Except for a single bulb burning over the reception desk, the lobby is dark. The elderly night-clerk snores bolt upright in his chair and the telephone dangles loosely from its cord.

'*Hier ist Schtern*,' he says.

'*Ich möchte Ihnen sehen*,' says Lydia.

Her voice sounds wispy and in the background, faintly, he can hear the shunting of trains. '*Wo sind Sie?*' he asks and she says she is speaking from a public booth in the Lehrte Station near the Invalidenstrasse entrance.

'Wait in the refreshment bar. I'll be there in half-an-hour,' he says in German, curtly, and hangs up the receiver.

When he arrived she was sitting alone at a table in the gloomiest corner of a large gloomy room, lethargically stirring a cup of grey coffee. As a matter of routine, Peter carefully scanned each of the early morning travellers before slipping into the seat at her side. Morosely gazing at her averted profile, he said: 'Did you get lost?' thinking that she looked like someone who had travelled unhopefully and arrived at the wrong destination.

She gave a quick, uneasy smile. 'I'm sorry. You have every right to be angry.'

'Have I?' He stared bitterly. 'Why?'

'Because I kept you waiting for the call.'

'Is that the only reason?'

'No,' she said. 'It's not the only reason.'

Like two strangers forced into an unwilling conversation, they turned away from one another. Lydia sipped some of her unappetizing coffee and glanced through the grimy window at passengers crowded round the Bremen platform. Dread settled on his heart. What she would say was going to hurt and, with savage perversity, he willed her to say it. The night's torment was not yet complete.

'Are you going to tell me about it, or is it something you can't discuss?' he asked.

'I have to tell you everything, although you're never going to forgive me for it. According to the rules there's no choice.' She played nervously with the spoon and recited: 'A member of the Cheka who becomes sexually involved while on foreign assignment must report the circumstances without fail to avoid the risk of blackmail.'

The hiss and shudder of trains filled the silence, hoarse cries of porters, the slamming of doors, a guard's shrill whistle: melancholy noises that belonged to dislocation, to throat-constricting moments of goodbye.

'Go on,' he said tersely.

'Von Huberhof recruited me into his exclusive club,' said Lydia in a wry, detached voice. 'Let's say there was a kind of initiation. I'd feel better if I could tell myself it was something I had to do. It wouldn't be true. I slept with a man I detest who stands for things I hate, and I did it of my own choice.'

Every word she spoke stripped a piece of skin from his heart. He was gripped by a powerful, utterly useless hatred. For more than ten years he'd been obsessed by this woman. For every hour of happiness there had been weeks of longing, anxiety, terror even. Why did he put up with it? Why couldn't he settle for a woman capable of an ordinary, selfish, domesticated conjugality? Once again he thought of love with all its jealousy, fear and aching separation as a sickness. And the more intense the suffering, the less one could bear to be cured of it. Infidelity sharpened the hunger of love.

'To say that I did it of my own choice,' Lydia amended painstakingly, 'is not quite true. I don't know why it happened. Nothing as simple as lust, no violent infatuation, not enough drink to lose control. It just . . . happened.'

He looked at her in frozen dismay. He was back in the hotel room, trapped between waiting and silence, and everything was going on in the harsh glare of his insomniac brain.

She stared at her clasped hands. 'It's an appalling time to say it, but I love you.'

He gripped the edge of the table, bearing down to stifle the pain, then got up and walked blindly out of the buffet. Thrusting through the crowded station, he made for the lavatory and bent over a water-closet. Spasms of nausea wracked him and he broke out in a cold sweat. The stench of vomit clung to his clothes. He leaned against the greasy yellow wall, breathing heavily, then washed under the running tap and dried himself on a pocket-handkerchief. The face in the corroded mirror was pale, unnaturally calm.

Lydia was still there when he returned, smoking nervously. He looked at her with cold dislike and said: 'I have to ask you this, even if it sounds melodramatic. Supposing you were ordered to kill von Huberhof, would you do it?'

She took the cigarette from between her lips, blew out a thin stream of smoke and replied in one clipped monosyllable: 'Yes.'

'Without hesitation?'

Pushing a strand of hair away from her wintry eyes, she said: 'Provided that it's not ordered as an act of revenge.'

'The question is strictly professional,' he said in chill reprimand. 'I have to be satisfied that this involvement has not created a conflict that undermines your oath of loyalty.'

'The only thing undermined is my self-respect.'

A gesture of sympathy would have been in order, but there was no consolation in it for either of them and he did not have the strength to make it. Lydia was the kind who savoured her bitterness to the last drop. No excuses, no self-justification. If there was a debt to be paid she'd pay it in full, out of her own resources. That fierce independence was the secret both of her strength and her frailty and he'd got used to it. His brain felt paralysed by fatigue. He wanted to return to the hotel, draw the curtains, stumble into the black forgetfulness of sleep.

'Now that you've been recruited into this nest of conspirators, what have you been asked to do?'

'Nothing as yet.' Lydia dropped her cigarette into the dregs of coffee and stirred it absently until it disintegrated. 'There's to be another meeting. Von Huberhof is to try and arrange something for later today. I'm to be introduced to somebody, he didn't say who.' She glanced up hesitantly. 'Peter, if you have any doubts about me, I'm ready to go back to Moscow.'

In simple human terms there would have been only one answer, but as her commander he must force himself to be utterly dispassionate and put duty first.

'No, we can't spare you now. This is too important for us. With German aid we can build up an arms industry to the levels attained by the most advanced Western countries. A technical delegation from the *Reichswehr* is due to arrive in Petersburg to inspect factories in nine days from now. We are sure an attempt will be made to sabotage it. In a way,' he pointed out wryly, 'you've made yourself indispensable. You've won the confidence of the enemy. We have to rely on you to find out what von Huberhof's plan is.'

An act of madness, he thought disconnectedly. They will try something desperate and she'll get hurt. Jacob Peters should not have insisted on sending her. After so many years, the change had been too abrupt. She was bound to be thrown off-balance. More than one battle-tested Soviet emissary had failed to survive exposure to the soft corruption of Western luxury. 'They sniffed real coffee,' Moscow cynics said. Why should Lydia, scarred by the abject miseries of Pushkino famine victims, be immune?

He closed his eyes, rocked by a wave of dizziness, and the sound of locomotives brought an illusion of hurtling through an endless tunnel. The stations of his life glimmered and were gone, a journey between nowhere and nowhere . . .

'I must get some sleep,' he muttered. 'You go now. Telephone when you have some news.'

'Peter,' she said, touching his arm. 'I'm sorry.'

'Yes, I know,' he said, too tired for rancour or reconciliation.

She looked back wretchedly as she left and an unexpected stab of pity went through him. It was not a good feeling for Lydia to arouse: it diminished her. He forgave her because there was no other choice, but she would not forgive herself. He pitied her own unmerciful judgement.

A newsvendor entered the buffet. He bought a copy of the *Berliner Tageblatt* and glanced out of the window before opening it. Lydia hurried through the rush-hour crowds with an erect, forlorn defiance, and it was as if another rope had lassoed his heart, binding him closer to her than ever.

2

'Very kind of you to motor down with Ernst to see us, Countess Alexandrova,' smiled Colonel Oskar von Niedermayer, leading them out to the garden. He patted the rump of a mastiff with a huge sad head and signalled to a servant who led the reluctant animal away.

Birds flew and bees danced in the droning, flower-scented air. A green and perfect lawn fringed by poplars stretched to the banks of the Havel, sparkling in afternoon sunshine. Colonel Niedermayer, good looking and sunburned in a well-worn brown Norfolk suit, laughingly repeated the story about the English lord whose recipe for a decent lawn was to plant some seed, then cut and roll the grass for three hundred years. 'An Englishman would turn up his high-bridged nose at such an upstart German meadow,' said von Niedermayer, wrinkling his own aristocratic nose. Lydia, whose polite admiration had provoked the anecdote, said the English were masters of ironic understatement and Ernst von Huberhof recalled a young English officer, minus an arm after being blown-up by a shellburst, who exclaimed: 'I say, it isn't my bowling arm, is it?' With a touch of malice, von Huberhof commented: 'It has style. At least you must admit that, Oskar,' and the Colonel conceded that it had.

'However,' he said, 'I wonder if the Countess would agree with me that the English, who believe God is an English gentleman, are also masters of the passionless art of hypocrisy?'

'I would rather God were an English gentleman than any kind of Frenchman,' said von Huberhof laughing softly and squeezing Lydia's arm. She repressed an inward shudder and the involuntary memory arose of his naked body approaching the bed, smooth and soft-bellied, a silver-grey bush of hair around its pubis.

Flanked by the two protagonists, her light frock lifted by the breeze and wisps of wind-blown hair softening the sculptured bones of her face, she looked much younger than her years and deceptively carefree. But a sullen and despairing gloom permeated her as von Huberhof's musing fingers on her bare arm stirred the sediment of the loathsome erotic nightmare that left her feeling bruised and humiliated. 'Let us really get to know one another,' he'd murmured, beginning the insidious tactile conquest of her senses with hands, tongue, fingers, his voice thickening, his flesh hardening, the language of sex becoming brutal, staccato and Germanic as he commanded her submission.

Oskar von Niedermayer continued his satirical disparagement of the English as they strolled about the garden and von Huberhof countered with ironic admiration of the victorious enemy; but below the surface of badinage ran a deadly serious difference of opinion concerning the right direction of Germany's future. Colonel Niedermayer, the so-called 'German Lawrence' who had conducted a dashing wartime intelligence campaign against the British in Persia and Afghanistan, was the principal negotiator of *Sondergruppe R* in the secret armaments plan and one of its boldest initiators. He gave the impression of a man not easily deflected from his purpose. The same went for von Huberhof. Lydia caught an echo of chivalry, two gallant Teutonic knights preparing for a clash of lances.

'Ernst tells me you have kindly offered your services to us as an interpreter,' von Niedermayer said, steering her to a wrought-iron table under a striped garden umbrella. It was hot in the shade. A manservant of military bearing wearing white gloves brought a tray of chilled Moselle. 'Did he explain that it would mean going to Russia?'

Von Huberhof watched her and smiled confidently. She'd been well briefed during the drive from Berlin and he had reason to believe she was a good pupil.

'To Russia?' Lydia widened her eyes in simulated astonishment.

'Surely you were told,' von Neidermayer said, quizzically returning her gaze.

'Not at all! Ernst has been very mysterious. He mentioned only confidential conversations *with* Russians, not *in* Russia.'

'I hope it doesn't alarm you?'

'It does, a little. I've heard they throw people like me into prison.'

'Naturally,' said Colonel Niedermayer, 'we would not permit such an outrage to a charming lady under our protection.'

'But perhaps the Bolsheviks will be unwilling to discuss secret matters in the presence of an expatriate member of the former upper classes?'

The Colonel thoughtfully sipped some wine. 'They will be surprised, of course. Perhaps suspicious.' He gave a thin-lipped smile. 'But they will put up with such a minor irritation. The army is the only power in Germany which retains real authority and the Bolsheviks have become more pragmatic. Ernst and some of his friends disagree with me, but I am of the opinion that Lenin is no longer obsessed with the idea of converting the world to communism. Like any other national leader he is interested in power, in making his country strong.'

'They see themselves as the wave of the future and they will drown us all unless we build an impregnable dam,' von Huberhof editorialized.

Oskar von Niedermayer's smile broadened and he turned back to Lydia. 'As I was saying, they have become pragmatic. Ernst tells me you have his entire confidence, so I will let you into a secret. Soviet intelligence has brilliantly stage-managed the use of expatriates for its own purposes.' He paused and looked keenly at her. 'I'm sure you know that many of the White emigrants have begun to yearn for their homeland and some have been enticed into its service. Nowadays,' he said, laughing heartily, 'the problem is to distinguish White from off-White.'

Boats drifted lazily along the river with a soft splash of oars. Branches lifted in the breeze. A flock of birds flew over the flat landscape and rose towards the sun. The Colonel gazed at Lydia, laughing, and ripples of menace disturbed the placid surface of the afternoon.

'Many of us,' she said, 'agree with Ernst. The wave of the Revolution threatens to engulf Germany. Berlin 1921 is Petersburg 1917. When people have no bread they become rebellious.'

'You are a pessimist,' laughed von Niedermayer and drank some wine.

'No, she is a sceptic,' said von Huberhof. 'Lydia's scepticism will be very useful to the mission. We are fortunate to have her assistance.'

'I've no doubt about it.' The Colonel bowed ironically in her direction. 'We have our own qualified interpreters, of course, but they cannot be expected to have Countess Alexandrova's insight into Russian mentality. Mind you' – he glanced slyly at his adversary – 'I suspect Ernst is interested in getting an objective account of our discussions in Moscow. He lacks confidence in our frankness.'

Von Huberhof looked offended. 'My dear Oskar, how can you say such a thing?'

Colonel Niedermayer chuckled and slapped his knickerbockered knee. 'As an admirer of the English you should appreciate an English sense of humour,' he said. He lifted his glass. 'Let us drink to the success of our important mission. *Na zdrovie!*'

'*Viel Glück!*' von Huberhof responded softly.

They all clinked glasses. As Lydia was about to drink, a bee hovered close to her mouth, then settled on the rim of the wineglass.

'You are promised honey and immortality,' whispered von Huberhof.

'An excellent omen,' Oskar von Niedermayer declared with huge satisfaction.

That same afternoon General Nikolaev sat up in bed in his cluttered Charlottenburg apartment nursing his stomach and entertaining a shrewd, black-eyed little Frenchman. '*Execrable!*' he yelled, swallowing a tablespoonful of white medicine and immediately gulping down some whisky to take the taste away.

'*Le mal au ventre?*' inquired Breton-face.

'*Oui, le mal au ventre,*' General Nikolaev groaned self-pityingly. 'Quack says I eat and drink too much. Damned leech wants to starve me! Not much pleasure left when you get to my age, M'sieu Dubois.'

The Frenchman smiled respectfully with the lower part of his face. Dressed in neat, conventional style, trousers a little baggy at the knees and small hoof-like feet shod in black patent leather boots, he had the wide rubbery mouth and knowingly furtive look of a racing tout.

Clearing his throat, he said: 'My instructions, *mon Général*, are that the credentials of Lydia Nikolaievna Alexandrova, Countess, of Russian nationality, have been checked. As far as they go, the details she gave you are accurate. She lived in Paris for three years and four months. Her last known address was rue Broca 29. She left France in the summer of 1911. No criminal convictions are recorded but she was a known associate of militant anarchists under suspicion of conducting armed robberies.'

'That's all right, then, eh?' grunted General Nikolaev.

'Excuse me, my instructions are that it's not all right. The woman should not be trusted. Not in the interim.'

'What interim, Dubois?'

'Our agents working in Moscow are still checking.'

'Nonsense!' bellowed the General. 'Those fellows at the *Sûreté* make a fetish of suspicion. High-spirited young lady. Sowed a few wild oats. She made a clean breast of everything, didn't she?'

'Of everything that can be verified. What was she doing after 1911?'

'Lived in America, for God's sake! I put it all in my report.'

Breton-face shrugged. 'We only have her word for it. Remember, *mon Général*, what happened the day I saw her leaving this apartment. One of our men reported a woman answering her description outside our secret-meeting place in Bayischerplatz. She left when he spoke to her.'

'Must have been somebody else. Besides, any decent woman would do the same.' General Nikolaev drank some whisky and smacked his lips. 'Women raped every day in this city. Papers full of it, full of it!' He tugged ruminatively at his whiskers and gazed at the bullet-scarred wall facing the bed with a faraway look. 'Shot a fellow in the balls for insulting her maidenly modesty. Wild little thing! Sixteen-year-old Russian girls reading that bloody German Marx and running amok with bombs and firearms.'

The Frenchman laughed out of the side of his wide, derisive mouth then thought better of it and coughed.

'There was a rather notorious adventure in London,' he said. 'Did she tell you about that?'

'You're going to tell me, aren't you?' said General Nikolaev, staring fiercely at him.

'She was one of a gang who attempted an armed robbery at a jewellery store. Several policemen were killed and some of the robbers. The interesting thing, *mon Général*, is that among her confederates was Jacob Peters, now a chief of the Cheka. Another gangster went under the pseudonym of Peter the Painter. We have reason to believe his real name is Piatkov, head of a secret department of Soviet intelligence involved in espionage in Western Europe. Through a cipher-clerk in Piatkov's section, information was received of a spy network active in our French naval dockyards. It would be a mistake to underestimate Countess Alexandrova.'

The General massaged his painful stomach, his face purple with strain. A loud rumble occurred beneath the bedclothes and a strong sweetish stench filled the room. 'Ah! . . .' he sighed 'Forgive the gas, M'sieu. Best to get it out of the system.'

'*A bientôt*,' said Breton-face hurriedly, holding his breath. 'I am expecting more information any day. Perhaps it would be best if I passed it to you at the usual place. *Au revoir*.'

'The usual place, yes. But the girl's all right. Good blood!' General Nikolaev lay back on the pillow and closed his eyes. 'Don't slam the door,' he muttered.

In a few moments he was asleep. Blue flies cruised in the odoriferous air, landing on his hairy face to browse like cattle on rich pasture. He twitched his nose and began dreaming. Back in the prime again, he galloped his charger up the terrace slope of the Imperial Palace at Peterhof and dismounted at the Samson Fountain. 'Lydia Nikolaievna!' he said, advancing with outstretched arms to the ripe little minx of sixteen. She ran away, and he chased her in tantalizingly lewd guises through labyrinthine chambers until the dream turned bad like a battle that malevolently reverses the strategy of victory. Towering figures of stone, falling pillars, cockroach armies in stealthy advance, black-veiled nuns burying the narrow coffin of an era. An outrage had been perpetrated upon him: he looked in the mirror and saw a shambling, decayed old man. Trouserless, he fled. Lydia, the Bolshevik, stood at the foot of his bed, and from her scarlet lips came the Judgement. He pulled a gun from under the pillow and levelled it at her breast. Nerveless trigger finger, paralysis of will. He could not shoot her . . .

General Nikolaev awoke with bristling hair to find a baleful yellow eye glaring through the window. Clammy pyjamas clung to his loins and the sheets were soaked. Damned incontinence! The black sky outside confused him. What time was it? Where had the day gone? Was it still yesterday or already tomorrow? As the old wives' tale goes, sleep in the rays of the moon and wake up an idiot.

Still punished by his rebellious belly, he took off the wet pyjama trousers and wandered into the kitchen to eat a morsel of pickled Westphalian pork with pumpernickel and a glass or two of Liebfraumilch. Barbaric provender, but damned tasty. The doorbell rang. Still chewing, he struggled into a dressing gown and went to answer it, brandishing a carving knife.

'Who's there?' he yelled, ready to disembowel any sneaking assassin who might burst in on him.

'Fyodor Yegorovich, open up. This is Ernst,' replied von Huberhof. He came in, smiling buoyantly, a big healthy man in the prime of life. General Nikolaev, trapped in fleshy senescence, could gladly have stuck him like a pig out of sheer envy. 'Pleased with yourself, I see,' he grumbled, flinging the carving knife down on the littered desk.

'Everything is arranged,' said von Huberhof, keenly regarding his flushed, disgruntled face. 'Dyspepsia again?'

The General farted agreement and brought out glasses and a decanter of whisky. The tray jiggered in his hands as he placed it on the table. He sat down, jaw sagging, thinking that there'd be no fuss when the Grim Reaper came for him. Ready to go anytime. How could this smug German understand that the ache in his gut was homesickness, homesickness for his house on the island of New Holland in Petersburg, for the dank smell of the Kryakov canal and the flower-girls of the Gostini Dvor crying: '*Tzvyeti, tzvyetochki!*' with rough honeyed voices, for Saratov where his name as military governor was posted on proclamations all over the province and his private yacht lay anchored in the Volga? If only it were possible to go back to it all the years would melt like winter snow. Certain things, things like that, were dearer than life itself. You remembered them always. Maybe they were waiting for you on the other side; maybe that was heaven, all the filth of life rinsed away and only the happiness shining out.

'You are not feeling well at all, are you?' said von Huberhof with concern.

'Not feeling so good about many things,' Nikolaev said gruffly.

'My dear old friend, it's rather late to have second thoughts.'

'Ha! second thoughts. In old age they come crowding in all the time.' Retreating into ambiguous snorts, the General fortified himself with some whisky, trimmed a cigar and huffed smoke through his hairy nostrils. 'I'm worried,' he said, staring querulously into the other's clever, cynical face. 'Niedermayer's no fool. He must guess you're up to some mischief.'

'Oskar has made up his mind that he knows what I'm after. He is a brilliant man, a true patriot. That's the pity of it. For the best of motives he's prepared to lead Germany into disaster. Of course, he does not believe for a single moment that Lydia is needed as an interpreter. Our *Reichswehr* is not short of proficient linguists with an expert grasp of military technology. He assumes she is being sent as my personal spy, and because I represent an influential body of opinion he's prepared to humour me. That's good, eh?'

General Nikolaev drew the skirt of his dressing gown over one white flabby thigh that had become exposed. 'Ernst,' he said, 'to tell you the truth, I'm not sure.'

'Be frank with me, Fyodor Yegorovich. You have second thoughts about the use we are making of Lydia.'

The old man carefully laid his smoking cigar on the ashtray and rubbed his palms together as though testing the palpable reality of his flesh. He could lie down to sleep with the pain in his stomach and never wake up. Conscience buzzed in him like a troublesome insect.

'Yes,' he said. 'I have.'

'I thought so,' Von Huberhof nodded sagely. 'There is something I have to tell you, too. This afternoon, before I left with her to return to Berlin, Oskar drew me aside and said, "Ernst,

I have a feeling that this charming girl of yours may be a Bolshevik agent".'

Good God, another one! General Nikolaev was struck witless. First the *Sûreté*, now Colonel Niedermayer! It was sheer nonsense! Ridiculous!

'Of course, I don't accept that,' von Huberhof said, shrugging. 'Oskar's feelings in other matters are not reliable, either.'

'He was trying to annoy you. If he really believed it, he wouldn't let her go along.'

'On that I disagree. Supposing, merely for the sake of argument, he is right. What harm can it do? Provided the members of the mission are careful to say nothing indiscreet in her presence, she can tell the Bolsheviks nothing they don't already know.'

'Poor Lydia!' The old General swallowed a huge gulp of whisky and his red-veined eyes filled with tears. 'Become very fond of her. Not a pretty thing to dirty one's soul with, the death of a girl like that.'

'*Mein lieber* Fyodor,' said von Huberhof in a deep, sincere voice, 'when it comes to personal feelings, don't you think it distresses me just as much as you? We are at war. Terrible things happen in war. The finest action, the most sacred God-given cause, claims its innocent victims.' He twisted the ring on his little finger and a sad smile blossomed on his lips. 'It's painful for me to admit it, but I believe I've fallen in love with Lydia. She is a woman one would be proud to make the mother of one's sons.'

General Nikolaev lumbered to his feet and slouched to the bathroom. Flexing his trembling knees, he strained to make water.

'Bloody Germans!' he groaned.

3

Waiters ran under the coloured lanterns carrying huge trays of foaming Berliner Kindl and the beer garden resounded to band-music and lusty choruses. Peter's attention wandered. He felt the powerful gravitational pull of the crowd, the desire to become submerged. The impulse rasped against the tough grain of his stubborn solitude and he remained an onlooker, wry, envious perhaps, but indissoluble.

Near by, a swaying group of flushed middle-aged men, arms linked, roared out a drinking song. People celebrated as though there were no riot and rebellion, no shell-shocked men with empty sleeves, no widows, no orphans, no hungry prostitutes selling themselves for dollars: no tomorrow. Mass euphoria, an antidote to despair. Just above the trees sailed a prodigal full moon; chatter, song and contagious hilarity came from adjoining tables; the fumes of cheap but potent brandy swirled in his brain. His mood swung through an arc of ninety degrees from misanthropy to a kind of tolerant, almost affectionate, understanding. It was also the effect of detaching himself from pain. In his sleep, he'd cut it adrift, seeking subconsciously to exclude it from his version of the future. That was his own antidote to despair and it made him more sympathetic to other expedients.

'And that's all that happened,' he said, staring hazily at Lydia across the table.

'Believe it or not, yes,' she said.

They sat under a plane tree, some distance from the lighted podium of the band, the estrangement of the morning unbridged. Her dark, shingled head was outlined against a ghostly white magnolia. She tilted her face towards the sky. Moonlight carved hollows in her cheeks and turned her luminous grey eyes blue and owl-like as she gazed reflectively at the summer stars. She was someone he did not know, no longer the humorous, decisive Lydia with her taut impatience for action but a languorous, mysterious stranger, Kokoschka's fantasy 'Woman in Blue', Berlin's Countess Alexandrova whose aloof grace as she walked along the Unter den Linden tormented beholders with a vision of unattainable felicity.

The dream-image disintegrated as she gave a characteristically low exasperated laugh and said: 'I can't make sense of it at all. The idea of turning up in the Kremlin as an interpreter for the German army is so absurd that I'd find it impossible to keep a straight face. Can you imagine it?' She parodied a deep, pompous voice. 'The Herr Kamerad says to tell the Herr General he will settle for nothing less than one hundred submarines mit full torpedoes. *Jawohl!*'

Peter laughed excessively. That was better. That was very much better.

'The colonels of *Sondergruppe R* think they're playing a devious game with you,' he said. 'They'll find they've picked the wrong person.'

'I hope you're right. Niedermayer scarcely bothered to disguise it. I had the distinct impression of being treated with contempt.'

'They are treating Russia with contempt,' said Peter. 'I prefer von Huberhof's outright enmity. He's afraid of us. It's less insulting.' Striving for a casual tone, he asked: 'Are you seeing him again?'

There was a tiny hesitation. 'Yes, tomorrow.'

'Alone?'

'No, with Fyodor Yegorovich. We're going out to Dalldorf, ostensibly to bring gifts for the inmates. I'm hoping it will make some things clearer, at least.'

The awkwardness remained. Partly to dispel it, partly out of genuine curiosity, Peter asked if she knew von Huberhof's opinion of the sick girl who imagined that she was the Grand Duchess Anastasia.

'Yes, I spoke to him about her. He says she is suffering from auto-suggestive amnesia. She has a terror of recognition and gets very disturbed by questions about her childhood. Claiming to be of royal birth is a subconscious device to conceal her true identity and, at the same time, dramatize herself.'

'I'll put that in her dossier when I get back,' he said.

Lydia stared. 'Don't tell me you actually keep a file on the poor girl?'

'Indeed, we do. On all of them. After all,' Peter declared frivolously, 'she may be genuine. There was a devil of a mess in Ekaterinburg when they shot the Romanovs. I investigated it. The execution squad were drunk to a man.' He grinned. 'That's a piece of secret information you couldn't have been given if you hadn't taken the Chekist oath of loyalty.'

'There were rumours.' A retrospective bitterness entered her face and she looked away. 'That's the dark side of the Revolution. It doesn't make me proud.'

'A handful among a million dead. I don't have to tell you that, Lydia.'

'No,' she said, 'you don't have to tell me.'

It was an old bone, and gnawed enough. Peter clicked his fingernails against his empty glass in time to the devil-may-care rhythm of brass, drums and rasping fiddles. The bandsmen, dwarfish on the distant podium, jerked like demented puppets. A suitable madness, he thought.

Lydia had withdrawn again. His glance rested on her bare throat and the slight swell of her breasts under the clinging silk of her dress. He saw her, as von Huberhof had, for the first time; but superimposed upon this jealous perspective was his own intimate knowledge of her nakedness. Familiarity had never dulled the shock of delight he experienced as the outwardly spare body stripped off its masculine garb. The androgyny was deceptive. Her long slender legs swelled unexpectedly into shapely fullness at the thighs and buttocks and, stroking her firm curved belly, he encountered the soft hairy mount of venus that moved under his hand like a live warm animal. An unpredictable lover, she could be languid or perfunctory, or frank and ribald; but there were times when she became savagely erotic, caught up in a primal demanding lust as irresistible as a July thunderstorm. The next morning no trace remained of the astonishing upsurge: if anything, her limpid eyes were cooler, her manner more wary and sceptical. And, so rare that it remained with him as a singular act of grace, he recalled one night of tenderness when she'd begun to live again after the debilitating sickness of typhus. Strolling by the river at Davidko, she'd talked of life as if it were a new discovery, of her hopes for the future of Russia and the Revolution. They leaned on the wooden bridge watching the autumnal sun sink into the fiery water, then returned to the cottage and drank spiced buttermilk. 'I owe you my life, Peter,' she said. He'd gone down on his knees and clasped her fever-wasted body against his wet cheek. It was more than seven years since their tormented honeymoon in a slum house in East London. He felt like a boy of eighteen, clumsy, shy and reverent, and Lydia made love to him with tact and sensitivity as if truly he were an innocent. Afterwards he thought of Pushkin's melancholy poem 'Autumn', with its climax of reawakening to a fresh voyage. Perhaps it might have been like that. But the winter of 1918 came with its iron frost, its famine, the cities plunged into darkness as terror and civil war rampaged through the land. A chance was lost and it had never quite come again. No, it was not possible to bury the bone of the past. Not altogether.

Impulsively, he took her hand and pressed it. She smiled ruefully and said, bringing the conversation back to the present: 'You know, Peter, I've come to the conclusion that Jacob made a mistake in sending me here. You think so too, don't you?'

'I'm keeping an open mind,' he temporized. 'Jacob believes you'll do well. He thinks you have a flair.'

'It appealed to my sense of humour. If you'd ask me for a definition of espionage, I'd have said it was comedy played in deadly earnest.'

'With some reservations, that's as good a definition as any.'

'The first few days here were overwhelming,' she said. 'I thought I was rediscovering myself. Everything seemed possible again. It was like arriving in Paris at the Gare du Nord expecting all that happened to be marvellous. But I've changed too much. I can only be what I've become.' Her old husky, ironical laugh returned. 'As Ernst von Huberhof might say, at thirty I'm too old to learn to fly.'

Peter tightened his grip on her captive hand. It was a desperately late discovery. She was already airborne, alone at the controls, flying an unpredictable route with nothing but instinct and nerve to steer her to a safe landing.

'Lydia,' he said, 'when this is over and you come back to Moscow, please move in with me.'

'You'd regret it, Petya. I'd disorganize your life completely.'

'Don't you think you've already done that?' he asked quietly.

She could have replied that it was not at her choice; that from the very beginning she'd felt threatened by his engulfing power and sought to escape it; that his relentless devotion had gradually eroded her freedom as it destroyed his. He'd shaped his life around her: she was never absent from his thoughts. With all its reservations, love of a kind was born in her, the love and responsibility she must feel for someone who'd accidentally become her victim. She could have said all this, but because the balance between them had shifted and given her dominance, all she said was: 'I know, Peter. Sometimes, I think the worst thing that happened to you was meeting me.'

His watchful brown eyes lingered on her face, serious and intent. 'It was a rendezvous I had to keep. I recognized you at once. All my life I'd been waiting and there you were. It was simple and inevitable.'

'Just like that?'

He smiled sombrely. 'Exactly like that.'

The band struck up a foxtrot. Laughing couples staggered on to the wooden dance-floor, stamping their feet, slithering, holding on to each other for support. Tobacco smoke eddied around the coloured lights. Whipped up by the music, waiters hurried frenziedly to and from the spouting beer-barrels. Peter seized one as he passed and commandeered two brimming tankards. He drank thirstily and night spun faster. A suitable madness.

'We'll get a large apartment overlooking the river.' He threw out his arms. 'As big as this. With a studio. I'll take up painting again. I'll paint pictures that will make Malevich, Kandinsky, Burlyak and Tatlin tear the hairs from their brushes in sheer envy. And you know what you will do?'

'No,' said Lydia, raising her eyebrows.

'You, madame, will dance.'

Peter pulled her to her feet. She looked startled, then laughed. With volatile and very Russian abandon they whirled among the unsteady, hilarious fugitives from reality.

4

'*Danke schön*,' said the woman in Dalldorf, watching with defenceless eyes as Lydia handed her a jigsaw puzzle. '*Danke schön*,' they said, one and all, taking the magazines, water-colour paints, story books, pencil sets and coloured wools. Grudgingly, all their defenceless eyes said: 'Danke schön.' 'Anastasia', whose dossier was stored in the Lubianka, received a reproduction of the Novogorodian icon of St Elias and the Fiery Chariot, but the cropped-haired pugnacious woman of many incarnations, whose condition had deteriorated, remained with other petrified souls in some lower purgatory inaccessible to visitors.

The same dull, echoing corridors, sickly smell of disinfectant, distant shrieks that could have been laughter or terror. Only the weather had changed. Clouds in thunderous phalanxes rolled in from the north, the first skirmishing gusts of rain slapped the windows, a dull rumble approached as if the sky was shaken by celestial herds of stampeding elephants. 'I don't like storms,' said the hospital nurse. 'It either frightens them or gets them over-excited.' She shuddered. 'I can feel the electricity myself.'

General Nikolaev sulked in the consulting room's padded leather chair, half-asleep, and von Huberhof turned from the mauve light outside the window looking troubled.

'My dear Lydia!' He touched the inside of her wrist with his lips, smiling sadly. 'You are very precious to me. I wish I could explain everything to you, but the rule is that each knows only what is expected of him. What you will tell us on your return will have much bearing on our future activities. Isn't that so, Fyodor?'

'What? What?' The General glanced up uneasily. 'Yes, of course.'

'There is another thing, though, and I believe it will appeal to you very much,' von Huberhof resumed in his warm, confiding baritone. His cheeks dimpled with private amusement.

Ah, here it comes, she thought, watching closely as he opened a cupboard and pulled out a large much-travelled leather portmanteau bearing the labels of expensive hotels in several European capitals. Neatly stencilled in gilt just below the handle was her own name: 'Countess L. N. Alexandrova.' Pains had been taken to tarnish the legend and disguise its newness.

'You want me to take this along?' she asked.

'Yes. It will be delivered to you just before you leave for the station.'

'Am I permitted to know what's inside?'

Von Huberhof politely inclined his head. 'Naturally, it is right that you should,' he said smoothly. Before unlocking the case, he took the precaution of turning the key in the door. He threw open the lid. It was stuffed to the brim with pamphlets in Russian.

Lydia picked one up. 'Pamphlets?' She sounded incredulous.

With a grin of mischief, von Huberhof pushed his hand into the portmanteau and produced a hessian bag large enough to hold a couple of kilos of bread. It jingled merrily. 'Gold roubles,' he declared triumphantly, spilling a shiny heap of coins on the desk. 'I suppose you can guess what we want you to do with this?'

'Pass it to somebody?'

'Excellent!' He rewarded her with a schoolmasterly smile. 'The money and literature are for an underground group of patriots with whom General Nikolaev is in contact. Am I right, Fyodor?'

Fyodor Yegorovich harrumphed noisily to clear his throat and said yes. The loose flaps of his elderly jowls quivered and his watery eyes were glum. Muttering an excuse, he heaved up from the chair in evident distress and asked if he could be let out of the room.

'Dyspepsia, poor fellow,' von Huberhof observed briskly, re-locking the door after him.

Lydia spun a coin and caught it in her palm. Tsarist gold. With paper roubles almost as valueless as refuse in gutters, in cities ravaged by the lethal diseases of hunger, gold was a powerful weapon. It could be exchanged for the currency of souls, undermine loyalties, sabotage factories, buy the services of assassins. Yes, this made sense of her recruitment. They needed her as a smuggler, not an interpreter.

'Why me?' she asked, knowing that he would expect her to ask it.

'Because you are the ideal person,' he said. 'You see, at the frontier station Soviet security will be exceptionally heavy. There will be a strict search of all passengers' luggage except, of course, that of the German mission. And you are travelling as an official member of the party.'

'Will someone contact me when we arrive in Petersburg?'

Von Huberhof scooped up the gold, replaced it in the hessian bag and, securing the locks, disposed of the portmanteau.

'My dear girl, it will be gone by then.' He turned from the cupboard and paced before her as if delivering a lecture. 'Listen carefully. You must see that the porter in Berlin places the case just inside the door of the special compartment reserved for the mission. The train stops briefly at Pskov. Precisely ten minutes after it has restarted, pick up the case and leave the compartment. A man will be standing in the corridor outside. There may also be a Soviet guard on duty. The man will distract his attention while you slip into the toilet. Wash your hands and return to your seat, leaving the case behind.'

'It seems very simple,' said Lydia. It also depended a bit too much on chance. Supposing the toilet was already occupied? Supposing there was more than one guard, or a number of passengers chose that particular moment to stretch their legs in the corridor? She'd had a certain experience in such undertakings. In her anarchist youth she'd smuggled subversive contraband across guarded frontiers. Effrontery, luck, careful planning had ensured success. She would then have regarded von Huberhof's planning as slapdash. Now, of course, it didn't matter. This would be her first smuggling failure – by arrangement. For the moment von Huberhof's unlucky courier stepped off the train, Peter's shadows would follow him, an unwitting germ-carrier of disaster to the secret counter-revolutionary group.

'Everything is clear except for one detail,' she said. 'How shall I know which is the right man?'

'When the time comes you'll have no difficulty in identifying him.'

'No password, no signal?' she persisted.

'It will be someone you'll recognize,' he replied cryptically.

Why was he being so evasive? Suddenly she suspected his bland self-confidence. Was it possible that he intended her to be caught? Deliberate slapdash, in fact. What purpose would it serve? . . . Dimly, the outline of a strategy presented itself. The best way to subvert *Sondergruppe R*'s negotiations would be to play on Soviet suspicions. This would certainly be accomplished if the luggage of a member of the mission was found to contain illicit gold and pamphlets preaching insurrection against Soviet power. There might even be a mysterious courier of an underground group, also set-up as a victim. If the Cheka was led to an active conspiratorial organization it would give substance to fears that a secret alliance existed between the *Reichswehr* and internal counter-revolution. Lydia knew enough about the morbid apprehensions of besieged Russia to realize what effect this could have.

If such was the plan it was a good one. But it contained a fatal flaw, as Peter would gleefully say. They had chosen a double-agent to play the principal role. The Cheka would know everything in advance.

'This is very tantalizing,' she said, smiling inwardly. 'I shall begin to think that when I step out of that train compartment, I shall come face to face with you.'

'Perhaps.' Von Huberhof laughed. 'You really ask far too many questions, young woman.' He came round the desk and leaned over her, fondling her arm. 'Tell me, are you free this evening?'

'No, I'm not free,' she answered.

'I wish you were.' The ice-blue eyes were insolent. His slow, lingering hand brushed against her breast.

Again, with a shuddering revulsion, she felt a perverse stirring of lust for this hateful enemy. It was like the gathering storm outside that hurled raindrops as large as pebbles against the glass membrane of the locked room and turned the atmosphere sultry and oppressive.

'I'll never forget our night together,' he said, staring at her with the mad blue eyes of his mother, and suddenly kissed her hard on the mouth.

She stood up, shaking. 'Ernst, I really must go!'

'Why are you afraid of me?' he asked, smiling wryly.

What she feared was the dark compulsion to abase herself. Like someone peering into an abyss and struggling against the impulse to fall, her only defence was to retreat.

General Nikolaev and a wiry, saturnine man with a sharp narrow face were standing at the corner of the passage outside, conversing in Russian. Confused by the violence of her feelings, she registered the fact subconsciously. It was some moments before the men became aware of her silent presence.

'Ah, Countess! A pleasure to see you again,' the dark man fulsomely exclaimed, switching hurriedly to German.

Although his appearance was vaguely familiar she could not place him.

'I am Egon Otto Schmidt. We had met in Professor von Huberhof's consulting room on your last visit,' he explained, smiling a strained smile, an odd-looking man with one piercing black eye on each side of his jutting, beak-like nose.

Now she knew why recognition had eluded her. It was a matter of language. The German had not merely been speaking Russian, he'd spoken it flawlessly, with a true Muscovite accent as to the manner born.

Egon Otto Schmidt, the German, was as Russian as sour cabbage soup.

She was suddenly certain that this was the man who would be waiting in the corridor when the train left Pskov on the last stretch of the journey to Petrograd.

An amateur Expressionist, wielding a cruel pencil, had turned the blonde Gretchen in the Pilsner poster into a lascivious old hag; and immediately beneath, so beautiful it hurt, sat Lydia. Peter hated these goodbyes.

'I was worried when I came and I'm even more worried now,' he said. 'Quite an accomplishment for a four-day visit at the expense of the Soviet people.'

Tucked away in a small side-street, the shabby *weinstube* smelled of empty barrels and burnt-out nicotine. A handful of morose tipplers, dim as troglodytes, awaited it seemed the slow disintegration of time. It was an appropriate place for their last meeting before his return. The waiter hovered, a furry mole on his right cheek like the imprint of a demon's thumb. Showing eagerness, he poured the last of the wine into their glasses and asked if they required another bottle.

'*Nein danke*, we are soon leaving,' Peter told him, staring until the man backed away.

'It's important to me that you came,' said Lydia, her face clouded in cigarette smoke, already drifted into memory. 'You've put my feet back on the ground.'

'I wish I could be sure of that.'

The familiar complex feeling of tenderness, regret and exasperated mistrust moved him. He wanted to shake her like an intractable child and shout: 'For God's sake, the world is treacherous! You must be able to read the signs. Take care!'

'Please, Peter . . .' she began, but her voice trailed away. It was no use trying to frustrate his protective concern. He was convinced that unless he was there to command it, the sky would fall on her defenceless head.

'Just let me repeat one thing,' he persisted. 'Watch out for your little *spic*, Breton-face. He's a member of the *Sûreté* and knows his business. All the details he got about you from Nikolaev will have been sent to Paris. We must reckon with the possibility that they may decide you're a Soviet spy. If you only have the slightest suspicion that that may have happened, go immediately into hiding and contact Spichalsky. *That's most important.*'

'Yes, I promise, but –'

'But nothing!' he snapped, glaring at her. 'I don't give a damn if you dislike his face. Spichalsky's reliable. I've given him strict orders that he's to protect you and he'll do it, whatever his personal feelings. You should be safe on the train. The chief danger is here, in Berlin.'

'All right, Peter.' She gave him a humorous look. 'I'll obey your instructions to the letter. I won't move without looking over my shoulder, I'll wrap up warm, keep clear of wild horses and try not to drink the local water. Satisfied?'

Her eyes stopped smiling. Eloquently, they said: 'And please don't be jealous. All that is over.'

'Time to go,' he said ambiguously. Cellar dust on racked wine bottles, wooden ribs showing through a broken patch of plaster, scratches on tables, 'Gebrüder Eppner' in faded Gothic lettering on the wall clock petrified at a quarter past four: random details impressed on the moment of separation.

'I'll see you in Moscow,' Lydia said.

'No,' replied Peter. 'You're not allowed to know me in Moscow. You're a right-wing member of a secret German mission, remember?'

'Can't I even wave hello?'

She won a smile from him at last. 'Only if nobody's looking,' he said.

A short while later, just as he was paying the hotel cashier before leaving, the telephone rang.

'For you, Herr Schtern,' said the desk clerk.

His heart jolted, but the voice was Spichalsky's.

'Just to say goodbye,' it said deferentially.

Overcoming his sharp disappointment, he murmured into the mouthpiece: 'Please keep in mind what I told you. The work takes priority over everything. My firm regards it as of the utmost importance.'

'You can rely on me one hundred per cent,' Spichalsky's voice insisted sturdily, as if standing to attention. '*Gute reise*, Herr Schtern, a safe journey.'

Chapter Thirteen

All very well for Piatkov to send his prima donna, thought Spichalsky resentfully, but when it got too hot for that female bum-waggler who was called on to do the dirty work? The stiffness in his wounded shoulder did not improve his mood. Scaly fish glided away with sulky grace and freshwater marine animals writhed deadly pink tentacles as though they sensed in his baleful eye the dull gleam of a predator when he prowled among the glass tanks of the Zoo Aquarium searching for Fritz Erkner.

For six days and nights, snatching a bite here and there and sleeping with one eye open like a bear on guard against hungry wolves, he'd concentrated on a single task: protecting Selena like a precious piece of china. For another sixteen hours, until the minute the Nord Express left Berlin, no one could relax. 'No harm must come to her. Her mission is of vital importance,' said Piatkov. The way he talked, her highness was the heroine of the Revolution. Dig a bit, take a good sniff, and you'd get down to the stink of the class enemy. In the written words of Comrade Commissar Latsis, one of the biggest Chekists, no need to look for toilers' blood on white hands to smash the bourgeoisie. Ask what class he comes from, then stand him up against the wall. They were getting soft with former aristocrats in Russia's mother city, smashing the peasants of Tambov and honest Red sailors, while ladies and gentlemen, all girlish manners, began to dance again.

Still no Fritz. Glowering with sullen rage, he ascended to the first floor gallery and scanned the crowds, staring in amazement at crocodiles lethargically crawling on short reptilian legs. It was hot enough for a steam bath. Spichalsky saw sea-snakes, tortoises, water-fleas, several varieties of crustacean and a few score assorted humans, but no Erkner. Sentenced to the firing squad for dereliction of duty, a voice within him barked as he stamped downstairs. Bicycle clips on the ankles of his overall trousers, Fritz stood open-mouthed on the fringe of a party of schoolboys listening to some four-eyed spindleshanks with a little pointed red beard on his receding chin.

Spichalsky strode irately past, halting beside the lifelike model of the iguanodon in the entrance hall. 'Respected Mamushka, such animals used to be on the earth thousands of years ago,' he wrote in his head. She would put the picture postcard in a frame and place it on the mantelpiece, proud that it came from her successful son, vigilantly protecting the workers' holy republic against enemies in a faraway place.

Fritz joined him. Having torn himself away from an account of the wonders of nature, he spoke of thunderstorms of fish that rained from the skies of ancient Greece, of frogs leaping from clouds on to the island of Ceylon, of a hailstone as large as a hen's egg with a frozen Crucian Carp inside it that fell on Essen during one violent storm. Spichalsky's granny would laugh at such simple miracles. Besides, the mind of a commander was occupied by important things like the treachery and cunning of the human species.

'You are ten minutes late and I am waiting for your report,' he interrupted sternly.

Unabashed, hands thrust negligently into his overall pockets, Fritz informed him that everything was quiet on the Nikolaev front. The General spent the day in his apartment. Servants and tradesmen came and went. At eleven a.m. he was visited by an elderly man carrying a small black bag, apparently his doctor, who left after twenty minutes. Later, an elegant young woman whose description fitted Selena arrived and stayed a little over half an hour. Fritz handed over to Ivan, his relief, and would return at midnight to continue surveillance.

Sweating in his thick dark clothes, Spichalsky rode a crowded streetcar to his next rendezvous. The man at the French Consulate had nothing of significance to report, either. Bretonface entered the building early in the morning and did not reappear. Spichalsky then checked on Selena: she had not been abducted, run over or physically molested except by a man who sought to attach himself when she sat in the Café

Josti drinking coffee and reading a newspaper. At 11.30 a.m. she went by taxi-cab to General Nikolaev's, which confirmed Fritz's observation, leaving shortly before one p.m. Several telephone calls satisfied him that all loopholes were manned, troops vigilant, that in this little war of stealth he was not outgeneralled.

The heat had gone out of the day when he climbed four flights of rickety stairs of an overcrowded tenement in the working-class suburb of Neukölln and knocked softly on one of the doors. Grubby children rolled glass marbles in dusty passageways, slid down banisters, ran yelling into the street. A sewing machine stitched seams in the cross-textured fabric of noise – the frayed voices of women, infant screams as shrill as the tearing of silk, patterns of footsteps, running water, laughter, quarrelling – the patched and threadbare noise of poverty.

'Comrade Pochhammer,' said Anneliese Kaufman in pleased surprise. Her neatly cluttered room smelled of dumplings cooking on a kerosene stove, Lenin framed on the wall was in a mood of benevolence, a lively pennant of washing fluttered from the clothes line that stretched from her window to an outside drainpipe.

Anneliese, a plump Party member of a good ripe age for a woman, widowed by the war and childless, gave him a gap-toothed smile. Spichalsky had no taste for the broomstick type with joints like nutcrackers who said to you the nearer the bone, the sweeter the meat. A nice fistful suited him better. He beamed at her shyly, knowing she'd gladly share her dumplings with him.

After coffee he said a silly thing or two and they slapped one another playfully, getting a bit red in the face. Somehow, they shifted on to the bed. 'Comrade,' said Anneliese when nature put him in the mood to be a bit rough, 'in our village of Ochtrup we have a saying. "No need to shove with all your strength against an open door." Be so kind and close your eyes.'

He heard the skirt come off, the cotton drawers, the blouse. Shoes dropped on to the floor. Shut-eyed, he heard the sound of bare skin rubbing on skin and got the female smell in his nose. A man just undoes his buttons and he's ready for it.

'Can I look now?' he asked, so thick in the throat the words could hardly come out.

She came and lay backwards on the bed, a lovely big meaty woman as broad in the haunch as a healthy mare, and opened her good sturdy legs. For five minutes, while he did his manful duty, he got shot of them all – Nikolaev, Selena, Breton-face, von Huberhof, Piatkov, the lot. Afterwards, he gave her a bit of tenderness because, although he was no more in the mood for it, females have a need for a cuddle and Spichalsky wasn't a pig, after all. Then, feeling as light and easy as if he'd knocked off a couple of kilos, he went back to work.

The Nord Express rolled across Europe towards Berlin, but the night could still bring mischief. Ten hours at least must pass before he'd really be able to get between the blankets and relax. From Spichalsky's experience, life always knocked you off your feet when least expected. Turn your head, take a step in the dark, walk round a corner, and in the blink of an eye – trouble . . .

Everything began peacefully enough as he arrived in Matthäikirchstrasse. Dusk settling on the suburban street, Evensong floating out of the grey stone church, a man smoking a pipe in the porch, calling out a cheerful greeting. Responding with a reserved '*Guten Abend*', Spichalsky crossed the road and pretended uninterest in Vlado who sat at the wheel of the hired Mercedes. Lights burned in the handsome house of the French Consulate. He continued to the end of the street and waited, breathing fresh air from the leaf-rustling Tiergarten like a man out for an innocent evening stroll.

When the smoker knocked out his pipe on the wall and re-entered the church, Spichalsky hurried back and got into the motor-car. Vlado, bored, scratched his bristly chin and said: 'Nothing doing. Still hasn't come out.'

'Hungry, eh?' commented Spichalsky, grinning. He pulled a newspaper-wrapped package from his pocket. 'Bread and sausage. Get that inside you, my lad.' He patted the other's bony shoulder. A good commander was a father to his men. 'Give me the binoculars, Vlado, I'd like to have a peep.'

It had not escaped his notice that a certain window on the Consulate's first floor remained carelessly uncurtained. A corner of the room zoomed up as if he had his nose pressed to the glass. Two figures moved soundlessly back and forth like fish in an aquarium. One stops, unhooks the telephone. Oho! Jean-Pierre Dubois, alias Breton-face. He speaks briefly, half-smiles, speaks again, rings off. Spichalsky watches intently as he goes to a heavy green metal safe, unlocks it, takes something from inside and closes it again. Some moments later the light in the room goes out.

'Vlado, start the car,' Spichalsky said.

Vlado crammed the sausage into his mouth and got out to crank up the engine. Vibrating pleasantly in every fibre, Spichalsky stared with magnified vision at the Consulate door. Breton-face emerged alone, larger than life. The powerful lenses even picked up the gleam of his black patent-leather shoes. He stopped to light a cigarette, gazing swiftly along the street under the wide brim of his hat. The hired Mercedes, concealed in the shadow of the church, slipped out as Breton-face drove off and turned into the wide, dimly-lit Tiergartenstrasse.

Saturday night in Berlin. Crowds, rowdiness, electric signs, everybody rushing to places of pleasure. Vlado swerved along the roads in and out of the traffic like a drunkard. 'Take it a bit easy!' snarled Spichalsky as they skidded into the path of a clanging tramcar. The Frenchman nearly got away. He disappeared down a side-street and when they found his motor-car it was empty.

'Stop!'

Running to the corner, praying for luck, Spichalsky caught a glimpse of him in the light thrown by a garish dance-hall. Jazz blared from the doorway. A beggar thrust matches into his face. Shouldering him roughly aside, Spichalsky broke free in time to see Breton-face vanish into the wall. It was the side entrance of a photographer's, Gustav Reiner. Wedding couples posed in the dingy window. Girls simpered in balletic poses. Low-grade civil servants, chests puffed and bemedalled; faded pre-austerity pictures of nude fat babies; brilliantined youths with manly fuzz adorning their smirking faces. Peering into the interior, all Spichalsky could see was a crack of light under a closed door. He crossed the street diagonally and melted into a shadowed portico. Sweetness in the mouth helped him to think.

He sucked a *bon-bon* and waited. When the Frenchman reappeared, Spichalsky made no attempt to follow him. Of one thing he was certain: there would be another visitor.

Inebriate with lust, a man came from the dance-hall clutching a powdered girl and shamelessly began coupling in his hiding place. He moved into another doorway. After some minutes a droshky turned into the street, the horse ambling along in no particular haste. It stopped outside the photographer's. A bulky, infirm passenger alighted with assistance from the cab-driver, straightened himself and marched stiffly if precariously into the side entrance. Old soldier Nikolaev.

Too drunk to have his picture taken for the family album, Spichalsky reflected with ponderous humour. He unwrapped another *bon-bon* and sucked thoughtfully waiting for Nikolaev to re-emerge and drive off, then walked slowly back to the Mercedes. A message had been passed and he must find out if it concerned Selena. Instinct told him it did, professional instinct. He relied on that: it had never let him down yet.

2

The snub-nosed fellow ambled into the Café Josti and settled down to have a good look round. His guileless Russian eyes took in everything but travelled blankly over Lydia as if she was no more than a hole in the air. Lydia poured some *ersatz* Mocha from the metal coffee pot and went on reading the emigré newspaper *Novoye Vremya.* Unmistakably Spichalsky's man, and not too good at his job. She'd noticed him first four days earlier. Nature had equipped him with rather unfortunate ears. They stuck out red as tomatoes as he stared intently into a haberdasher's window, and when she saw them blazing again after leaving a tobacconist's to buy cigarettes it could have been a coincidence. But since then he'd popped in and out of sight, looking vague and preoccupied, wherever the whim took her. Even without the big monkey ears his ubiquity, the fact that he always glanced in another direction at her approach, would inevitably have aroused suspicion. A nice enough lad by the looks of him: she was sometimes tempted to stop for a while to chat, but that would probably hurt his professional pride.

Novoye Vremya made lively reading and she quickly became

immersed. Among the human driftwood washed up on the banks of the Spree by the storms of October were some maliciously satirical talents. They burned brightly, witty as sparks in the wind and just as ephemeral, but it was cheerful enough while it lasted. One couldn't say as much for the grim sloganeers, the foot-slogging statisticians, who marched across the mouse-grey acreages of Soviet newspapers. The editors of *Pravda* would have taken a very severe view of one parody in the manner of Mayakovsky on Lenin's arrival in Heaven.

Hm! . . . Hm! . . .
God, eh, old man? Be so kind,
  step down, we'll give you a golden bullet.
All the holy paraphernalia
  finished, we say. Quits.
We're expropriating the people's opium.
Down below, toilers
  are taking over the Universe.

'What is amusing you so much?' a furtive voice insinuated.

Herr Doktor Neubert, long yellow teeth bared in a frugal smile, met her glance over the edge of the newspaper. He bowed.

'What a surprise, Herr Doktor!' she said, making an effort to sound pleased.

'A nice one, I hope.' He touched his lips coyly and settled his string shopping bag on his knees. 'I noticed you all alone, pensive, a little sad.'

'It's the coffee,' she said. 'They've changed the flavour. It now tastes of burnt cork.'

'Ach, so.' Doktor Neubert laughed rustily like someone exercising a forgotten talent. 'You must give me the pleasure of buying you a pastry.'

Sweeping aside all protestations, he summoned the waiter with a peremptorily uplifted finger and barked: 'A selection of pastries, if you please, *Herr Kellner*.'

A tray of sweet cakes made of frost-bitten potatoes was brought. Lydia chose the least objectionable and writhed inwardly while Doktor Neubert paid the waiter with some grimy marks. An involuntary sigh escaped as he returned the depleted purse to his pocket. With careful management, the money could have bought enough cheap groceries to last a whole day.

'You really shouldn't, Herr Doktor. They are so expensive.'

His hand flipped at the wrist, flinging away gold. 'Why not? Life, my dear Countess, is – how shall I say it? – more than a pocket full of *groschen*. Sometimes one is entitled to a little treat.' Dividing the pastry on his plate into small rectangles, he lifted a section to his mouth and chewed slowly, prolonging the satisfaction. 'You are enjoying it, yes?'

'Yes, it's quite – delicious.'

'Good.' He bent forward and spoke in a confidential whisper. 'For health's sake, I don't drink the coffee. Never! Camomile tea morning and night, that's all. People are good enough to say I'm very young for my age. This is because nothing goes inside my stomach unless it's pure. Absolutely pure!'

His adhesive glance fastened on her. On the other side of the café Spichalsky's man listened with his eyes.

'A very good principle,' she murmured.

'Inner purity is the great secret,' the Herr Doktor insisted, coming even closer. 'Disease starts – if you will excuse me – in the bowels. It is absolutely categorical. Purity. Regularity. Health.' He cleared his throat for a further important announcement. 'This afternoon I am going to the Schlossgarten. The band is playing Strauss, Mendelssohn, Verdi and Liszt. Would you do me the honour of allowing me to escort you?'

'I would have liked that, but I really must do some packing,' answered Lydia. At least, she thought remorsefully, it wasn't entirely a lie.

Doktor Neubert picked a crumb from his plate with bird-like concentration.

'Ah, yes! Frau Flügel, our landlady, remarked to me that you are off on a journey tomorrow morning. May I ask, are you going for business or pleasure?'

'Just a short vacation.'

'A vacation, *ach so*!' The animation could not disguise the poor man's envy. 'Are you spending it at a seaside resort?'

'No,' said Lydia, unexpectedly reminded that she'd been landlocked for years. Her last holiday by the sea, at Yalta, was in the summer before the war. Now, sitting in the crowded, smoky Berlin café, corroded by time and experience, she was overcome by a craving as sharp as the longing for freedom for sand, rocks, the sting of salt water.

'No, I'm going to visit relatives,' she said.

'You are keeping a secret from us. You have a husband.' The Herr Doktor clutched his string bag and gave a false laugh. Suddenly embarrassed, he changed the subject. 'What is so amusing in your Russian paper? Please translate it for me.'

Lydia wistfully shook her head. 'It wouldn't sound funny in German.'

The big-eared young fellow remained discreetly close when she left Josti's to go to General Nikolaev's. Before getting into an auto-taxi she made sure he had time to hail another cab. She owed that to Peter. For all that he was now back in Moscow, his husbandly shadow pursued her, vigilant as ever.

As she paid off the driver, her protector's taxi continued round the next corner and the man got out to await her departure. Fritz Erkner in workman's overalls tinkered with a street gas-main, checked his watch and logged her arrival. Elsewhere, Boris Spichalsky was just about to begin his rounds, the clock ticking away in his blunt, obedient head.

'It's a beautiful day outside,' she said. 'Why are all the curtains drawn?'

General Nikolaev shrugged. Apathetic, clad in a soiled gown and loose slippers, he evidently regarded the weather as reclusively irrelevant. 'Damnable place! I hate this country!' he groaned. Shoulders bowed, he shambled back into the stifling gloom of the apartment and collapsed into an armchair. His elderly obese dog, Zuki, waddled after him, settling drowsily at his feet.

'What you need is fresh air. I'm not surprised you feel like that. How can you breathe?' Lydia pulled the drapes briskly aside and flung open a window. Somnolent flies swarmed awake in the sudden sunshine. The General blinked. In full daylight he looked terrible, matted hair all over his crumpled old face, eyes bloodshot, a rime of dried spittle at the sagging corners of his purple lips. 'Did Frau Gottlieb give you breakfast?'

Frau Gottlieb, who lived in the basement, was his housekeeper.

'Couldn't touch a morsel of it,' he said. 'Couldn't put a thing into my stomach,' he said, tenderly stroking the pendulous bag of his gut and gazing at her piteously. 'Gave it to the dog.'

'Nonsense!' She picked up a half-empty whisky bottle and laughed. 'I bet you've had your usual medicine.'

'Mustn't touch a drop. Pill-peddler says it'll finish me off.'

'You've got to eat something,' Lydia said firmly. 'How about a boiled egg, bread and butter and a nice hot cup of coffee?'

While in the kitchen, the furtive clink of glass told her he was at the whisky again. Well, the disorderly old Slav could hardly be expected to preserve himself on an austerely healthy infusion of camomile like desiccated Doktor Neubert. Misuse had taken irreparable toll of his monstrous flesh. Without whisky to oil the decrepit machinery there'd be no puff left in it.

Egg yolk trickled down the General's chin like a baby's as he spooned it shakily into his mouth. 'You're too good to me, Lydochka,' he mumbled. 'I don't deserve it.'

There were tears in his eyes.

'Fyodor Yegorovich, don't be such a humbug,' she said, moved.

'No, I mean it. I'm not a good man, you know. The things I've done in my life . . .' His voice trailed away and he blew a great blast into his handkerchief.

'That was in your prime,' Lydia said. 'I expect they've forgotten all about it upstairs.'

Her ironic sympathy served only to unsettle him more. Getting fond of General Nikolaev was a nuisance. She had a positively bourgeois sense of guilt about deceiving the old rogue. Just as well Peter hadn't asked her what she'd do if orders were given to kill him. From the Chekist point of view it might be considered necessary. Sitting there watching the dribble of egg congeal on his chin, she thought it would be like murdering a senile child. Yet, given the chance, the General would unhesitatingly hang every Bolshevik he could lay his palsied hands on. An enemy was an enemy. Fortunately, there was no good reason to interfere with the process of nature. Whisky wouldn't keep him going much longer.

The General drank his coffee and kept glancing at her after each sip as though there was something he wished to say but couldn't quite summon up the courage to do so. Sad congested eyes made a last erotic assessment, watching the rise and fall of her breast, the curve of hip and slenderness of ankles, returning to memorize the contours of her face as though he saw in her all the women he had known and lost.

'When you were in America, did you ever consider settling down there?' he asked. 'I hear it's the only place in the world where a person who's lost his country can take root again.'

'I couldn't be anything but Russian,' she said.

'You're young. You could make a new life with an American husband and children. A woman's homeland is her family.'

'I'm not that kind of woman,' she said.

General Nikolaev reached out and unsteadily splashed some whisky into his glass. 'The old times will never come back, my dear, whatever we do.' He drank in brooding silence for a while then came to an abrupt decision. 'Lydia, you don't have to go,' he said. 'I've been thinking things over. Ernst rather rushed you into this. It wasn't right not to give you time to consider it properly.'

'What are you trying to tell me, Fyodor Yegorovich? That it's dangerous?'

'Possibly.' He avoided looking at her.

Lydia smiled. 'Now, you're not to worry. I've packed my toothbrush and have every intention of leaving in the morning as arranged. Niedermayer promised me his full protection if anybody tries to arrest me.'

'And who,' said the General in a wry undertone, 'is going to protect Niedermayer?'

She felt the sharp contraction in the atmosphere that comes with suspicion. A montage of impressions passed through her mind – secretive glances, enigmatic silences, laughter that had the cold ring of mockery, the curiously resonant contest in the Potsdam garden between Huberhof and Niedermayer where little was said but much implied; she recalled the flawless Russian spoken by Egon Otto Schmidt in the corridor at Dalldorf.

'Why did you say that, Fyodor Yegorovich?' she asked, striving to sound casual.

He shrugged, drained off his whisky and stared into the empty glass.

'What can possibly happen to people on an official mission?' she persisted.

The General gave her a bloodshot stare. 'Idiotic questions! For God's sake, we're dealing with Bolsheviks, the worst scum in the world! Who knows what devilry they'll try?'

Cool and crisp, she said: 'We shall soon find out, shan't we? I'll say goodbye for now, Fyodor Yegorovich. Won't you wish me a good journey?'

'Lydia, dear one!' He laid a blotched, protective hand on her shoulder and spoke brokenly. 'Think it over, eh? Sleep on it. Not too late to change your mind.'

'I will.' She paused at the door. 'Tell me one thing before I go, who is the man to whom I must pass the portmanteau when the train leaves Pskov?'

'Eh, what?'

'Never mind,' Lydia said. She could recognize terror when she saw it.

'You won't tell anybody I tried to persuade you not to go.'

'No, of course not,' she said. 'Good-bye.'

As she left the apartment, General Nikolaev poured himself another large measure of whisky.

The day continued in an unfocused blur. Frau Gottlieb took Zuki for a walk and brought up some post. He must have gone through it, judging by the torn envelopes on the carpet. He must also have eaten some food because the luncheon tray on the table bore the remains of a meal. He recalled spending time at the desk glancing aimlessly through the cluttered drawers. Letters in faded ink; faces of old comrades, mistresses, dead relatives, photographs of festive groups smiling with no foresight of impending doom; and battle souvenirs, the gazette entries of Imperial honours, bits and pieces saturated in a nostalgia that made his life seem as distant and improbable as a vision of Byzantium.

Pain came spasmodically, a distant discomfort. He journeyed to the medicine cupboard and administered the prescribed white stuff to his stomach as though nursing a suffering relative. Thoughts unwound and snapped like weak thread, but mostly random pictures drifted through his mind and he thought of nothing. The whisky bottle stood half-empty. Without recollection of how he'd got there he found himself in bed under the distinct impression of awakening in Petersburg to brass kettle-drums and bugles of marine guards on parade. When the illusion faded and his heart stopped hammering, his stubborn will gave up. He wanted to pull the blankets over his head and sleep for ever. To hell with it! . . .

It was the telephone that woke him. Blue light from the darkening sky filtered into the room. The telephone kept ringing. Cursing, he grabbed the receiver.

'Yes, who the devil is it?'

'*Mon Général*' – the voice had the soft hiss of steam: it was Jean-Pierre Dubois – 'regarding the matter we have been discussing, I have an answer.'

'I'm sick, M'sieu. Not at all well. Let it wait until tomorrow.'

'But, *mon Général*, tomorrow will be –'

General Nikolaev cut him off in mid-sentence. A sharp agony, the length of a sword-thrust, pierced his left side from the chest through to the sciatic nerve. He found it difficult to breathe and limped into the drawing room for some whisky to ease the pain. The glass in his hand slipped, shattered. Trembling with impotent rage at the clumsiness of his infirm body, he gazed down at the splintered debris and struggled against a mawkish impulse to cry. Instead he went to the bathroom, relieved his bladder, stared for long moments with perplexed bitterness into the savage mirror. Meanwhile the telephone rang on and on until he could stand it no longer.

'Tomorrow will be too late,' hissed Dubois. 'There can be no question of delay. It is of the utmost urgency.'

'*Comment, Dubois? Je ne comprends pas.*'

'The message will be at the usual place. Collect it this evening. Please leave at once. *Immédiatement.*'

This time the Frenchman rang off. A lifetime's military discipline had made the General responsive to the tone of command. That is how a soldier half-dead of fatigue is driven into battle. The stern voice connects to the nerve centres: limbs move in automatismic obedience: Fyodor Yegorovich dressed himself, left home and drove off in a horse-cab to the backstreet photographic studio of Gustave Reiner.

Reiner did not look like a practitioner of illusion. A stocky man, with the heavy blue-scarred face of a miner, he stared intently at the General as if trying to penetrate a skilful disguise before admitting him. It was dark inside. The big mahogany camera stood on a tripod hooded by a black cloth, set before it a padded leather chair. There was little conversation. The General sat down and blinked as Reiner switched on the fierce electric eye, draped his head in black vestments and pressed a rubber bulb. Click. A baffling procedure, always the same. Presumably the photograph was visible proof that the message had reached the correct recipient, but he invariably experienced a vague sense of dread, an irrational fear that his innermost identity was being snatched away for burial in some impersonal archive. To complete the ritual, he signed his code name to a receipt bearing the date and precise time of the transaction before delivery was effected.

On reaching home he lit the lamp and laid the envelope, oblong, white and disquietingly thick, on the black surface of the desk. *Utmost urgency*, Dubois had said with scalding sibilance, words that stung like whips, hissing alarm, crisis, speed, action. He was too old for it. Imprisoned in the creeping paralysis of senility, time alone went fast for him. Circling the room in indecision, he paused by the liquor cabinet and poured a deep whisky to prepare for the shock. The drink warmed his ailing stomach, spreading its spurious vitality through his veins. The leaden weight in his head eased. He gripped the paper-knife and with one stroke slashed open the envelope.

Fingers shaking, Nikolaev drew out a typed sheet of paper wrapped around a yellowed photograph. The back of the picture was uppermost. It bore the stamp 'St Petersburg Department of the Okhrana', the date 14 March 1908. Carefully written in ink was the following: 'Alexandrova, Lydia Nikolaievna, Countess. Anarchist. Born 3 February 1891, at 5 Ulitza Gogolya, St Petersburg. Photograph made at age sixteen.'

He turned the picture over, an oval portrait embossed with the seal 'Studio Avanzo, Nevsky 5'. Arrogantly poised on its curved slender neck and framed in waist-length hair, the schoolgirl innocence and promise of the young face arrested his heart. Fingertips rested on her cheek in a pose fashionable during the period while she gazed unsmilingly at the camera with the defenceless candour of inexperience. It brought Fyodor Yegorovich the grief of a lost love. For although the cool devastation of those great, luminous Russian eyes had not changed in the intervening years, this was the Lydia he was sure he remembered meeting in the palace garden at Peterhof (the very same year she posed for the portrait), the Lydia he'd pursued in his dreams ever since her older persona reappeared so suddenly in Berlin. Lydia at sixteen, the perfect age of blossom, unblemished: pure as spring water.

General Nikolaev brushed the moisture from his eyes, put the photograph aside as though returning from a long journey, and began reading the typescript. Addressed to him from the *Sûreté* in Paris, the message was brief and to the point. Their sources in Moscow had completed inquiries. Countess Alexandrova, former anarchist, had joined the Bolshevik faction of the Russian Social Democratic Party in summer 1911. For several years she had been an active subversionist, arrested in March 1914 and sentenced to Siberian exile. After the Revolution she fought as a commander of Red guerrillas. The sources confirmed that Alexandrova was now a Soviet secret agent on special assignment in Berlin. The woman was dangerous. She must be frustrated at all costs, if necessary by physical elimination. His contacts in *Reichswehr* intelligence were to be immediately informed.

Alas, the General thought mistily, laying the paper aside, an apt parable of life's disillusion. However tender and promising their beginning, women soon became deceivers then, in the end, unforgivably ugly, gross, coarse in mind and body. Lydia, of all people! He simply had to have another drink. Its benign influence helped him to view the matter with melancholy detachment. Now everything seemed obvious. The Bolshevists damn near poisoned him once. Had to have his stomach pumped out after eating some doctored fish, since when poor old faithful Zuki had been promoted to food taster. They'd sent assassins after him in vain, so a pretty woman was despatched as an agent provocateur, taking advantage of his innate chivalry. With typical Hebraic cunning, the woman was one for whose father – some official at the Tsarist court – he had an affection and who, as a sweet young girl, had captivated him. They had cleverly calculated that she could tell him quite a lot about her rebellious youth and he'd put it down to nothing worse than immature idealism.

An involuntary convulsion of laughter seized General Nikolaev with such abrupt violence that he almost choked in his own phlegm. The irony of it had suddenly occurred to him. Russia had fallen into the clutches of a clever breed of foreigners: this time they'd been too clever by half.

The spasm of merriment subsided and he reviewed the situation. Von Huberhof's associates had approached him with a plan to destroy all possibility of secret agreement between the Soviets and the *Reichswehr*. It suited his own interests, but he'd first obtained approval from friends in the *Sûreté* and westernizers in Germany's Foreign Office. The plan required someone to act as the trigger. After careful analysis, a profile of a suitable subject was produced. Least suspicion would be aroused by a girl; one with initiative, a sense of adventure and a strong incentive to join in an anti-Bolshevik conspiracy. Who better than a young Russian woman whose family had been ruined by the revolution? For weeks the General searched for a suitable candidate without success. There had been qualms. The girl chosen could not be told that she stood little chance of emerging safely. It was a heavy responsibility to bear.

Then Lydia introduced herself. Everything fitted: an impeccable member of the ruined aristocracy, temperamentally daring, linguistically and intellectually accomplished, even her brief, bizarre terrorist background was in the circumstances an advantage. Yes, everything fitted beautifully, but his conscience chafed. Could he send this unsuspecting girl who had given him her trust to almost certain death? The decision had been no: within the limits of secrecy by which he was bound, he'd sought to warn her. Now the situation was quite different. She had come to him treacherously, an agent of Felix Dzerzhinsky, Satanic master-mind of the Cheka, Polish mass-murderer of her rightful sovereign, Tsar Nicholas the Second, his family and an entire élite generation of Russians. Who knew what innocent blood stained her own renegade hands? Now he feared that she might take his advice and, by withdrawing at the last moment from the *Sondergruppe R* mission, escape her deserved retribution.

The General took up the telephone and gave the operator a number. A calm, judicial severity stiffened his ponderous frame: he had recovered the faculty of command.

'*Achtung*,' said von Huberhof.

'Ernst, something very important has happened. Can you come here at once?'

Von Huberhof asked no questions. He evaluated the tone and diagnosed trouble. 'I'll leave immediately,' he said.

Fyodor Yegorovich hung up the receiver. His glance was drawn to the portrait of sixteen-year-old Lydia. Indefinably, the face had changed expression. He could not put a name to the difference, but the eyes followed him and it made him feel distinctly uncomfortable.

He turned the photograph over and settled down to wait.

3

Maybe he dozed a bit. Maybe time slipped by while he was thinking about something he'd already forgotten. Whatever the reason, when the doorbell rang it seemed only a few minutes since he'd put down the telephone. No need to call out and ask who it was, as one usually did. Germans could always be relied on to turn up promptly. The General hastened to admit von Huberhof. He certainly had sensational news for him this time. Drawing the bolts, he pulled open the door.

A thickset stranger stepped into the hall. Fyodor Yegorovich stared in shocked silence as the man addressed him in his native tongue.

'*Dobry vecher, General.* Good evening,' Spichalsky said with a queer smile, closing the door. '*Kak pozhivaite?* How's your health?'

Insultingly polite, his Russian had the nasal coarseness of a village *muzhik*. General Nikolaev recoiled a step. '*Kto vy?* Who are you?' he muttered, but he already knew. There was an archetypal menace in the intruder, the unmistakable brutality and slyness of the Bolshevik in his thick-skinned features. He'd been expecting him for a long time. Guns, knives, heavy clubs had been strategically prepared for such an encounter, but they were out of reach. Heart pounding, the General stealthily put a hand behind his back and grabbed the only available weapon. An umbrella. He struck out as he would at a mad dog.

Spichalsky sadly shook his head and took the blow on his forearm. 'Now, *Gospodin*, who needs the rough stuff?' he asked, wrenching the umbrella away. He returned it tidily to the rack then, in a swift move, seized the old man by the scruff of his neck, propelled him to the drawing room and pushed him into an armchair. Pressing the flat of his broad palm against Fyodor Yegorovich's chest to hold him down, he said: 'Let's have a quiet chat and not get excited, eh?'

Instead of responding pacifically to this reasonable suggestion, Fyodor Yegorovich spat out all his hatred. 'Assassin! Scum! Bolshevik cut-throat! Shithouse!' he cursed, the veins almost bursting through his sagging skin.

Spichalsky was offended by the filth. Without the slightest grimace, quite stolidly, he lifted his powerful right arm and punished the offender with a hard fist. Blood spurted from the General's heavy nostrils: his lower lip burst like an overripe plum and his head slumped sideways. A dense mist descended upon him. After the shock, he felt no pain, only dazed incomprehension.

The concussed glaze in the old man's eyes assured Spichalsky that he'd have no more trouble there for a while. Except for a pool of light over the desk, darkness spread through the apartment. He wondered where the message from Breton-face was hidden: perhaps in the bedroom wall-safe he'd noticed when he and Fritz searched the place. An odd snuffling made him turn sharply, but it was only Nikolaev's mild fat dog creeping in from the kitchen. The animal looked at its comatose master, whimpering with distress.

'There, there! old fellow.' Spichalsky stroked it gently and gave a reassuring pat to its flank to prevent it barking. The dog gratefully licked his hand and allowed itself to be led back to the kitchen, curling up in its wicker basket. He shut the door and returned to the drawing room. A small moan came from the General's smashed mouth. Spichalsky growled: 'Be quiet!' and picked up the photograph from the desk. 'St Petersburg Department of the Okhrana.' He read the details, turned the pasteboard over and stared at the skinny young Countess with disfavour before carefully placing her portrait into his wallet. The letter in French baffled him: not his language. As he was about to fold it up and put it with Lydia's photograph, his eye alighted on the words '*agent secret soviētique*'. A smile encroached on his grim, compressed lips. A kid could understand that.

Nikolaev suddenly broke into a weak fit of coughing. Blood thickened by mucus trickled down his chin and he half-struggled out of the chair. Spichalsky thrust the cumbersome body back with his boot and kept his foot on it while he thought. Not that there was much to think about. The old man had an inadmissible knowledge. In such matters Boris Spichalsky was allowed a certain initiative. It happened now and then.

He removed his boot from Nikolaev's stomach, gripped his coat with both hands and jerked him upright.

'*Gospodin*, you need a long rest,' he said, dragging him towards the bedroom.

Consciousness began to return to Fyodor Yegorovich. It returned in the form of a familiar claustrophobic nightmare, the suffocating apprehension of terror and impending doom. He writhed his limbs as helplessly as a fly impaled on a pin. He could not escape the suffocating softness that pressed down on his face, stifling breath, damming the blood of his pumping heart. The dream was death. It left him no name. Waking with agony and relief, he sometimes felt a paradoxical regret at facing the world again; a scarred old soldier, tired of the knife-sharp cold of exile, when death finally came he was ready for it.

But as he drowned and drowned in unrelenting softness, a terrible awareness came to Fyodor Yegorovich Nikolaev, General, former military governor of Saratov, Colonel of the Seventh Imperial Hussars, the awareness that he was not yet ready to die: and he died . . .

As long as the faintest movement of struggle remained, Spichalsky kept his backside squarely on the pillow, reflectively picking his nose. It finished quite soon. He stood up, uncovered the dead man's congested face, then returned to the drawing room. With premeditated assurance, he examined the contents of the well-stocked drink-cabinet, selected a bottle a quarter full of brandy, uncorked it and sniffed approvingly. He splashed some liquor on the corpse's mouth, the rest on its chest, and glanced carefully through a chink in the curtain at the street. It was a quiet part of town. Some pedestrians passed on the opposite side. When the street became empty, he dragged the obese body over to the window, swung it open and hoisted up the corpse, allowing it to topple over by its own weight. It struck the pavement three floors below with a thud like that of a heavy sack of potatoes splitting on impact.

Spichalsky picked up the pillow soiled with blood and mucus, tucked it under his coat for subsequent disposal and left by the back door, descending to the courtyard. Before a full minute had passed he disappeared.

Through the open window came a cool night breeze. Deserted except for the dog quietly sleeping in the kitchen, the apartment looked much as it always did, a little dishevelled by the disturbance of living but peacefully awaiting its occupant's return. In due course, a horrified crowd gathered around the General's body. Von Huberhof arrived in his automobile just as the body was being lifted by stretcher into a hurriedly-summoned ambulance.

He glanced at it, shrugged, and returned to the car. He understood everything. Looked at in a certain way, considering certain misgivings that had arisen, the tragedy could be viewed as not altogether inconvenient.

Chapter Fourteen

Halfway through the fifty-hour journey across Europe from London's Charing Cross to Petrograd's Warsaw Station, the Nord Express stood under the grimy glass roof of Bahnhof Stettin waiting to resume its run on schedule. One sleeping car and an adjoining carriage were marked 'RESERVED'. In the vicinity stood several sharp-eyed men.

The stationmaster and a uniformed chief-inspector of police watched through the window of an office overlooking the platform. 'Who are they? Why all the security?' asked the former.

'Matters of state,' was the cold, formal reply. The chief-inspector implied possession of important secrets, but that was all he knew. He cleared his throat. 'Another fifteen minutes.'

'Precisely,' agreed the stationmaster.

Passengers dazed after a day and night of travel paced up and down to get the cramp out of their limbs or crowded kiosks for beer and tobacco; the engine took on coal, water and a fresh crew; parcels and mailbags were loaded; Berliners travelling east humped their luggage aboard and leaned out of compartments for a last chat with people seeing them off.

Ernst von Huberhof, a white rose in his buttonhole, glanced at the minute hand of the platform clock, craned his head towards the station entrance, and went on talking affably. Colonel Niedermayer paid absent attention and consulted his pocket watch. Major Tschunke, an officer of General von Seeckt's staff dressed in a well-cut civilian suit, rubbed his hands together nervously but tried to appear unconcerned.

'Where is our charming Russian interpreter?' von Niedermayer voiced at last.

Von Huberhof smiled a trifle edgily. 'As a lady, she has the privilege of keeping us in suspense.'

'Not for more than nine minutes, I hope. The iron horse has no sense of chivalry.'

The conversation continued rather disconnectedly as the margin of time dwindled. Major Tschunke said: 'Traffic is rather bad, of course, this time of the morning,' a remark his companions greeted with silence. Von Huberhof's head was now almost permanently screwed in the direction of the entrance.

'Ah, there she is!' he exclaimed with undisguised relief.

'There she is, comrade,' the man said to Fritz Erkner, his lips scarcely moving. He rolled his eyes to the left and pulled the corresponding lobe of his large red ear.

Sitting on a bench at a safe distance from the platform, Spichalsky frowningly lowered his newspaper and said to himself: 'Thought she wasn't going to make it,' and stood up to get a better view.

The young woman whose arrival had aroused this interest showed no haste as she came towards the train, accompanied by a porter. Dressed in a close-fitting black costume, her eyes covered by a short veil, she stopped to choose some magazines at a newspaper kiosk before proceeding in the direction of von Huberhof's group.

'*Guten Morgen, Madame*,' said Colonel Niedermayer and Major Tschunke whom she had not previously met, raising their hats. Major Tschunke introduced himself.

'Lydia,' said von Huberhof softly, also raising his hat.

Each in turn kissed her gloved hand.

Gazing into her veiled eyes, von Huberhof said: 'Your sleeper is Number Three. I will see to your luggage.' He signalled to the porter to follow him into the *Schlafwagen*.

'Well, Countess, I cannot say how delighted I am to see you. The rest of our party is already aboard,' said Colonel Niedermayer, adding insincerely: 'I was beginning to fear that we'd have to manage somehow without you.' To prevent further delay, he captured her elbow in a firm grip and assisted her into the train.

Waiting in her compartment was von Huberhof. 'It's in the corridor recess just by the carriage door,' he whispered. Her own luggage rested on the rack. 'So off you go to Red Russia. You are very brave,' he said.

'Unless you intend to go too, you'd better hurry.'

'You are right.' He affected a tremulous smile that nauseated her. 'Dear Lydia, I shall miss you more than you know. Open your window so that I can say goodbye from the platform.'

He plucked the rose from his buttonhole, presented it, and kissed her mouth on leaving. She took out a small lace handkerchief and wiped her unclean lips.

The engine shuddered, Fritz Erkner and his colleague jumped aboard, passengers called last farewells, doors slammed. As though speaking tender sentiments, von Huberhof said: 'Please be punctual at Pskov. The contact will be waiting. Ten minutes after leaving the station. If you are not on time it will put him in greater danger. He is also brave.'

'Who is it?' she asked again, and again the reply was: 'Someone you will recognize.' A lump seemed lodged in his throat and his blue eyes looked troubled. '*Liebchen*, I hate to tell you this, but I think you must know. It is the last service you can do for poor Fyodor. A last blow for his cause. He fell out of the window and was killed.'

'What? What did you say?'

The engine blast obliterated her voice. 7.58 a.m. The Nord Express moved majestically past waving handkerchiefs, past sad and smiling faces, away from Ernst von Huberhof, hand upraised in salute. Security men relaxed and walked off. Boris Spichalsky took out a *bon-bon*, unwrapped it and sucked appreciatively. That was over. His shrewd eyes followed von Huberhof's progress to the station exit. No sooner had one job been finished than it was time for the next. Spichalsky enjoyed his work.

As they pulled out of the station Lydia stared blankly at railway yards, warehouses, men cycling along cobbled streets in morning sunshine. Fyodor Yegorovich fell and fell to his death through the numbed hush of her mind. At their last meeting in his disconsolate apartment – only yesterday? – he'd been a frightened man. She saw again the egg dribbling down his chin, felt his unsteady hand on her shoulder. Guns under the pillow, firing into the bullet-scarred wall at dream assassins, fear had never left him by day or night. Had he been his own assassin in the end? It was, in a sense, irrelevant. Terror remained terror, whether imaginary or real. An old Russian bear dancing on a chain, however he died, it was homesickness that had really killed him and something coarsely robust and human had passed away. Fellow exiles would sing the sonorous Slavonic funeral service and mourn the time when their own remains would lie in alien soil. All she could feel was an inadequate pity.

Streets went by, a patch of trodden grass, the brief dark roar of a tunnel, grey stone crosses casting horizontal shadows in the Liesenstrasse cemetery. Lydia closed the window on the episode. Unconsciously, her feet trampled the white petals of von Huberhof's fallen rose. She sat before the washbasin mirror, took the rouge from her handbag and repaired the smudged shape of her fashionable mouth. In a pocket separate from the cosmetics was the small pearl-handled revolver kept loaded for emergency. Once more she wondered if Fyodor Yegorovich had killed himself, then his death joined the unconsecrated casualties of the revolution and receded with Berlin.

'Goodbye, Berlin,' said Major Tschunke to the smoking factories of the northern industrial quarter. He drew up the window. 'Well, Oskar, now we're on our way, do you think we're going to make history?'

Disdaining rhetoric, Colonel Niedermayer replied: 'I shall be quite satisfied if we make guns.'

The two were much of an age but the Colonel regarded himself as more representative of modernity. Robert Tschunke's duelling scar was symbolic. His own cheek had no sabre-cut. The spirit of *Börsenschaft* was still too prevalent among the German officer class. Useless. Old-fashioned. Blown to bits in the trenches. He held out an engraved gold cigarette case and they both lit up. 'Tell me, Robert, what impression does Countess Alexandrova make on you?'

'Mm! highly favourable.' Major Tschunke grinned boyishly. 'Of course, I've seen her before. One doesn't forget such a pretty woman.'

'Really? I didn't know you'd met.'

'I didn't say we'd met. But I laid my sights on her on two occasions without a chance to get a shot in.'

'Where and when?'

'First at a charity performance for Russian refugees. Several weeks ago, I suppose. Frau General Seeckt was patroness, so the C-in-C detailed me to round up a detachment of music-loving officers, and wives if available.' He grinned again at the recollection. 'No wonder I'm not the most popular member of the Staff. Quick march! Off we went and just got settled down to be bored when this girl strolls in, glances round scornfully with those splendid eyes, and our fellows sit up like a cavalry troop on royal inspection.'

'*Hoch der Kaiser?* Surely not?'

'If anything, more swagger,' insisted Major Tschunke. 'It didn't do us any good. She made a bee-line for that ancient ruin General Nikolaev and they left together. By the way,' he asked with a puzzled frown, 'what do you think she sees in Ernst?'

Colonel Niedermayer scratched his nose and shrugged negligently. 'Interested in his medical work, I expect. And the next occasion?'

'A *soirée* given by the C-in-C. She turned up with Nikolaev again. I didn't get introduced then, either. Outranked. She'd captivated General von Haase. That's not difficult, of course.'

The Colonel gazed absently out of the window as the piece clicked into place. Von Haase, head of the *Truppenamt* and chief negotiator with the Russians. Disturbing. Very disturbing, indeed. His mind dwelt on hidden submarine flotillas, secret airfields, powerful guns concealed in underground armories. Russia's vastness offered space and silence for war-games as nowhere else in the world. Much was truly at stake. In five years the balance of power in Europe could be restored, the infamous Treaty of Versailles turned into a worthless scrap of paper. They were about to take the first practical step towards putting that ambitious plan into effect. France, Britain and America would stop at nothing to avert it.

'Perhaps she'll captivate the Bolsheviks,' said Major Tschunke. 'Ernst is convinced we're too simple-minded to cope with their Asiatic cunning. I expect he's hoping that Countess Alexandrova's long slim flanks and splendid grey eyes will distract them.'

Colonel Niedermayer said: 'With due respect to Professor Huberhof, I feel he has made an inadequate study of commissar psychology. An occasional nip at a shapely behind is all right in its place, but female curves cannot compare in excitement with the alluring graph of rising production.'

Major Tschunke rewarded the remark with more laughter than it deserved. Cows cropped the sun-dried grass of a field; a cylindrical gasometer spun off westward where the city petered out in ramshackle dwellings and patchwork vegetable plots. The Colonel's body swayed with the movement of the train. The woman threw a shadow in his mind. He thought: we are taking a spy with us, but refrained from communicating the suspicion. An old hand at intelligence, he'd learned the value of reticence. Another thought surfaced: she is an agent of the French.

Because of Ernst's fanatical anti-Sovietism, he had mischievously suggested she might be a Bolshevist, but the devious Cheka would see no sense in smuggling its own agent into Moscow disguised as a member of the German technical mission. But an alliance between Russian Bolshevism and German nationalism was the monstrous nightmare of the French General Staff. For the *Sûreté* it made a great deal of sense.

In strictly logical terms, Colonel Niedermayer saw the following sequence: General Nikolaev's links with the *Sûreté* were not taken sufficiently seriously in Berlin; he introduces a clever young Russian countess to Generals von Seeckt, von Haase and other high *Reichswehr* officers, also to von Huberhof, leader of a group bitterly opposed to the Soviet negotiations; von Huberhof, exploiting influential friends at GHQ, foists the woman upon the mission. His supporters argue that she will be able to reassure him that no underhand clauses would be included in an agreement with the Soviets and, once he was satisfied that Germany's interests were not in jeopardy, he would withdraw his opposition.

As easily withdraw rot from the core of an apple, Colonel Niedermayer reflected cynically. He said: 'Robert, I think we ought to ask the Countess to join us in the dining car for breakfast. Let us say in fifteen minutes.' Major Tschunke was only too delighted. 'And Robert,' the Colonel added casually, 'please instruct Müller to carry out a security check of her luggage.'

Something in the tone brought Major Tschunke's shoulders back with a jerk. '*Jawohl*,' he said.

He was gone for longer than expected. Lydia was not in her compartment. He couldn't see her anywhere. Colonel Niedermayer, putting two and two together, found his suspicions procreating like rabbits.

A uniformed railway guard, big around the shoulders, made as if to stop her leaving the reserved section of the train but touched the peak of his hat instead. His orders were limited to preventing unauthorized people entering. Her aim was reconnaissance: a sound guerrilla principle. Passengers lolled at ease in first-class carriages, noisy family parties picknicked in the crowded squalor of cheaper accommodation, men smoked in corridors. Above the racketing of wheels, a polyglot mixture of European tongues. Starched napkins delicately wiped grease from well-fed faces in the dining car that smelled of porridge, bacon and coffee. Overalled men perched on packing cases ate thick sandwiches in the goods van, staring in silence and suspending mastication until she passed from sight. Strangers all, interchangeable with strangers anywhere.

Apart from the assiduous red-eared Russian, accompanied by a friend, who followed with dog-like devotion as soon as she appeared, along the entire caterpillar length of the Nord Express the passengers had the protean anonymity of transient populations in any crowded city street. The recognizable face von Huberhof had promised her was not to be found. In particular, she did not find the darkly earnest German who spoke in the perfect accents of a Muscovite. Either he was well hidden or not yet on the train. Lydia checked again on the return journey: no Egon Otto Schmidt. Yet she remained convinced he would keep their appointment when the express left Pskov.

Awaiting her in the dining car, paternalistically stern, Colonel Niedermayer said: 'I really would prefer that you do not leave the carriages reserved for our party. We are travelling in secret. There are people aboard who are probably undesirably curious. Not least, we have a responsibility for your safety.'

After this reprimand, he exercised considerable charm and jested that she would henceforth be regarded as their prisoner. '*Natürlich*, you are fully protected by the provisions of the Geneva Convention.' He paused. 'That means you may only be shot while attempting to escape.'

Major Tschunke grinned boyishly and waved a warning forefinger. 'We have our sights on you,' he laughed.

Breakfast took a long time. The waiter, a young soldier seconded from duty in an officers' mess, served each dish unhurriedly. Colonel Niedermayer pointed out the beauties of the passing Brandenburg countryside and related some amusing wartime experiences in Persia and Afghanistan. Her opinions on the new craze for jazz, the Russian theatre in Berlin, French cooking, Russian cooking, the merits of different Alpine ski resorts, and other assorted topics were solicited by Major Tschunke, who had the disconcerting habit of leaning back and studying her from different angles like an odd piece of sculpture.

The entry of a swarthy, crop-headed German interrupted the tedium. Colonel Niedermayer briefly introduced her. 'This is Kurt Müller, on the staff of our mission.' Müller's blue, much-razored cheeks were flecked with spots of blood. He had a mechanical smile and a controlled reticence. Lydia was in no doubt about his function.

'Robert,' said the Colonel abruptly, 'we have some paperwork to do. I'm sure Countess Alexandrova will excuse us.'

When she returned to her compartment they had crossed the Oder and were racing alongside the sun towards Landsberg. Everything was exactly as she'd left it, magazines on the hinged table, the crushed rose, her cases neatly stacked. Lieutenant Müller of *Reichswehr* security was an expert.

2

At the precise moment the Nord Express began to leave Berlin, eight hundred miles away in Moscow, Peter Piatkov struggled up from the depths of sleep and broke surface, instantly alert. The map of its journey, one he had often travelled, was engraved on his brain. Through Lydia's eyes he watched streets flash by, the encroaching suburbs, telegraph wires linked across the sky as tautly as the nerves that signalled his psychic message of love and support. If, indeed, she had succeeded in joining the train. If she had not . . . his mind reflected in panic, stopping short as the censor blotted out the unthinkable.

This was the second awakening. At 2 a.m. in the midst of a dream came the faint intrusion of a distant motorcycle. He stared into the dark, plotting its route through the muted night traffic. An instinct for singling out the vibrant thread of danger warned him it would stop outside the house. Tolya Lieberman's long legs flew up the stairs bringing Spichalsky's laconic telegram. His fears were fulfilled – Selena exposed: the first death: ponderous hints of calculable consequences. The hints were gratuitously tormenting, inspired by malice. Everyone knew that an agent unmasked in the midst of a vital operation had contracted a crippling, often fatal, disability. Traps were set, invisible marksmen took aim and fingered their triggers, bloodhounds picked up the scent. Spichalsky should immediately have smuggled Lydia into hiding and set in motion the well-drilled emergency procedure of escape. Because of obtuseness, a failure of initiative or perversity he had not done so. Now it was too late.

Tolya understood. A shy compassion made him look away. Forcing a reassuring matter-of-fact tone, he said: 'She's under twenty-four-hours surveillance. Two good men are travelling with her on the train. In Pskov, picked Chekists will go aboard under the personal command of their district chief. Every security precaution has been taken in Petrograd. It will turn out well.'

He only repeated what Peter, who had planned and ordered these arrangements, knew in great detail. In Königsberg, Wirballen, Kovno, Vilna, Dvinsk, vigilant men disguised as porter, newsboy, customs official, sweetmeats vendor, engine cleaner, were briefed to check the smooth and unimpeded progress of the express through each vital stage of its journey. Once Lydia was aboard there should be no problem, but Lieberman also feared disaster and no censor intercepted his sombre imaginings: a body dragged from the water of the Landwehrkanal; police called to a naked corpse found in a bedroom with every sign pointing to suicide; an inexplicable disappearance that left no trace.

'Thank you, Tolya. We can do nothing now but wait,' said

Peter with grim composure. 'If anything more develops let me know at once.'

He heard the motorcycle backfire and recede into a series of distant explosions. An oppressive heat gripped the city like a clenched fist yet he was cold. Coldly, he willed himself to sleep.

The short night flickered with weird images of disquiet, his slumbering voice uttering cries of fragmentary alarm in the solitude of his room. Cryptic warnings reached him to which the code had been lost. Through labyrinthine dreams the relentless Adversary appeared in multiform guises. But Peter awoke to the knowledge that his nightmare had only just begun.

The sun ascended its molten arc as day progressed, scorching reminder that fate had laid on afflicted Russia a cruel summer of drought. Moscow laboured, suffered and sweltered. Mosquitoes swarmed in the heat feeding on blood thinned by years of deprivation. Bony horses, their flanks dripping sweat, staggered under monstrous loads, some faltering under the whip, falling on their sides to die. In city parks, ragged human bundles lying on the grass too still for sleep were carted away. Americans of the Hoover Relief Mission and other foreign volunteers in the Hotel Metropole organized philanthropic deliveries of grain, soup, dried milk and medicine as charity for a beggared nation. Yet factory machines turned, workmen hammered wood and metal, dilapidated typewriters clattered in Sovnarkom, Sovnarkhoz, Gosplan, Glavki, the Lubianka offices of the Central Cheka and other state institutions, driving on, planning the future, laying down with pitifully inadequate resources the massive foundations of Socialism on one sixth of the land surface of the earth.

... While Peter fought its enemies, guile against guile, commanding agents in distant capitals of Europe, divided between his desk in Moscow and the train bringing Lydia closer with every moment to the fateful encounter ten minutes of miles beyond Pskov. At 5.50 p.m., nine hours into her journey, the Nord Express entered Eydtkuhnen, on the Prussian frontier, and he thought of the fifteen minutes halt before it started again, the view of white-painted houses from the carriage window, the stream glinting through larch and beeches, chickens pecking the backyard earth of a cottage by the railway line as the drowsy motion of travel resumed. It stopped again across the frontier at Wirballen for an hour of Polish customs checks, passport examination and a change of coaches. Frontiers were always perilous, zones of suspicion and hatred, none more so than the one dividing Poles and Germans. Peter felt tense. His diaphragm contracted as though an officious hand was about to descend on his shoulder.

Lieberman came from the cipher room straight into his office and held out a message: 'I think you ought to see this at once, Peter,' he said in a voice full of gravity. Peter glanced through it, lifted dazed eyes, went over it again word by word. Like the cryptic warnings that had invaded his sleep, it was vague, ominous, oracular – tangible only because it could be deciphered and read. It advised him of a rumour that an imminent act of sabotage with international repercussions was to take place on Soviet territory.

Tolya Lieberman sat down and nursed his bony knees. Earnest intelligent eyes blinked rapidly behind the wire-framed spectacles, conveying more nervousness than he pretended. His points were brief and persuasive. The source was tainted: their double-agent in Paris who functioned at a modest level of French intelligence and had been unwillingly recruited by blackmail and bribery. Rumours were common and this one had the flavour of inauthenticity. It had more relation to psychological warfare than information: too generalized, impervious to corroboration by normally accessible methods, calculated by vagueness and innuendo to generate a helpless sense of fear. An army of millions could not guard the vastness of Russia against every shadowy group of conspirators. France was Lieberman's territory. He had an expert knowledge of the *Sûreté*, unrivalled insight into the mentality of its intelligence branches. The message bore the hallmarks of an exercise in French disinformation, he insisted.

'Can you imagine?' he said derisively. 'Our "François" heard it from a colleague in the Eastern Directorate who swallowed too much Pernod at luncheon. I can see that colleague reporting back to *M'sieu le Directeur*. "Rumour communicated as ordered," and his boss replying, "Good, now let's get on with some real work".'

'You may be right.' Peter shrugged pessimistically. 'The message is everything you say, but' – his eyes took on a cold, abstract look – 'imagine for a moment that it's genuine. If one wanted to create an international scandal by an act of terror here there are two obvious targets. One, the Hoover Relief volunteers. An assassination there would cause uproar in America and threaten the entire programme of aid. The other,' he said, his breath tight, 'is the secret German technical mission. The *Sûreté* would gladly arrange to machine-gun every single member of it. We must take every precaution. I'll discuss it with Jacob Peters at once.'

Jacob agreed with this evaluation. He ordered the immediate strengthening of guards watching over the foreign relief workers and a stringent tightening of security to protect the *Reichswehr* visitors on arrival. But little could be done about the hazards of their journey. It was after 8 p.m. The Nord Express had left Kovno, racing through the long tunnel that emerged by the river Niemen. Beyond lay Landvarovo, the rail junction for Dvinsk, Pskov and Petrograd.

An arrow in flight cannot be deflected.

The heat was little abated, the sky still light, when he got home, stripped down to the waist and plunged his head under the lukewarm rusty water of the tap. Footsteps tripped lithely up the stairs as he towelled. A neighbour's twelve-year-old daughter by the sound of it. Then the knock, far too peremptory for a child, contracted his heart. Cursing himself sardonically for over-reacting, he called through the closed door: 'Yes?'

'A comrade from the Theatre Cooperative,' came the demure reply.

It was a child – nineteen-year-old Galya. 'I'm glad to find you in at last,' she said, tossing her wild black curls and making a dramatic entrance.

Relief gave way to a spurt of rage. 'You've been told never to come uninvited. Get out!' he scowled.

Unabashed but pretending fear, Galya circled him warily. 'Ooh! Savage! You look as though you eat people.' She moistened her plump, pretty lips.

He was touched by a certain innocence. People did eat people. 'Galichka, please go home,' he said wearily.

'It's hot,' Galya said. She reckoned up on her fingers. 'I haven't seen you for three weeks and five whole days.' Sitting on the bed, she unbuttoned her blouse, threw it off and let her full young breasts spring free. 'Tomorrow we start rehearsals for a new play and I won't have any time for love. A dedicated artist puts all her energies into her work.' Skirt, patched cotton knickers, shoes were discarded and Galya jumped up, naked as a colt, exuberant, in fighting trim. By what ingenuity did she keep her curves so well-nourished?

Peter chased her, manoeuvred her into a corner and carried her squealing to the bed. Slapping the round, dimpled buttocks, he said: 'Get yourself dressed. I have to go to a meeting.'

Galya pounded his chest. Sharp white teeth sank into the flesh of his shoulder. From hunted to predator: the reversal of roles was not to his taste.

'Ouch! You should be locked in a cage.'

'You're not going to a boring meeting.' She fastened her pelvis against him and wriggled wickedly. 'You've excited me now and I won't let you go.'

Regretfully and with difficulty, he disengaged himself. 'It's a party, not a meeting. We'll drink water flavoured with caraway seed, pretend it's vodka and talk about the state of the revolution.' Anxiety throbbed under the wolfish lust. Even at such a time his mind travelled on the Nord Express, now stationary in Vilna while passengers took dinner in the restaurant car.

Galya had felt his swelling desire against her belly. 'You're in a very erotic state and it belongs to me because I made it. I won't let you give it to another woman.'

'Female comrades,' he corrected her. 'And all old enough to be your mother. You will be very bored, and very distracting to the elderly Party members. Go back to your room and have fun with your Polish poet.'

Very perversely, she said: 'You can come back with me and have fun with him afterwards. Maybe he will like you better.'

They made their way to the Shulkin's apartment through night streets thronged with restless Muscovites driven by the heat from overcrowded tenements. People were feverish with evening gaiety despite chronic pangs of hunger and the poor, monotonous appearance of the city, its shop windows drab, empty, shuttered. There was an heroic quality in the hope they brought to the dim, impoverished capital. Only the skyline retained splendour, spires, domes and cupolas soaring towards the spendthrift glitter of stars as if God, the archetypal millionaire, had scattered barrels of diamonds over the black floor of heaven. Perhaps it inspired the busy Nepmen at market stalls in Petrovka who enthusiastically yelled the praises of dusty rags, wilted cabbage leaves and time-battered, decomposing objects that stank of long disuse in airless cupboards.

Galya prattled her incomprehensible theatre jargon. Like a compass needle pulled to the magnetic north, Peter's thoughts returned to Lydia, much of an age with the child at his side when they first met but already caught in the net of a sombre destiny. 'What do you want of the Revolution? What do you expect it to achieve?' he'd once asked in those early days. Twenty years old, vivid, romantic and, he'd thought, sentimental, her answer was immediate: 'Human dignity.' She was not then a Marxist, nor ever really became one despite her journey into the Communist Party. She had set out in the same direction as Bolshevism. Despite the horrors of revolution, civil war and famine, the agonizing struggle had been about freedom and human dignity. Young and rebellious, precocious enemy of her own class, a foot soldier slogging through every campaign, Lydia emerged battle-hardened. But the core of her idealism, her obstinate, uncompromising independence, remained intact. Peter was afraid for her. Russian history broke idealists on its relentless wheel. Especially the idealists of freedom, for in Russia freedom was measured by its absence. Like absolute beauty, it was unattainable. The great disorderly country would fly apart unless held in tenacious control. Power was ugly yet necessary; it had its own impersonal momentum. Those who stood in its path upholding human dignity left only bloodstains on the snow like the doomed sailors of Kronstadt. Survival in Russia was the art of living within the limits of possibility.

'Galichka, tell me,' he asked, bruised with love for another woman, 'what do you want most out of life?'

'To be a great actress, of course, the greatest in Soviet Russia.' Candour shone in her bright bewitching eyes. 'And I will be. I will be greater than Sarah Bernhardt.'

Another generation. He walked on, the stiffness of experience in his joints.

Noise bounced down the stairs of Nina Shulkin's communal apartment. Not of music, laughter or voices accelerated by alcoholic lubrication. It was the loud assertive babble of a conference antechamber where everyone argued opinions simultaneously.

'I said it would be boring. You can still go home,' Peter told Galya at the door.

'Why did you come then?' she demanded logically, leaning her hip against his thigh. A persuasive softness made him hesitate: the logic was seductive. Why, indeed? Vilna, Novo-Vileisk, Novo-Svyentzyani, the river Dvina, Dvinsk – lights of towns streaking past in the night, the train drawing closer to Pskov . . . If he wanted to forget it for a while, that fleshly softness promised amnesia.

His hand moved slowly along the sensual curve from slim waist to full breast and squeezed gently.

'Because I intend to get really ravenous before I eat you,' he said and pulled open the door.

As an effective entrance, Galya could have asked for nothing more dramatic. Her flushed and amorous face crowned by its black curls, the dreamy concupiscence of her eyes, the youthful ripeness that seemed to offer itself for plucking, drew every gaze in the overcrowded room, even that of the ten-year-old boy, Poolka Murontzeff, who had the falling forelock and sulky mouth of the dead terrorist who had been his father.

Nina hurried over, kissed Peter's cheek and assessed Galya with brooding jealousy on behalf of Lydia. After the introductions were made, she glanced round in harassed distraction and said: 'How nice to have someone so pretty and young. I wish there was somebody your own age to introduce to you, but we are all veterans, I'm afraid.' Jacob Peters, immaculate in a black silk Russian blouse tightly belted round his expanding waist, approached fingering his small blond beard. Nina brought them together and led Peter to a gaunt Hungarian, wife of one of

Semyon Shulkin's fellow economists in *Vesenkha*, the Supreme Council of National Economy. She was a shy woman with a scrubbed red face that perspired freely and, mistaking him for another economist, asked: 'What do you think, comrade, about drought in the Volga Basin region? They say it will bring the worst famine since 1891. Do you agree?' Her anxiety was clearly genuine. Whose wasn't? Murmuring that they could only hope for rain to come soon, he extricated himself. Semyon Shulkin, brilliant head stuffed full of plans that could produce miracles of socialist development, slouched untidily against the wall surrounded by a flock of seminarists quick to recognize a coming man of power. Shrinking from the prospect of a learned lecture, Peter turned and was trapped by the transfixing gaze of Nina's eldest son.

'Hello,' said the boy. Tall for his age, preternaturally serious, something about him caused Peter to stumble into a stagnant memory. St Petersburg, October 1910, and he sat in the building of the Tsarist secret police, an Okhrana lieutenant studying the photograph of a Bakunist youth, Polovski Murontzeff.

'You grow more like your father every time I see you,' he said.

The boy frowned, increasing the resemblance. 'You were his friend. My mother says you and Aunt Lydia were his comrades. One day she's going to take me to London to show me the house where my father lived.'

'He was very brave,' said Peter.

'I know.' The young face clouded. Troubled brown eyes reflected perplexity, a guarded apprehension. 'No one,' he said, 'can be exactly . . . I mean, everybody's different.' The boy reddened and became silent. 'Do you like swimming? I came first in the hundred metres, at school,' he resumed hastily, and Peter discussed backstrokes, diving, techniques of life-saving until the shadow of the hero-father gradually receded.

The dreadful party became increasingly tedious and the heat of the packed bodies suffocating. Nina served a liquid called vodka that tasted of paraffin and left a foul coating on the tongue. Small cakes of baked grated carrot and another indefinable ingredient were handed round on plates, each guest taking only one with practised self-denial. The acrid smoke of adulterated tobacco stung Peter's eyes and he looked round for Galya. Jacob had manoeuvred her into a corner and grimly exercised his wit and charm, but she seemed unimpressed. With or without her, Peter was ready to leave. Then he saw Joseph Frumkin.

Joseph sat cross-legged on the floor. His military tunic, elbows frayed, was a thing of rents and patches. He looked like a man accustomed to being alone in a crowd, composed, meditative, self-sufficient. He also looked emaciated, which was common enough. Slowly and avidly he drew on a *papirosa*, holding the smoke in his lungs a long time before reluctantly letting it escape through his nostrils.

The unexpected sight of him struck Peter like a blow in the chest. They did not know one another well but they had shared the same woman, still shared her divided affections. It was a kind of kinship: it could link men in sympathy or hatred. For Peter, Joseph Frumkin represented a decade's corrosive jealousy: he had murdered him over and over again in his dreams.

Joseph met his glance and stood up. The first thing he said was: 'I believe you saved my life.'

'When were you released?' Peter spoke without expression.

'Eight days ago. A military commission turned up in Solovetsky, reviewed my case and found me innocent of everything but the crime of survival. I was the only one of the Kronstadt prisoners left alive. They issued an open travel warrant and unlocked the gates.'

'It must feel good.'

Frumkin rocked his head from side to side and held out his hands in a Jewish gesture. 'Good and bad. I shall miss my friends.' He smiled with wry humour. 'Prison is a positive experience. It gives one a strict but salutary education.'

'So they tell me,' said Peter. According to the conventional Soviet wisdom, punishment must be firm, just and reformative. That was not what Frumkin meant at all and they both knew it. But Solovetsky had wrought a change in his rival. He remembered him as passionate, argumentative, volatile, a man torn by inner conflicts. Now the deep-socketed eyes were strangely peaceful. An unexpected thought came to him. If he ever painted a saint it would be with that world-weary tranquillity, that tired, patient look of endurance.

'Have you any plans?' he asked.

'I've considered several. Political journalism, my old profession, no longer attracts me. Russia needs teachers more than politicians. I am qualified in history and literature. Either will do. The Arctic has left me with a longing for the south. Perhaps I'll settle in Kharkov where there is a university.' Joseph's glance wandered away, sadly cruising over the faces in the crowded room. He was about to reopen a wound and wanted to be merciful. 'I came to Moscow in the hope of seeing Lydia,' he said. 'Nobody seems to know where she is.'

The old scar broke. Peter felt the blood well out, yet the effect was paradoxical. He almost blurted out: 'Joseph, Lydia's in danger! I'm terribly afraid, but there's nothing I can do. I'm helpless! It's unbearable!' Sweat as salt as tears trickled down his face. Crushing the impulse, he spoke with enmity, harshly. 'I can't help you. I did nothing to save your life but send a message to your prison commandant. Even that was against my principles.'

Joseph spread his arms again. 'It's the deed that counts,' he said without rancour. 'And I thank you for it.'

But Peter was already pushing towards Galya. 'Are you coming?' he demanded furiously, yanking her arm as if she was at fault for everything.

Jacob Peters grinned lazily. 'Don't treat the girl like that. She's not state property. She wants to stay with me, don't you, my darling?'

'Well, make up your bloody mind,' Peter snarled at her.

Galya's black eyes sparkled. The party wasn't boring her at all. She stared at Jacob Peters, whose soft hand had signed the death warrants of hundreds, who smiled at her so affably, and he had no appeal for her. For one thing he didn't look the slightest bit interestingly cruel.

'Oh, you're hurting me!' she protested loud enough for the entire company to hear. They watched them leave in shocked silence, except for Jacob, shrewd enough to recognize he'd played the wrong game, and Joseph Frumkin, whose soul bore the teethmarks of a real and vulpine cruelty.

Later, in Galya's tiny room under the garish posters of Constructivism and the rebellious poems in coarse vernacular scrawled on its walls, Peter fought the future greatest actress in all Russia to lustful, sweating surrender. They lay entwined through the heat of the night and the train in his head ran into a long, silent black tunnel.

The inner alarm jangled him awake. Wan morning light penetrated the curtained window. Galya lay on her back, one arm outflung in the rhetorical gesture, the hand of the other modestly shielding her plump, voracious cleft.

Almost four hundred miles, a diagonal crow's flight to the north-west, the Nord Express raced through open country towards Pskov.

3

Colonel Niedermayer wiped his lips on his napkin and turned an acquiline profile towards the window. Dusk settled on the low hills of eastern Poland: the dark green waters of a lake glimmered with failing light. 'It could be East Prussia,' he remarked. A controlled meditative smile creased his lean cheeks and he pointed his knife at a small town whose lights shone in the distance. 'Wilkowyszki, Napoleon's headquarters in 1812 before he marched on Moscow. The lesson he learned at great cost remains valid more than a century later. Russia can be defeated but not conquered.'

Blond, square-built Colonel Schubert stopped eating to give the matter thought. His tongue searched a hollow tooth. 'Except,' he temporized, 'from within.'

The waiter cleared away their dishes and served *Käsetorte* and coffee. In descending rank he did the same at other tables. First Major Tschunke and Herr Ruthardt, the senior industrial expert, then Lieutenant Müller and three engineers, finally military interpreters and clerks. Lydia's inclusion at the top table was, she guessed, a social concession. A woman of title must be treated according to rank, not function.

'Revolution is a different matter,' said Colonel Niedermayer. 'Russians remain Russians whoever seizes power. Do you agree, Countess?'

All through dinner he had conducted a devious interrogation.

She did not take it lightly. Niedermayer impressed her as witty, serious, humane, but firm of purpose and, if necessary, ruthless. His searching look made no secret of the fact that he regarded her as a problem and was determined to arrive at a solution.

'How do you define "Russian"?' she replied.

Colonel Schubert nodded vigorous agreement. 'Quite right. Who are the Russians? The people at the top are a mongrel collection. Not a race at all, a mixture of breeds.'

'How would you define it?' Niedermayer asked, pointedly ignoring the intervention. 'Quite apart from the present Russian experiment.'

Experiment. The expression repelled her. It indicated, if not sympathy, a spirit of scientific detachment. There they were, civilized people digesting a rich four-course meal and indulging in intelligent speculation over what would be left in the test-tube after the human chemical substance had been thoroughly agitated and held over a flame.

She forced a laugh. 'You won't get a thumbnail sketch of our Russian character from me. Gallic charm, Scottish thrift, Spanish *machismo*. All rather silly, isn't it? Actually, there were quite a few Russians who were ready to be conquered by Napoleon. Our aristocracy were half in love with the French and despised their own language so much they regarded it as only fit for giving orders to servants.'

Colonel Niedermayer noted the deprecating reference to the French. It could be a diversionary ploy. 'You're very difficult to know, Madame,' he said, wry and enigmatic. He lit a cigar in philosophic surrender. 'As for national character, in these days of swift travel – aeroplanes, airships, express trains – nations are growing more alike. Not to speak of the cinema and the wireless.' Frowning at the glowing tip of his cigar, he said in a tone of amazed disapproval. 'Do you know, people tell me that the most popular song of the moment in Berlin dancehalls is a barbaric American jazz tune called "Yes, we have no bananas".'

Back in her sleeping compartment, Lydia settled down to kill time and relieve suspense. Returning home filled her with excitement and dread. Berlin had diverted her, relegated the agony of Russia to a less immediate zone of the mind. For a while she'd allowed herself to become someone else, someone who laughed easily, enjoyed her own sensuality, who took the taste of bread for granted. Like an exhausted athlete after a short rest, she'd have to force her muscles into effort again. Hunger, lice, refugees, the whirlpool of the 'experiment' sucking into its vortex those who were weak and defenceless. She tried to read. The sound of the wheels intruded. *Too fast, too fast, too fast, too fast . . .* The train hurtled through the night towards Russia: the air rushed past like an endless scream: it was going to be unbearable.

Major Tschunke knocked and entered, grinning with boyish embarrassment. Eyes glistening and slightly unfocused, hair greasily pomaded, he had the air of a student who had contracted an alcoholic wager to attempt the virtue of a lady. Something bottle-shaped bulged under his jacket. He clicked his heels.

'Please forgive the intrusion,' he began in a most dignified manner. The carriage jolted, almost throwing him into her lap, and a vintage bottle of champagne rolled on the floor. Retrieving it, he stood up, clicked heels again. 'Madame Countess, will you do me the honour – yes, the honour – of drinking a toast to the success of my mission. Excuse me. The success of *our* mission?' His tongue had difficulty in coping with sibilants.

'*Nein danke*, I have a headache,' she said. The excuse was in key with the old-fashioned charade.

'Oh, that is a pity!' Major Tschunke's face lengthened in commiseration. It was rather overdone and difficult in his state to sustain. Brightening again, he began to unfasten the cork of the bottle. 'One glass of champagne will make you feel better.'

'I don't want it,' Lydia said tersely. 'I'm going to bed.'

The sabre-scar on the Major's cheek showed up white against the sudden flush of erotic excitement. He leaned for support against the wall. 'Just a little one,' he wheedled, holding up two fingers in token of moderation.

'No,' she said very firmly indeed.

There was another knock at the door. Lieutenant Müller came in and stood stiffly to attention. He clicked his heels at Lydia, staring over her head, and barked: 'Excuse me!' Executing a left turn, he clicked his heels at Major Tschunke. 'Colonel Niedermayer's compliments and will the Major join him in his compartment at once.'

He marched his superior away like a prisoner under escort. Lydia suspected that Niedermayer was less concerned to save her annoyance than to forestall a possible drunken breach of security. She locked the door to prevent further invasion of her privacy and spare him anxiety.

A few miles out of Vilna her eyelids became heavy and the magazine page blurred over. The cradling motion, drowsy impressions of polished mahogany, lamplight, warmth, induced regression to a childhood sensation of being borne in strong, safe arms into the future. Sleep brought fragmentary images of Berlin, her mind digesting the city and turning it into memory. She slept through Dvinsk; stared vaguely at the ceiling when the carriage rattled over points at the rail junction of Korsovka. Asleep once more, she did not feel the gravitational pull of her homeland as the train crossed the Latvian frontier into Russia. Slowly a rim of light appeared on the horizon. Here and there, an early-rising peasant began work in the flax fields or trundled through the half-darkness in his wooden cart.

Like a forest guerrilla, Lydia awoke at the first touch of dawn.

She emerged from sleep as if struggling to escape drowning. A vague sense of dread like a clinging premonition of death was located in her stomach. She lay motionless for a few moments, thinking that in half-an-hour they would arrive at Pskov, and sluggishly registered unease, as an invalid notes malfunction of the imprisoning body. The engine's steam-whistle let out a mournful blast.

Impatiently throwing the blanket aside, Lydia got up and opened the window to dispel the stale fumes of night. Dew glistened on grass; birds swam like fish through the translucent mist; without a dwelling in sight the earth looked newborn. She turned away with reluctance to encounter her own mirrored reflection, the morning stranger whose oyster-grey eyes conducted a cold, disparaging assessment. Shrugging, she slipped on her dressing gown. Bowels and bladder were making their gross demands. A fastidious distaste for squatting on chamber pots called for a trip to the W.C. Besides, the trip would shortly have to be made for another purpose. It could serve as a rehearsal.

In the corridor of the sleeper lights burned overhead and

night still prevailed. One door stood slightly ajar, affording an informal view of the cabinned interior. Lieutenant Müller stood in his undervest, braces hung over belted trousers, scraping blood-flecked lather from his hard, pimply jaw. Within handy reach on a hook was his shoulder-holster, black gun-butt protruding. The reserved eyes carried a warning: you are under observation. She smiled, glancing away to the portmanteau undisturbed in its recess. Soon it would be handed over to von Huberhof's courier with its death-sentence load of counter-revolutionary gold and pamphlets. Once more she wondered at the identity of that doomed man, thinking of him with respect: an enemy soldier carrying out his dangerous, lonely mission.

The uniformed train-guard's nodding head jerked upright as she entered the adjoining compartment. He stood up drowsily and straightened his hat. Further down the corridor a man in a crumpled suit leaned against the frame of an open window smoking a cigarette. She could see only his thin, stooped back and hesitated fractionally before entering the toilet, wondering if he would turn. When she left the man was gone and the train-guard paced an empty corridor. Lieutenant Müller buttoned up his jacket, the hook that held his gun now empty, and peered at himself in the mirror with no hint of self-question. Lydia closed the door of her cabin and lit up the first cigarette of the day. It was time to get dressed. Now that the moment of action approached, she felt she'd arrived home at last and was resuming her role in the revolutionary struggle.

Pskov rose out of the plain like a mediaeval fortress still defying the marauding armies of Mongolian khans and Teutonic knights. The domes of its cathedral, copper-green above the Kremlin's limestone walls, overlooked a town of crooked rooftops weathered by five turbulent centuries. Peter was born in one of those dwellings in a narrow street so secretive, he said, it concealed itself from the sun. As a child, he said, Pskov had given him a false sense of security. No danger seemed able to penetrate its fortress walls. It was a place where things could be hidden away safely, secret and precious things. Then, in his eighth year God, the thief, stole away his mother whose voice had the same husky timbre as Lydia's own. She thought of Peter not only because this was the place of his birth but also in an attempt to disconnect, to keep her mind resilient, ready to meet the unexpected. Tension narrowed the focus: one must always reckon with the possibility of ambush.

Coated in cosmopolitan dust, the Nord Express rolled to a halt in the drab provincial Russian railway station. A few passengers got down. No porters besieged the train clamouring to carry their luggage. No newsvendors appeared (newspapers were stuck on walls – *Pravda, Izvestia, Komsomolskaya Pravda* – presumably the local paper had to be bought); no one offered hard-boiled eggs, potato pancakes, fruit, sugary drinks. Faded Party slogans flapped uneasily. A mixed group of male and female labourers staggered beneath the weight of wooden crates near the usual giant poster of a mighty-thewed Soviet worker smashing verminous enemies with the hammer of Socialism.

Lydia lit a fresh cigarette and settled back to wait. Some young Red Army men in shabby cotton tunics lounged near the deserted railway restaurant, rifles slung on shoulders, staring at her elegant profile behind the carriage window as though she were a creature from another world. They exchanged sidelong comments, scratched red sunburnt necks and grinned in good-natured amusement. The sight of them revived memories of rough-humoured partisan comradeship in the nostalgic forests of the civil war. Already it seemed an age ago. Yesterday seemed an age ago. Time resents impatience. Its sullen rebellion had long stopped the rusty station clock at the perpetual hour of four.

Eventually a detachment of Chekist border troops arrived. One of them accompanied by Lieutenant Müller entered her carriage. A slow, methodical, sharp-featured man, trained to mistrust, he examined her papers and compared her feature by feature with the passport photograph. Dissatisfied, he said in a drawling unfriendly tone: 'You were born in Russia, yes?'

'It's all in the documents,' she replied coldly, not entirely because her appointed role required her to show hostility.

'Documents,' he said, 'are sometimes forged.'

Lydia repressed a smile. In the present instance they had been forged by experts of the Central Cheka.

The man scrutinized her papers again. 'Alexandrova, Lydia Nikolaievna, rank of Countess.' He transfixed her with a look as militant as a sword. 'I must ask you. Do you have in your possession any weapons or counter-revolutionary propaganda?'

'I'm an interpreter, not an assassin,' she said.

Lieutenant Müller's eyes flicked worriedly from one to the other, not quite following the conversation. It did not require fluency in Russian to sense trouble.

'We are here at the invitation of your Government,' he intervened, speaking German. 'This lady is a member of our mission.'

'*Einen Augenblick*, just a moment!' the Chekist snapped and turned back to Lydia. 'I must examine your luggage.'

She shrugged. Either he had not been briefed or he too was playing out a role. He went through her cases systematically, asked her to open her handbag, glanced into it, then riffled the pages of her German magazines.

'You are forbidden to pass these to any Soviet citizen,' he said and made a scowling departure.

Even as a simulated performance the episode left a sour aftertaste. More to the point, it distracted her attention from a disciplined party of ten men in civilian clothes, ten fingers of Peter's outstretched protective hands, picked representatives of the Pskov Cheka led by their district commander, who boarded the train while her luggage was being searched.

Presently, the guard whistled and waved his flag. A Red Army boy with a cheeky face touched his cap in ironic salute. She looked at her wrist-watch. Somewhere, perhaps in the very next coach, she thought with a tightening of breath, a man was doing exactly the same. Counting off each minute from one to ten. It was he who had reason to be nervous. Her part in the affair was merely to pass a contraband portmanteau; for him it would be the moment when the eagle's shadow swooped across his path. The heart instinctively tilts towards the victim: she felt the contraction of pity. Taking the decorative little revolver from the secret pocket of her handbag, she slipped it into the hip-pocket of her travelling suit. Life began to be measured in seconds. Best to be prepared.

Out of the station gloom into a dazzle of sunlight. They crossed the bridge over the river Velikaya, white gulls, green willows, boats ruffling blue water, a distance ahead the sun floating like a blazing ship where Lake Peipus flowed into the sky, images indelibly printed on the tension-sensitized membrane of her mind. And the face of the man in the next coach. Sad deep-set eyes, cadaverous, wearing that look of intense preoccupation one finds in someone whose gaze is concentrated inwards upon a fixed, obsessive purpose. Darkness and light. Man's bitter manipulations and nature's rhythmic response to the pendulum seasons.

Six slow minutes left. A cigarette burned unnoticed between her fingers. She picked up a magazine and tried to read, threw it aside; stared at empty fields; vibrated to the throbbing motion of the speeding train. The door opened quietly and a man stepped into the carriage. A faint shiver passed through her spine as though stroked by a feather. The gun in his hand was a Mauser. He wore the leather jacket of a Chekist.

Stupefied, she began to say: 'I've already been ...' but something in his eyes froze her tongue. The look and the uniform did not go together. His eyes were neither insolent nor confident of authority. The man was frightened.

'Don't move! Keep quiet!' he said desperately.

In the next instant a second intruder entered and swiftly locked the door, the man von Huberhof said she would recognize, Egon Otto Schmidt from far away Dalldorf. In his hand was the heavy portmanteau which bore her gilded name. He was also dressed as a Chekist.

The shock was inevitable, a brief, stunned blankness, a total suspension of belief. She had been flung headlong into the unexpected. Egon Otto Schmidt gave her a non-committal stare. 'Good morning,' he said in Russian. The first thought to struggle through was that he could walk along the corridors of Lubianka without challenge. Saturnine features, moulded by fanaticism, bore a resemblance to Felix Dzerzhinsky. He had the devout look of one who would serve state security with priestly dedication. Far from reflecting fear, his sombre eyes held a smouldering ecstasy.

Her voice came through with difficulty, sounding puzzled, apprehensive. 'We must have received different instructions,' she said.

'I'm sure of that.' He grinned very faintly. 'Please don't scream. This will not take more than a couple of minutes.'

'You are Russian, aren't you?' she said inconsequentially. 'I looked for you on the train.'

'Vanyusha and I only boarded at Pskov.'

He laid the portmanteau on its side, took a key from his pocket and kneeled on the floor.

'I don't understand,' Lydia persisted, glancing at the Mauser pointed at her head. 'Why is it necessary to threaten me like this? I was told to leave the case in the toilette for you to collect.'

'Yes, I know.' His manner was curt but civil, as if only lack of time prevented him from giving a full explanation. Deftly, he undid the locks and threw back the lid. Spread over the contents of the portmanteau were pages from the *Berliner Zeitung*. She recognized the picture of a sex murderer: it was an edition of the paper that had titillated café society three days earlier. Egon Otto Schmidt swept the pages aside and Lydia had her appalling answer. It would make deep black headlines in newspapers all over Germany, if not the world. The portmanteau contained no counter-revolutionary pamphlets, no gold roubles: packed close together inside were bundled sticks of explosive. Schmidt intended to blow up the train with dynamite.

'My God!' she whispered, starting to her feet. Nervously Vanyusha prodded her with his gun. 'Sergey Ivanovich, please hurry!' he pleaded.

'Keep still!' Egon Otto Schmidt spoke in a tense, angry undertone, as though both were equally insubordinate. He produced tiny scissors and a spool of magnesium fuse, talking quietly and compulsively. 'Yes, naturally I'm Russian. Born in Moscow, Kruimsk Naber, overlooking the river. Do you know it? Studied philosophy in Heidelberg. Nothing I wanted more than to be a professor.' He chuckled dryly. 'Instead I became a Colonel in General Wrangel's defeated White army.' Taping the fuse to the explosive, he snipped off the required length and said thoughtfully: 'That should give us twenty seconds.'

Twenty seconds. Lydia went very cold, so cold it cauterized the instinct of self-preservation. All her energy became concentrated in holding back the onrush of time. Her right hand was in her jacket pocket. Slowly she gripped the pearl handle of her gun and felt for the trigger.

In a low scared voice, she said: 'I can understand that you want to blow up the train, but why me? After all, I did help.'

'Not the train.' An abstract expression showed in Egon Otto Schmidt's dark brown eyes. 'Only the *Reichswehr* part of it.'

'Please, I've done you no harm,' she pleaded.

He brought out a box of matches, opened it and paused, holding a match ready to strike like a man arrested by a thought when about to light a cigarette.

'We may all have to die,' he said sombrely.

'Sergey Ivanovich!' Vanyusha cried in an agony of suspense.

'All right, Vanyusha.' Schmidt turned to Lydia and said rapidly: 'I'll light the fuse and push the explosive into the corridor. We make for the coach-door on the left. You may jump first, then it's up to you. But if the corridor is not empty, if someone should be there, no one will escape. We'll have to fight. Right,' he said taking a deep breath. 'Here we go!'

The match was struck, flame spurted and he stooped. As Vanyusha watched, Lydia fired from her hip pocket into his blond sweating face. Egon Otto Schmidt dropped the lighted match, jerked round and reached for his Mauser as blood came from a hole below Vanyusha's left nostril and his eyes glazed over. The gun exploded as it slipped from its holster, smashing the carriage window. Vanyusha's falling body, thrown forward by the movement of the train, trapped Lydia in her seat and Schmidt's next bullet hit his comrade's chest.

Violence, always dreamlike, gave her the sensation of reliving a recurring nightmare. Blood soaked into her clothes, Vanyusha's blood, Murontzeff's blood, the dying blood of her doomed generation. Through the vague traumatic mist, she struggled to free her arm and fired across the burdensome weight of the dying man, his breath gurgling as he inhaled the internal bleeding.

Egon Otto Schmidt groaned and grasped his shoulder. His baffled desperation was also generic. He was a man facing the dilemma of how to die. In an instant it was grimly resolved, methodically executed. First he unlocked the door. Then he scooped up the spilled box of matches and dragged the portmanteau out of the carriage. A pellet from Lydia's small revolver ploughed into his back. His lean, swarthy face contorted in pain but, undeterred, he crouched and put a lighted match to the fuse.

Alerted by the shooting, the doors of sleeping compartments flew open and faces stared in horrified bewilderment as the red spark ate into the strip of magnesium. Lieutenant Müller alone responded actively to crisis. Charging in from the restaurant car where he'd been enjoying a quiet breakfast, he ran down the corridor gun in hand and shattered Egon Otto Schmidt's face at point blank range into a torn mask of blood. Lydia freed herself from Vanyusha's body and leaned against the door-frame.

'The case!' she screamed. 'It's going to explode!'

Instinctively she had spoken Russian. Lieutenant Müller could only follow the language of her pointing finger. Colour fled from his clean-scraped cheeks leaving only the bright-red scabs of lacerated pimples. The logical thing would have been to stamp out the spluttering fuse, but terror drove out reason and courage drove out terror. Gathering the portmanteau in his powerful arms, desperate seconds ticking by, he carried it to the end of the coach, with difficulty opened the door, and hurled it down an embankment.

After a slow count of three, a blast like the detonation of a fifteen-inch shell reverberated across the sunlit fields.

Almost two hours later, wearing a different dress, the blood washed off her hands, Lydia sat in the dining car and stared bleakly at the distant Gulf of Finland. Colonel Niedermayer observed her with curiosity and respect, more puzzled by her than ever. Her silence was bitter and mournful. Tact counselled him not to attempt to break it. The Nord Express would soon reach the Warsaw Station in Petrograd and conclude their journey. Not altogether uneventful, as the English, with their reputation for understatement, might say.

Lydia's eyes were suddenly flooded by tears and she clenched them hard, the muscles of her slender throat convulsed. The Colonel wondered if he should put out a hand to comfort her, but being a reticent man not given to impulsive gestures he refrained. Overwrought, naturally, he thought.

The tears continued to force themselves through her shut

eyelids. She felt she was weeping blood. Vanyusha, she thought. And Sergey Ivanovich who went by the name of Schmidt. Two more heroes dying for a lost cause. The wrong side, the right side: how soon it became meaningless! All that mattered finally was the waste of it, the ugliness. Men had died hideously at her hands, and all her own countrymen, Russians.

'Why do we kill each other?' she asked herself in despair. 'What terrible cross are we nailed to? What kind of people are we?'

And, like prayer, her meditation turned from bitterness to hope. Surely the cruel age was reaching its end? Though it clawed down the innocent, the brave, the misguided, its paroxysms were those of a dying monster. Russia had emerged from revolution, the century was young. She prayed that the starving children of Pushkino should grow up firm-fleshed, free of terror, tender towards each other.

Her heart grew stronger. At last Lydia felt able to open her eyes.